THE CULT OF THE BLUE PARROT

By

Sandra Hulstrom

Dear Venera
Thanks so much for your
support!

Your friend,

Sandra
Hulstrom

To Mark, my Scrabble buddy who set me free. Thanks.

Thanks to my beta readers for all their support and encouragement:
Loral Ann, Claudia, Kim, Kat, and Randy.

And a special thanks to my poetic sister, Rebecca, for her advice and
editing help. You inspired me to try; and, wow, what an amazing journey!

Contact the author at:

sandratalltrees@gmail.com

Prelude

The sound of a child's laughter filled the air, spilling from her in giggles of delight and peals of joy as Danny spun and tossed her again into the air. His laughter joined hers as he easily caught her, this time kissing her cheeks then tickling her. Seven-year old Sarah now held Danny's hand as she pirouetted down the dock, then she dropped his hand and raced him to the boat. "I win!" she crowed, as she danced a little victory jig on the deck. A glance at Danny's face stopped her in her tracks. "What's wrong?" she demanded. "You didn't even try to beat me."

"I just want to make sure you understand." He had that big-brother look on his face. Danny was seventeen and very grown-up suddenly. "Today is our secret, Sarah. No one must know, not even Martin." He was very somber as he looked at her. "No one, Sarah. You understand?"

"Julie knows," she said objecting, her voice taking on that stubborn tone. She did not keep secrets from Martin and she didn't know why everyone was making such a big deal about today.

Danny was her big brother and he was in charge, Martin had said so. Martin was Danny's age, seventeen, but he was her best friend. The three of them had always been together but now Martin was in the Army and she and Danny were in Hong Kong. She missed Martin terribly. Danny was not as good at bedtime stories and he pulled her hair unmercifully when her curls got all tangled. Danny was always off in the clouds somewhere, thinking about his studies. Martin was patient and listened to her. Besides, Danny had Julie now and it wasn't fair that she didn't have Martin with her all the time. Martin couldn't come to see her for weeks and weeks even if he did manage to contact her every evening to say good night. It wasn't fair.

"You and Julie talk all the time," she said accusingly, remembering their blonde heads close together, their quiet murmurs to each other. Danny and Julie were in love and, while Sarah was fascinated by their relationship, she was still a bit confused with how quickly the sophisticated blonde with the shoulder length wedge of straight, shining hair and cool, assessing, green eyes had entered their lives.

"I know, but not about this," he said firmly. "And there's no need to tell Martin. You'll just worry him and it's over and done with." He looked anxiously into her eyes and she realized he was worried about Martin's reaction.

"Why did you and Martin get mad at each other?" Danny and Martin had never argued like that before and it had frightened her. "Why did Martin say I shouldn't take any tests? You take tests at school."

"It doesn't matter, bunny. It's over and done with. We won't do it again and Martin doesn't need to know about this."

"Are you sorry?" she asked primly. "You shouldn't have lied to him," she said with the moral authority of a child's black and white view of the world.

He just looked at her, his eyes questioning. "We have a deal? Our little secret?" She nodded. "Good," he said smiling. "Now, do you want to help me with dinner?"

"Yes!" She was jumping up and down with excitement, the boat bobbing slightly in the water. "I want to do the sizzling rice part! Let me do the rice!"

He smiled and pulled out the stool that little Sarah sat or knelt on when helping in the galley. "You like it here, don't you, on the *Moonsong*?"

"I love it," she replied happily. "It's so much better than the dorm," and she shuddered when thinking of all those people, all in her space, invading her privacy zone, way too close for comfort. It was inevitable that the mostly Chinese students at the University of Hong Kong would be intensely interested in the blonde, English boy who spoke impeccable Chinese, and his little sister who accompanied him everywhere.

The boat was small but it was a bubble of space that was all theirs. The city of Hong Kong, the bustle and constant barrage of images and smells and noises faded somewhat to the background and Sarah could breath on board the *Moonsong*, could hear herself think. "And here we can cook whatever we like, we don't have to eat their yucky food." She wrinkled her nose in disgust and Danny laughed at her.

A thread of alarm ran through the adult, sleeping, Sarah. This was the part of the dream where she wanted to wake up. Oh, how she cherished this first part of the dream, her last memories of her brother. While she was still deeply asleep, her subconscious struggled to wake. The alarm became anxiety; the anxiety spiked higher. She had to wake up! She had to! But she slumbered on, watching the unaware, happy child chatter on to Danny. Now she would put the sizzling rice into the bowl, laugh with glee as it danced and sang in the soup. It was her favorite but she had not eaten it since that night. She could taste the nutty flavor of the rice in the rich vegetable broth. This was all as real to her as the day it happened.

Anxiety escalated into panic. She had to wake up! But she slept on, the dream speeding up through the next part, as though it wanted to punish her, wanted to make sure she saw what she didn't want to see before she woke up.

Danny told her to get ready for bed and she was below in the tiny bathroom, already in her pj's, brushing her teeth. She still remembered the melody that she'd been playing with in her head that night. It was forever Danny's song. She had never written it down and never would.

Then she heard it, the sounds from up on deck. Someone on board, confronting Danny! In a full-blown panic attack, she struggled and thrashed in her dream, trying desperately to wake herself up. She felt the shock of the cold water as she slipped through the porthole in her pj's, into the water as silent as a baby seal, just like Martin taught her. She swam easily underwater to the underside of the dock opposite the *Moonsong* and clung to the piling there, watching carefully. She knew she must see the faces of these men, remember the car, remember which way they went, dragging Danny with them. But, oh god, she didn't want to see, didn't want this to be happening. She didn't want to be brave, she wanted Martin, and she continued to thrash and moan in her sleep in her attempt to end the dream. Suddenly, salt water filled her mouth and she gasped and choked and finally woke.

Sarah staggered from her bed so wet with perspiration that she thought for a moment she really had been in the water again. Sometimes she wondered if she could actually drown at this point if she didn't manage to wake up. She paced silently, arms wrapped around herself, trying to calm her trembling limbs, grateful she had at least woken before the worst part, before she started screaming and couldn't stop.

She thought of Paul. Paul was her psychiatrist, had been for thirteen years now. Sarah pictured his face, his darkly handsome Irish features, his blue eyes, the intelligence and warmth there. He reminded her of what Martin might look like as he got older and wondered again if that's why she hadn't ended the therapy and the relationship years ago. It was comforting to look at Paul and she did like him. But Sarah knew she would not tell him about the dream. Not today, not ever. She had promised Danny and had never broken that promise.

Sarah smiled tiredly. Paul was at least helpful to her little 'family' and knew she would continue to see him just to keep them happy. She would just keep Paul at arm's length as she always did. Now that Julie and Paul were a couple, Paul was even more entwined with Sarah's life, for Julie was now an integral part of Sarah's life. The cool, sophisticated, blonde had become a first-class doctor, Sarah's medical doctor, and the closest thing to a friend Sarah had. Julie had been a virtual stranger to her when Danny died. She realized now she knew Julie for almost twice as long as she had known Danny and the realization filled her with a quiet dread. As much as she hated the nightmares, her dreams were her only connection to Danny.

There would be no more sleep tonight so Sarah curled up in a chair to await the dawn, her face pensive. The window, for now, only reflecting darkness and her lonely vigil back at her.

Chapter One

The sound of applause startled Sarah out of a deep reverie. Gazing around her oceanfront garden in momentary confusion, she then chuckled inwardly. It was the wind; it was high this early in the morning, rustling through the very tops of the tall trees. Sarah sat and listened intently, sipping her tea. It did sound a little like applause, how the sound ebbed and grew, seeming to come from all directions at once. She smiled ruefully. Applause. She wasn't likely to hear that sound again. Just as well, it wasn't necessary. The stage, she realized, was her high. That wonderful feeling of finally being able to connect with people, show them the good side of herself, the things she was proud of. Time which was, after all, totally under her control. Showing only what she wanted, never revealing anything else. 'Keep her secret, keep her safe', flitted through her mind. Funny, she hadn't thought of that phrase in a long time.

Sarah shook herself out of and away from those memories. Her new mantra, keep busy. Idle thoughts were bad. Who knew where they might lead...

Her gaze swept over her treasured garden, a riot of color and rich, earthy smells. The hummingbird feeders should be cleaned and filled, time to pick up after the dog and to check on the new baby ducks out by the pond. New tracks need to be laid on the new song. Practice the new dance routine, it still wanted work, something didn't feel right there. Time to film it today, see why it didn't feel right, didn't flow. Lots to do today, enough to fill the entire day, she thought with satisfaction.

Sarah remembered that Alexander was coming for dinner tonight and her stomach contracted with anxiety. Clutching her teacup tightly, Sarah stared out over her garden to the beautiful view of the Pacific Ocean beyond and tried to calm herself, concentrating on deep, even breaths.

It would be all right. Alexander would talk. He needed that. He needed to feel like he was doing something. She would listen, just as she had every other time this past year. She would listen then say no. No to New York. No to Yuri. No to any appearances. No to all of it.

Alexander didn't realize it yet but Sarah had no intention of ever leaving Tall Trees again. The estate was aptly named, she mused, as she looked at the small stand of huge sequoias with the wind rustling their tops. It was rare for these trees to grow so far south on the California coastline; but, this estate in Malibu was situated on a point, a bluff with protection and the perfect climate for the sequoias, which had somehow found their way here and prospered. They weren't as big as their giant cousins to the north but they were beautiful and impressive. Between the ocean, the trees, the restored stone abbey, and the eighty acres of beautifully landscaped grounds, it was a lovely, tranquil retreat... or prison, depending on your point of view. Anyway, she shook off the morbid thought. It was a lovely place to hide and she had no intention of leaving, no matter what Alexander thought or said.

Sarah stood and stretched, faced the sun, and luxuriated in the wonderful, warm feeling it gave her skin. It was too bad that when people touched her, it didn't feel like this. Perhaps then she wouldn't flinch, pull away. Unlike people, the sun didn't feel intrusive.

Sarah wandered back into the bedroom, changed into workout clothes, and glanced into the mirror. In an attempt to tame her wild tangle of curls, she combed through her hair with her fingers and wove it quickly into a loose braid. She usually avoided looking at her face in the mirror but today she stopped and stared at herself before flushing and looking away. 'The Most Beautiful Woman in the World'. That's what the headline on the magazine cover said over the picture of her face. Inside, the article said she had been voted the most beautiful, sexiest woman alive. Sarah snorted in derision. Voted on by whom? Who decides these things? How ridiculous. Out of all the women alive? She wondered idly how Alexander had managed it. Who did he pay off? Was it money or a favor? Which magazine was it again...? Oh yes, *People*. Was it a female editor in charge... did he seduce her into it...? Sarah shrugged, what difference did it really make? None. Alexander was going to do what he did best, promote her. All she had to do, she told herself, was to keep making music. That's all. All the rest of it was Alexander's problem. Whether or how well the music sold... well, Alexander was a genius at that and it mattered little to Sarah how many people listened or bought her music. It was the making of the music that counted.

Sarah stood and did something she rarely did; actually looked at her entire body in the full-length mirror. She saw a slender young woman. Twenty years old was a woman, she thought, no longer a girl or a teenager. She realized with a slight shock that Alexander had probably been planning the 'Most Beautiful' award for sometime. Because it also came with 'The Sexiest Woman Alive' tribute, he had waited until she was out of her teens. She had turned twenty just two months prior... She wondered, with a sinking feeling, how long he had been planning this particular media coup. Probably ever since the infamous photo of Magnus, Alexander, and herself in 'the dress' on her nineteenth birthday. That cover had created a sensation; Alexander's message to the world that she was growing up. It was a very sophisticated cover with both Magnus and Alexander in tuxedos and herself in a beautiful, slinky, sexy gown that, of course, Alexander had personally selected. Magnus, her guardian, was seated, kissing Sarah's hand while Alexander, her manager, perched on the edge of the bar, had his arm casually around her shoulders. The photo was as full of old world charm and 1940's *film noir* as Magnus, her guardian. And the message was clear; he was handing his ward off to his son, Alexander, who would now be in total charge of her exploding career.

Sarah continued her perusal, examining her face closely. All the elements of beauty were there, the clear skin, small classic nose, full lips and the huge violet eyes that the article called 'enchanting'. Her golden blonde curls fell almost to her waist. She was a natural blonde as the downy patch between her legs could testify to. She wondered idly if she should wax or something down there. From what she was reading in women's fashion magazines, it seemed virtually no woman went natural anymore. She smiled ruefully at the thought. It wasn't as if anyone was likely to see her pubic hair.

She studied her face again. She saw the tiredness in her eyes. The lack of sleep was catching up with her. But mostly what she saw in her eyes was despair, melancholy, sadness, and grief. She didn't feel beautiful; she felt empty and sad most of the time but that was better than feeling twisted and guilty. If those people reading the magazine knew her, knew what she had done, they wouldn't think her beautiful. They would look at her with disgust.

Sarah turned away. It frightened her that someone so wrong, so broken, could look so beautiful. She shivered thinking that evil often comes disguised as beauty. She wondered for the millionth time if it was possible to be evil and not even know it, not be able to help it. She didn't want to even think these thoughts. Surely evil had to be a choice? She tried so hard, so very, very hard to be a good person. But it didn't matter. What she did know was that anyone she had ever loved, really loved, had come to a bad end because of her.

Magnus, her beloved guardian, was the latest victim. The man with the magic of music in his fingers. The man who had saved her. The courtly old man she had loved with all her heart since the day she met him at age seven and he sixty-five. They became the best of friends. He took care of her, helped raise her, loved her, taught her... and it had cost him his life. She knew that Alexander thought his father's death purely accidental, a small plane crashing in the jungle. But Sarah knew better, knew that the plane had been tampered with, knew that Magnus had been murdered.

And it was her fault.

The weight of it felt crushing. She had trouble breathing sometimes it was so heavy. But it would never happen again she promised herself. Never. She would stay here, at Tall Trees. She would make no friends, be close to no one, endanger no one.

She didn't know why Flint had killed Magnus except to take him away from her. She sensed Flint wanted her weak and alone. The fear that always flickered through her when she thought of him caused her body to tremble and shivers raced through her as if she was assaulted by tiny icicles. Flint was coming for her. She sensed it and dreaded it and feared it. Yet there was still a thread of curiosity.

He was evil, that much she knew; monstrous and evil, devoid of any compassion or feeling except power and dominion. She had never seen him, only felt his eyes of fire on her. She called him Flint because his mind felt as hard as steel and sparks flew from him whenever she sensed his presence. Why he wanted her, she didn't know. She must be like him. The thought repulsed her... can a person be born evil? Like calls to like... she pushed the thought away. She would be a good person, the kind of person that Martin would be proud of.

She realized with a shock that she had thought of Martin's name. *Never do that again,* she scolded herself. At least she hadn't spoken his name out loud, but it was dangerous to even think it. She must be more careful. She must guard him in her heart so that no would know how much she had loved him, loved him still.

It was funny. When she was little, that was what Martin had always said to Danny about her, 'Keep her secret, keep her safe.' Now, it was what she repeated to herself over and over, *Keep him secret; keep him safe.*

Chapter Two

The powerful Ferrari purred underneath him as he cleared the gates to the estate and swept up the long drive. Alexander barely noticed the beautiful scene before him, it was familiar and the car was new. He concentrated on his driving, the ease and speed with which he was able to maneuver the curved drive. He admired objects of beauty, especially when they performed as perfectly as this vehicle did, he thought with satisfaction. The Ferrari made a good addition to his auto collection.

He was a connoisseur of beauty: in people, art, architecture, and especially music. And Alexander liked to collect what he loved. The Ferrari was his tenth car. His art collection was world-renowned. He owned four homes, each an architectural gem, and had an endless supply of beautiful young women to adorn his arm when he went anywhere.

As he exited the car and nodded to Sebastian at the door, he stopped to admire the view. The sun was setting over the Pacific; golden light bathed the formal gardens in a soft glow. Father had loved this place, had spent millions restoring the old abbey and grounds, all to provide a safe and peaceful haven for his charge, Sarah.

Alexander spoke aloud to his father, a habit he'd acquired after Magnus' death a year ago. "You did your job too well, father. Now she won't leave here and I don't know what to do." He shook his head at his folly. Did he actually expect an answer? Alexander spoke to Sebastian as he entered the house. "How is she today?"

"Fine," Sebastian replied carefully. "She's waiting for you on the terrace."

Alexander nodded. "Thanks. Have Max put my car away. I'm planning on spending the night here. Hold dinner for an hour or so. Give me a chance to try to talk some sense into her."

Alexander headed for the terrace and saw Sarah watching the sun lower itself into the Pacific. Her beauty caught him by surprise again, it was especially so when he hadn't seen her in a couple of days. She was unaware of his arrival so he just stood and watched her watch the sunset. She was, as always since Magnus' death, alone. She was sipping one of those endless cups of tea she seemed to drink, herbal teas, definitely no caffeine. She looked so young, so defenseless, so heartbreakingly alone. It was strange, he thought, how much she caught his eye, how he could think of nothing else. He had always been a ladies man, loved them in all shapes and sizes, but had always been especially drawn to tall, buxom women. He was 6'2" and liked a woman who could look him in the eye. But ever since Sarah had developed from a skinny, shy kid into a beautiful young woman, he found himself comparing all other women to her and finding them wanting. When Magnus realized that his son had eyes for Sarah, he sat him down for a serious talk. That had been over five years ago, when Sarah was fifteen.

"Son, you are twenty-one years older than that young girl. She is not now nor will she ever be one of your playthings. I need to know that you understand this." Magnus had pierced him with a steely look in his eyes that brooked no argument. "I know you haven't touched her, that you are the gentleman I raised you to be. But even the way you look at her, son, is making her uncomfortable."

Alexander hadn't protested. He knew his father was right. It was just so difficult. She was only fifteen but was as smart and talented as anyone he had ever met. Musically, she was a genius. He worshipped that talent of hers that wove the very molecules of the universe and turned thin air into magic of the most amazing kind. So, to stop himself from even innocently flirting with her, he concentrated on the music. Sarah finally became comfortable enough with him to spend time with him – again making music. It was all about the music. And it had served them all well. Alexander and Magnus had become rich beyond their wildest imaginings and all because of this talented, beautiful, difficult, tortured young woman who was now his sole responsibility and he had no fucking idea what to do.

Well, time to try a new tactic tonight. Tomorrow it will be one year since she's left this estate. That's long enough he told himself. A year to grieve is enough. He wondered for the hundredth time if he should have talked this plan over with Paul first. Then dismissed the thought for the hundredth time. Paul had been Sarah's shrink since she came to them

11

when she was seven. She had arrived on their doorstep, shivering, wet, and frightened beyond all speech. She didn't speak a word for over a year. Paul had been her psychiatrist for thirteen years now and she had still never spoken of what happened, her past, her fears, nothing. What possible advice could Paul give him? Father and Paul had discussed endless strategies over the years of how to deal with Sarah. Nothing had ever worked as far as Alexander could tell. Only work helped Sarah. The music. The dance. That's what I need to concentrate on, he thought. That's the only thing that will get through to her.

Sarah looked up at his approach and the look of wariness, even fear in her eyes, sliced him to the bone. He knew better than to touch her. Sarah hated human contact and shunned it as much as possible. Father had known that and respected it. He insisted they didn't need to know why she couldn't bear it, they just all had to respect her feelings and refrain. It seemed to cause her physical pain and Alexander couldn't begin to guess why. He knew she could tolerate it. After all, she was the finest ballerina in many generations. It seemed to be the only place that Sarah tolerated touch and it was the only reason Alexander tolerated the ballet. He thought it a monstrous waste of her talent and resented the toll it took on her time and her body.

He had argued endlessly with his father over what the ballet took away from Sarah's music but had lost every time to the simple answer, "She loves it, Alexander. She's amazingly talented and she wants to do it. It's the only place and time where she has to interact with others and I feel it's important for her to continue as long as she wants to." And so she had, just one short season a year, the Fall, with ABT in New York. And that was fast approaching.

He grimaced when he thought of what he was about to do. Talking her into dancing in New York was the last thing he wanted but he could think of no other way of getting her out of Tall Trees and back out into the world. It made him sick to think of the waste. It actually cost them a small fortune for Sarah to dance. Ballerinas, even prima ballerinas, weren't exactly paid a lot of money. And considering what it cost in staff and time to keep her there and healthy, not to mention the risk if anyone screwed up, well it didn't bear thinking about. However, even with all the drawbacks, Alexander did believe it was important that Sarah was at least seen, live and on a stage. Too many rumors started flying when she spent this long completely cloistered.

Alexander took a deep breath, straightened his tie and shot his cuffs. He was always impeccably groomed and dressed and today was no exception. He approached and stopped just before her. "Hello, Princess. How is my beautiful girl this beautiful evening?"

Sarah flushed and dropped her eyes. She seemed to find any hint of flirtation from him distasteful. He reminded himself for the thousandth time not to take it personally. He consoled himself with the thought that at least she seemed to like him better than most other people. It was just so damn hard. Whenever he didn't know what to say to a woman, he reverted to his playboy persona. It had worked like a charm with every woman he'd ever met but Sarah.

"Hello, Alexander. It's good to see you. How have you been?" Sarah answered with her usual courtesy. Her politeness with him angered him at times. She could be free, funny, relaxed with his father, or even with Sebastian or Jonathan, but not with him, virtually never with him – not unless they were working.

"I'm good, Sarah. Couldn't be better. Your new album - #1 with a bullet! Told you so." He beamed at her with undisguised joy and satisfaction. She made the music, she wrote the songs, she was in total control of the material, but he was the one who made it happen. Since Alexander had started managing her music career, Sarah had become the #1 recording artist in the world. Everyone clamored for her time, her attention, any part of her they could get. And access to Sarah was one hundred percent through Alexander, especially since his father had died. Magnus had been Sarah's legal guardian since she came to them at age seven. Even though she was nineteen when his father died, and technically no longer in need of a guardian, Alexander had started the legal process within hours of his father's death. It was unusual, but due to the scope and size of the estate, and Sarah's agreement to the arrangement, he now had full legal responsibility for her until she was twenty-one years of age at which point she would automatically be emancipated. He was also her manager and her agent. Fat lot of good it did him, he thought. She did what she damn well wanted and nothing else. And she never gave him a reason for not leaving the estate. Just simply said no and went about her business.

"Good, I'm glad." She smiled at him. Just a small smile but it gave Alexander hope. "I'm working on something completely different now. Wait 'til you hear."

He groaned. "Not off in a completely new direction again, are you?" He realized that the music that had just been released held no interest for her any longer. She really didn't care how well it sold. She never seemed to listen to the numbers, the business side of the music business. She would just smile and tell him that was his job, his problem. And she seemed to absolutely hate any and all award ceremonies, events that Alexander loved. What he treasured the most, out of everything he collected, wasn't really his; they were Sarah's awards. Two Academy Awards for Best Actress, both before she turned fourteen. Fifteen Grammies in six years, the most by any recording star of any age, including Best New Artist and six Album of the Year awards. And she was the highest selling recording artist of all times – having taught him about the wonders of using the internet to not only sell music but salvage the entire sagging music industry. Alexander now managed a vast music empire and a variety of other artists, all thanks to Sarah.

Sarah looked at him appraisingly. "Why did you want to have dinner tonight, Alexander? You usually like to stay in town during the week." He didn't answer and she looked away. Her voice was small as she said, "I'm fine, Alexander. You don't have to worry about me and you don't have to come here to babysit me. I know you'd rather be out socializing, dinner and drinks with your friends."

"I'm the only family you have left. I care about you, I like spending time with you, and it's my job to make sure you're OK." Alexander almost reached out and touched a strand of her hair that was blowing in her face. He ached to touch her but he didn't. He had to look away though. Guarding himself against her was so difficult. Sometimes, if he made a wrong or thoughtless move, it was weeks before she was comfortable with him again. He couldn't afford that now, too much was at stake. "I do want to talk to you about New York though."

There. It was out. The gauntlet flung.

"I know you want me to go," Sarah replied carefully. "I've already said no. What's changed? What's different?"

"Sarah, you need to talk to Jonathan for an in-depth description of the role Yuri wants you to dance. Better yet, let Yuri come here and tell you about it himself! He's dying to talk to you. Please, Sarah, at least just listen." He heard the pleading note in his voice and despised himself for it. Goddamn it, he wasn't going to beg!

Sarah just looked at him. "Yuri always has the role of a lifetime for me." She shrugged. "It doesn't matter, he'll find someone else to dance it. I'm not dancing anymore, Alexander. I thought that you, of all people, would understand and approve. I'm going to stay here and concentrate on my music."

"Sarah, Yuri's done something completely new, something based on Steinbeck's 'East of Eden' and the whole biblical thing. He's insisting that only you can dance a role this demanding; that he choreographed Eve just for you. After all you two have been through, don't you think you owe it to him to at least listen?" Alexander was quiet for a moment. "Please, Sarah, just listen to him."

There was resolve in Sarah's eyes as she looked at him. "No, Alexander. I don't want to listen. I don't want to dance. Yuri doesn't need me; there's a line of ballerinas drooling for their opportunity to dance with him. He'll find his Eve." She walked away across the terrace and resumed her watch of the setting sun.

Alexander felt he had been dismissed. Like some fucking servant, he seethed inside. She says no to me and turns away and I'm supposed to just take it! He felt anger surge through him and resisted the urge to shake her. He'd been having that urge for a while now and knew it would be foolish to act on it. He shut that thought down quickly and completely. A lot was riding on this; he had to be successful.

Sebastian approached him with a drink and Alexander told him to go ahead and serve dinner. Hell, this conversation on the terrace was getting him nowhere. Maybe he could have a more rational discussion with her over dinner. Maybe table the whole thing during dinner, see if he could get her to relax with him. Then, after dinner…

Alexander was hopeful again. Dinner went surprisingly well. He and Sarah chatted about anything and everything. He realized, with a sharp pang of pleasure, that Sarah was trying. Trying to please him, trying to be the family they were when Magnus was alive. She had always been animated, full of discussion and ideas when talking to Magnus. It gave him hope for phase two of his discussion tonight. He moved from the table and asked Sarah to join him for an after-dinner drink in the library. She liked the library, it had been Magnus' favorite room in the house. As they settled in front of the fire, both in separate chairs, Alexander carefully selected his next words. "Sarah, why does going to New York seem to bother you so much?" He'd almost said 'terrify you', but 'bother you' seemed less confrontational.

Sarah was quiet for a long moment. Then, with a sigh, "I knew this conversation wasn't over. It doesn't bother me, Alexander. I just don't want to go."

"Why? You've always loved the ballet, loved New York. Is it because you're afraid we can't take care of you there?"

"No." Sarah laughed softly, dismissing that idea. "Sebastian, Jonathan, you – even the ballet company, you all have my MCS down cold. I'm not afraid I'll be exposed to something; and, if I am, all of you will spring into action like some comic book trio and I'll be saved. It's not that." She sat back in the large chair and tucked her legs up under her on the seat and turned to face him.

It was true. Sarah's Multiple Chemical Sensitivity disorder was nothing to be taken lightly. Sarah had no allergies to anything found in nature; however, chemicals of any kind were dangerous and even possibly fatal for her. It was the primary reason she lived so isolated, so alone. Father, Sebastian, and he had learned through expensive and painful trial and error how to care for this strange child they inherited. Food had been the first hurdle to overcome. Sarah could eat only organic. After a few near death experiences, they had learned that this rule must be absolute. The only way to control the quality of what she ate was to control the source. For well over ten years now they had owned a farm which operated under strict instructions and supervision and was run by one of the top organic growers in the country. Sarah was also a vegetarian by choice; Alexander swore she liked animals better than most people. So, the farm solved the food issue as long as she never ate anything from any other source. This was solved by shipping everything from the farm to wherever Sarah was.

Additionally, the estate inside and out was set up for her specific needs. All natural materials were used as much as possible: stone, wood, glass, etc., all OK. Carpets, upholstery, and clothing all went through rigorous testing before being allowed on the estate. No chemicals were ever used in cleaning or gardening. The house and the estate were safe zones for Sarah as was the apartment in New York, any car she rode in, and the private jet; all designed with Sarah's safety in mind. Going out in public was very, very difficult and carefully orchestrated. An advance team went in just prior to Sarah's arrival using spectroscopic equipment to monitor for the chemicals most dangerous to her. She never went anywhere without a survival backpack close at hand; oxygen tank with filtering mask should the air she was breathing be contaminated, and an EpiPen in case she was exposed to a chemical that affected her skin or air passages. Luckily, most contaminants only caused mild reactions, rashes and asthmatic breathing problems; but, some fairly common chemicals such as tetrachloroethylene, used in dry cleaning, caused disastrous reactions that happened frighteningly fast.

It still gave Alexander palpitations when she went out, but he felt it was important that she do so. He remembered the last incident all too vividly though. Sarah had been walking with Magnus and Sebastian a few years ago in New York. She had been recognized and mobbed in the street and they sought refuge in a close-by shop which turned out to be an on-premise dry cleaning establishment. Within seconds of exposure, Sarah had collapsed into seizures and began bleeding from all the soft tissue in her body. Even with the oxygen on hand and medical help arriving within minutes, she had almost died. He and father had decided then that Sarah could never be allowed to go anywhere out of her safe zones without that advance team checking first. So far that had worked well. Sarah seemed to accept the conditions imposed on her and never, to his knowledge, tried to circumvent them.

Hell, maybe that was it, the entire problem. Who wouldn't be afraid of touch if it meant that you could die? But Alexander knew he didn't really believe it. There was something else, something more that terrified Sarah and that she never spoke of. Actually, the MCS turned out to be a convenient cover for Sarah's scant public appearances. The public's interest in Sarah was intense. The MCS would have been impossible to hide, at any rate, and now she had the public and her fan's sympathy for her reclusiveness. No one but the close inner circle knew the rest, the real reasons she never gave interviews, never appeared on talk shows, never promoted her own work. No one knew of the psychotic breaks, the self-mutilations, the suicide attempts; and, if Alexander had his way, no one ever would.

The year between Sarah's sixteenth and seventeenth birthdays had been the worst. That breakdown had been severe and Alexander had despaired of her ever recovering. Only Magnus had not given up hope. And because his father asked it of him, and because he loved his father, he had hidden what Sarah was going through from the world. She had such an incredible backlog of work that he was able to bring out two best selling albums that year. He promoted her work as if she was just fine at home, working away on her music. In fact, she was strapped to a bed, being fed through a tube, with nurses wiping her ass, keeping her fixated eyes from drying out, exercising her limbs so she wouldn't stiffen.

He pushed the memory away. Not again. None of them could endure that agony again. She had been catatonic for almost a year and that had been the good part. Then came the terrifying nightmares, the screaming, the suicide attempts, the self-loathing. And still, after all these years, no answers as to what drove this behavior. Paul could speculate all he wanted but Sarah said nothing. If only Sarah could tolerate drugs they might have had some success in trying to control what was happening to her. But almost all medications, especially anything that affects the brain, were impossible for Sarah to take. Thank god for Julie. His cousin, Julie, was a damn fine doctor and Alexander knew with certainty that Sarah was only alive because of Julie. And Julie was family; she could be trusted to never say a word.

Alexander took an appreciative sniff of his brandy and settled back comfortably in his chair. Sarah was staring into the fire and he watched the shadows dance across her face and body. He chose his next words with great care. He could not afford to push her towards that dark place, whatever or wherever that was. God, he wished his father were alive to advise him. But he wasn't and Alexander had to do the best he could. He could almost hear his father's voice. 'Do what's best for Sarah, son. Not for her music, not for her career, not for her fans, but for her.' And Alexander couldn't help but think that staying on the estate for the rest of her life was not good for Sarah. The longer it went on, the harder it would be to get her out. Had she added agoraphobia to her list of problems?

"Sarah, is it possible that you're reluctant to go because you despise all the unwanted male attention and Father won't be there to shield you from them?" He waited quietly to see how she would take this question. Ever since Sarah had accepted that damn Juliet role when she was not quite fourteen, men had been ape shit over her. He couldn't blame them. She was exquisite and innocent and ever so sexy without even realizing it. It was something about the way she moved, it was so graceful, so alluring. And her proportions, she was small but she was perfect: long neck, long legs, high breasts, the most perfect ass he'd ever seen... he shook himself off that train of thought. Not now. *Eye on the ball, Alexander*, he reminded himself.

Sarah was horrified by male attention, hated it so much that she never made another movie. Even when she won her second Oscar for playing Juliet, she could not be persuaded to accept another film role. He smiled to himself just thinking about it. Only fourteen years old and she said there wasn't enough control over the process for her. His thoughts wandered for a moment to another favorite occupation of his; trying to decide just how smart Sarah was. She had never taken an IQ test, refused to, but Alexander was willing to bet big money that the number would shock him if he knew it. She was one of the smartest people he had ever met and he and his father were no slouches in that department. What really made Alexander uncomfortable was the thought that Sarah was only showing him a fraction of what she was capable of. That he didn't understand even a tenth of who she was. That she knew everything he was thinking before he even said it... this was another unproductive train of thought. He put that thought away as well... eye on the ball.

Sarah looked at him a long moment before she answered his question. "Yes, that's part of the..." she searched for a word and finally came up with "issue." She darted an accusing glance at him, as if he were to blame for the entire male population's hormones. "It doesn't help that you orchestrated that stupid magazine article."

Alexander raised his eyebrows. "Me! You think I bought off People Magazine, a division of Time Magazine and the Time Warner Corporation?"

Sarah laughed aloud. It was so good to see. It'd been so long since he'd seen her just throw her head back and lose herself in laughter like that. He laughed with her although he hadn't meant it as a joke. He was serious. Did she honestly think he had anything to do with their choice?

"Alexander," Sarah teased. "Was the editor perhaps a woman? Perhaps a friend of yours? Perhaps someone who owed you a favor?"

"Absolutely not. It was a guy, Gabriel Peterson, who heads up that team and they have an entire process they go through and I had nothing – I repeat nothing – to do with it except supply them with the photos after you won. And they almost scrapped you and went to the next person on the list because you wouldn't pose for the issue."

Sarah looked surprised. "You didn't ask me to pose for them."

"Would you have if I'd asked?" he asked.

"No," she replied.

"Well, there you have it. That's why I didn't bother to ask. I told them to use what I gave them or pick someone else. I guess they finally decided that selecting the most beautiful woman in the world shouldn't be dependent on her being willing to pose for them."

Sarah smiled but said nothing.

"Sarah, I realize that article made things more difficult for you." Frustrated, he carefully straightened the crease in his trousers. "But, here's the thing, article or no, you're grown up now. You're probably the most eligible, desirable female out there. There's going to be a line of guys for you no matter what. Almost no girl alive knows how to cope with that much attention, much less one like you. You've led a very, very sheltered life but that's no reason to withdraw from life completely."

He played his trump card. "What do you think Father would want you to do?"

Sarah glanced sharply at him but decided to let the manipulation slide. "I'm not a girl. I may be young and sheltered, but I'm a woman, not a girl."

"Fine. Young woman," he corrected himself. "Look, Sarah, I have an idea." She just looked at him. "Hear me out before you say anything." He took a deep breath. "What if you were engaged?"

"Engaged?" she replied, puzzled, shaking her head negatively.

"To be married," he said. "To me." He spread his hands in a placating gesture at the expression on her face. "Now, hear me out like I said. I know you're not in love with me. I know I'm twice your age. But, Sarah, I do love you. I love you with all my heart and I would do anything to help you." He looked earnestly at her. "It wouldn't have to be a real engagement. If you showed up in New York with a big ring and my announcement that we're to be married, well, then the pressure is off you. No one can start nasty rumors, no more twitters about the Ice Queen of the ABT, and any guy who dares to come on to you will have me to answer to."

Sarah stared at him in surprise. "You mean we would pretend?"

"That's entirely up to you," he replied. "I'm asking you to marry me and I'd like nothing more than for it to be real, to actually happen. Perhaps we could use the engagement as a test period, to see how we could make it work, to see if it could be acceptable to you. If not, at the end of the season when we leave New York, I can make an announcement that the engagement is off. I won't be angry, Sarah, if that's what you decide. But, it will give you space to breath while you're in New York. You won't have to deal with three thousand suitors. And maybe you just need to get your confidence back, realize that you can go out in public without Father at your side. I can be that shield for you, Sarah."

Her eyes shimmered with tears as she looked at him, really looked at him for the first time in so long he couldn't remember when she had last looked into his eyes. "You would do that for me?" she whispered.

"Of course," he said simply. "I would do anything for you, Sarah. Anything."

She began to shake her head. "I can't marry…"

"Wait," he cut her off. "Let me finish, please let me finish," he pleaded. "Sarah," he paused awkwardly. "I'm well aware that you don't desire the intimacy of marriage." He was dancing on dangerous ground here. He didn't want to insult her, wasn't sure of the language to use, but he plunged ahead. "I've talked to Paul about what your aversion to touch means as it applies to sex, and I'm aware that that is not something you care to engage in, with me or anyone else. And it's also not something you care to discuss. I know you and I have never had this discussion," he shifted uncomfortably in his seat, "but Father and Paul told me."

Sarah flushed and turned her face away but said nothing.

"Sarah," he hoped she could read the sincerity in his eyes. He sometimes felt she could. He so hoped it was true now. He needed her to understand and believe him. He needed her to trust him as she had trusted his father. "I would never, never force, or even ask you to do anything you didn't want to do. If you'll have me, I'm offering you love. I'm offering you protection. I'll be your shield from the rest of the world. I'm offering you everything I have and everything I am, Sarah. We can have separate bedrooms. Your life doesn't have to change. Just let me love you and take care of you. I can't bear for you to think of yourself as alone. You'll never be alone, Sarah. You'll always have me."

He stopped talking. There was nothing else to say. It was a preposterous proposal and he prayed she would say yes. He silently reached into his pocket and handed Sarah the ring, dropping it in her palm rather than putting it on her finger.

Chapter Three

Sarah stared at Alexander in surprise. She knew he'd been thinking of marriage but thinking of it in a legal sort of way. She was aware that how to take care of her once she became emancipated was a concern of his. But she hadn't expected this, this sincere declaration of love and sacrifice. She was more touched than she realized she could be by Alexander. Sarah was well aware that he had lusted after her, albeit in a gentlemanly polite sort of way, for a long time. Most of her discussions with Magnus about sex and relationships had come because of their discussions about Alexander's natural feelings for her. People were so often a mystery to Sarah. Too much information was sometimes worse than none she thought. Especially since what people thought and what they said and did were often two very different things. And, no matter what men said, Sarah knew what they were thinking when they looked at her. It was so difficult to know which was more representative but Sarah suspected it was as the old saying went, 'It's the thought that counts.' But she also knew that Alexander did love her as well as desire her. She just hadn't expected him to offer to make this kind of sacrifice. To enter into a one-sided marriage with a woman who was not in love with him and couldn't offer him sex or children would be a huge concession for a man like Alexander, an unabashed, hedonistic, never married, playboy. She had always suspected that one day Alexander would be glad to give up the party life and settle down with the woman of his dreams and raise perfect children. She never suspected he would offer to give up his party ways to stay home and babysit her.

She stared at the ring lying in the palm of her hand, a large, four-carat, square-cut, yellow diamond with two triangular white diamonds on either side. "Alexander, that's a very kind and gentlemanly offer but I couldn't let you do that." She smiled wryly at him. "Wouldn't that cramp your style, Mr. Smooth?" She used the title of her hit song that the entire world recognized as being about Alexander.

He smiled fondly at her. She knew he complained about the notoriety the song gave him but secretly loved it. "I told you, Sarah, I will do anything for you. And," he added with a twinkle in his eye, "I didn't say I would give up sex. But I would give up my bachelor ways and I would be very, very discreet about any women. I would never embarrass you, Sarah."

She was surprised again. He really had been thinking about this. "But what about children, Alexander? Don't you want children someday?"

"I don't want some imaginary, future children more than I want you," he said simply. "We can always adopt."

"Oh yes," she said sarcastically. "Because that worked out so well for you and your father." She could tell by his face alone that Alexander was stung by that remark. She softened her tone. "I only meant because I was such an easy child to raise," and suddenly they were both laughing. It did feel good to laugh again with Alexander. She wished she could love him like he loved her. It would be so much easier. She felt about Alexander the way she felt about her brother, Danny. She had been only seven when Danny died but she remembered him in perfect and wonderful detail. He was big and really, really smart but sort of clueless, and she had loved him the way she now loved Zander. Well, it had taken some time to get there with Alexander but now she did think of him as her brother, her family. She loved him but was not 'in love' with him, a crucial distinction. She realized she had never even shared her private nickname for him and impulsively decided on the wave of their laughter to do so. "You know, in my mind I always call you Zander. I've never said it to you because I know you hate nicknames." She gave him an impish look.

His turn to be surprised, he looked at her inquiringly. "Really? You call me Zander?"

She giggled. "I think of you as Zander. It's two syllables shorter, saves a lot of time."

He smiled at her. "I do hate nicknames because mine invariably ends up as Al, which I hate, or Alex, which is only marginally better. No one has ever called me Zander." His brown eyes twinkled with fun. "You can call me that. It can be our secret, our code." Then he reached out and nearly touched her face.

Sarah flinched and Alexander caught himself in time, but she could see what it cost him. The moment between them was ruined. She had done it again and it was just a sample of what a disaster a marriage between them would be. She prepared herself to dash his hopes, but he spoke first.

"I'm sorry, Sarah," he said softly. "I shouldn't have done that. Maybe someday you'll trust me enough to let me touch you. I can wait. I can wait as long as it takes."

Sarah felt her heart contract for him. It was more his tone than what he said that touched her so. He had no clue why she wouldn't, couldn't, let him touch her, and she had no way of telling him. "It's not that I don't trust you, Zander," she replied softly. "I do trust you. I trust you completely. It's myself I don't trust."

He looked at her with wonder. "I don't understand, Sarah. What about yourself don't you trust?"

"Everything," she replied.

Sarah got up and stood in front of the fire. Suddenly she didn't want to dash his hopes. She didn't want to continue to befuddle and confuse the one person who was trying his best just to help her. Of course he didn't understand. How could he? She had never told him anything real about herself. And suddenly she realized that she never would. She would never have to if she abandoned that Sarah right now. That Sarah she had been could be left behind, right now, if she just vowed to herself to forget about Martin. After all, he was never coming back. He had ended up hating the person she was. Not one word, not in over four years. Zander would never have to know about that Sarah. He would never have to know she was responsible for his father's death. Maybe that's what she needed to do to atone: give up, once and for all, her ability to travel using just her mind; never again go to Top of the World, and those things about herself that she could not control - the mind reading, the flood of unwanted information when a person touched her - those things she would continue to hide. If she never used her abilities again, Flint would lose interest in her. She would be worthless to him; he would forget her.

Suddenly she was exultant, happy. She didn't need to hide from the entire world, only from Flint. And she was practically certain he couldn't see her unless she used her mind to leave her body and travel.

But could she do this? Was she strong enough to resist those temptations? She didn't think so.

She impulsively turned to Zander and said, "If I married you, you would be in charge, right?"

Alexander looked at her cautiously. "I'm not sure what you mean, in charge of what? Your career? That wouldn't change," he said slowly, trying to read where she was coming from.

"I mean, in the marriage vows I would have to promise to love, honor AND obey you? Right?" she queried.

"You don't have to make that vow. In more modern ceremonies these days, the obey part is left out." He smiled at her. "This is the 21st century, Sarah."

"But I want to make that vow. I want you to make the rules and I'll have to obey them. And, if I don't obey, you can punish me." She looked at him pleading for understanding but she didn't need her mind reading abilities. She could tell just by his expression that he was lost.

"What kind of rules are you talking about, Sarah?" He looked bewildered. "Punish you? I don't understand. Besides," he laughed nervously, "you never obey me now. You virtually never do what I ask."

"But if I was married to you, if I took a vow to obey you, I would have to. Don't you see?" she added, a pleading look in her eyes.

"No, not really." Alexander shook his head. "You'll have to explain yourself."

"Alexander, don't you see! This could be the perfect answer. I don't trust myself. I shouldn't be making decisions – not decisions that affect other people. I don't know what to do, how to be normal around people, how I'm supposed to act. I can't be trusted to do the right thing." She took a deep breath to steady herself, to keep her voice from shaking. "Alexander," she pleaded with him, "you could tell me what to do and I would have to do it. And if I don't, as my husband, you could punish me. Then I would know that I have to obey. It would be easy. Just follow the rules, that's all I would have to do." Sarah could tell by Zander's expression that he was still confused. "I don't know how to be normal," she said simply. "I've never known. I've tried and tried but I don't understand people. I don't know how to be like them."

"Sarah, I think you understand people much better than you realize. For god's sake, you write best selling music and lyrics that resonate with people all around the world. Millions of people adore you." He looked at her perplexed, his eyes troubled.

"They don't know me," she replied simply. "And I understand certain things about people, certain situations, but I almost never understand why people do what they do. Why they make the decisions they do. Why they say one thing but mean another. Why they value this thing over that thing. Why this person is important to them, but these people are not." She shook her head. "Everything in my life seems too loud, too close, and really, really fast, Zander. It makes me cringe most of the time. Most of the time I want to hide. And it makes me tired, so very, very tired and I can't sleep." Sarah turned away. She had never revealed so much of herself to Zander before, never had this kind of conversation with him before. She thought fleetingly of Paul; he was going to have a field day when he heard about all of this. Sarah had no doubt Zander would talk to Paul about it. Zander seemed afraid to deal with her since his father's death without checking with Paul first. No wonder.

"Zander, there's something else." She stepped closer to him. In for a penny, in for a pound, she thought. She did love and respect this man, even if she wasn't in love with him. She wasn't stupid. It was highly unlikely she would ever get an offer from anyone she could tolerate better than Alexander. She had often thought that perhaps sex, for her, was like taking medicine or getting through a physical from Julie. Just get it over with. Maybe it wouldn't be so bad. After all, millions of women have sex every day with people they don't necessarily love and they get through it. "If I agree to marry you, I'd like to be a wife to you. A real wife." She stepped even closer and lifted her face to him. "At least I'd like to try," she said softly.

There was confusion in Zander's eyes. She could feel his panic, his indecision. "What are you saying?" he asked softly.

"That you can kiss me if you want to," she replied as softly. "You can touch me, Zander."

Alexander looked deep into her eyes, confusion warring with desire. Desire won, her lips were so close. He leaned over and kissed her softly. His heart nearly stopped when he felt her kiss him back. Desire flared hot through his body, he put his arms around her and kissed her more deeply. He then felt her tremble. He wasn't sure, was it desire or fear she was feeling? He pulled back to look in her eyes and realized that she was afraid. "You don't have to do this, Sarah," he said softly. "You don't have to prove anything to me."

"It's OK," she said, putting her fingers over his mouth to stop him from talking. "I want to. I'm just a little scared. Aren't most girls their first time?" She slipped the ring on her finger.

An electric shock went through Alexander's entire body. "You want me to make love to you?" he said stupidly.

She smiled shyly at him. "Isn't that what husbands and wives do?"

"Sarah, are you sure? Baby, don't..." Sarah put her lips over his and all rational thought fled Alexander's brain. Almost all. He knew he had to move slow; he didn't want to scare her. But she was in his arms, he was kissing her, stroking her face, and she was allowing it. He was shaking with need and sat them both down on the edge of the couch. He kissed her slowly, her face, her eyes, her cheeks. He stroked her beautiful full lips with the tip of his finger and kissed her again. He looked at her carefully, trying to gauge her reaction. She wasn't responding ardently, but she was allowing it. He could see resolve in her eyes and realized she intended to go through with this.

Alexander was torn. It appeared Sarah was determined to lose her virginity tonight, here with him. He knew that she was a virgin because during the time of the terrible breakdown they had feared she had been raped, or abused, or perhaps just fell in love and was abandoned. Her crisis was so severe; and, again, she wasn't speaking, so she had been examined by Julie. No evidence of any sexual activity was noted. No trauma of any kind was found on her body. And she certainly hadn't had any opportunity since then to meet any likely candidates. Alexander and Paul had discussed Sarah's problems many times, especially since his father's death. He supposed Paul was more of a consultant to him than a shrink to Sarah. But he and Paul had never discussed what to do if Sarah came on to him. That seemed as unlikely as aliens landing.

He remembered his father's advice, 'Do what's best for Sarah.' She was initiating this. She was getting her nerve up now, for whatever reason, and trusting him to do this. He would seduce her as slowly and gently and lovingly as he could. And he would stop the instant she asked him to. He couldn't think of what else to do. To turn her down would be an insult to her feminine charms; her self-esteem was fragile at best. He was a skilled lover. He would do everything in his power to help her achieve an orgasm. If she was frigid, as Paul suspected and he was practically certain of, well perhaps he could help her at least enjoy the experience instead of dreading it so much. Sometimes the fear of something was much worse than the thing itself. Perhaps sex was like that for Sarah.

He resumed kissing her, now lightly stroking down her graceful neck and kissing the small hollow at the base of her throat. She smiled at him at bit tremulously and her eyes encouraged him to continue. He could see the pulse in her throat and kissed it. God, those gorgeous violet eyes, so frightened but so trusting. He kissed her throat down to the edge of her blouse and slowly unbuttoned the first button. He looked at her again, was he moving too fast? No, she was actually responding now, she turned her face to his and kissed him on the lips. Encouraged, he kissed her back, then slowly stroked one finger over the top of her breast as he started to open the second button of her blouse. Sarah exploded out of his grasp with a muffled cry of fear and anguish. Her blouse ripped in his hands and he hastily let go of her, signaling with his upheld palms that he would not attempt to touch her again.

She backed away from him, pain, humiliation, and fear on her face. "I'm sorry," she sobbed. "I'm sorry. I don't know what's wrong with me. I'm sorry." She wept and held her blouse together and backed away from him until she met the opposite wall. She then collapsed, holding her arms around herself, rocking and weeping.

Alexander was aghast. He realized she must have steeled herself to accept his touch and had attempted to tolerate it as long as she could. He was horrified at himself. What a fool he was! Knowing her deep psychological problems, why in the world had he thought this was a good idea? He had just wanted her so badly for so long that he deluded himself into thinking this was what she wanted. Sarah didn't know what she wanted. She had made that abundantly clear when asking him to set the rules and make her obey.

He approached but didn't come too close, then crouched down to talk to her huddled form on the floor. "I'm not going to touch you, Sarah," he promised soothingly. "Don't worry, Princess, I'm not going to touch you. I'm the one who's sorry. I should never have done that. I frightened you and I'm very, very sorry about that." He wished he could comfort her, ached to take her in his arms and hold her, wipe her tears away, but he knew better than to try. Then would come hysteria, then god knows...

"Oh god, baby girl. What happened to you? Who hurt you so badly that you can't bear to be touched?" His eyes filled with tears as he softly asked, "Was it Danny, Sarah? Did Danny hurt you?"

Sarah looked up at him in surprise and he saw anger surge through her. "Danny! Danny loved me! Danny was your friend! How could you say that! How!" She all but hissed at him.

"Sarah, sometimes people we love hurt us the most," he replied softly. Sarah slapped him across the face. She was furious. He had never seen her so angry.

"Danny never hurt me," she stated flatly. "Never! You're accusing him of being some sort of pedophile, hurting his little sister. He never hurt me!" She rushed past him out of the room.

Alexander rocked back on his heels. Well, that was a fucking disaster. Who the hell did he think he was playing amateur shrink? He actually couldn't believe he had said that about Danny out loud. The thought had slipped into his mind a few times, only because of how unnaturally close seventeen year old Danny was to his seven year old sister at the time he first met them. But he had dismissed those thoughts as uncharitable. Of course they would be close; they were orphans. And little Sarah, who was a bit strange even back then, obviously adored her big brother.

He thought back to those days in Hong Kong. He hadn't really paid much attention to Danny's little sister other than to notice that she seemed more like a four or five year old than seven in size and maturity. She was painfully shy, stuck to Danny like a barnacle, and spoke to no one but her brother. He remembered that Danny had assured him that Sarah could speak. 'She's actually very smart,' he'd said, 'just really, really shy. She hasn't been around people much.' Danny said they had grown up in a small missionary in rural China. Sarah had never been anywhere but that small village until their parents died and the unbelievably smart Danny managed to get himself a full, doctorate-level scholarship at the University of Hong Kong. In Physics no less, at age seventeen! He brought his little sister with him because they had no other family. The little girl had not been adjusting well to the noise and bustle of Hong Kong. Everything made her sick. She couldn't tolerate living in the noisy, crowded, student-housing situation he was given. He couldn't leave her with anyone, she was too shy and freaked out. She tagged along to all his classes and went everywhere Danny went. Alexander pictured her as she'd been then, quietly reading the books Danny gave her or drawing in the tablet she had. Sitting there as quietly and patiently as a little blonde mouse during the advanced physics and mathematics classes that Danny attended.

That was actually how he and Danny met; he sat in on the tail-end of one of those classes at Julie's insistence. When Danny heard through Julie, a medical student at the university who he had a major crush on, that her cousin, Alexander, ran an illegal high stakes poker game, he'd finagled his way in. Alexander actually thought it was funny and kind of cute that Julie would bring this kid to his game. The kid brought along his baby sister for Christ's sake. He told Julie no way but Julie said she was willing to stake him. Which had to mean something, Julie was no fool. So, he had let Danny play even though he knew the kid had never tried his hand at poker before. He figured at best it would be interesting, at worst an expensive lesson for Julie. But Danny had won. Not huge, but he had won and observed everything with that computer for a brain he had. He then came back, having earned his own stake into the next game. This time he went for Alexander with a vengeance. It was uncanny, like the kid could read minds or something. He couldn't lose. He finally went after what Alexander realized he had come for all along, the *Moonsong*, Alexander's 40', wooden beauty of a sloop. A sailboat of dreams, albeit a bit slow for racing against modern, lightweight craft. When Danny tapped him out for cash and he put the *Moonsong*'s title on the table, he knew for sure that he had made a mistake. It was the look in Danny's eye; the only tell he'd seen from the kid. The boat was what he wanted. The boat was why he came and Alexander knew then that he had lost. He'd been outmaneuvered and outplayed, and by a seventeen year old kid fresh from the missionary. The memory still made him laugh.

At the time, he and his father were the two biggest jewel thieves and con artists in Europe and Asia, and this kid had taken him without a struggle. He good-naturedly gave up the boat and found out that the kid desperately needed a better living situation for himself and his little sister. The University had a marina. He could live there, on the boat, with his little sister. He had admired the *Moonsong* when Julie pointed it out to him as belonging to her cousin. He then simply went about finding a way to acquire what he needed. That was Danny. Despite the over ten-year age difference, he and Alexander had become fast friends. But, he reflected ruefully now, how well could he actually have known Danny in the few short months they spent together?

He realized that meeting Danny was the one act that totally changed the course of his and his father's life. Because that was how they ended up with Sarah. And that changed everything. After Danny's gruesome murder, he realized how little he actually knew about the kid and his little sister. Perhaps there was a side to Danny he never suspected. They had certainly never learned any more about Danny and Sarah's past from Sarah. They knew only what Danny told him and Julie and that was painfully little.

The sound of the garage and a car startled Alexander out of his reverie. He ran out the front door certain it couldn't be Sarah but saw her in Sebastian's Audi, her chocolate lab, Roscoe, in the passenger seat, heading down the driveway. He ran after the car, shouting her name, but she didn't stop. He was incredulous. Well, he got his wish. Sarah left the estate. But she had never driven a car to his knowledge. She certainly didn't have a driver's license, and she never, but NEVER left the estate alone. It was a cardinal rule. He watched the tail lights disappear, whirled around and shouted for Sebastian who stood ready at the door. He must have heard Alexander chasing the car, shouting like an idiot.

He threw the keys to the BMW; it was the closest car to Sebastian. "It's Sarah! In your Audi! Quick man; no time! Follow her! Bring her back, Sebastian."

"My God, Alexander! What happened?" Sebastian huffed as he hustled himself into the BMW. "Why aren't you going after her?"

"Because she's pissed as hell at me right now. Hurry, Sebastian, bring her back!" he ordered.

Sebastian roared down the driveway. He could be pretty responsive for an old man of over seventy. Sarah loved Sebastian. She would listen to him. He would bring her back. Alexander repeated this to himself over and over as he paced, waiting.

Chapter Four

Sarah tensed behind the wheel of the Audi. It helped that she rode as a passenger many times in the front of this car with Sebastian driving. The Audi was the car the major-domo of the house used for running errands. Before Magnus died, Sarah accompanied him many times, usually on trips to the farm, which made her familiar with the controls and how to operate them. It was all pretty straight forward and she relaxed slightly. She sensed rather than saw that it was Sebastian who was coming after her and she relaxed even more. It would be OK. He wouldn't be angry, just concerned. Where did she think she was going anyway? She had no idea, just away from Zander. She shouldn't have gotten so angry with him. He was just grasping at straws when he said that about Danny. Zander hated being in the dark. He always liked knowing more than anyone else and playing his own cards close.

The truth was, she had nowhere else to go, no one to go to. The thought made her pull off the road into the Paradise Cove small parking enclosure and turn off the car. Why did she act so insanely with Alexander? She stared at the ring on her finger with revulsion and pulled it off. How could he not know she hated diamonds, especially huge blood diamonds like the one in her hand? Because you've never told him, stupid, she reminded herself. She was the closet mind reader, not him. And Alexander loved the biggest and the best of anything. Of course he would buy her a trophy ring like this.

She finally admitted to herself why she had reacted as she had. It was irrational but she couldn't help but believe it. If she gave herself to another man, she would forever destroy any chance of Martin coming back into her life. And she couldn't do it. She couldn't give up on him entirely. Sarah wept again as she got out of the car. It was crazy to think like this and she knew it. He was never coming back. It's been four years, Sarah, four years, two months and twenty-four days. And not a word. Not a single word! And he's married anyway, she raged.

He. Married. Someone. Else.

She had to get that through her thick brain. Even if he did come back into your life, he wouldn't be yours, you stupid ninny. He's married, has a baby. My god, he probably has more kids by now.

She knew what obsession was. She'd had plenty of discussions on the subject with Paul without ever letting him know who the object of her obsession was or revealing anything at all about him. These were rhetorical discussions although she knew Paul was too bright not to see through most of that. Still, it was he who called it her obsession the first time and she realized he was right.

Martin had never led her on or professed to love her like that. She blushed with shame remembering some of her actions at age fifteen when he was twenty-five and headed off for his last deployment in Afghanistan. He probably thought she was such a child. No wonder he broke his promise and didn't come for her when he got out of the Army. He was already in love with a woman his own age, a baby on the way. She didn't blame him. Not in the least.

He had taken care of her all of her life. Martin's face was the first face she ever remembered seeing. At only ten years old, he assumed total responsibility for this little baby girl that his friend, Danny, thrust upon him. From the time she was born, it was Martin who she remembered caring for her, feeding her, bathing her, laughing with her, singing to her, keeping her safe and warm. It was Martin who hugged her and kissed her and called her his girl. Martin and Danny were the same age but Danny always had his head buried in a book, too lost in his contemplation of quantum mechanics to pay much attention to a baby. But Martin talked to her all the time. Martin listened to her. Martin loved her. She knew this unequivocally. Martin loved her so much that, as a baby, she was sure he was just like her. But as she grew older, she realized with dismay that it wasn't true. Much as she wanted to believe that Martin could do the things she could, she realized he couldn't. Not without her anyway. Other people, even Danny, couldn't do any of the things Sarah could do. They couldn't leave their bodies and travel anywhere they wanted, see anything they wanted. They couldn't enter the mind and body of a bird or whale and be that creature for a while. They couldn't read other people's minds. They couldn't move objects with their minds and they couldn't go to places like Top of the World. Martin could do some of these things with her. At least, he could go places with her when she went. He couldn't read minds, though, or move objects with his mind. He had cautioned Sarah since she was old enough to talk to never, never tell anyone about these things she could do. He also told Danny, "Keep her secret, keep her safe."

Sarah broke down sobbing. He had done his best to care for her as long as he could. Sixteen years was a long time to bear a heavy burden like herself, she thought. When he knew she was safe, secure, and loved, he finally walked away. Walked away to a life of his own, a life he had always dreamed of, a life he deserved. She knew of his secret longing for a family, the white picket fence, a normal life. He craved it, having never experienced anything even remotely close to it. And he deserved it, he really did.

So, she let him go. It almost broke her in two but she let him go. She never tried to find him, to go after him. Didn't that prove something? That she really loved him? She loved him so desperately that she had driven him off. Obsession/love, another distinction the confused Sarah had trouble making. And she realized when he left that she was really alone. No matter how much she looked, researched, studied, she never found proof of anyone else remotely like herself. She was a freak, an oddity. Considering the circumstances of her birth, did she even know if she was fully human?

Her tears came faster as she stormed around the rocks, Roscoe close on her heels, and headed towards the water, the hated ring clutched in the palm of her hand. She would throw it in the ocean. It was madness to think she could marry Alexander. Freaks like her didn't get married; they hid. She must have been insane.

Suddenly Roscoe growled a low warning sound deep in his throat and Sarah realized with a jolt that she wasn't alone. It was after midnight and there were two men on the beach, suddenly in her face, confronting her. Her heart went into overdrive at the same time she froze in shock. It all happened so fast.

"We weren't supposed to do anything, just watch," the big guy whined.

The smaller, weasely guy snarled, "Yeah, well she just fucking fell into our laps. We'd be fools not to take advantage of that," and Sarah saw the glint of a knife in his hand.

In the blink of an eye, Roscoe charged. She threw the big man away from her with her mind and screamed as she realized that the smaller man, the one with the knife, had stabbed Roscoe who howled in pain and fell as Sarah reached out for him. She never even felt the knife as it sliced a gash through her forearm. Grabbing a handful of sand, she flung it in the smaller man's face. He stumbled. She heard a shout from the parking lot. Sebastian! Thank God! She screamed again, "Help! Sebastian!" The smaller guy took one more look around for his partner, saw he was out cold, and ran off into the darkness away from the parking area.

Sarah was crouched over her dog as Sebastian arrived brandishing a tire iron. Covered in blood and sand, she begged him to help her as Roscoe died in her arms. "My god, child, are you all right?" He dropped to his knees to examine her more closely. She didn't appear to be injured except for a nasty cut on her arm. Most of the blood seemed to be her dogs' but he couldn't be sure in the darkness. He pulled his handkerchief out and bound her arm. He then got up, checked the large man to make sure he was still out, and grabbed his cell phone. "Alexander, get here now" he ordered into the phone. "Paradise Cove, just down the road. Sarah's been attacked. She's injured, I can't be sure how badly. One assailant down, one escaped. Get here fast. We need to get her out of here now!" He could hear Alexander running even as he spoke, then heard the roar of the Ferrari through the phone as Alexander flew down the road, still talking to him.

He was there in two minutes, tires squealing as he came in fast. He was up and running, armed, moving towards them instantly. Alexander took in the scene immediately. "Where'd the other one go?" he asked Sebastian, his eyes scanning the darkness.

"That way," Sebastian pointed to the direction away from the parking lot. "I only ever saw the back of him as he disappeared. He was smaller than this one," nodding his head towards the unconscious man, "but that's about all I could see in the darkness."

Alexander went to Sarah, knelt beside her in the sand and touched her dog. The dog was gone, dead.

"Sebastian, get something to secure him with." Alexander gestured at the unconscious man. "I'll call the police, you wait here for them. I'll get Sarah home." He touched her arm lightly, just for an instant, to get her attention. "Sarah, honey. We have to go. Now. You have to go with me now, Sarah." He took her arm and tried to pull her to her feet.

She pulled away. "Roscoe," she said pleadingly. "We can't leave Roscoe here."

"Sebastian will take care of him, Sarah. We won't just leave him. But you have to go now. Please baby," he begged her. "Please let me take you home now." He pulled her toward the car. She jerked away from his touch again but she did follow him to the car. He bundled her in and headed up the road to the estate, dialing Julie as he went. His next call would be to Paul. Paul was going to earn his fucking fee tonight. He was getting his ass out of bed and getting up here now, damn it. Alexander was in over his head and he knew it. His last call would be to Police Captain Frank Parker, an old friend of his father's. Parker owed his father a favor; time for Alexander to play that card. He didn't want Sarah's name connected with this incident in any way, shape, or form.

Chapter Five

His eyes blazing with uncontrolled rage and fury, the man Sarah knew as Flint lashed out and struck the nearest thing to hand, an acolyte known as Garbage. Bleeding profusely from the gash in his head delivered without warning or provocation, he now lay still. When Flint, barely aware of the man, tripped on his inert form, he angrily kicked him aside. Garbage was aptly named by him. They were all useless garbage, these acolytes of his. The two idiots watching the estate at the beach just proved that point. At least their idiocy gave him a glimpse, a flash of the girl. He was now certain this girl, this celebrity, could lead him to his quarry. It was unfortunate that she was so well known, so wealthy. It made it harder to get to her and those two fucking, dickless, assholes of his had just tipped his hand early.

He vowed they would both die a slow, painful death for not following his orders to the letter.

Chapter Six

Alexander stared at Sarah, rubbing his face in frustration. She still had said nothing since he got her back to the estate. A single tear ran down her face and she seemed oblivious to Julie, finishing up the last of the dozen or so stitches in her left arm from the knife wound. When he thought about her wound, what could have happened out there, he got queasy and looked away. He'd never even taken a knife wound and to think that some bastard went after Sarah with one enraged him.

When Julie finished, he thanked her and asked her to leave them. Alexander turned to Paul, sitting quietly in the corner, observing, and said, "Talk to her Paul. Goddamn it, make her see that she can't do shit like this, can't just run out of here like that. My god, Sarah, you could have been killed!"

Sarah seemed not to hear.

Paul spoke. "Sarah? Can you hear me, Sarah?" When she still did not react, Paul said matter-of-factly, "I need to know if you can hear me. Please respond." He waited.

Sarah finally stirred and looked at him. "Yes, I hear you, Paul," she said dully, her voice listless.

"Good," he replied. "That's good. Can you tell us, please, what happened?"

She turned away. "I don't want to talk right now. I'm very tired."

She was tired and frightened. Frightened of what had happened but of what she had done as well. Not more than an hour after she made her vow not to use her abilities, she had thrown that man on the beach away from her. She was thoroughly shaken. She could have killed him and she hadn't even thought about it, she had merely reacted. She desperately wanted to find a place to hide and dug her nails into her hand to distract herself in an effort to repress the urge.

"Sarah, you have to tell us what happened." Alexander felt a thread of panic. Oh shit, was she going to stop talking again? "The police will be coming. We have to know what happened on that beach."

Paul interrupted, "Give her time, Alexander." He smiled encouragingly at Sarah. "She knows she'll have to give a statement to the police."

Sarah did not reply.

Alexander burst out again with, "Christ, Sarah, you could have been killed!"

Sarah finally reacted. "Roscoe was killed!" she cried out, "and it's my fault." The tears were flowing again as she rounded on Alexander. "This is what I meant, Alexander! This is why you have to set the rules! This is why I need to learn to obey! I can't do this by myself anymore!" and she collapsed on the bed, sobbing.

Both men considered going to Sarah to comfort her; both rejected the idea. They knew she would not tolerate it. Paul turned to Alexander. "What's she talking about?"

Alexander explained what had transpired earlier that evening and described Sarah's unusual request for rules and punishment.

Paul looked at Alexander with consternation, his brow furrowed. He then turned to Sarah. "I understand your need to have a clear set of rules to follow. You find social interaction very difficult. It's reassuring to have someone you trust tell you what the acceptable custom is, what is the correct thing to do. But tell me, what do you mean when you tell Alexander that he must punish you if you disobey?"

"I mean," she turned to Alexander with heat and defiance in her voice, "that if you're the husband, if you're in charge, you're supposed to be the strong one! If I disobey you, like I did tonight, you should beat me." She walked to the corner of her room and picked up an old cane of Magnus' that she kept and handed it to Alexander. "Here," she said.

Alexander stared at her in shock, the cane loosely held in his hand. "You expect me to beat you with this?" he said stupidly.

"Yes, you should," she replied, her voice challenging him.

"You can't be serious!" he said, incredulous, and threw the cane across the room.

"Then I can't marry you." Sarah turned away. "If I make the rules," she said, "then I say I stay here, at Tall Trees, alone."

Alexander felt he was in a surreal farce of some kind. Paul said nothing. Alexander looked at both of them and finally said to Sarah, "Let me understand you. My choices are we marry and I punish you whenever you break a rule or you stay here at Tall Trees and see no one."

Sarah replied simply, "Yes."

Alexander gaped at her then turned to the expert. "This is not right, Paul." He'd almost said this is crazy, but caught himself in time. "You have to talk to her, you have to make her see reason."

Paul replied, his voice calm, "I actually think this is progress, Alexander."

Alexander stared at him. "You're fucking kidding, right?"

"Sarah's telling you what she needs, Alexander. That's a huge step forward."

"Not when what she needs is to have me beat her with a fucking cane!" Alexander was furious.

Paul took Alexander's arm and said to Sarah. "We need to talk privately for a few minutes. We'll be back shortly." He led Alexander from the room.

As soon as they were alone, Alexander rounded on Paul. "You can't be serious, Paul! There is no fucking way I'm beating Sarah with that cane. I don't care what she wants!"

Paul looked at him calmly for a moment then said, "I know this is upsetting to you but think about this. Do you want Sarah to start cutting again?"

Alexander was floored. God no. The discovery of that straight razor and what Sarah had done to her inner thighs with it shortly after Magnus' death stopped him cold. He wanted no repeat of anything like that. "I can't do it, Paul," he said, despair in his voice. "I could never beat her like that."

Paul replied crisply, "I'm not suggesting you beat her with that cane. That is far too aggressive, too violent. However, perhaps you and Sarah can find a middle ground. Something that satisfies her need to be punished with something you can tolerate administering. Believe me, whatever you do to her will be far less severe than what she'll do to herself if she gets desperate."

"Why? Why does she need to be punished?" There was real sorrow in Alexander's voice. "What could she ever have possibly done to feel this way?"

"I don't know," Paul replied. "I'm fairly certain this goes back to her early childhood, possibly something to do with her brother's death." He shrugged. "We may never know, Alexander. You and I have discussed this many times. It's much more fruitful to try to help her manage her fears and anxieties."

"How could she possibly feel guilt over Danny's death? She was seven years old, for god's sake, and she wasn't there when it happened."

"You'd be amazed at what children think and believe," Paul replied. "Alexander, this is the first crack I've seen in thirteen years in that armor Sarah has wrapped herself in. This is important."

"So, what are you suggesting?" Alexander asked tiredly.

"Spanking," Paul replied.

"Spanking?" he repeated, his voice incredulous. "You want me to turn Sarah over my knee and spank her?"

"Yes. You must do it vigorously enough to satisfy her need to be punished, but not harm her of course."

"Are you serious?" Alexander actually started laughing. "I don't know. The only spankings I've ever administered have been to luscious bare bottoms just prior to a lusty fucking. I've never really spanked someone, as an actual punishment I mean. I wouldn't know where to start."

"Have you ever been spanked?" Paul asked.

Alexander thought back. "Yes, when I was about twelve or so. Father took a switch to me for something I'd done. Totally deserved, as I remember it."

"What else do you remember about the event?" Paul asked. "How did it make you feel?"

"Well, I remember that it stung and hurt for a couple of days afterward. I remember that I was pretty embarrassed and humiliated that my father had to do this. Let's just say that I knew better than to do what I did to earn that spanking."

"So, you felt the beating your Father gave you was justified?" Paul clarified.

"Well, I wouldn't call it a beating. It was a switching and, yes, I guess it was justified."

"Then remember that experience when dealing with Sarah," Paul suggested. "Try to spank her hard enough so she will remember the event, but always keep in mind that this isn't really about punishment. It's to satisfy her need for punishment. No matter what, Alexander, never, never punish her when you are angry. These are very upsetting and strong emotions and the last thing you want to do is lose your temper."

Alexander sat down heavily. "So, you actually think I should do this. What about the rest of it? The rest of what happened tonight."

"I think your idea of an engagement is a good one. It also puts a time limit on the rules and punishment trial in case that behavior turns out not to be beneficial." Paul looked frankly at Alexander and continued, "Further, I believe that you have to take sex off the table during this engagement. Alexander, I know that you seem to believe Sarah suffered from some sort of sexual abuse, most probably as a child. However, I must warn you that we have absolutely no idea if there is any truth to that or not. And since we have no idea of the root of Sarah's sexual issues, and there are so many issues to deal with here, I suggest we set that aside for now. You can always add sex into the relationship later," he said with a smile, "if things are going well. But it's tough to take it out if it's already there. I believe that Sarah will only relax with you if she knows that sex will not be expected of her at this juncture."

Alexander nodded and realized he felt relieved. There were only so many landmine fields he was prepared to negotiate at once. "So, am I to do this now?"

Paul nodded. "That would be best for Sarah. I believe she's desperate for some relief tonight. Sarah has never talked to me about her compulsion to cut, but other patients have described it as lancing a boil. It's painful but the release is said to be worth it." Alexander rose to his feet and headed for the door. "I'll wait here for you," Paul said, "in case you need to talk after." Alexander nodded, subdued.

Alexander knocked quietly on Sarah's bedroom door then entered. She was sitting on the edge of the bed staring into space. He pulled a chair over and sat facing her. She finally looked at him. "I choose option number one, Sarah," he said. She looked surprised but said nothing. "You and I are officially engaged," he announced. She still said nothing. "Furthermore," he took a deep breath, "you know what the rule is about going out. You are never to go out alone. You know that?" She finally nodded yes. "You are in for a spanking, young lady," he said as firmly as he could. "I want you to bend over the bed."

Sarah just looked at him for a moment. Then she rose and bent over the bed as instructed. Alexander never saw the tiniest ghost of a smile that crossed her lips as she bent over. She was not happy about the spanking she was about to get. In fact, she was a wee bit worried about that, but she doubted Zander would actually hurt her. No, she was happy because she had won. Zander was going to help her. He wouldn't know how he was helping her, but he would be all the same. The new Sarah would be born starting right now. She would never use any of her abilities again; and, if even tempted, she would make Alexander punish her.

Chapter Seven

At seven am the following bright and sunny morning, two homicide detectives, Lt. William Terrell and his partner, Lt. Martin Stone, headed up the road, past Paradise Cove to the Tall Trees estate. Will checked the address in his note and confirmed, "This is the place. Captain said to meet him here as quick as we could. Also told me to tell you to keep your mouth shut, Stone. Let me do the talking." His partner merely smirked, his eyes amused. They were buzzed in and drove through the gates. Will's eyes opened wide as he took in the grounds.

"Holy shit!" Martin offered as they exited the car and walked up to the entrance. "This place is a fucking palace. What happened, Will? Some celebrity get himself killed?"

"Shut up, Stone," Will murmured under his breath as the door opened and a small Asian woman of about sixty, clearly a servant of some kind, let them in. As they followed her through the house, Will told his partner once again, "I don't know what's going on here, Stone. Captain said to meet him; we're meeting him. Keep a lid on it."

Martin made a zipping motion across his lips as he continued to goggle his way through the house. Their guide left them in a large library and asked them to wait. Martin continued to stare and ogle the house, going over to the window to look at the spectacular view of the Pacific Ocean. "This is like a frigging hotel," he said to Will. "What do you think the square footage is on this dump?"

Will looked around appreciatively. "I wouldn't exactly call this a dump. Someone has good taste. This place is beautiful. Look, Stone, I know how you feel about celebrities but the Captain is involved here personally somehow."

"How do you know that?" Martin snorted derisively. "Thought you said you had no idea what this was about."

"I don't. But when was the last time the Captain was at a crime scene or with a victim before us? Him being here and asking us to come personally rather than going through channels tells me he knows someone here. So just keep your mouth shut 'til we find out what's going on. That's all I'm saying."

"So, how much square footage do you think this bastard has?" Martin asked again, looking around and laughing at his partner.

Will shook his head in warning as they heard voices approaching. He glanced at his partner again but Martin seemed frozen in place, listening intently. Several people filed into the room. A tall, good-looking guy, snappy dresser, who Will suddenly recognized as Alexander Gregory, the music mogul. With him was the Captain and he realized, with a shock, that the slight blonde following the Captain and talking to another woman was none other than Sarah Eastin. Sarah fucking Eastin! Was there a bigger star today? He didn't think so. Holy shit! Will looked at Martin uneasily. His partner had a notoriously short temper when it came to dealing with spoiled celebrities. The Lindsey Lohan thing would never be lived down. To his utter surprise, Martin was staring straight at Sarah Eastin with shock on his face, rooted to the spot. Will turned and looked at the girl again. Pretty thing, little thing. She, too, stood frozen, staring at Martin in shock, her face pale, her eyes wide. The woman speaking to her said something else, Sarah ignored her. Everyone had noticed by now and looked mystified at Sarah and Martin.

Martin spoke first. "Hello Smallest."

Sarah's teacup shattered as she dropped it and flew across the room into his arms. "Martin," she breathed. "Oh my god! It's really you, Martin!"

She clung to his neck and the best feeling Martin ever experienced in his entire life washed over him. He hugged her tightly and breathed in her scent. She smelled heavenly, like jasmine with hints of vanilla, a faint but intoxicating odor. He buried his nose in her hair and hugged her again. Happiness shot through every fiber of his body. He wanted to jump for joy but he just held her, looked at her face, then stroked her cheek gently with two fingers and said, "Damn, Smallest. It's good to see you again."

"What are you doing here?" Sarah said to Martin at the same time that Captain Parker said, "I see you are acquainted with Lieutenant Stone, Miss Eastin."

Sarah looked at him in confusion. "Lieutenant Stone?" she repeated, not understanding. There was silence for a moment.

"I'm a cop, Sarah," Martin finally said. "Captain Parker here is my boss." He looked at her with a smile and saw, by her shocked reaction, that she just got it, realized he was there about a police matter, not a social visit at seven am.

He saw her go deathly pale and caught her before she hit the ground when she fainted. Martin carried her to the couch, gently laid her down, and stepped back as everyone surged around Sarah in concern. Martin recognized Julie now as the woman Sarah had been talking to when she entered the room. Julie wouldn't recognize him, of course. She was taking Sarah's pulse, feeling her forehead. Sarah stirred and came to. She sat up shakily and Martin poured a glass of water from a decanter on the table and held it out to her. Her eye caught his wedding ring for a moment then she looked away and accepted the water. She drank a few sips and handed it back.

"I'm sorry everyone. I'm fine. I just need some air." She rose to her feet, still shaky, and Alexander tried to stop her. "I'm fine. Really I am." She pushed past him and walked out onto the terrace and sat facing away from them, looking out at the ocean.

Martin realized his legs were shaky as well and sat down abruptly. Alexander looked at him in puzzlement with a healthy dose of suspicion on his face. "Do you always have this effect on women?" he asked.

Martin ignored him. "She didn't ask for me, Frank?" he quietly asked Captain Parker. "She didn't have any idea I was coming here?"

"No, Stone. I had no idea you two knew each other."

"He ask for me?" Martin inclined his head towards Alexander.

"I don't know who the hell you are," Alexander snapped. "How could I ask for you? So how do you know Sarah?" he asked with some heat in his voice.

Martin still ignored him, addressing his questions to Captain Parker. "So, this is just a coincidence? No one asked for me? You just happened to call me?"

"Technically, no," Frank replied. "I called Will and asked the two of you to come here. I had no idea you knew the girl, I certainly never heard you mention that. If this is a problem, Stone, tell me now. I'll get someone else."

Martin said nothing for a moment, thinking.

Alexander could contain himself no longer. His eyes snapped with anger and he bristled with indignation as he demanded, "Who the hell are you and how do you know Sarah?"

"Shut the fuck up, Al. I'm not talking to you," Martin growled.

"The name's Alexander," he shot back, "and you will tell me how you know my fiancée or you will leave here immediately. Frank," he turned to Captain Parker. "Who is this asshole?"

"Alexander Gregory, this is Lt. Martin Stone and his partner Lt. Will Terrell. These two are the finest team I have. I trust them to get this handled and to keep their mouths shut." He turned back to his men. "Technically, this isn't our case. There's been no homicide. However, Ms. Eastin was assaulted last night at Paradise Cove and I want to get to the bottom of this and fast. Her guardian, Magnus, was an old friend of mine. I do not want this blown all through the papers and the tabloids. I do not want to hear about this in the news." He turned back to Alexander. "Stone and Terrell are the most media-shy team I have; and, since Stone here is singularly unimpressed with celebrities, I thought they might be just the team to get this done and get it done quickly. They won't waste time trying to get someone's autograph."

Alexander looked at him then pointed a finger at Martin. "This guy isn't getting anywhere near Sarah until I know how he knows her."

"Shut the fuck up, Al," Martin said again. "It's not your decision, it's Sarah's. I need to talk to her." He stood up and walked towards the door.

Alexander blocked him with his hand. "No you don't pal. You stay away from her."

Martin just stared down at the hand on his chest then looked at Alexander. He took a deep breath. "Look, Al," he said, his tone of voice even. "I'm just going to talk to her. Right there where you can see me." He pointed out at the terrace. He lifted Alexander's hand and looked over at Captain Parker. Was Sarah really engaged to this ass? Alexander finally moved aside reluctantly and Martin went out to Sarah.

"I'm sorry about all the drama in there," she said. "I guess I've made things difficult for you. Awkward, as they say."

"Not at all." He pulled a chair around and sat down facing her. "Who cares what they think, anyway. I sure don't." He took Sarah's hands in his and looked her in the face. "What happened, Smallest? Who hurt you?" He fingered the bandage on her arm.

"You don't have to get involved in this, Martin," she said, shaking her head. "It's no big deal. You know," she said softly, searching his face with her eyes, "I thought of a million ways I might see you again. What I would say to you if I ever got the chance." She laughed shakily. "But I never dreamed it would be by accident, like this. I never thought you'd be dragged back into my life because of your work. It's OK, Martin. I know you didn't choose to come here. Go back to your life, your family."

His eyes were warm, his smile sincere. "Sarah, I want to help. Believe it or not," he laughed, "I'm good at my job. Don't worry about my life," he glanced at his ring, "or my family for that matter. I want to help. Please tell me what happened."

So Sarah did. She couldn't think of anything else to do, short of sending him away and she wasn't prepared to do that. He was here and that was all that counted. She didn't tell Martin about the argument with Alexander that sent her to the beach, just what transpired once she arrived there.

She stared at Martin the whole time she spoke, drinking in the sight of him. He was just as perfect as she remembered and she remembered everything about him. The blueness of his eyes, how they crinkled with laughter and fun but could turn steely and cold in an instant when someone angered him. His black hair and how he would run his fingers through his hair and push it off his forehead when he was thinking. The strong line of his jaw. The perfect strength of his body. His capable hands that could be so gentle and yet break a man in two. She realized that he had turned himself into a formidable warrior over the years she had known him. There was nothing he didn't know about combat, hand-to-hand fighting, weapons, and explosives. Yet, she had never feared him. She was afraid of many things, but never, never her Martin. He would protect her with his dying breath. But he couldn't love her, not the way she longed to be loved by him. That thought threatened her hard won composure but she pushed the sadness back. He's here now, she told herself fiercely. That's what matters. At least he's here. Happiness flooded through her at the same time the fear she fought to control raised its head again. But would he stay? That was the question. Sarah clung to the hope that perhaps they could at least be friends. It would be better than nothing; it would be something. She could at least talk to him, hear his voice, look at him. It would be enough.

Martin listened carefully to her account, nodding occasionally, saying nothing until she was through then, "Why did you go to the beach at Paradise Cove?"

A thread of alarm ran through Sarah; this was going to be difficult. Sarah knew she couldn't lie to him but dreaded him finding out so soon about how she lived. Oh well, there was no hope for it. If he spent any time with her at all, he was going to find out anyway. "What do you mean?" she asked, adding hesitantly, "I wanted to go for a walk on the beach."

"Why not walk on your beach here?" he nodded towards the ocean. "It was after midnight, Sarah. You went to Paradise Cove alone. Do you often go out alone?"

"No," she answered in a small voice. "No, I don't."

"So, why did you go last night?"

"Does it matter?" she asked.

"Maybe not," he shrugged. "I just know, as a cop, that it's as important to listen to what people aren't telling me as to what they are saying. It's usually the stuff they don't say that ends up mattering." He smiled encouragingly at her. "I'm going to find out the whole story anyway, Sarah. I usually do. It'll save time if you just go ahead and tell me."

She looked at him and finally said, "I had an argument with Alexander last night. I was angry. I wasn't thinking. I just wanted to get away for a while. So I got in the car and drove but then I realized that I had no idea where to go. So I just stopped at Paradise Cove."

"What was the argument about?"

"What difference can that possibly make?"

He just gave her a quizzical grin. "Come on, don't make me drag it out of you," he teased. "He's not at all what I expected. Al, I mean," he added.

Sarah looked at him for a long moment and realized she couldn't very well pray to have him back in her life and then refuse to tell him anything that had transpired in the last four years. She took a deep breath then said, "Alexander asked me to marry him last night. At first I said yes but then I changed my mind and we argued. I ran out. I actually stopped at Paradise Cove because I was angry and I wanted to throw the ring in the ocean. Please don't tell him that part," she added in a small voice. "That I wanted to throw the ring away. I don't want to hurt him like that. It was foolish of me." She flushed and looked away from him. "There, now you know why I went to Paradise Cove. Does it matter?"

"Where is the ring now?" Martin asked. "Did you toss it?"

"No, I never got the chance."

"Did they see the ring, Sarah? Was this a robbery attempt? I'm guessing old Al in there gave you a pretty impressive rock. Is that what this is about?"

"I don't think so," she answered slowly. "I'm pretty sure they never saw the ring. I wasn't wearing it when I encountered them. It was in my hand."

"So, where is it now?"

"I'm not entirely sure. It all happened so fast. I'm pretty sure it was still in my hand when I picked the sand up and threw it in that man's face. I must have thrown the ring as well, or I dropped it when I picked up the sand." She shrugged. "I guess I forgot about the ring until this morning when I heard Alexander tell Captain Parker it was a robbery and they had stolen my engagement ring."

"Did you tell them that wasn't the case?" he asked.

"No," she admitted. "I haven't really said anything to anyone yet. Alexander and Sebastian were there after the fact and surmised from what they saw what must have happened. I didn't say those men took the ring," she added.

"Describe the ring to me." She did and he whistled softly. "Wow, rock like that must be worth a lot. Half a mill or so, wouldn't you say?"

Sarah had no idea; she just shrugged.

"Well, if it wasn't about the ring, then it's pretty strange isn't it? But, no matter. Don't worry. From what you said, we've got the one guy in custody. We'll find out who the other guy is and what they were doing there. Sarah," he added carefully. "You know you were damn lucky that Sebastian came along when he did. Things could have turned out very differently. I'm not trying to scare you but you can't be running off alone like that. Not as well known as you are. It's too dangerous, Smallest."

She smiled at the use of her old nickname. It was what he had called her when she was very young and headstrong and refused to mind him. "You have to, Sarah," he'd say. "Because you're the smallest and I'm the biggest and you have to listen to me." It was irrefutable logic from a thirteen-year-old boy to a three-year-old girl.

"Yes sir, Biggest," she replied now with a smile, her heart swelling with love for the one she had called 'the dark boy with the laughing eyes', the center of her universe when she was young. "What's strange?" she asked. "Before, you said if it wasn't about the ring, it was strange."

"Well, it's all fairly strange if you ask me." His eyes were kind but he said, "You get engaged to Mr. Billionaire in there, then get unengaged the same evening. You had that ring for all of what, an hour or so, before it gets lost or stolen. Keep in mind, this is half a million dollars worth of lost or stolen." He looked frankly at her then grinned, "And you don't seem to care about that at all."

"I told you I didn't like the ring," she said, flushing uncomfortably.

"Again," he added, "half a mill's worth of don't like. For that, you return it, Sarah. You don't chuck it in the ocean. Then there's the fact that you never go out alone but the very first time you do, bam! There were two guys on the beach just down from your estate and just waiting to waylay you. How long were you out before this happened? Ten or fifteen minutes?"

"About that," she admitted uncomfortably.

"Sarah. I'm sorry, but you know there's no way this was random. Those guys were watching for you. What did you say that big guy said, 'We were only supposed to watch'?"

"You don't know that. Besides, what would be the point of them watching for me? I almost never go out."

"Until you did, Sarah. You said you never went out alone but you did last night and they got lucky. You 'fell into their laps'. Hey, it's OK," he reassured her. "You're famous, Smallest. I'm surprised there aren't squads of guys watching this place. Hell, maybe there are. Anyway, your guy Sebastian got the one and we'll get the other. We'll get to the bottom of this. Just don't go out alone again. Promise?"

She nodded. "Promise."

"OK, we'd better head back in before Mr. Billionaire in there has a hemorrhage," he said, nodding his head towards the house. "Hey, where's the old man anyway?" He would like to finally meet Magnus, although he must admit that the son seemed to be a pompous ass.

"Magnus died last year, Martin," Sarah said quietly.

Martin was stricken by the look in her eyes. "I'm sorry, Sarah," he said gently. "I didn't know. I know how much you loved him." He took her hand again then kissed it. "I'm so sorry, Smallest. I didn't know you were all alone."

"I'm not alone," she said carefully. "I still have Alexander and Sebastian and Julie, even Paul and Jonathan are part of my little world now."

"Why'd you change your mind, Sarah? Why don't you want to marry him?"

"Actually, we are to be married," she said. At the surprised look on his face she added, "Last night was a very up and down night. I did and said some foolish things. I don't know what I was thinking," she said with a small laugh. "He and I are very different people but it works for us."

"Yeah, he's the playboy of the western world and you're the girl who stays home," Martin teased. "You weren't thinking of trying to keep up with his partying, were you, because that guy is legendary, you know, in the annuals of the LAPD. You'd never make it, Sarah." He smiled at her.

She laughed again as she said, "We are totally different people and I could never hope to keep up with Alexander, wouldn't care to try."

"So, the engagement, it's back on?"

"I've told him I will marry him. We still have some things to discuss, but he knows that much."

"Do you love him, Smallest?" Martin asked.

"He loves me very much. He has for a long time. And he's very, very good to me."

"I didn't ask if he loved you, Sarah. I asked if you love him?" Martin looked into Sarah's eyes and saw that the question made her uncomfortable. Interesting, wonder why?

"Yes. I love him." Sarah replied carefully.

"OK." Martin nodded brusquely. "Come on then. Let's go face the music, you and me."

"What are you going to tell them? You can say whatever you want," she offered. "I'll back you up."

"Thanks. I usually find that some version of the truth works best," he answered with a smile. "Don't worry, I won't tell them too much."

He held on to her hand as they walked back inside and Sarah was perfectly happy for the first time in a very long time. Martin gave her hand a little reassuring squeeze before he let it go. He nodded briefly to his partner, Will, and then said, "No problem, Captain. Will and I can handle this easily. Sarah told me what happened. We'll get on it right now."

Alexander went to stand beside Sarah and said in a tightly controlled voice to Martin, "Are you going to tell me how it is that you are acquainted with my fiancée?"

Sarah's face flamed but she said nothing. Martin stared at Alexander for a long moment and finally said, "I knew her brother, Danny. We all grew up together. I've known Sarah since she was born."

Alexander was flabbergasted. This guy had known Sarah as a child! He knew Danny? Almost no one was aware that Sarah had once had a brother. He turned to Sarah, a question in his eyes.

She smiled and nodded. "Martin helped raise me when I was a baby. He, Danny, and I were the three musketeers." She stopped.

That's it? Alexander thought. That's all either of you is going to say? Neither Martin nor Sarah spoke again. Alexander turned back to Martin. "So, tell me, how long has it been since you two have seen each other?" No one spoke. Alexander looked back and forth between Sarah and Martin.

Finally, biting back a smile, Martin replied easily, "Oh about three, four years maybe. Since I got out of the Army. Guess that's when we lost touch."

Alexander was surprised. "How is it I've never met or heard of your friend, Sarah?"

"She never told you about me?" Martin asked with a smile. "Funny. I know all about all of you. Hi there, Julie," he said with a little wave at her. "And Sebastian there," he nodded politely at Sebastian. "And you, of course, Al," he said with a sardonic grin. "Congrats on your recent engagement," he added politely.

"Well, you and I will have lots to talk about," Alexander said in a friendlier tone to Martin. "I want to know all about you."

Martin shot Alexander a look. "You want to know anything else about me, ask your fiancée," he retorted. "I'm sure she'll tell you anything you want to know. Gotta go to work now," he said turning to Sarah. "I'll see you again soon. Here's my direct cell number. What's the best number to reach you at?" She gave him her cell number and he and Will left with Captain Parker.

Alexander, Julie, and Sebastian all turned towards Sarah, expectant looks on their faces. Julie was the first to speak. "So, dish girlfriend," she said in a mock teen accent. "Seriously, Sarah, who is that gorgeous hunk of a man and where have you been hiding him?"

Sarah flushed uncomfortably. Had Julie forgotten she was engaged to Zander now? She glanced at Zander. Julie's comment did not seem to bother him. Was Julie making a play for Martin? She was horrified at the thought and then realized she was taking Julie too literally, a problem of hers. Julie was joking. Martin was good looking and she was just commenting on that. Keep this lighthearted, she thought. "Forget it, Julie," she said in a teasing voice. "He's married now."

"Ah, too bad. All the best ones are. Even my cousin, the eternal playboy, is soon to join their ranks." Julie wasn't sure what she thought about the engagement she had just heard about that morning. She was of two minds. She didn't think Sarah was well enough, stable enough to get married, but she knew why Alexander was so anxious about it and she

56

didn't blame him. Sarah was a pretty shaky foundation to build an empire on. Not just millions but billions at stake. And she knew Alexander had Sarah's best interests at heart. With Sarah, it was tough to know what to do.

Julie thought about her secret, the thing that only she knew now that Danny and Magnus were dead. She wondered if she should tell Alexander, maybe after he and Sarah were married. Then she realized with a jolt that if she was going to tell him, it should probably be before the wedding. Would she want to know something like that about someone she loved? Julie didn't know. She rubbed her eyes tiredly. She had kept silent all these years. Best just to take it to the grave with her.

"So tell me, Sarah," Julie continued in a sympathetic tone of voice. "Is that why you and your friend lost touch? He got married."

"Something like that." Sarah was careful to keep her tone light. "He got married when he got out of the Army," she added.

A frisson of alarm went through Alexander. The guy had said he lost touch with Sarah when he got out of the Army, three or four years ago. Turns out he also got married then. Four years ago was Sarah's most severe breakdown... is it possible any of those events are connected he wondered?

Sarah turned with an impish smile and said, "Well, I have work to do, so I will see you all later." She waltzed off towards her studio and Alexander watched her walk. She was going through the garden rather than through the house to get to her wing of the estate. She was practically walking on air and he realized he didn't think he'd seen her like this, happy like this, in a long, long time. Since before that terrible time, he thought with another frisson of fear. Well, hopefully they would finally learn something about Sarah's past. He should be relieved but he felt only anxiety. He pulled out his cell and called Paul. "You're not going to believe what happened this morning," he began.

Chapter Eight

Martin, euphoric as he and Will drove down the drive of the estate towards Paradise Cove, couldn't refrain from pounding on the roof of the car in sheer exuberance as Will looked on in amused tolerance. "So, you going to tell me?" Will asked.

"Tell you what?" Martin laughed. He knew damn well what his partner was asking.

"Tell me how it is you're my partner and I've spent more time with you in the last three years than I get to spend with my wife, and yet you don't mention that you're on hugging terms with Sarah-fucking-Eastin," Will replied.

Martin just laughed. "I don't talk about her much," he said, shaking his head.

"Much!" Will retorted. "How about not at all!"

Martin ran his fingers through his hair then turned his gaze to his partner. "Look, Will, when I got out of the Army after that last tour in Afghanistan, I was in pretty bad shape. Mentally I mean. Well hell, Will, you know. I met you about a year after that. I was still pretty fucked up." Martin scratched his neck and squirmed uncomfortably. "Sarah had just turned sixteen when I got out. We had always kept in touch, but during those last couple of deployments...well, I just didn't realize what a big star she'd become back stateside. I didn't want to intrude on her life. She didn't need me anymore." He paused then continued ruefully. "Hell, I wasn't even sure if she'd want to see me and I knew damn well that bunch wouldn't welcome me. Al and Magnus and Sebastian, they would have reacted like I'd just dropped a live cobra in Sarah's lap. Can't say I'd blame them. What the hell did Sarah need with an unemployed ex-soldier with a psych discharge and no prospects? So, I did her a favor. I stayed away."

Will glanced over at his partner, then back at the road. "Well, you two seemed mighty happy to see each other now."

"Yeah, it was great," Martin said, grinning from ear to ear. "She missed me too. I could tell."

"So, what's she like?" Will asked.

"She's great." Martin couldn't stop grinning. He felt like an idiot but a happy idiot. "She's really great," he said again.

"Great? That's what you got for me? Great?" Will shook his head in amusement. His partner's usual powers of description seem to have deserted him. "How do you know she's not a spoiled brat now that she's a big star? You haven't seen her in four years."

"No, not her," Martin answered immediately. "She hasn't changed. I can tell just in the short time we spent together. She's nothing like that bunch we were dealing with around the Lohan chick. You'll see, Will. Sarah's different. You'll see."

"So, you really grew up with her and her brother?" Will asked.

"Yeah. Danny and I were the same age, ten, when Sarah was born. Their Mom was real sick and their Dad wasn't around a lot, so Danny and I basically raised Sarah from the time she was born. Both their parents died when she was about three. Danny was an egghead or an airhead, depending on how you want to look at it, so it was really me that did most of the care for Sarah when she was a baby up until she was about seven. That's when I went in the Army." He felt almost lightheaded talking about this. He had never, never spoken of Sarah to a living soul but Danny, and that was years ago.

"What happened then?" Will asked.

"Well, that's when everything changed. The year Danny and I turned seventeen and Sarah was seven, I went to West Point and Sarah went with Danny to the University of Hong Kong. He got a full scholarship there and Sarah could live with him. But Danny was murdered after about six months in Hong Kong and Sarah went to live with Magnus and Alexander."

Will whistled. "That's tough. What happened?"

Martin shrugged. "Four goons came on the boat he and Sarah were living on, dragged him off, took him to a warehouse in the jungle outside Hong Kong, tortured, and killed him. We never figured out what it was about, who they were, why they were after Danny."

"Why'd she end up with Magnus and that bunch? Who were they to her and you?" His partner was still a mystery to him. Will realized that this was pretty much the most Martin had ever told him about his life in the three plus years he'd known him.

"No one," Martin answered. "They just stepped up to the plate. Danny met Al through Julie. Danny and Julie were an item, they met at the university. She was in med school there. Actually, Danny was gaga over Julie. So, anyway, that's how he met Al. He's Julie's cousin and they became friends even though old Al was about ten or eleven years older than we were. Through Al, Danny and Sarah met Magnus, his father. Sarah and the old man became fast friends almost immediately. Very unusual for Sarah, she's very shy. Magnus introduced her to the piano. She'd never seen one before. When he realized the kind of talent she had, he got her one of those 'to scale' baby grand's. Did you know they make those for kids? Sarah was pretty small at seven, tiny hands. Man, she loved that piano." He shook his head ruefully.

"When Danny was killed," he continued, "Sarah took it hard, really hard. She was sick for a long time. I was in a real bind. Sarah had no other family. Both her parents were dead. There was only me. But Sarah's not technically my family. She's Danny's sister, not mine. I had just joined the Army six months prior. They weren't going to let me out to take care of her. Besides which, I was seventeen with no money or job and Sarah needed doctors, lots of expensive help. Sarah loved Magnus. She trusted him and she was pretty good at reading people. So, I made a decision. I let them have her." He was quiet, remembering. "But she is my family, Will. I don't care what the law says. That little girl is mine. I love her, always have and she loved me. I always kept in touch with her, checked up on her. Every leave I ever had the entire ten years I was in the Army was spent with Sarah, every single one. She's the only family I've ever really had."

"So, Stone, how come none of them knew about you? You're that close to Sarah, you spent all that time with her, why don't they know you?" Will turned off the ignition. They were at Paradise Cove but Will was more interested in finishing this conversation than he was in getting a look at the crime scene. It had happened around midnight last night. It could wait a few more minutes for them to view.

60

Martin, silent a long moment, looked out the window at the ocean. Finally he said, "Because I asked Sarah not to tell them about me. I didn't trust them at first. They appeared to be very rich. Al ran with a pretty fast crowd." Martin glanced over at his partner then seemed to come to some sort of decision. "Look, Will, I may have glossed over some of the details there when I was talking about our childhood. Danny, Sarah, and I, we had one of those bad, def com 4 childhoods." He used the term that was code between himself and Will for when they encountered severe child abuse cases in the course of their jobs. "When you grow up like we did, you learn not to trust. Danny had his head in the clouds but I was the planner. And I always had a back-up plan to keep Sarah safe. When Danny died and Sarah wanted to stay with Magnus, I wasn't sure what to do. If he was a good guy, like Sarah thought he was, well it was the best solution. But if he was a bad guy – I mean, really, think about it, this guy was in his sixties befriending this little seven-year-old girl. And this was in Hong Kong, Will. Lots of rich guys go to Asia to buy little girls. I didn't think that's what this was about or I wouldn't have let Sarah go near him. But I just couldn't trust him that easily either. So I told Sarah not to tell Magnus, any of them, about me. That way, if he turned out to be a bad guy, I could come and take Sarah away and they would never know where to even begin to look. They didn't know I existed.

After awhile, after I finally began to trust that Magnus was just what he said he was and really did care about Sarah, well, by then it seemed weird to spring me on them. I mean, at first she was so sick. Then, when that all finally got sorted out, she was suddenly doing all this Hollywood stuff and music. It just seemed better to keep it to ourselves."

Will had a host of other questions he wanted to ask but sensed his partner was done talking for now. They both got out of the car and walked towards the yellow taped crime scene area on the beach.

Chapter Nine

When his partner dropped him off and finally headed home, Martin gunned it up the road to the Tall Trees estate on his motorcycle to fill Sarah and Alexander in on what they'd found that day. And a strange day it had been, he reflected. He wasn't sure what he'd expected to find when they started digging into this case, but it sure wasn't what they had found. Damn. He shook his head in frustration. The blue parrot thing was troubling. He didn't know why it bothered him as much as it did, but it did.

He got buzzed into the gate immediately and drove the long winding drive to the front of the mansion. Sebastian opened the door before he could even get off the bike and welcomed him in.

"Good evening, sir. This way please. Mr. Gregory and Miss Eastin are waiting for you."

Martin looked at Sebastian with humor in his eyes. "You don't need to call me sir, Sebastian. Martin will do."

"Of course, Lt. Stone," Sebastian replied. Martin laughed aloud and shook his head, following Sebastian.

Alexander and Sarah were in the library in front of the fireplace. Sarah jumped to her feet when she saw him but didn't run to embrace him this time. She smiled deeply, though, and said hello.

Martin touched her cheek hello then turned and he and Al actually shook hands. This was going to be oh so civilized. Martin sat then cleared his throat.

Sarah interrupted. "Would you like something to drink, Martin?"

"Sure," he replied.

"Join me in a cocktail?" Alexander lifted his glass.

"No. How about a soda or something? I'm still working here, Al," Martin said dryly.

"I doubt we have soft drinks here," Sarah said, coloring slightly. "We do have juice, seltzer, tea, or coffee," Sarah said.

"I'll have a cup of coffee, Sebastian," Martin said, "black, please."

Martin reached into his shirt pocket, pulled out a ring, leaned over and dropped it into Sarah's hand. "I'm betting that's your ring," he said.

She nodded.

Alexander reached for it. He looked at Martin in wonder. "Well, I never thought we'd see this again. Where did you find it?"

"On the beach pretty much exactly where you said it would be, Sarah. Only took a few minutes to find it," Martin replied.

Alexander looked at Sarah in confusion. "I don't understand, they didn't take the ring, Sarah?"

"I never said they did, Alexander. You did." She was quiet.

"Well, what happened to it?" Alexander asked.

Sarah said nothing and then Martin said, his voice easy, "It must have fallen off when she picked up the sand to throw in the guy's face. Maybe the ring is a little big or something." He shrugged. "Anyway, it was right there at the logical spot based on where she was standing at the time. What's that rock worth anyway, if you don't mind me asking?" Martin questioned Alexander in his cop voice.

Alexander said nothing for a moment, just looked at him. Then he replied, "One point six million."

"Whewww!" Martin whistled softly. He looked right at Alexander as he said, "Hunka, hunka burning love. That's a lot of ring."

"Sarah's a lot of woman," Alexander replied. He rang for Sebastian, handed him the ring and asked him to have it cleaned and brought back to Sarah.

Sarah did not seem happy to see the ring back, Martin reflected. She still said nothing.

Martin stretched his legs out and tried to decide how best to proceed. Finally he said, "Does a blue parrot mean anything to either of you?"

"Blue parrot?" Both Sarah and Alexander looked puzzled.

"Yeah," Martin said. "Any significance to either of you?"

"No," Sarah and Alexander both shook their heads in the negative. "Why?" Alexander asked.

"Because the big guy we picked up on the beach from last night was obsessed with them," Martin replied.

"So," Alexander said, "What does that mean?"

"I don't know," Martin said. "I guess I was just wondering if it meant anything to either of you, or perhaps to your fans, Sarah? You know, like Buffet fans are called 'parrot heads', does a blue parrot mean anything to you guys? Maybe a club you frequent?" he asked Alexander.

Sarah and Alexander both still shook their heads no.

"Oh well," Martin shrugged. "Maybe the guy's just weird. Plenty of that going around," he said with a lift of his brow.

Martin watched Alexander and Sarah carefully. They were the most restrained engaged couple he'd ever seen. There were no little gestures of affection, no shared glances. Martin was pretty sure he had not seen Alexander touch Sarah at all, not this morning, definitely not now. Nor had Sarah touched Alexander. Interesting. He pulled his thoughts back to what he and Will had learned today. Well, they both appeared to be honestly perplexed by the blue parrot reference, although Sarah was getting more and more nervous. She was hiding it but he knew her too well. Her stillness alone was indicative of how on edge she was.

"Who are they?" Alexander asked. "Did you get the bastard that hurt Sarah?"

"The guy on the beach, the big one, is George Fulton, an auto body mechanic that works at the Culver City Auto Body & Repair on Lincoln. Either of you know him by any chance? Any chance you have work done on your cars there?" he asked Alexander.

Alexander shook his head. Martin continued. "Will and I checked out his apartment, talked to some of his neighbors, went to his job, talked to the people who worked there. Other than a shit load of blue parrots everywhere, we didn't learn much about the guy."

"Why do you keep talking about these parrots?" Alexander interrupted.

"Cause I've never seen anything quite like it before," Martin answered. "I expected to find that the guy was obsessed with Sarah. Instead, this guy had blue parrot trinkets, you know, souvenir shop type of stuff, everywhere. He had pictures of blue parrots; he had an entire mural wall in his apartment of a blue parrot. In his locker at work, where most guys keep the pin ups or the photo of their girlfriend or whatever, more blue parrots. He also had a blue parrot tattoo - over his heart. That's the spot most guys with tats reserve for Mom or Jesus or their girlfriend or the flag. Not a blue parrot, unless it's really important, which it obviously was to this guy."

"What did he say?" Alexander asked.

"Not much." Martin shrugged. "He's dead." Martin noticed that Sarah went very pale but said nothing.

"Dead!" Alexander exclaimed. "He wasn't dead when I checked him on the beach. Just knocked out."

"No, the blow to the head didn't kill him. That was a minor concussion. He spent the night in the lock up ward at the hospital and was released this morning. How did he get knocked out at the beach, anyway?" Martin was very curious about this. When he examined the crime scene, it just didn't make sense to him. According to what he'd been told, when Sebastian showed up, the big guy was already down. How? Who? He'd seen the spot where Sarah was standing, where her dog's body was found, and the big guy was lying at least twenty to twenty-five feet away at the base of some large boulders. Furthermore, Martin had found the spot on the rock, at least fifteen feet off the ground, where the big guy had undeniably hit his head, as the blood and hair found there testified. How the hell did that happen? That guy was big, over 6'3" and weighed in at about two hundred and fifty pounds. Who tossed him on that rock and knocked him out? But Martin said none of this, just waited to see what Sarah had to say. She was intensely uncomfortable, he could tell that much.

Sarah was evasive for the first time. She squirmed in her chair and finally said, "I'm not sure how it happened. It all happened so fast."

"Sarah," Martin asked gently. "Was there anyone else there that night?" He wanted to take her hand and reassure her but didn't want to be too familiar with Al sitting right there.

"No," she answered immediately. "It happened just like I told you. I think that when Roscoe started to attack, the big man backed up. I think he must have just tripped and fell and hit his head on the rocks."

Martin knew this wasn't plausible but he said nothing.

"If the blow to the head didn't kill him, what happened to him?" Alexander asked. "And, did you find his partner, the guy with the knife?"

"No," Martin admitted. "We've drawn a complete blank there. No one seems to know any of Fulton's friends or acquaintances. We floated the weasely guy's description around Fulton's apartment and his job. No one admits to knowing who it might be."

"What did Fulton say about who he was with?" Alexander asked.

"Fulton was dead before we could question him," replied Martin. "Suicide."

"Suicide!" Alexander exclaimed. "Didn't you guys have this creep in custody! How did he manage to kill himself!"

Martin flashed back on the grisly scene that greeted him and Will when they arrived at the station after visiting the crime scene this morning. Martin noticed that Sarah seemed to be a bit better, was recovering her equilibrium, but there was no way he was describing what happened to Fulton in any detail. Made him queasy to think about and he was a cop.

When he and Will arrived at the station, they were told that Fulton was just being brought in for questioning. They headed down to the interrogation room to find bedlam and blood everywhere. Fulton had his hands cuffed behind his back and his throat was gashed so deeply he'd almost been beheaded. Captain Parker was there and motioned for them to come forward the moment he saw them. "What the fuck, Captain?" he'd said when he realized the dead guy was their suspect. "Who killed this guy?" Martin looked around at all the cops gathered there. No one said anything for a moment.

"No one," Frank answered.

"Then how the hell did he get dead?" Martin demanded.

"He did that to himself," Frank answered.

Martin's jaw dropped. "He did that," he pointed to the guys' throat, "with his hands cuffed behind him! That's a neat trick." Martin noticed the broken glass to one of the offices, the blood on the edge of the jagged shard and realized the guy must have stuck his head through the glass and cut his own throat. Must have been deliberate, it would be hard to do that kind of damage accidentally.

Martin squatted down and examined the body. Big guy, looked to be early thirties. Hands looked like a workingman's hands. He was still wearing the hospital/jail issued jumpsuit. Martin looked up at Frank. "Captain, I want a good look at this guy. Can we strip him down here?"

Captain Parker said, "The morgue will give you any info you need."

"I don't want to wait that long, Captain. You know how backlogged they are, that could take a couple of days. I want a look at this guy now. He's our only lead." Martin motioned at the lab techs who had finished their photos and were packing up their equipment. "These guys look like they're done."

Frank nodded and Martin motioned for someone to help him take the cuffs off the body, then they removed the jumpsuit. He was a large, powerful man, even in death. Martin examined him carefully then had someone help him turn the body over so he could see the back of the guy. Martin even looked between his toes to see if the guy was a junkie. The only distinguishing mark on the body was a small tattoo, about three inches high, of a blue parrot right over the guy's heart. Weird, Martin thought at the time, weird place to put a parrot tattoo.

Captain Parker asked the two officers who brought Fulton in that morning to accompany them back to his office. Once they were behind closed doors, Frank ordered Stultz and Conners to give a full report of everything that transpired since they picked the suspect up that morning at the hospital. Seems like the big guy had been very nervous, jumpy, scared of something.

"Scared out of his gourd if you ask me," offered Stultz. "He kept looking around like he was afraid of ghosts or shadows or something."

"Someone after him, you think?" asked Martin.

"Who knows," Stultz shrugged. "We didn't see anyone or anything unusual. He actually seemed a bit calmer when we got to the station. We booked him in then Conners and I were escorting him to the interrogation room. We followed protocol," Stultz interjected for Captain Parker's benefit. "One in front, one in back. He was secured with the cuffs."

"I saw you bring him in," Captain Parker confirmed. "You guys are fine. There's no blow back for you on this." Both Stultz and Conners relaxed. "Continue," Captain Parker ordered.

"Well, Conners and I were just talking on the way, you know, shooting the shit. I said something like 'this ahole will probably be out of here before lunch' and the dude starts losing it again. He's getting all agitated. He wouldn't keep walking. Keeps saying that we have to keep him, we can't cut him loose. I'm just thinking that maybe we should have had a taser along for the walk after all, when Conners here says something like 'we're not running a fucking hotel here' and the guy goes completely ballistic. Conners jumps on his back. I'm trying to take him down from the front and he's just tossing us around like confetti. Next thing I know, he sticks his head through that plate glass window; and, I swear to god, the dude deliberately cut his own throat."

No one said anything for a long moment. Then Frank dismissed Stultz and Conners, turned to Martin and Will and said, "That's pretty much what I saw go down. I wanted to get a look at this guy, that's why I went down when they brought him in. What the hell do you think is going on here?" he asked.

"I don't know," Martin replied. "But I don't like it, Frank. I don't like it at all."

His unease had only grown throughout the day. What he thought would be a pretty simple open and shut case of finding the guy that skipped away was turning into something else entirely. He just didn't know what. Everything he had expected to find in a case like this was missing. Fulton did not appear to have been a crazed fan or a fan at all. There were no photos of Sarah in his apartment or at his work. He didn't have much of her music, just a few of her biggest hits on his computer and iPOD. There was that issue of People with her on the cover; but, hell, that magazine was everywhere, and Fulton's copy hadn't been open to the section on Sarah. He actually thought the guy had been reading the article the magazine was left open at, the one about the injured football player. The magazine wasn't annotated or worn out from being looked at repeatedly. Hell, stalkers usually have little shrines to the objects of their obsession. There was no indication Fulton was obsessed with Sarah. Of course, he could have hidden his obsession much more carefully than their initial search today revealed. Martin would dig deeper, much deeper. But this case didn't feel like that's what it was about anymore. Over the years, he'd learned it best to listen to those feelings.

Martin pulled himself back to Alexander's question. "During transport to the interrogation room this morning, George Fulton put his head through a plate glass window and cut his own throat." He said this matter-of-factly and watched Sarah and Alexander for their reactions. Sarah said nothing, just looked down, but she did seem a tiny bit relieved.

Alexander burst out with, "Aren't suspects handcuffed during transport?"

"Yes," Martin confirmed. "His hands were cuffed behind his back and he had two officers attempting to restrain him at the time. He was a pretty big guy," Martin added.

"Why would he do something like that?" Sarah asked.

"I don't know, Sarah. He had no record of mental illness, actually, no record at all. Just a loner who worked in an auto body shop." He smiled encouragingly at her. "Just day one. We'll find out everything there is to find out about this guy." He glanced at the bandage on her arm. "I will find the guy who did that to you, Sarah. Don't worry, I'll find him." And he meant it. No lowlife bastard was going to slice up Smallest and not answer to him. That piece of shit was in for a world of hurt when he found him.

"Well," Martin said, polishing off the last of his coffee. "That about sums up today." His stomach growled loudly. It was after eight pm and he'd only eaten a hotdog grabbed on the run about noon today. He stood, "I'd better be going."

"Would you like to stay for dinner?" Sarah impulsively asked. "You must be hungry." She smiled, they had all heard Martin's stomach growl.

Martin chuckled. "Well, no, I wouldn't want to intrude on you two love birds," he said as he looked at Alexander.

Martin could see that Alexander was surprised by Sarah's invitation but he recovered quickly as Sarah looked at him.

Sarah was gripped by uncertainty. Was this a rule? She'd completely forgotten about Alexander when she invited Martin to dinner. Perhaps engaged women didn't invite other men to dinner without their fiancée's approval. And Martin was a married man. How could she keep conveniently overlooking that fact? "I'm sorry, how thoughtless of me," she said coloring slightly, trying to hide her embarrassment. "You've had a long day. Of course you'll want to get home to your family."

Martin looked at her fondly then with a wry smile said, "That's not a problem, Sarah." He needed to find a way to talk privately to her for a few minutes. He realized he didn't want to talk to her about this in front of Al.

Alexander cut in with, "Then it's settled! You'll join us for dinner. Sarah and I would be delighted; we're getting ready to sit down shortly. I'd like the opportunity to get better acquainted with you."

Al all but slapped him on the back, all jovial good cheer. Martin thought, why not? He was hungry. He did want a chance to observe them a bit more closely and he could talk to Sarah after dinner.

He turned to Sarah. "Actually, I think I will take you up on that invitation after all. I am hungry." Then turning to Al, "that is, if I can ask for a few minutes after dinner to speak privately to Sarah?"

Alexander seemed taken aback at first but then said, "That's entirely up to Sarah."

"Wonderful," Sarah said, all smiles. "I'll let Sebastian know we'll have another for dinner." Sarah left the room in a little cloud of happy confusion. She wasn't sure if she should have invited him but he was staying! He said yes! This was even better than she'd hoped.

Martin turned to Alexander. "I'd like to have a word with you anyway, Al."

Alexander looked at Martin then said, "I really do prefer to be called Alexander, if you don't mind."

Martin chuckled. "Well, that's quite a mouthful, Al. I'll work on it."

Alexander was irritated but tried to shut it down. The guy was deliberately trying to get a rise out of him and he wasn't going to take the bait. He wanted to know about Sarah's childhood; and, if he had to put up with this jerk for a while to do so, well that's the way it goes. He waited.

"Any chance that what happened out on that beach last night was about you, Al?"

"What do you mean?" Alexander asked.

"I think you know what I mean," Martin said.

"No, I don't," Alexander said coldly. "You're going to have to spell that out for me."

"What I mean, Al, is that this guy didn't look like he was obsessed with Sarah. And those guys were watching the estate. For some time now is my guess. Found their spot on the beach, perfect view of anyone coming in or out of the gates of this place. Hell, their binoculars were still there. The only thing they said in front of Sarah was, 'We were only supposed to watch,' and the other guy said, 'She fell into our laps'. I also find out from Sebastian that Sarah hasn't left this estate, at all, in a year or so except for last night. A year is a long time to watch and wait, Al. No, they weren't expecting Sarah. Were they maybe expecting you?"

"That's preposterous!" Al exclaimed. "I don't know what you're talking about."

"Come on, Al!" Martin said impatiently. "Cut the crap. You're the playboy of the western world, man about town, Mr. Music Mogul. I know about the partying, the women, the drugs. I don't give a shit; I'm not here to bust your chops. But if anyone's in trouble in this house, if anyone's stirred up a hornet's nest somewhere, like a jealous lover or unpaid drug debt, it's far more likely to be you than Sarah." He stared Alexander coldly in the eye.

Alexander stared back then said in a controlled voice, "I can think of no situation, such as you described or otherwise, that could in any way be connected to what happened to Sarah on the beach. My god, man, do you think I would ever expose her to that kind of danger!"

"Sorry, but I don't know you all that well, Al. A lot of guys think with their dick, not with their brain. You'd be surprised at the trouble it can get you into." Martin looked frankly at Alexander, appraising him, trying not to judge. "And it's been my experience, Al, that rich guys, really rich guys like you, tend to think the rules don't apply to them."

"I can assure you that is not the case here," Alexander said crisply. "After all, I'm the one who called Captain Parker, brought the police into this. Were I the man you just described, and keeping in mind the considerable resources available to a man as wealthy as I am, I would have simply handled this myself and had those two men found and exterminated, because that's what they are, vermin. But I did not. I am a civilized, law-abiding man and I followed the rules. I called the police."

"So, you follow the rules, obey the law now, do you, Al? I remember when you and your father weren't exactly law abiding."

Alexander's eyes were as icy as his voice. "I'm sure I don't know what you're talking about. And I'm about to rescind that dinner invitation and ask you to leave now."

"Relax, Al. Like I said, I'm not here to bust your chops." Martin brushed his hair back off his forehead as he said, "What you need to understand is that what Sarah knows about all of you, I know. I've always known. Sarah's never kept anything from me. If I wanted to bust you, I could have done it years ago." He tugged at his hair again then looked at Alexander with a bit less heat than before. "Guess Sarah used to think of you and your father as modern day Robin Hoods, but I doubt the authorities would have the same take on it. Look, Al, I don't care about what you used to do and if you say you guys are completely legit today, that's fine. But I want you to think about this. Is there anyway this could be some kind of blow back from those old days? Something that Sarah just got caught up in by accident?"

Alexander relaxed slightly. Fuck, this guy was surprising. So, he knew about his and his father's former career. Alexander was surprised that Sarah knew anything at all about it but it continually amazed him to learn what Sarah knew. "I cannot see how this could be in any way connected to our former occupation." He inclined his head as he admitted, "but I hadn't considered that before. I have not been active in that life for some time now."

"I know Sebastian, Jonathan, all you guys were part of that network back then. Hell, probably your gardener used to be part of that network," Martin said. "Don't know, don't care," he continued. "As a matter of fact, I'd prefer not to know the details. But if you've still got contacts, use 'em. Any markers to call, now is the time to call them in. Check it out, Al. I swear to god, if she gets hurt again because of some crap you're into, you are going to be a very sorry man." Martin looked Alexander right in the eye as he delivered the last statement. Alexander nodded and they went in to dinner.

Considering the tone of the conversation the two men had just had, dinner was surprisingly enjoyable due to Sarah who sparkled and shone. She dazzled both men. Neither could take their eyes off her as she beguiled them with the tales of the intricate lives of all the wild creatures who lived on the estate. Sarah knew them all, the den of foxes, the eagle's nest, the rabbit holes, the ducks, the swans, the nest of the barred owl. She seemed to know every animal who lived on the large estate, how many young they had, who was mating, everything. Martin was enchanted. She was just as happy, carefree, and untamed as he remembered her. She was like a little feral creature herself, he thought. She'd always been more at home with her animal friends than with most people. He noted she was wearing the ring again. It did look like a lot of rock for her small hand.

Sarah shifted slightly in her chair, her bottom still surprisingly sore from her spanking last night. She was grateful. While humiliating, it was well worth it. It kept her focused. She reflected wryly that had she been sitting, not standing at the time, she probably wouldn't have invited Martin to dinner. The pain in her posterior would have reminded her to keep her mouth shut. But, it had all worked out. He was here and it was divine. She saw that Alexander appeared to be enjoying himself as well and she relaxed a bit more. She couldn't get over it, dinner with Martin. Surely a landmark occasion. She wondered again what he wanted to talk to her about after dinner. Cosmic joke, she thought. She could read minds, couldn't stop people from bombarding her with unwanted information they had no idea they were imparting. All except Martin. The one person's thoughts she desperately wanted to know she couldn't read.

It had been that way since she was a baby. Danny, everyone else, was an open book to her. She could always sense what Martin was feeling, just as he could sense her. But she couldn't read his mind, his thoughts. She always knew his emotions, his feelings. If he was happy or sad or angry or hurt or hungry, she knew, just as he knew the same about her. And it didn't matter where they were. They didn't need to be together to feel these things about each other.

At least, as long as they were bonded, but they were no longer. That bond had been severed four years ago and the pain of it still staggered Sarah at times. She'd felt as if someone had taken an axe and split her in half lengthwise, from her head to her toes, and the half that had been Martin had walked away. She was left with a broken, bleeding half-life; and, the half that was Sarah wasn't very good at life on her own. Still, she was encouraged. She had taken the vow to not use her abilities and Martin had appeared the very next day. That had to mean she had done the right thing in agreeing to marry Alexander. Maybe that's all Martin needed to know is that she wouldn't be the same parasitic, needy creature she'd been as a child.

Alexander was amazed as he watched Sarah and Martin converse and laugh together. He had never seen this Sarah. Not even with Father had Sarah been this open and carefree. He realized within ten minutes that Stone was in love with Sarah. Not surprising, few men who met Sarah were not caught by her charms. What sent a bolt of jealousy through him was the feeling that Stone was in love with a different Sarah than the one he knew. As if his Sarah, Sarah Eastin, were a cloak of some kind and there was another Sarah hidden inside this cloak, one that he had never met but that this Stone guy knew well. The thought made him uneasy. What sent a bigger bolt of jealousy through him was the realization that Sarah might feel the same way about Stone. It had not escaped him that Sarah not only tolerated this guy's touch, she seemed to welcome it. He watched how Stone had touched her cheek when he first arrived. Not only had Sarah not flinched, she smiled. He had the feeling that gesture was very familiar to the two of them and his jealousy grew. He took another sip of his wine and cautioned himself to be patient. He was on a fact-finding mission and he had actually learned quite a bit this evening. He fully intended to use some of those contacts he and Martin had discussed. But some of that would be directed to finding out everything there was to know about one Martin Stone. This was another thing that Alexander was very, very good at.

As they rose from the dinner table, Martin said, "Can I talk to you for a few minutes, Sarah? Out there." He gestured toward the terrace.

"Of course," she replied and headed towards the door.

"I'll be right here," Alexander said reassuringly as he sat down in the library with a view of where Martin and Sarah were headed. The message was clear. He would give them privacy for a conversation but he would be watching. Martin was irritated; did the guy think he was going to cart her off? But he pushed his irritation down. Al was just being protective.

Martin and Sarah sat down on a bench facing the ocean. Martin leaned over, his elbows on his knees, looking at the waves and twisting his wedding ring. He finally stopped, sat back up, and looked at Sarah. "It's about my family, Sarah. I'm not actually married anymore."

She was surprised. "But you still wear your wedding ring."

"Yeah," he said and touched the ring again before putting his hands on his knees.

"I'm sorry," she said. "What happened?"

"They died, Sarah. Becky and Drew died in a car accident about three years ago."

Sarah was stricken. "Oh god, Martin. I'm so sorry. I didn't know. I'm so, so sorry. Oh, your baby too! You had a boy then?" she asked. "I always wondered." She threw her arms around Martin and hugged him to her.

After a few moments, he drew back and looked at her, brushing a strand of hair out of her face. "Thanks, Smallest. I appreciate it. I'm OK; it was three years ago. Guess I just haven't gotten around to taking the ring off yet." He smiled ruefully with a lift of his brows. "I didn't realize you knew about the baby," he said, and she just smiled at him. He felt foolish. Of course she knew. Not much escaped her. "Yes, Becky had a boy. His name was Andrew but I called him Drew." He stood and walked a few steps, then turned and looked at Sarah. "Anyway, I just thought you should know," he said and sat back down.

Sarah's heart broke for him. His family! His dream! Life could be so cruel, so unbelievably cruel.

Martin looked at her. "But, I'm glad you've found someone. Are you happy, Sarah? I gotta say, you two don't seem ideally suited."

Sarah stared at Martin as the implication sank in for the first time. Martin was unattached but she was not. Life was cruel, very, very cruel at times.

"As I said, we're very different, but we suit," she said.

"Not exactly a declaration of wild, passionate love," he said with a quizzical look at her.

"Not everyone gets wild, passionate love," Sarah said quietly. "Some of us take what we can get." She looked at the ring on her finger.

"Aren't you at least going to ask him to exchange it?" Martin asked. "You're going to be wearing something you don't like for a long time if you don't say something."

"No. It's fine. He likes it. The ring is more for Alexander than me anyway."

Martin shook his head. "Sarah, Smallest, is everything OK here?" he asked quietly. He pulled her to his side and put his arm around her. Fuck Al, let him squirm. He turned her face to him and looked her in the eyes. "I'm worried, Smallest. I get here and I find the old man gone. Turns out Al controls everything now, Sarah. He's your agent, your manager, and your guardian."

"I know that," Sarah said quietly.

"And now he wants to marry you too? And I gotta say, you don't strike me as a young girl in love. Doesn't he have enough control already? You want to give him even more?"

"He's not taking advantage of me, Martin. It's nothing like that."

"He controls all the money, all the finances, right?" Martin said carefully.

"He controls the business side of it all," she answered. "All I do is the music. I get total control over the music, the content, every note, every lyric, every image in a video. Alexander does everything else. We like it that way. It works for us," she said a bit defensively, beginning to turn away.

Martin held on to her, stroking her hair soothingly, saying "OK, OK Smallest. That's fine then." He held her for a moment. "Look," he said. "I don't give a flying fuck what Mr. Billionaire in there wants. I only want to make sure you're doing what you want to do Sarah. Have you two set a date?"

She gave a tiny nod. "My twenty-first birthday," she said softly.

Ha! The moment of emancipation thought Martin, but he didn't say that. "Good," he nodded. "That's good. That's months and months away. Who knows," he teased, "maybe I'll even end up liking old Al after all. If he's anything like his old man, he can't be all bad." Martin kissed the tip of Sarah's nose and released her. "Tell you what, Smallest. If your Al is all you say he is and you still want to marry him on your twenty-first birthday, I'll even walk you down the aisle if you like."

Sarah blushed down to the roots of her hair and Martin laughed good-naturedly at her. Ah, his Sarah. She was still such a funny little duckling.

76

Sarah felt her universe spiraling out of control. She was getting what she wanted, but everything was off a notch, as if a crystal was refracting and distorting reality. She had dreamed of walking down the aisle with Martin as her husband since she was a little girl. But never had she dreamed of walking down the aisle with Martin so he could give her away to another man. Spinning, spinning. Things were spinning out of control.

Chapter Ten

Three days later, in the early evening, Martin headed to Sarah's, again on his motorcycle. His frustration with this case mounted daily. They had turned over every rock, talked to every neighbor, every co-worker, every person at the bar where Fulton hung out on Wednesday and Saturday nights. Nothing. No connection to Sarah. No knowledge of any friend or acquaintance matching knife weasel's description. The blue parrots were a strange oddity, but other than the unease they gave him, he couldn't see they had any significance.

Martin contrived a way to see Sarah every day. First, he brought her dog's body back to her for burial. Then, the following day, he brought her his dog, Sam, early in the morning on his way to work. He was right; she was still an early riser just as he was. Sebastian always admitted him immediately no matter what time he arrived and took him straight to Sarah. She must have given him instructions, Martin realized, and was inordinately pleased. He knew getting access to someone like Sarah could be very, very, difficult and he was pleased she still felt as close to him, apparently, as he did to her. She still considered him family and his spirits soared. Sebastian didn't even lift an eyebrow when Martin whistled for Sam that day and the dog came bounding out of the truck. He simply showed them back to Sarah's private wing where he found her in the garden, apparently doing yoga or perhaps some kind of ballet thing; he wasn't really sure. She stopped immediately when they arrived and Sam bounded up to her.

"He's adorable, Martin!" she cried, down on her knees greeting the exuberant border collie. "What's his name?"

"Samson," Martin said. Then, in unison, they said, "Sam, Son of Tarly," and laughed, both remembering the name of a character in a fantasy game they played as children, and again Martin was extraordinarily happy that she remembered. "Sam for short. Just thought you might like the company for a couple of days. I'm at work all day and

Sam here gets himself into mischief if left to his own devices too long. Thought he might as well get himself into mischief here," Martin added with a grin, scratching Sam behind the ears. "I'll take him off your hands when you've had enough of him."

Yesterday, when he stopped by to take Sam back, she asked that the dog be allowed to stay awhile longer. They were fast friends already and Martin reflected that Sam made an excellent wingman... lots of excuses to come back. Mind your manners, Sam, he thought as he gave Sam his scratch on the chest. Maybe you'll get lucky enough to stay here for a while, boy.

Now, on day three, he was on his way to Sarah's, again with the excuse to take Sam home. Although a pretty flimsy excuse, he realized, since he was on his bike and couldn't take the dog home on it. Oh well, fuck it, he thought. What was wrong with just saying he was stopping by to say hi and let them know there were no further developments? The bright side is, it would probably get under Al's skin, realizing he was coming by every day. Good. He wanted to rattle the smug bastard's cage a bit. He still wasn't sure about old Al. And he found it interesting that he hadn't seen him the last two days he'd gone there. Turns out he owned another home in the Hollywood Hills and usually only came to see Sarah once or twice a week. Very interesting.

The other times he stopped by, Sarah had been alone. Today he noted a small group on the terrace when he arrived. Sebastian, serving drinks, turned to him for his order. What the hell, Martin thought. I'm off duty. "I'll have a beer, Sebastian. Thanks."

Sarah greeted him as Sam bounded up to say hello. Scratching the dog behind the ear, Martin said hello to everyone.

"Kind of you to lend Sarah your dog," Alexander said dryly.

"No problem," Martin laughed. "I'll take him off your hands if he gets to be too much. He can be a handful, I know." He and Sam tussled for a moment then Martin stood, surveying the group.

Sarah's eyes shone with happiness as she looked at him and he went to her for a more personal hello. Hell, let these guys think what they wanted. He hugged her then stroked her cheek delicately in his signature greeting. "Hi Smallest." Releasing her, he went back and picked up his beer, realizing the entire group was looking at him strangely. Fuck it. He didn't care.

Sarah came to herself with a small start and finally introduced Martin to Jonathan and Paul. "And, of course, you met Julie the other morning," she said.

Martin recognized Jonathan, an older, stodgy British guy from the estate in Hawaii; but, of course, Jonathan wouldn't know him. He remembered that Jonathan was an old friend of Magnus and he wondered if Jonathan had been a part of Magnus' old network of con artists. He wasn't sure, the guy looked like a straight arrow now. Martin had also seen Paul a number of times over the years although they had never met before.

Martin cursed his faulty memory again. He used to have a razor sharp memory. Not as good as Sarah's but very, very good. However, that final debriefing when he was leaving the Army, leaving the Special Forces after ten years, well that had been brutal. They had used a drug, Rhonopol, banned now, that had left him drooling in a straight jacket and with a memory more like swiss cheese. He remembered most everything but there were holes, things, events, he couldn't reconcile and he just about gave up trying to. All his memories from that day forward were intact, but pre Rhonopol memories were suspect, out of order, full of holes. He couldn't quite place when he had last seen Paul but he let it go. Probably didn't matter.

Jonathan spoke. "We were discussing the American Ballet Theater's offer of a plum role to Sarah for this Fall, that of Eve in a biblical version of 'East of Eden'. She'll partner Yuri Rominoff, of course."

Sarah said lightly with a small laugh, "Sorry, Jonathan, but I've already told Alexander no. I'm not accepting the role."

Alexander spoke up. "Ah, but you are, my dear. I've already accepted for you. We leave for New York in two days."

Sarah stared at Alexander in shock. "But I told you I didn't want to go, to turn down the role."

"Sarah," Alexander said firmly. "You told me I was in charge of your schedule and that you would cooperate." He'd been careful not to use the word obey but he knew she got his meaning.

She flushed with anger. "Yes, but not to go to New York for an entire season! I don't want to go."

"Furthermore," Alexander went on as if he hadn't heard her. "There are a couple of gentlemen I'd like you to meet." He nodded at Sebastian who ushered two large, muscular guys to the terrace. They stood at military attention in front of Alexander and Sarah. "Sarah, this is Bates and O' Donnell. They are your new security detail for your stay in New York."

Sarah stared aghast at Alexander. "You can't be serious! I'm not taking those men to New York. I'm not going to New York. And if I were, Sebastian and Jonathan will be all the protection I need. After all, it was always just Magnus and Sebastian before. I don't need these Secret Service guys."

"Sarah," Alexander said with infinite patience, "You are going to New York and you will be taking these gentlemen with you everywhere you go. They will be staying at the apartment with you. They will accompany you to and from the studio and Lincoln Center. Do I make myself clear." His tone brooked no argument.

Anger gripped Sarah as her heart beat faster. She didn't want to go to New York. Martin was here. She wanted to stay here. She had already said no. So, she said it again. "No."

Alexander slapped the table in front of her in anger. "Enough Princess! You will do as you are told!" He sat back.

No one said anything for a moment. None of them had ever seen Alexander speak like that to Sarah and they didn't know what to say. Interesting dynamics, thought Martin. The legendary working relationship appeared to be a bit rockier than Sarah had let on.

Sarah jumped up from the table. "Please do not speak to me like I'm a child," she said, her voice sharp, her eyes flashing in anger. "And I'm not going to New York." At that she rushed off the terrace, into the garden, and through the gate to her private garden.

No one said anything for another moment. "Well, that was a bit harsh," said Julie. "What's gotten into you?"

Alexander didn't answer.

Martin got up. "Smooth, Al, very smooth. And I got news for you," he gestured at the two bodyguards. "Big doesn't necessarily mean good. Actually, it usually means slow." He patted the two bodyguards on the shoulder in a friendly gesture as he said, "Where'd you find these two goons, 'Bodyguards R Us?' At that, Martin sauntered off the terrace across the lawn towards Sarah's private garden.

Alexander watched him leave with undisguised dislike on his face. He looked at Sebastian and nodding towards Martin said, "Where the hell does he think he's going?"

"Ms. Sarah gave instructions that he was to have free access to all parts of the estate at any time." Sebastian replied.

"She did, did she? Unfucking believable." He shook his head. Even he didn't wander into Sarah's wing of the estate without an invitation from her. Well, now that he was setting the rules, things were going to be different.

Martin found Sarah in her private yard. He liked her garden better than the more formal grounds they had just left. Hers was an English style overgrown garden, a kaleidoscope of color and textures all tumbling in joyful profusion, lots of flowers, lots of scents. He sniffed appreciatively realizing that what he really wanted was a whiff of Sarah. He found her scent addictive, he wanted more. Sam was with her, she was petting him absentmindedly. "Hi, Sam, you traitor." Martin said. "I see you like her better than me already." He gave Sarah a big smile. Sarah laughed and it did him good to see it.

"So, Smallest," he dropped down and sat on the ground near her chair then stretched out comfortably on the grass. "What's the deal with this New York thing?"

"Nothing," she said. "I just don't want to go."

"Why not? Isn't that what you usually do, dance in New York every Fall?"

"Yes," she admitted. "I didn't last year because Magnus had just died."

"Other than that, you've done this every year since you were what, twelve, thirteen years old?" Martin prodded. She nodded again. He put his hands under his head and looked up at her from his prone position on the ground. "So, how come you don't want to this year? I mean, it's no skin off my back." He shrugged. "I don't care if you dance or not, just curious. Don't you like it anymore?"

"Yes, I like it fine," she admitted. "It's just," she searched for an excuse, something plausible. She couldn't tell him she didn't want to leave him. She lit on the bodyguards. "You know how I am around new people, strangers." She laughed shakily. "I could never put up with those two going everywhere with me, being around me all the time. It would never work. And I know Alexander. He'll insist. He'll never let me get away with just Sebastian and Jonathan as escorts. You'll see. It's better if I just stay home," she concluded.

"Well, I wouldn't let you get away with Jonathan and Sebastian as 'escorts' either, Sarah. You don't need escorts," he said dryly, "you need bodyguards. Jonathan and Sebastian are both pushing seventy. Surely there's someone you and Al can agree on. It doesn't have to be Mutt and Jeff in there."

"Martin, you know how I am around people. It's difficult for me to be around people I know well for any length of time, much less strangers. It's just too… hard," she finally said.

"Tell me about what New York entails," he said. "Maybe I can come up with some ideas for you. It seems a shame you're not going to dance if you want to."

So, Sarah described her usual routine in New York when Magnus was alive. The apartment, on the upper West Side, overlooked Central Park. Sarah was driven from the apartment to either the ballet studios, also on the upper West Side, or to Lincoln Center where ABT performed. After the performance, she went straight home. There were a few appearances as well, such as the Benefactor's Ball, but she typically only stayed thirty minutes to an hour at such events. She might drink perhaps one glass of sparkling juice or champagne, provided by Magnus. She never ate or drank anything from the event itself. Usually she danced the opening dance number with Yuri, danced a dance or two with Magnus and even Alexander, if he was attending, and then whoosh, back home.

Other than that, she stayed home. She didn't go to restaurants. She didn't go shopping. She didn't go to movies with friends; she didn't seem to have friends. She didn't go to clubs. She didn't go to salons. She didn't do virtually any of the things that Jace, Will's twenty-year old daughter did. The difference between Jace and Sarah was startling and Martin's heart ached for Sarah.

He'd thought, when he'd seen her on the stage that fateful night, the night he decided to walk away rather than meet her as planned, that she finally had it all. She was incandescent that night. It was a huge outdoor concert of over thirty thousand people and she had them all in the palm of her hand. Her performance blew him away. He had never seen her on stage before. He'd been on so many tours of duty in so many bases around the world, they had just never connected before while she was performing. He'd thought that she had finally overcome most of her hurdles. She assured him she was outgrowing many of the MCS symptoms, that it was getting much better. It must be true, he thought, there she was on stage in front of thousands and doing great.

But it wasn't really true. Not only was Sarah not at all like the bunch of celebrity bozos he'd encountered around Lindsey Lohan, she wasn't remotely like any typical twenty year old young woman he'd ever met. He had to smile at her speech patterns. She sounded like she had just come from some finishing school for royalty, a by-product of her years of being educated by Magnus no doubt. He had never seen Sarah use her cell phone, any phone for that matter. She didn't text, she wasn't running around doing a million things: flirting, and driving, and working, and going to school. She stayed home. She worked from home, alone.

It would be interesting to see her in New York, he thought. Dancing with an entire ballet company, that's got to be more interaction than he had ever seen her have with anyone. He realized that while he saw her dance over the years, as she always shared with him what she learned, he had never seen her perform a ballet on stage before.

"So anyway, that's about it." Sarah was summing up. "That's why I don't need bodyguards. I don't really go anywhere," she said somewhat apologetically. "It's actually pretty boring, I guess."

Martin smiled at her. "OK, doesn't sound like too tough of a gig. Want me to talk to Al?" he asked. "Maybe I can get him to rethink those two goons in there, help him find someone more appropriate."

"It won't do any good but you're welcome to try. Alexander is pretty inflexible when it comes to security." She thought again of the spanking she'd gotten for rushing out of the house the other night and going to Paradise Cove. She realized, with a sinking feeling in her stomach, that she might be headed for another spanking tonight. She had defied Alexander again.

Martin rose and kissed her cheek. "I should get going, Smallest. I'll see you soon," and he left.

Sarah stayed seated in her garden. Suddenly, Alexander appeared at the gate. "May I come in?" he asked rather formally.

"Of course," she replied.

Alexander strode up to her. "Sarah, we had a discussion about you obeying me. Did you obey me tonight?"

"No." she replied simply.

"No," he repeated. "You did not. You defied me. Get inside and bend over the bed," he ordered.

Sarah stared at him a long moment, then rose from her chair, went in to the bed, and obeyed. This time, when she bent over the bed, Alexander lifted her skirt and bared her bottom in her panties. Her face flamed scarlet but she said nothing.

"I'm giving you ten slaps," he said.

Another suggestion of Paul's, "Let her know exactly what to expect. Tell her how many times you will strike her. Sometimes it's helpful if you both count them down."

Alexander felt ridiculous, but he followed the advice nevertheless. "One!" His first slap landed with a satisfying shock against his palm. Sarah gasped. "Two!" Again, the gratifying slap of his palm against her buttock. He had lifted her skirt for his own benefit. If he had to do this, damn it, he was at least going to look at the ass he was spanking. He badly wanted to pull her panties down and spank her bare bottom, but didn't dare. He knew he was already crossing a line just with lifting her skirt. "Three!"

Sarah smarted badly already and he'd only smacked her three times. She tried to brace herself, but against mostly bare skin, this was much more painful than last time. Seven more to go.

Alexander noted with satisfaction that her bottom blushed enticingly pink as his hand continued to move in a pattern of spanking each cheek high then low. "Eight!" Slap! "Nine!" Slap! Sarah began to cry out in pain. "Ten!"

Sarah, near tears, called out the last number with him. She lay there, quivering, then slowly pulled her skirt down. She decided not to sit but pulled herself to her side on the bed and lay there.

"Are we going to have any more difficulty about New York, Sarah?" Alexander asked sternly.

"No, Zander," she answered quietly. "I'll go to New York."

"Good," he said, his tone softer. "Do you need anything? Can I get you anything, Sarah?" His voice was kind.

"No," she answered softly.

"Do you realize," he asked, his voice sad now, "those ten slaps are more than I've touched you in the last ten years." She didn't reply and he turned and left the room. As he walked away, he realized he would need to find some relief tonight. He felt guilty, even angry with himself, but there was no denying how aroused he felt. He needed to bury himself deep in someone warm and wet and welcoming.

Sarah turned her face into the bed after Zander left. Her tears fell freely now. Well, she had wanted this. She had wanted a way to subvert her will, to give it to someone else, someone she trusted more than herself. She dashed her tears away. It was stupid to cry, it would gain her nothing. Zander had no idea of the real punishment he had meted out tonight. She was going to New York and therefore leaving Martin behind for over two months. Even though she knew it useless, she gave herself to her tears. What if Martin didn't want to see her again when she came back? Now, there was the police case, his reason for seeing her. If that were solved, would he leave again? She remembered his face, his voice when he told her about what had happened to his family. He was as lonely as she was, she realized. He had missed her, she could tell.

Perhaps it's for the best, she thought tiredly. She had not seen him in over four years. Now, after only the third day since he had come back into her life, she already felt hopelessly entangled in all of those feelings again. She had waited every second of the last three days for the sound of his voice, the touch of his hand on her cheek, the look in his eyes. She touched her cheek softly, imitating Martin's gesture. It didn't feel the same when she did it. When he touched her face, she felt the touch radiate throughout her body, ending achingly in her womb, setting off dozens of other confusing feelings and emotions. She wanted something, something so, so badly and she didn't even know what it was. But she was pretty sure Martin didn't want what she wanted. She needed to learn how to put some distance between her and Martin, how to give him some space. She didn't want to smother him with her neediness. Not like before.

Chapter Eleven

Paul remained on the terrace with Julie and Jonathan and stared into his drink, musing. After they all said their goodbyes to Martin, they watched Alexander head for Sarah's private garden. Earlier, Paul thought Sarah had been pushing for another punishment when she defied Alexander, but then he realized she had really been angry about New York. Not frightened; angry. He cautioned Alexander when he saw him head towards Sarah. He took him aside and quietly reminded him, "Don't talk to her when you're angry and don't even think of punishing her if you're angry."

Alexander nodded and seemed sincere when he said, "I'm still just trying to figure out what's expected of me here. What do you think, Paul? Do you think this little display of temper was just to see if I'll follow through?"

"Perhaps," he said. "I've no doubt she's expecting you, though." He watched Alexander walk away.

Paul thought back to his first involvement with this unusual family and wondered again how he managed to get himself quite so enmeshed in the complicated, messy, high drama mystery of this amazing, extraordinarily talented, and severely damaged young woman.

Magnus came to him over thirteen years ago now. They knew each other but not well. Magnus had helped Paul's family after the tragic aftermath of Paul's mother's suicide. Paul's father had been absent for years, unable to deal with his wife's depression and mood swings. That left teenaged Paul trying to deal with his mother and his younger brother. After it had all gone to hell, Magnus had shown up. Turns out he was a distant relative of his mother's, on the Hungarian side of the family, and Magnus believed in family. He took control of the horrible situation and had been a friend to Paul ever since. He put Paul through medical school and supported him in his decision to become a psychiatrist. Magnus understood how much his mother's problems haunted Paul.

But thirteen years ago, Magnus came to him for the first time in a professional capacity. He called, scheduled an appointment, and arrived precisely on time. He was dressed, as usual, in his dapper, formal style: exquisitely tailored suit, silver topped cane in hand, every inch the successful, charming, debonair 'Man About Town'. However, Paul realized Magnus seemed nervous, had difficulty sitting, and strolled around, examining various objects in the room. Paul was used to this. Patients were invariably nervous and agitated when they first came to him. He was just somewhat surprised to see it in Magnus.

Magnus finally sat, looked Paul directly in the eye, and said, "I need to talk to someone about some dreams I've been having. Very, very troubling dreams," he added, rubbing his face with his hand. "I've never experienced anything like this before. I can't sleep at all anymore. I couldn't think of anyone to discuss something like this with." He shifted uncomfortably in his seat. "Then I thought of you. You're a bright young man." He smiled at Paul who was just a few years older than his son, Alexander. Paul, practicing psychiatry for four years now, was building a thriving practice. "And I know I can count on your discretion," he finished.

Paul smiled at Magnus. "Privacy is a basic tenet of the profession, Magnus. You can count on privacy from any doctor you choose to visit; however, I am glad, and flattered, that you chose me. So, tell me about these dreams."

Magnus sat back, set his cane aside, straightened the crease in his trousers, and finally spoke. "They don't sound terrible, but they are," he said, looking at Paul, then looking away. "I see a young girl, a child. See appears to be about five years old or so. She's very small and defenseless. She has huge violet eyes that are so full of pain and fear that it chills me to my core." He stopped talking.

"Yes," Paul said. "Go on."

"That's it," Magnus had said. "I see this child, she stares at me with those eyes and I wake up sweating, my heart racing. I know I have to help her. I know she's in terrible danger, but that's it. That's all I see. Her face." Then he amended, "Sometimes I see her in a small huddle on the floor. She's wet, looks like she's in pajamas. Again, she looks up at me with that face." Magnus rubbed his hand across his eyes again then looked at Paul, his expression bleak. "I don't know what to do. I have the dream constantly, several times a night. I can't sleep. I see her face when I'm awake now. It's haunting me. I can't shake the feeling I'm supposed to help her but I have no idea who she could be. I've never seen her before."

"How long has this been going on?" Paul asked.

"Several weeks now. Like I said, they're getting worse, much worse." His hand shook as he straightened his trousers again. "What is this, Paul? What could this possibly mean?"

Paul hadn't known and they talked about Magnus' life, what was going on in the rest of his life. There seemed to be no reason, no stress, no incident which precipitated the dreams. Based on how troubling Magnus found the dreams, his difficulty sleeping, and the fact that the face of this mystery little girl was now haunting his waking hours, Paul scheduled several more appointments with Magnus. Over the course of the next ten days and three or four visits, they had learned nothing more. Magnus' agitation grew. He even sketched a portrait of the little girl for Paul. He was a fairly decent artist. Paul had to admit that the face of the little girl was compelling. Paul still had that sketch locked in the file in his office.

Ultimately, Paul had been unable to give any reason for the dreams but suggested the dreams and the little girl in them were most likely an emotional representation of something else that Magnus was just not ready to deal with yet. The lack of sleep and the dreams were taking their toll on Magnus. He told Paul he decided he needed to get away for a while. He was going to Hong Kong to visit his son, Alexander. They had an apartment there and Alexander had been living in Hong Kong for the past year or so while Magnus was still in New York. He missed his son; it was time to pay him a prolonged visit. Paul thought this a fine idea. Perhaps a change of scene was just what was needed.

Three days later Paul got a call from Magnus. He asked him to come to Hong Kong immediately, insisted he take a flight the very next day. When Paul asked if it was in reference to the dreams, Magnus replied, yes, but would say no more on the phone. Paul was a bit annoyed, but he did owe Magnus, and it was a free trip to Hong Kong, so he had done as asked and brought Magnus' file with him. He'd arrived at the apartment just before the dinner hour and asked for an explanation.

Magnus insisted that Sebastian get him settled in the guest room first, that he freshen up and then join them for dinner. He was expecting guests for dinner, there was someone he wanted Paul to meet. Magnus would say no more but Paul noted that he seemed more rested and happier than in New York. In fact, he seemed his old self.

Paul was flabbergasted when the dinner guests turned out to be Magnus' niece, Julie, Julie's new boyfriend, Danny, and Danny's little sister, Sarah – undeniably the little girl from the sketch. It was uncanny, there was no doubt this was the child. Magnus had even captured the color of her unusual violet eyes perfectly.

He and Magnus spoke quietly after the dinner guests had gone. Sebastian sat with them after he poured drinks.

"What do you think?" Magnus asked. They all looked at the sketch. Nothing had been said at dinner, Magnus had not even told his son about the dreams. The only person he had shared the dreams with, besides Paul, was his friend Sebastian.

Paul was still amazed at the child. "How did you meet?" he asked.

"The day after I arrived, Alexander had Julie over for dinner and she brought her new friend, Danny. I gather that Sarah, his little sister, goes everywhere with him."

Paul observed the little girl closely throughout dinner. She was extremely shy and spoke to no one but Danny, and then in a whisper. She was very polite and well mannered, but looked no one in the eye and would look away immediately if you looked at her. She did seem curious about Magnus, and Paul caught her observing him closely throughout dinner, but she didn't speak to him. Danny had brought dinner along for his little sister; a glass of juice, some fruit, and a cheese sandwich. Seems the little girl refused to eat meat and had a great many food allergies, so she only ate food that Danny knew she could tolerate.

After dinner, they went into the living room and little Sarah ran immediately to the grand piano and looked at Magnus, her eyes full of longing. Magnus sat down to play and the child was transported. It was enchanting to watch how she drank in the music, watching Magnus' fingers carefully, her entire little body caught up in the sound. At one point she crawled under the piano and lay, face up, prone on the floor, listening with a look of ecstasy on her face.

Her brother apologized for her but hadn't asked her to get up. "She's never heard a piano before the other night over here. She's crazy about it, as you can see," he said with a fond smile at his sister. "I appreciate the invitation tonight. She's been bugging me to come back here and hear that piano again."

But what astounded them all was when Magnus asked the child if she would like to play. She nodded yes, sat down, touched each key slowly, one at a time, then began to play what Magnus had just been playing, a Chopin Mazurkas from Opus 24 in G minor. It was ragged, the child's hands were far too small for the keyboard and therefore, there were some mistakes, but it was undeniably the Chopin piece Magnus had just played, note for note. No one knew what to say for a moment.

Her brother spoke first. "How did you do that, Sarah?" He walked over and stood beside her and she whispered something to him. Danny looked at Magnus. "She said she just watched you, what your fingers were doing." To Sarah he said, "But how could you remember it all, bunny? It's a long song." The child had just shrugged.

"What's their story?" Paul asked. "How old is she?"

"They're orphans. She's seven," Magnus said, "but don't you agree she looks younger? Her brother is seventeen. According to Julie, he's the most gifted graduate student in physics at the University. Julie is quite smitten with Danny, even through he's about five years younger than she. What can this mean, Paul?" Magnus repeated. They all looked at the sketch on the table before them again.

Paul shook his head and spread his hands in a gesture of defeat. "I have no idea, Magnus. I've never encountered anything like this before. At least she doesn't appear to be in trouble or danger," he offered. You're sure your son never mentioned her?"

"Quite sure," Magnus returned.

"Has she spoken to you?" asked Paul.

"Yes," Magnus replied. "When we first met. She said, 'You're the man with the music in his fingers.' That's why I went to the piano in the first place and began playing. It seemed such a charming thing for her to say and I was still trying to recover from the shock of meeting her. You could have knocked me over with a feather when she walked in the door."

"Has she said anything else?" Paul asked.

"Not a word," Magnus replied.

"Did she play the piano that first time?" Paul asked.

"No," Magnus replied. "I truly believed she had never seen a piano before the other day. Is that even possible?"

"There are musical savants," Paul replied, "so, yes, it is possible. Just rare. Do you know what's wrong with her?"

"Wrong?" Magnus questioned. "Her brother assures me she's just very shy. She's led a sheltered life in a small rural village here in China. Their parents were missionaries. He says she's not adjusting well to all the changes. She also seems to have many allergies, she's been sick a great deal since they arrived here. That's why he's being so careful with her food."

"That's a lot for a seventeen year old to take on," Paul said.

"Julie tells me it is just the two of them. They live on a sailboat in the marina at the University. A sailboat he won off my son at a poker game," Magnus added with a rueful chuckle and a shake of his head. "Paul," Magnus hesitated. "Why would she say that to me? She'd just met me. 'You're the man with the music in his fingers'. That's what she said, clear as a little bell."

"Did you ask her?" Paul replied.

"No." Magnus hesitated. "That's why I wanted you to come here. I'm uncertain of how to proceed and she is a very young child. I didn't know if I should say anything at all to her but I would like to ask her why she said that to me."

"Well, as long as you don't corner her, you ask her in a friendly not too inquisitive way, perhaps in front of or near her brother so she'll be more relaxed, it should be fine," Paul said.

Due to Sarah's obvious attraction to the piano, Magnus made arrangements for Danny to visit daily with his little sister for a piano lesson. The following day, Paul watched from a nearby chair as Magnus finished showing Sarah a new piece of music. Danny was across the room engrossed in a book. Magnus turned to the little girl and asked her why she had said what she said when they first met. Paul still remembered her reply. He thought at first she wasn't going to answer. Then she looked right at Magnus and said, "Because I saw you, too." Then she turned back to the piano and said no more.

Paul knew that was the moment that Magnus fell hopelessly in love with the child. He knew his old benefactor thought there was some cosmic reason he had been brought into the little girl's life, and Paul could say nothing to persuade him otherwise. He flew back to New York thinking it had been one of life's odder moments, but nothing more than that. Then, about three weeks later, Sarah arrived at Magnus' apartment in Hong Kong, late at night, in a huddle outside his door, wet, in her pajamas, and severely traumatized. She hugged herself, shivering, and would not or could not speak. There was a note with her. The note he and Magnus had gone over and over so many times. Who had written it? They never found out. The note, damp but legible, said, '4 guys took Danny. Maroon Lexus sedan, License URL 768. They went east out of marina. Please help.' Paul remembered Magnus describing what happened next, the frantic search which finally led to that building in the jungle just outside the city where they discovered Danny's gruesome murder. How Magnus had been certain that the child was in mortal danger as well.

Paul shook his head. He remembered that Julie agreed with Magnus, they must take Sarah with them back to New York. Get her out of Hong Kong immediately. Paul, horrified when they arrived in New York with the child and told him what had transpired, exclaimed to Magnus. "You can't just take a child! You know virtually nothing about her! What about her family? Her parents may be dead but she may have other family. What in the world were you thinking!"

It was Julie who said, "There is no one else, Danny told me."

Magnus told Paul that whoever took Danny was looking for his little sister as well. They trashed the boat looking for her onboard, they asked all around the marina about the little blonde girl... had anyone seen her? Based on the grisly scene that awaited them when they found Danny, Magnus felt that Sarah was in grave, grave danger. Julie agreed.

They never figured out why Danny had been murdered or by whom. It was a mystery to this day. Magnus somehow managed to forge a new identity for Sarah as the daughter of a suddenly deceased cousin and appointed himself as her guardian. There was no record of Sarah ever having a brother.

Paul became her psychiatrist and Julie her medical doctor. Little Sarah, so traumatized when she first came to them, didn't speak for almost a year. She had fevers, raging, high fevers that sometimes led to seizures, which resulted in the strange phenomenon of glass breaking and shattering nearby. Again rare, but Paul had heard of instances of telekinesis, usually by young children, usually in times of crisis or illness. A door being slammed shut, a lamp knocked off a table. There was little data, mostly anecdotal accounts, but it was interesting to observe the phenomenon personally.

Paul thought back now to this evening, the man, Martin Stone, he just met. Alexander was definitely right, he thought. There is something between them, some strong bond. That much is clear. Well, he thought to himself. I do believe we may be about to learn something about our mysterious Miss Eastin.

Chapter Twelve

That was surprisingly easy to pull off, Martin thought. He'd thought about it all last night after he left Sarah's. What really started him thinking, he admitted to himself, was the thought that he didn't want to lose her to New York so soon after just seeing her again. And he kept remembering he had never seen her dance on the stage. After he'd done some checking into Mutt and Jeff, the bodyguards Al hired, he found they were being paid ten grand a week, each, for an eight week gig. A serious chunk of change, Martin thought. Again he wondered why he liked being a cop so much. The money was shit. Well, he didn't do it for the money, that's for sure. Still, it got him thinking.

He'd talked to the Captain first thing this morning. He had over six weeks of leave the Captain had been bugging him to use, Will had more. If the Captain gave them permission, they would be allowed to accept an outside job, such as security consultants to Miss Eastin, for a limited amount of time. All he needed was another couple of weeks of unpaid leave, and the Captain had said yes to all that. Martin figured he would. Magnus was an old friend of his and he was worried about Sarah's safety.

Will signed up once he heard about the money. His first response had been that he couldn't leave his family for eight weeks. When Martin explained about the money, eighty grand each, and that Will could have his share, Will was astounded. "I couldn't do that, man. Hell, eighty thousand each, that's serious money."

"I am serious," Martin said. "I don't want Sarah's money and I won't take Al's, so I'll just burn my share if you don't take it. It'll be a good start on the college fund for your kids. Besides, with that kind of dough, Will, you can have them come to New York to visit you while you're there. You can make a little vacation out of it. This is not going to be a tough gig, I promise you." He'd added enticingly, "Private jet, penthouse, come on Will, chance to see how the one percenters live."

Next he would talk to Sarah, practically certain she would agree to have he and Will act as her bodyguards. Her eagerness to see him matched his. Then, he would tackle Al who would be fairly well boxed in. He wanted Sarah to go to New York. He would have to be reasonable about a switch in security if Sarah asked for him. After all, Martin thought with a grim chuckle, he knows I'm qualified.

Martin knew with certainty that Alexander was investigating him the last couple of days. Digging into his past, his military records, his employment records. Martin was virtually certain his home had been entered yesterday, while he was at work, and carefully searched; he knew it was Alexander. If not personally, then someone he'd sent.

As Martin drove through the gates of the estate, he marveled again at the beauty of the place, the manicured gardens, the majestic view, the graceful old stone building. Smallest, you've done pretty darn well, he thought. No surprise, he always knew she was amazing, like no one else. The first time he saw the estate he thought it beautiful, but he'd been contemptuous of it then, the conspicuous display of wealth. Now that he knew it was Sarah's home, he somehow felt different. Now he felt it was a sanctuary she deserved and he was glad she had it.

Sebastian greeted him courteously but still didn't call him by name Martin noted. He was told Sarah was in her recording studio. "Can I go up?" he asked.

Sebastian nodded formally. "Of course. Miss Sarah has asked that you be admitted immediately whenever you arrive here." He led the way to the bottom of the spiral staircase in Sarah's private wing that led to the upper floors of the large circular tower of her private quarters. The recording studio, on the second floor of the tower, featured a spectacular view all around. Martin found Sarah standing, headphones on, fiddling with a soundboard, bopping and weaving and dancing in place. Suddenly aware of his presence, she turned around.

"Martin!" She pulled the headphones off and went to him.

"Am I interrupting?" he asked.

"No," she said. Then laughing, "Well, yes, but I welcome it. I could use a break."

He looked around with interest but she headed back down the stairs and he followed her.

Walking out into her garden, she asked if he wanted anything. "Sure. A cup of coffee would be nice." It was ten am and he'd only had one cup of coffee this morning. Sarah rang Sebastian and quietly asked for coffee and tea. Martin approached her, "I didn't get a chance to say hi yet." He hugged her and touched her cheek. Then he stepped back and accepted the coffee Sebastian offered.

Sarah accepted her tea but didn't sit, still too sore from her spanking last night to sit comfortably. Just two more days, she thought miserably, then she wouldn't see Martin again for two months. Well, at least he was here today and she was glad of that. He had come to see her every day since they met again. She consoled herself with that thought.

Martin sat down and asked her to join him. "I've something I'd like to ask you," he said. She sat carefully and waited. "Sarah, how would you feel about me accompanying you to New York as your bodyguard? Me and Will," he amended.

She stared at him astonished and her heart leapt in her chest. *He wants to go with me! He wants to go with me!* She could only stare at him for a moment. She finally said, "But you have a job here. How can you go to New York?"

"Oh, that's all worked out." He waved his hand dismissively. "Both Will and I have a ton of leave we need to use up and the Captain gave us permission to seek outside, temporary employment as your security consultants, should you decide to hire us," he added.

Sarah stared enthralled. This was too good to be true. Alexander said the bodyguards would be staying in the apartment with her. They would accompany her everywhere she went. Eight weeks with Martin, the thought made her giddy. Her entire face lit up with a smile that warmed Martin's heart.

"Is that a yes?" he asked.

"Oh, yes!" Sarah replied and she couldn't resist giving him a hug.

"I'll find someone to take care of Sam, here," Martin said, stooping to pet his dog.

"He's welcome to come with us. Roscoe always went with me. We're all set up for dogs in the apartment," she added.

"Great," Martin laughed. "Sam, we're going on an adventure together!"

Alexander was surprisingly acquiescent telling Sarah that if Martin's qualifications checked out, well then it was just fine with him. He wanted his Princess to be happy. Yeah, Martin thought derisively, like you haven't already checked me out. Still, he was surprised the guy didn't kick up more of a fuss.

Chapter Thirteen

The acolyte known as Scum no longer held any interest for Flint. He watched as the life ebbed out of the man's eyes. He enjoyed Scum's painful death screams, made sure he made Scum's agony prolonged, that the rest of his acolytes would learn what it meant to displease him. His pleasure was short-lived, however. He learned nothing new from Scum about the girl, Sarah Eastin. The man stupidly thought that Flint would be pleased if he brought the girl to him when she unexpectedly appeared on the beach. That was the danger of controlling these weak minds, he thought contemptuously of his acolytes. He couldn't control them every minute of every day, and when he did give them mental commands and orders, they caught glimpses into his own mind. They knew of his obsession with the girl, but not the reasons why. So, they foolishly thought he would be pleased if they brought her to him. He was also angry that Dung had managed to elude his wrath by killing himself while in custody of the LAPD. His hands flexed instinctively as he imagined tearing out the man's throat with his bare hands rather than him killing himself. Well, in a way he had killed Dung, he thought with satisfaction. The piece of shit was so afraid of him, he had killed himself rather than face Flint's fury.

But, the girl. Flint nearly screamed with frustration when he thought of the girl. Who was she to the Blue Parrot? Why couldn't he see more than the occasional flash of her? He would have to be more careful. His acolytes would have to follow his instructions to the letter. He had to find out more about Sarah Eastin. He needed to know much more before he could form a plan, before he could act.

Chapter Fourteen

The Gulfstream G650 roared down the runway and lifted off smoothly. On board with Sarah and Alexander were Martin, Will, Sebastian, Jonathan, Julie, Paul, and even Max, the chauffer, along with a pilot, co-pilot, and flight attendant. Martin watched Sarah and Al from his seat beside Will. From the time of his and Will's arrival at the estate that morning, he observed a flurry of activity from everyone. Al seemed to be conducting business nonstop on his cell phone while barking orders at Jonathan and Sebastian, who scurried around, lists in hand, organizing an enormous amount of supplies. Only Sarah was still, in her garden with her iPOD, waiting to leave, her one piece of luggage packed and ready in her bedroom. After the final flurry of activity from everyone but Sarah, who seemed unconcerned with anything, they left the estate. Max drove the Lincoln Town Car with Alexander, Sarah, Martin, and Will, while Sebastian and Jonathan followed in the large SUV with most of the luggage and the huge amount of boxes and crates. "What do you suppose all that stuff is?" Will asked Martin quietly as they watched the car being loaded, surprised it all fit in the SUV.

"Food, medical supplies, and musical instruments mostly," Martin had replied.

Paul and Julie met them at the airport and Max drove them right up to the jet waiting on the tarmac.

Now that they were airborne, there was finally calm, but Al and Sarah still didn't seem to be talking much, Martin noted. Will checked out the interior of the jet appreciatively. Al seemed to be impatient to get back to his calls and did so as soon as they were at cruising altitude. He then got up and went and sat with Jonathan and Sebastian and they began a meeting of some type about schedules, it sounded like to Martin. Martin listened for a few minutes then tuned them out and got up and sat next to Sarah. She took off her iPOD immediately when he sat down and smiled at him.

"So what exactly does Jonathan do?" He asked, tipping his head towards the three-some in their huddled meeting.

"He's handling the ballet season for me," she explained. "Magnus used to but Jonathan offered." She shrugged slightly.

"Handling what?" Martin asked.

"The negotiations for my contract, the scheduling, any appearances, and the advance checks on the building and the dressing rooms, that kind of thing. I don't actually do anything but dance," she added somewhat apologetically.

"What about Julie and Paul?" Martin asked.

"Alexander is a bit overprotective," Sarah said. "He likes to make sure my doctor is close at hand."

"Paul, too?" Martin asked quietly.

Sarah flushed and looked away. After a moment she said, "Did you know that Julie and Paul are a couple now?" At his raised eyebrows, she nodded her head and gave a little laugh. "Yes, for over a year now."

Martin glanced over at them. Both were reclined back in their seats with their eyes closed. Martin saw Paul reach over and pick up Julie's hand. He turned back to Sarah. "Is it serious?"

Sarah shrugged. "I hope so for both of them. Paul got divorced over three years ago and I know he was lonely. And he's the first man in a while to catch Julie's eye. It took her a long time to get over Danny," she added quietly.

When Al returned, Martin politely gave him his seat back and returned to his own. The flight was largely uneventful; most were dozing, Sarah listening to her music, and Al on the phone. Martin sat still, quietly observing everyone in turn, studying them, his blue eyes thoughtful.

At one point Al got up from his seat and headed, presumably, to the toilet. He was gone quite a while. Martin decided to get up and stretch his legs and while walking down the center aisle got a look into the galley. Sure enough, Al was in there nuzzling the flight attendant. Martin waited a beat to make sure Al saw him then looked him in the eye, expressionless. He then turned and went back to his seat.

Fuck. Is this the way it was going to be for Sarah? He knew the reputation the guy had but it still pissed him off that Al would do that practically in front of Sarah. What if she had gotten up? Martin thought back to his conversation with Al that morning.

During the hustle and bustle of preparations to leave, Alexander called he and Will into his office. He stated without preamble, "I've been checking you two out. What I've found is that you're," nodding to Martin, "some kind of martial arts legend, a superb marksman with a gun, and mayhem is your middle name. Everywhere you go chaos seems to follow. I want to make it perfectly clear that if ANY of that occurs anywhere near Sarah, you're both out of here so fast your heads will be spinning."

"Hey, Al, I don't start that shit, I just finish it. I am a cop after all, and that kind of shit tends to happen in a city the size of L.A. As far as I'm concerned, that's the reason I'm here, to make sure there's no mayhem anywhere near Sarah." Martin glared at Al, then asked, "Find what you were looking for in my house?"

Al looked completely innocent as he replied, "I'm sure I don't know what you're talking about."

"You got brass balls, Al. I gotta hand it to you, breaking and entering a cop's house. Next time let me know before you drop by, I'll spruce the place up. Maybe I'll even do the dishes," he offered. Martin lived in a trailer on the beach near the Coast Guard Station in San Pedro. "My place is a bit smaller than this," he gestured around at Al's office, the estate in general, "but you must admit, I've got a nice view too." He laughed at Al and turned to leave the room.

"Just a moment," Al barked at him. "I haven't dismissed you yet!"

Martin turned back slowly and looked Al in the eye. "Let me make something perfectly clear to you. I don't work for you. I'm here for Sarah."

"I'm paying you," Al replied. "Make no mistake, you work for me and answer to me alone."

Martin shook his head. "You're not paying me, Al. You're paying Will there. My services are free to Sarah. She can fire me, not you. You can fire Will if you want," cocking his thumb at Will, "but you'll probably like him. Better than you like me anyway," he added with a smile at Alexander and left the room.

Martin brought himself back to the present and watched as Alexander settled back into his seat next to Sarah. He glanced at Martin who glared back at him.

Alexander also thought back to their conversation that morning. Stone had reacted pretty much as he'd thought the guy would. Alexander was glad the plan he and Sebastian developed meant that Alexander wouldn't be staying at the apartment with Sarah. He kept his own apartment in New York. When Father was alive, he'd insisted that Sarah be exposed to Alexander's hedonistic lifestyle as little as possible. He still virtually never introduced Sarah to any woman he was seeing. After all, they came and went with dizzying speed. Sometimes Alexander had trouble keeping them straight in his own mind.

Since that had always been Alexander's practice when his father was alive, they'd decided that the best way to get more information from Sarah and Martin was to remove Alexander from the scene so they would be more comfortable with each other. Sebastian would observe, eavesdrop as much as possible, and report back to Alexander. He thought back with frustration on his attempts to draw Stone out. The guy was even more closemouthed than Sarah, if that was possible. Alexander was also glad to put a bit of space between himself and Sarah. He accomplished his goal, she's left Tall Trees and is on her way to New York. Alexander hoped he would never have to punish Sarah again. The whole experience left him uncomfortable; aroused and ashamed and feeling like his father would look with horror at his son. Paul would also be there to keep an eye on Sarah. Paul and Julie would be giving him daily updates.

Alexander wondered if it had been too soon to let Martin catch him with another woman. No, the plan was a good one, he thought. Stick to it. Let's see if Stone's protective side really comes into play if he thinks Sarah's being misused. The hope was that Martin would confide in Sebastian, try to pump information from Sebastian about the nature of his relationship with Sarah. Sebastian thought he had a chance of befriending Martin. Martin was too antagonistic towards Alexander. They needed a new tactic. Sebastian is good, Alexander thought. If anyone can disarm that guy, it's Sebastian. Alexander was glad he wouldn't be staying at the apartment; he didn't think he could take eight weeks of being around the arrogant asshole.

There were two vehicles awaiting their arrival, this time a limo to accommodate Julie and Paul as well. Again, Max drove. Martin realized that Sarah's aversion to strangers must still be very strong if they even brought her driver from California. Sebastian and Jonathan supervised the unloading of the plane. They would follow shortly in another SUV.

The penthouse apartment was in the great, gothic, pile of a building called 'The Dakota' on the upper west side. Martin realized this was the building John Lennon had lived in, been shot out in front of. He vowed to himself that Sarah would never use that public of an entrance to the building. There was a group of about thirty or forty people hanging out at that entrance, most with pictures of Sarah or signs to catch her attention. "Don't go through there, Max," Martin quietly instructed. "There must be another entrance." Max nodded and continued around the block to the underground garage entrance. "Why were all those people there?" Martin asked Al. "How did they know she was coming?"

"Word gets out," he replied. "ABT has announced the Fall program featuring Sarah. They know where she lives when in New York." He shrugged, "That was actually a small crowd, wait until word gets out that she's arrived."

The apartment was huge. He and Will followed behind Sarah for a tour. Sam padded along, sticking close to Sarah. It must be about ten thousand square feet, Martin thought. The entrance was through a private elevator that would not rise to the penthouse level without a coded security card. The entry hall led to an enormous room with two grand pianos as its central focal point. The view was spectacular of Central Park and the cityscape beyond. To the right of the grand room, Martin didn't know what else to call it, was an impressive office/library, the dining room, kitchen, Sebastian's room and office, a maid's room, then a series of bedrooms, each a mini suite with its own bath. Martin counted four bedrooms in this wing, not counting the servants quarters. The massive bedroom at the end of the hall with an entrance to the wrap around terrace must have been Magnus' old room. It was very old world, masculine. Must be Al's room now, Martin thought. Martin noted the room assigned to Paul and Julie and one to Jonathan. The other room had two beds and was the one that had been designated for Will and him. Will shot him a look, the room was beautiful and the bath positively decadent.

To the left of the grand room was Sarah's wing. The hall led to a large music/sitting room with yet another baby grand piano and all types of other musical instruments stationed around including several guitars, a small drum set, a saxophone, banjo, mandolin, and flute. Alexander was waiting for them there, finishing up a phone call.

Again, there was an entrance to the terrace from here. The music room led to Sarah's bedroom, a large room that opened out onto the terrace again, this time into a beautiful, old, Victorian style greenhouse that enclosed the entire end of the terrace at Sarah's side of the penthouse. Sarah's bedroom surprised Martin. It was all mirrors and crystal chandeliers and floating fabrics hanging from the bed and even the ceiling in spots. Evidently it surprised Sarah as well. She stopped, stunned, then turned to Alexander.

Martin and Will stood quietly behind as Sarah said to Alexander, "Oh, Zander, what have you done?" She bit her lip and turned away.

"I wanted to surprise you, Princess," Alexander replied. "Don't you like it?"

Sarah said nothing for a moment, looking around. Finally she said, "What made you think I wanted to live in a harem?"

"You don't like it," Alexander stated flatly.

"I'm sorry, Zander," she said softly. They still had not touched Martin noted. "No, it's too much," Sarah continued, shaking her head slightly. "Too busy. I do like this," she finished, standing before a painting hanging over the bed that she'd noticed when she pulled the flimsy white gauze fabric hanging from the bed aside. It was a stunning painting of a huge flower. Martin didn't know much about art but Sarah seemed transfixed by the painting. "It's incredible, Zander!" she exclaimed, climbing to kneel on the bed for a closer look.

"I know you love O'Keefe's work. I wanted you to be able to look at it whenever you want. It's your engagement gift," he added.

Sarah was chagrined. Was she supposed to get Zander a gift? She would have to ask Sebastian. "Thank you, Zander," Sarah replied, her eyes shining with pleasure. They still did not touch.

Will grabbed Martin's arm on their way out of the room and whispered, "Georgia O'Keefe? If that's an original, it must be worth a couple million!"

Martin just shrugged.

Sebastian and Jonathan arrived and Sebastian came straight to Sarah. Alexander looked at him and said, "You were right, Sebastian. She doesn't like it, all except for the painting." He walked off, dialing his cell phone as he went.

"Why does he do these things, Sebastian?" Sarah asked quietly. "Why would he think I would like this?" she gestured at the interior of her bedroom.

"He's just trying to find ways to please you. He thought you might want a change, something different to look at." Sebastian also glanced around at the gaudy bedroom. He'd known when Alexander described what he was having done that Sarah would be appalled. Sebastian hadn't seen it before; it was worse than he'd anticipated. And what was Alexander thinking, to have so much glass and mirrored surfaces in Sarah's bedroom... "Don't worry, Miss Sarah. I made sure all your old furnishings were put into storage in case you didn't care for the new look. I'll get rid of all this tomorrow when you're at the studio. When you come home, it will be your old bedroom restored exactly as before," he promised.

"Thank you, Sebastian," Sarah replied, relieved. "The painting can stay over the bed," she continued. "That I do like very, very much."

"This way, gentlemen," Sebastian said to Martin and Will. "Let me show you to your room." He proceeded to lead them to the wing of bedrooms on the opposite side of the penthouse.

Martin didn't like that idea at all, it was too fucking far away from Sarah. He stopped, backtracked a bit, and said, "How about this room here? This will do fine." It was a small room off Sarah's music room that he'd noted when Sarah was showing them around. She had not opened the door and he assumed it was a closet. But when he peeked inside, he found a small, windowless bedroom with two twin beds. It had a door that opened directly into Sarah's bedroom and a small but full bath on the other side of the room. Martin opened the door and tossed his bag inside. "This will do for Will and me," he said.

Sarah said nothing but Sebastian interjected smoothly. "That is a very small room, seldom used. I have a much more comfortable room arranged for you this way," and began to lead them towards the other wing again.

"This is perfect for me, Sebastian," Martin replied. "How big is this apartment?" When no one replied, he said to Sarah, "I'm not leaving you alone all night in this wing. Hell, we'd have trouble hearing anything from way over there, much less getting to you quickly. If no one else is using this room," he indicated, "it's just fine. Whose room is it anyway?" Again no one said anything for a moment.

Sarah finally replied, "When I was younger and sick, Magnus and Sebastian used this room to stay close by. It hasn't been used in awhile," she replied. "But Sebastian can have it prepared for you. You're welcome to use it if you like." She seemed pleased at the prospect.

Sebastian looked very uncertain.

"Look, if you're worried about me, Sebastian," Martin said, "you can give Will another room and bunk with me. Either way," he added with a grin, "you or Will are welcome to chaperone Sarah."

Sarah blushed to the roots of her hair but said firmly to Sebastian, "It's fine, Sebastian. Please have this room prepared for Martin and Will."

Sebastian nodded.

Sarah went to speak to Alexander in his office. Martin and Will set off for a closer inspection of the security. Martin liked the security to the front entrance of the apartment but he didn't like the look of that terrace at all. With the gothic rooftop impediments, any idiot with half a brain could get onto that terrace. Once on the terrace, Martin counted four entrances to the apartment, one in Alexander's room, one in the grand room, one in Sarah's music room and one in her bedroom through the greenhouse. That one concerned him the most, so he inspected it carefully. It appeared that almost one entire wall of Sarah's bedroom was made of panels of glass that accordioned open to make the greenhouse virtually part of the bedroom. Martin was relieved to see that these glass panels were extremely strong, that the entire glass wall bolted firmly when shut, and it was alarmed to the security system. Good thing, he thought, because the greenhouse appeared extremely easy to penetrate. Inside the greenhouse, the door to the rest of the terrace was fairly solid, but it didn't look that tough to break any one of the panels in the greenhouse, Martin thought, tapping on the glass. Not thick, tempered, insulated glass like in the sliding glass wall. That would be tough to break through. This greenhouse would be a piece of cake to break into. He noted there were panels in the ceiling and glass panels all around the sides that could be opened to vent the greenhouse. He would have to make certain that the glass wall was closed and locked when Sarah slept and that she never went out into her greenhouse without letting him know. He looked around a final time, this time at the furnishings. There was a small Jacuzzi in the greenhouse along with a comfortable seating area with cushioned wicker furniture and a small table for four. Pretty, with all the plants and orchids, but Martin didn't like it at all from a security viewpoint. He wondered who cared for all this when Sarah was gone.

Martin looked at Sam still out inspecting the terrace. Sarah was right, they were totally set up for dogs. Outside Sarah's greenhouse, there was a small 'dog park', a raised square of grass about eight feet by ten feet in size, with bushes, a fake fire hydrant, and benches along the side. A perfect, miniature dog park. Sam approved, Martin noted.

Martin and Will continued their inspection. Will shook his head slightly. Chuckling and looking at Martin with wonder in his eyes he said, "All this for one little girl." He gestured around at the great room where they were inspecting the door to the terrace. "Think about it Stone, two bodyguards, two managers, a butler, a driver, two doctors, and that's just the ones we've seen so far. All for one little, itty, bitty girl. She must be one valuable songbird," he concluded. Martin glanced around again. That fact was really just beginning to sink into him as well.

Sarah and Alexander walked out of his office. "Goodbye, Princess. See you in a couple of days." He nodded at Sarah, then at Sebastian. "Take care of my girl," he said to Martin and Will before leaving.

"Where's he headed?" Martin asked Sarah.

"Oh, Alexander doesn't live here," she explained. "He has his own apartment here in New York."

Of course he does, thought Martin. He was beginning to wonder if Al planned on changing anything about his lifestyle in deference to his upcoming marriage. But Martin was inordinately pleased anyway. This was getting better and better. No Al to put up with all the time.

They spent a pleasant evening getting to know one other. Sebastian prepared dinner for them, served, then sat down to join Sarah, Jonathan, Paul, Julie, Martin and Will. Sarah had insisted that Sebastian join them and he had acquiesced saying, "Only with family."

Martin had been trying to decide how much to say when the inevitable questions arose about his and Sarah's relationship, but Sarah surprised him by replying first to Paul and Julie's query of how they knew each other. "As Martin said, I've known him since I was a baby. After I was born, my mother was too sick to take care of me, so Danny and Martin did."

"What about your father?" Paul asked.

"I never really knew him, either of my parents," she amended. "They died when I was about three. Then Danny and I became orphans at the mission along with Martin who was already there."

Ah, she's using the exact cover story he and Danny concocted for Danny and Sarah to use when they arrived in Hong Kong. She just added him to it. Smart girl, he thought. Martin picked up the story. "When Danny and I were seventeen, I was accepted into West Point and Danny got a scholarship in Physics at the University of Hong Kong. He took Sarah with him to Hong Kong, to the University. But Sarah and I always stayed in touch. I always came to see her whenever I had any leave."

"How is it possible that you stayed in touch," Sebastian asked, "and saw Sarah, yet we knew nothing of you?"

"It's easy to stay in touch," Martin replied. The last few years there we'd text virtually every day, unless I was on a mission."

"But how is it possible you saw Sarah, spent time together without our knowing?" Jonathan asked. He was Magnus's oldest friend and had known Sarah from the time Magnus adopted her. His stern, schoolmaster's demeanor hid his soft spot for Sarah.

"Some of that time was on the beach at your place in Hawaii, Jonathan," Martin replied.

There was shocked silence. Sarah's circle, as Martin was beginning to think of them, looked at Sarah.

She nodded her head in confirmation and smiled at the looks on their faces. "You remember I was always pretty insistent about the dates I wanted to go to Hawaii," she said to Sebastian. "It was so I could meet Martin when he was on leave."

Jonathan remembered her and Magnus' visits. How young Sarah had insisted on spending most of the day on the estate's deserted beach, alone. Her favorite spot was completely out of view of the house. She insisted she needed the time for her music, and since she was already writing best selling songs, they had agreed as long as she promised not to swim alone. Jonathan and Magnus even observed her surreptitiously a few times, curious about what she did for so many hours alone. She walked, danced, waded, sat, sang to herself, had conversations with herself, and generally cavorted about completely carefree. She then laid down to take an extended nap in the shade of a palm tree on the beach. They finally left her to herself on those trips. They were very productive times musically for Sarah.

"Sarah was a very young girl," Jonathan said severely to Martin. "You mean to tell me you met her alone on the beach without her guardian's knowledge?" He turned his severe glance to include Sarah. He remembered that Sarah had only been fifteen the last time she visited him in Hawaii and she had been coming there for visits for several years before then.

"I've been spending time alone with Sarah since I put nappies on her when she was a baby. She's family," he said with a note of warning in his voice to Jonathan.

"Why did you tell Sarah to keep it a secret?" Sebastian asked. "She was a very young child when she first came to us," he added. "It must have been you who asked her to keep silent."

Martin nodded his assent. He was quiet for a moment, appraising Sebastian, then said, "I didn't trust you guys. Sorry, Sebastian," he said with a shrug, "but I didn't."

"I don't understand," Sebastian said.

"Look, Sebastian," Martin said, "When I went into the Army was the first time Sarah, Danny, and I split up. I came back to see them after Basic and was really pissed at Danny. Sarah wasn't doing well in that dorm housing he had. She was sick all the time and he and I kind of had it out about how he was taking care of her. I was worried about that to begin with, Danny could be a real airhead sometimes. So, that's when he met

Al, got the boat, they moved out of the dorm, and things seemed to be going much better. Keep in mind, I hadn't met you guys. I heard all about you from Sarah, especially about Magnus," Martin chuckled. "The man with the music in his fingers. Sarah was wild about the piano from day one, weren't you, Smallest?"

Sarah smiled at him and nodded.

"Why do you call her Smallest?" Paul interjected.

Sarah answered. "When I was little," she said with an impish grin, "when I wouldn't listen to Martin he would tell me that I had to do as he said because he was the Biggest and I was the Smallest and that meant he was in charge. I guess he had to say it a lot," she laughed, "because Smallest stuck."

Turning back to Sebastian, Martin continued. "Anyway, when Danny died, I didn't know what to do. I had just joined up; I'd only been in for six months. I wasn't going to be able to get out and take care of Sarah for at least four years. Sarah loved Magnus and you guys had the means to take care of her, she was so sick back then after Danny died." Martin looked at Sarah and took her hand for a moment. Then releasing her, he continued. "That was part of the problem for me, Sebastian. You guys seemed so rich and I just didn't trust you right away. Sarah was a little girl. She didn't have anyone but me to look out for her."

"I still don't understand the need for secrecy," Jonathan said.

"So he could take her away if needed," replied Sebastian, looking at Martin. "Correct?"

Martin nodded. No one said anything for a moment.

"What is the age difference between you and Sarah?" Will asked.

"Ten years. Sarah was born on my tenth birthday. Best birthday present I ever got," Martin said with a laugh.

Paul was finding this very interesting, they all were. He looked at Sarah again; she positively glowed under Martin's attention. He had never seen her look so relaxed, so natural.

"Well, young lady," Julie said to Sarah. "You are very good at keeping secrets but I'm glad we've finally met another member of your family." Julie used the word Martin had used about Sarah.

Sarah colored slightly then said, "I always meant to tell you someday," she said to Sebastian. "But then, after Martin left, there didn't seem to be any point."

"Why did you leave?" Julie asked, curious.

Martin gave a wry smile. "I went to see Sarah at that big outdoor concert in LA when I got out of the Army. She was sixteen. You remember the concert?"

Sarah nodded but said nothing.

Martin smiled. "You blew me away. You were fantastic, Smallest. I realized you had everything I ever wanted for you. You didn't need me anymore. Magnus and Sebastian here were obviously doing well by you, Al too." He was silent for a moment. "I was pretty screwed up after that last deployment, Sarah. You didn't need me in your life. So, I did you a favor and left." He looked at Sarah. "I'm sorry, Smallest. I know that must have hurt. But I knew if I came backstage to see you, I'd never be able to leave. I hope you can forgive me."

Sarah said nothing for a moment, looking down at her plate. Then she looked up at Martin, her eyes shining with some hidden emotion. "I've always needed you, Martin," she said simply.

Sebastian was in an inner turmoil. What to do? This conversation confirmed what he suspected. Martin Stone was the dark boy with the laughing eyes. This could be wonderful, he thought, looking at how happy Sarah was. This could also be a disaster. Alexander would be livid. He didn't believe in the existence of the dark boy.

By the time they all turned in for the night, Martin was almost uncomfortably aroused. Watching Sarah all day, eating meals with her, just being with her put his libido on overload. He wished he had a switch he could use to turn off sex. He especially didn't want to think of sex in relation to Sarah. But he couldn't help it, that ship sailed. Sarah grew up and there was no denying how she appealed to him. He wanted her, badly. Had wanted her for years now. He vowed again, however, that he would never touch her sexually. Not Sarah. She deserved much more than the fucked up mess that he was sexually.

He wondered again if she was sleeping with Al. He honestly didn't think so. He had yet to see Al and Sarah even touch and Al hadn't kissed her goodbye when he left. Sarah's aversion to touch still seemed strong. It didn't extend to all people, she had no problem with Danny or him and little problem with Magnus, Sebastian and Julie. He wondered why she would even consider marrying someone she did have an aversion to.

He heard Sarah moving around in her room next door, preparing for bed. He imagined her undressing; his erection became painfully hard now. This was the first night. How the hell was he going to do this for eight weeks? His erection now so insistent, his cock so brutally hard, he rose from his bed and went into the shower. Even a cold shower couldn't take care of this. So, he set the water on warm, grasped the shaft of his thick cock at the base and stroked up, giving in to the fantasy of Sarah. He leaned his forehead against the shower wall, closed his eyes and thought of her. Thought about how watching her walk was like watching sunlight dance on water. He stroked firmly up and down the shaft of his penis, reveling in the feeling while reviewing every detail of Sarah that day. How playful she had been when showing Sam his private outdoor park. How he loved, just loved, to hear her musical laugh.

His hand moved faster, his balls aching with the need for release. Christ, he wanted to bury himself deep inside her. He then recalled the emotion in her eyes at dinner when she had looked directly into his eyes and said, 'I've always needed you, Martin,' and suppressing a groan, he exploded. His buttocks clenched, he arched his back and released his load onto the shower wall. His orgasm left him shuddering and breathing heavily. He pumped his cock a few more times, milking every last drop of his cum.

As he aimed the showerhead to wash his fantasy away, he realized he might have seriously underestimated how difficult these eight weeks were going to be.

Chapter Fifteen

Martin awoke at five am, as soon as he heard Sarah stirring. So, she didn't need much sleep either. They had gone to bed after midnight and he heard her moving about in her bedroom for over an hour after that. Less than four hours sleep didn't seem like a great idea for the strenuous day ahead of her but Martin, not much of a sleeper himself, sympathized. Will stirred and groaned. "Don't bother, Will," Martin told his partner. "Sleep in. We won't be leaving here until just before nine." Will closed his eyes again.

Martin went into Sarah's music room at about the same time she did. She did not seem surprised to see him. "Would you like some coffee or tea?" she asked. "Sebastian is bringing me some."

So, Sebastian's up early too, Martin thought. "Sure," he replied. "Coffee would be great." Sarah picked up the phone to let Sebastian know and Martin then helped her open the glass wall to her bedroom. They both went into the greenhouse and Martin looked around carefully. Everything seemed to be fine. He checked the door to the rest of the terrace, fine as well. Sam slept in Sarah's bedroom, a move Martin heartily approved of though he had chastised the dog as a traitor again. He now petted him in approval before Sam headed out to his private toilet. Martin relaxed, then turned as Sebastian entered with a tray.

Sebastian was still in his robe and the tray held three cups but he said to Sarah, "Would you prefer to have your morning tea alone with your friend?"

"No, please join us," Sarah replied. Then to Martin, "Sebastian and I usually have a cup of tea together first thing every morning."

"Would you two prefer some time alone?" Martin offered. "I can get out of your hair."

"Oh no. I'd love for you and Sebastian to get better acquainted," she said seating herself at the small table in the greenhouse.

Martin and Sebastian joined her, Martin finishing with, "OK, but we're going to be together a lot for the next eight weeks, Sarah. I have thick skin," he said with a grin. "Just tell me to get lost if you need some privacy, some space. I don't want to interfere with your work."

"You won't," Sarah said, selecting a pear from the bowl of fruit that Sebastian also brought and biting into it. It was juicy and she reached for a napkin. Martin watched as she licked pear juice from her lips and a sharp stab of lust shot through him. He took a pear as well, mostly to distract himself from watching Sarah eat hers.

"Has Sarah always been a vegetarian?" Sebastian impulsively asked.

Martin nodded his head, wiping the pear juice from his mouth. "Ever since she was old enough to figure out that meat used to be live animals. I guess when she was about two, well, that's the last time she took a bite willingly. I finally told Danny to stop trying to force her." He shook his head fondly at Sarah. "I think she was willing to starve rather than eat another bite of an animal."

Sarah just laughed. "At least I don't cry or vomit anymore if someone else around me eats meat. I have grown up," she said to Martin.

"And beautifully," Martin said. "As shy as you've always been, I could never have predicted all this for you, the stage, the music. I take my hat off to you, Smallest. You've done great."

"I just sing and dance," Sarah said deprecatingly. "Alexander and Magnus did everything else."

"That's kind of like saying Einstein was just a patent clerk," Martin said. "Don't sell yourself short. If you didn't make music, Al wouldn't have anything to sell."

Sarah smiled but said nothing more and Sebastian left to get dressed and started on his day. "Breakfast at eight," he reminded Martin.

"And what will you do until breakfast?" Martin asked Sarah as Sebastian left.

"My workout; yoga, stretches, and an hour or so at the barre'. Would you like to join me?"

"Actually, yeah. I need to stay in shape while I'm here. I'd love to work out with you if you don't mind. I warn you," he said laughing, "I can't dance, but I'll try yoga with you." Martin had noticed the small gym in the other wing of the apartment. Although not nearly as large as the gym Sarah had at Tall Trees, it would do for him. Other than that, he would find a chance to run in the park. Martin practiced parkour as well as martial arts and boxing. Parkour had come in very handy, as he'd known it would when he first observed the phenom coming out of Europe. He knew of no better, faster way to chase a suspect through a urban landscape then the jumping, flipping, diving moves of parkour. And more and more, these young suspects were skilled at it as well, forcing Martin's game even higher.

Sarah rolled out a yoga mat on the greenhouse floor and handed another mat to Martin. He rolled it out then proceeded to copy her movements as closely as he could. Damn, but she was limber. This did feel good, he thought, as they quietly went through the movements, the silence broken only by the very distant muffled sounds of the city. They felt isolated and alone in the greenhouse rather than in the midst of a huge city of millions. Martin had to hand it to Magnus, he'd really figured out how to give Sarah a tranquil living situation that nurtured her, an escape from the stress of crowds and noise that so easily affected her.

They joined everyone else for breakfast at eight with the exception of Jonathan who had already left to do the advance check of the dance studio where Sarah would be headed in little more than an hour. Sarah ate only fruit again with a small amount of yogurt. Martin dug in hungrily, eggs, bacon, potatoes, the works. He was hungry after their morning workout even if Sarah wasn't.

At nine am sharp, Martin and Will escorted Sarah down to the parking garage where Max waited with the car. Sarah carried her ballet tote, Will her survival backpack. Martin carried nothing; he wanted his arms and hands free. The drive was short, only about ten minutes. Jonathan called them in advance with an all clear but met them at the entrance to advise Sarah not to proceed up to the third level to watch the younger classes for any reason. They refinished some floors on that level about two weeks prior and the polyurethane levels were still far too high for Sarah. Jonathan reassured Sarah that her dressing room and all areas on the second floor where she would be rehearsing with Yuri were fine.

Yuri, delighted to see Sarah, wasted no time in getting down to business. "You always say you will know steps in time," he said, his

Russian accent heavy, "but I never believe. Show me," he commanded.

Sarah stretched and twisted her body first. She had a good workout that morning, but still needed a bit of a warm up first. She then rose on point and flexed her feet several times. Martin sat over to the side in the rehearsal room which, so far, held just a pianist as well as the three of them. Sarah had been sent a video of Yuri dancing the steps in rehearsal with Sarah's understudy. Now was the test of whether she had mastered the part. Finally, Sarah rose on point, assumed a pose with hands held twined over her head, and waited. The pianist began and Sarah twirled and leapt as Martin watched dumbfounded. She transformed herself into a literal extension of the music. Her body became music and Martin realized what she loved about dance: she used her entire body to celebrate the sound. She stopped at the end of the movement and Yuri grudgingly allowed that perhaps, with tremendous effort, he could get her ready for the role in time for opening night. They began to work together, going over each and every step and Martin settled back to watch.

Yuri was possibly the most fit man Martin had ever seen. He couldn't determine which looked stronger, the guy's arms or his legs. Watching his leaps that defied gravity, watching him lift and turn Sarah over and over again, he realized why. Martin didn't know a damn thing about ballet except what Sarah had shown him over the years but this proved to be more interesting than he'd thought it would be.

Back at the apartment, Sebastian straightened up Sarah's music room. Martin and Sarah played a game of Scrabble the previous evening, the old fashioned way with a board and tiles rather than an online version. Sebastian saw Martin use a pad and pen to test out the spelling of some words. He looked in the wastepaper basket and, sure enough, found a page off the pad. He took it to the office, opened the safe, removed an envelope, and pulled a piece of paper out. He sat down and compared the two pieces of paper side by side, the Scrabble words and the paper he'd removed from the safe. Sebastian, an expert forger and, therefore, very good with handwriting, examined the documents carefully: the downward slanting cross of the letter 't', the 'x' with the second leg longer. He was positive. Martin Stone was the author of the note that had been left with Sarah on their doorstep. It could be none other than he that brought Sarah there. They always wondered who had delivered Sarah to them that night.

Based on her condition, it seemed inconceivable she arrived on her own.

Sebastian functioned as a butler and valet to Magnus, but very few people knew the relationship had been much more complex, more equal than that. That was the front the two men had shown to the rest of the world. They had, in fact, been partners in some very complex and varied criminal enterprises, including jewel theft and fencing of stolen goods. Magnus and Alexander were the most successful jewel thieves in quite some years. Interpol and police in many countries despaired of ever catching the thief known as 'La Chat': the cat. What they didn't realize is that it was actually two different men, Magnus and Alexander. Sebastian was their accomplice and very skilled at selling whatever they stole along with his talents as a forger.

Those days had been left behind not long after Sarah became their responsibility. They stumbled into a career for Sarah quite by accident. The well-known film director, Franco Monterelli, was a friend of Magnus' and had been visiting them in New York. He talked of his difficulty in finding the right young actress for his remake of 'The Miracle Worker'. Young Sarah, who had been with them for almost a year at this point and had yet to speak, was sitting quietly nearby. Sarah suddenly left the room and when Magnus went to see where she had gone, he found her in her bedroom walking about, her arms and hands outstretched, stumbling into things and feeling her way about. She moved as if blind and when he called her name, she hadn't responded. Magnus finally touched her arm to get her attention; and, when she turned her face to him, real fear stabbed through him. Her eyes were blank and he realized she couldn't see. It was only when he shook her slightly in his fear and called her name several times that he saw focus return to her eyes, and she acknowledged him.

She spoke for the first time since Magnus found her on their doorstep. "It's OK," she said. "I was just pretending. I wanted to see what it would feel like to be blind and deaf."

"My God, Sarah," Magnus exclaimed. "I thought you were blind and deaf!" He noticed his friend, Franco, watching from the doorway.

"No," Sarah replied. "I just turned off my eyes and my ears to see what it felt like."

She then turned away and withdrew back into herself but Franco talked Magnus into letting Sarah audition for the role. To their surprise and relief, working on the film seemed to draw Sarah out of herself and she slowly began to speak again. When Sebastian and Magnus saw the quality of her work on the film, they realized they would have to change. If Sarah was to be exposed to the public, as she undoubtedly would be by this film role, then they had better be squeaky clean. So one life was left behind and another began, that of caring for, mentoring, and loving this strange child left in their care.

And, Sebastian did love Sarah deeply. He never married, never had children of his own. At seventy-two years of age now, he was grateful for the career change and still humbled by the fact that he was part of her life. Sebastian saw Sarah through some very, very bad times, but somehow he still knew she was amazing, special, unique, destined for greatness, and not just as a musician, composer, and entertainer. There was more to young Sarah, Sebastian felt certain. Meanwhile, she was his responsibility, his and Alexander's, and they had some tough decisions to make.

Alexander arrived at the apartment a few minutes later and the two men met in the office. "How is she?" Alexander asked. "Are she and Stone relaxing a bit?"

"Yes," Sebastian replied. "I've learned two important facts already. First, I'm fairly certain that Martin Stone is the author of the note left with Sarah, meaning he most likely is the one that brought her there." He showed the two papers to Alexander saying, "Here's a current sample of his handwriting." Alexander looked at the two pieces of paper then handed them back without comment.

"What's the second thing?" he asked.

"I'm also certain that Stone is 'the dark boy with the laughing eyes', Sebastian replied.

Alexander's mouth tightened. "Explain," he requested.

Sebastian repeated what Martin said about deciding not to meet Sarah after that outdoor concert. They remembered that concert well. Sarah's incredible performance shattered all previous endeavors and vaulted her into superstardom. However, they couldn't get her to leave her dressing room afterward. They'd waited for hours, Sarah's agitation growing, and still she refused to leave.

Finally, there was no choice. The venue was shutting down; they had to leave. Sarah disintegrated before their very eyes. She gave the most vibrantly alive performance of her life, crackling with energy and passion, but now withdrew totally into herself, curling into a ball, refusing to speak. When they got her home and Magnus begged her to tell him what was wrong, she finally replied, 'The dark boy with the laughing eyes is gone and he means to never return.' The despair in her voice broke Sebastian's heart. By the following morning, Sarah was catatonic and the worst breakdown of all began. They never knew what to make of Sarah's strange statement. Magnus and Sebastian felt sure she referred to an actual person, someone she knew and loved had left or abandoned her.

Alexander scoffed at this notion. "Who," he demanded of his father? "Who could this dark boy possibly be? She's been with us for nine years now. She doesn't go out, she doesn't go to school. You or Sebastian or Jonathan are with her all the time. This is another one of her fantasies, there is no dark boy."

Now, Alexander got up, went to the safe, and pulled out a file. He looked through it, obviously looking for something specific. His finger found it. "Stone couldn't have written that note or left Sarah on our doorstep. He was still in Officer Training and on a ship in the North Atlantic at the time. A huge amount of his military records are classified, but this is early on and his records are specific. He couldn't have been in Hong Kong."

Sebastian didn't ask how Alexander acquired a copy of Stone's military record. He and Alexander both had close connections to one of the most talented hackers in the world. Anton undoubtedly worked his magic for Alexander again.

Neither man said anything for a minute or two. "Sorry, Sebastian, you're wrong about the note and I think you're wrong about the 'dark boy'. We still don't know what precipitated that breakdown. I don't care what she said. Just because she said 'the dark boy is gone' doesn't mean it means anything. She was in a bad way by then," Alexander concluded.

But Sebastian remembered exactly what she said and the despair in her voice when she said it. 'The dark boy with the laughing eyes is gone and he means to never return,' and he silently disagreed with Alexander. Martin Stone broke Sarah's heart by leaving four years ago.

Sebastian was sure of it. Now he was back. Was this a good thing or a bad thing? Sebastian said a silent prayer for Sarah, for all of them.

Alexander left and Sebastian met the building's maintenance crew at the door. He'd made arrangements with the manager to have some men come to remove Sarah's new bedroom furnishings and return her old furniture from the storage area. Of the four men who arrived, Sebastian knew three of them, had worked with them previously. The one new worker the manager said had been with him just over a year. Sebastian supervised them carefully the entire time they were in the apartment, then spent the next several hours returning everything in Sarah's room to how it had been prior to Alexander's remodel, including putting all of Sarah's clothes back into her former dressers and chests.

Sebastian finished and was on the phone with Max who said Sarah was on her way back to the apartment with Martin and Will. The service doorbell rang and he asked Max to hold a moment and answered the door. It was one of the building maintenance men, the new one. He said he'd left a small tool, an angled screwdriver in the room. Could he please retrieve it? Sebastian continued his conversation with Max as he let the man in and began to move towards Sarah's room to find the tool himself. Max distracted him with a question and he turned to find that the man had already gone into Sarah's room. He signed off with Max, and with a sigh of exasperation, went to fetch the man who was already coming out of Sarah's room, tool in hand. Sebastian looked carefully around the room, nothing appeared to be out of place. He showed the man out of the apartment.

Sarah arrived with Martin and Will a few minutes later. Her first day had gone well and she glowed with good health, her mood one of exhilaration. She's happy to be dancing again, Sebastian noted.

Martin watched with interest as Sarah described her day to Sebastian. He knew the relationship between the two was not that of a servant and employer even though Sarah no doubt paid Sebastian well for his efforts on her behalf. No, she treated Sebastian as a trusted friend. She did not appear to be as close to him as she had been to Magnus, but it was a very similar relationship Martin realized.

Sarah went to her room to change; and, when she opened the door, she exclaimed with pleasure, "Oh, thank you, Sebastian!   You remembered. My old room is back." She twirled about with delight, her arms open to encompass the room. Martin saw that the room was now much more simply furnished with beautiful, rounded edged, dark wood furniture and simple, plain but luxurious bed coverings and curtains. He smiled at Sarah's obvious pleasure to have her old room back and noted she even hugged Sebastian when she thanked him again. I was right, he thought, Sarah had no problem touching or being touched by Sebastian.

The three men left and she closed the door to her bedroom. Martin reacted quickly a few moments later when they heard Sarah's soft cry of distress. He was in the room and by her side in a flash, the other two men following close behind. Sarah stood in front of an open dresser drawer, staring with revulsion at her hand held before her face. Martin looked at her hand, looked in the drawer, and his blood ran cold as he grabbed Sarah to him in a defensive move and looked around the bedroom. "Someone's left their calling card," he said to Will, holding Sarah to him, his arms around her protectively. "Check the bathroom, Will."

Will did and called out, "All clear in here."

Martin pulled Sarah into the bathroom, turned the water on, and held her hand under the faucet and rinsed it off. Sarah still looked shocked and confused.

"What is it, Martin?" she asked quietly, hating the slight quiver in her voice.

He looked directly at her before answering as quietly, "Some guy whacked off in your dresser, Sarah." She began to tremble. "Don't worry, Smallest. Probably one of the men who brought all this furniture back in. I'm sure he's long gone," but thought to himself that this had happened pretty recently. The sperm was not warm, but was not beginning to dry either. He brought her back into the bedroom, sat her on the bed, and asked her not to move while the three men searched the room. Martin examined the dresser drawer carefully without touching anything. The drawer held Sarah's lingerie. He noted that the contents of the drawer seemed disturbed. Using a pen from his pocket, he lifted some of Sarah's panties. Sure enough, along with the sperm the guy left behind, buried under Sarah's panties was a Sarah Eastin doll, nude, with a knife plunged between its legs. Martin felt a chill go through him. The handle of the knife was a blue parrot. This wasn't just some masturbation fantasy. This was a threat. And the bastard had been in Sarah's bedroom.

Martin didn't want Sarah to see the doll. He asked Sebastian for a couple of Ziploc bags and carefully, using his pen for leverage rather than his fingers, placed the doll in one Ziploc and a soiled pair of Sarah's panties in the other. He then turned so Sarah couldn't see and handed the bags to Will. To Sebastian he said, "You and Al got a faster, private route to check these for DNA and fingerprints rather than me going through channels? I know someone in LA that could help us but not here." Sebastian nodded. "Good," Martin said. "Get right on that." Martin was a bit pissed at Sebastian, but kept it tamped down. "But first, what the hell, Sebastian! Didn't you supervise these guys?" He gestured around the bedroom.

"Of course," Sebastian replied.

"Martin," Sarah said reprovingly, "this is not Sebastian's fault."

Martin nodded and let out a sigh. She was right. Much calmer, he turned to Sebastian and said, "What happened?"

Sebastian, thoroughly shaken, explained about the worker who had returned for the tool. "He wasn't in Sarah's bedroom more than twenty, thirty seconds unsupervised," he finished, still incredulous at his stupidity.

"Guess that was all the time he needed," Martin replied. "Find him, Will," he said to his partner. To Sebastian he said, "You're absolutely certain the guy went no where else in this apartment?"

Sebastian nodded, then thought. They had all been back and forth from the rear service entrance several times. Sebastian was sure he accompanied them every time, all the way. But had he? Had he watched carefully enough? Perhaps I am slowing down, he thought with a sense of anxiety. Had he put Sarah in jeopardy? "I'm ninety-nine percent certain," he amended. "But it's possible I didn't see them all every second." He turned to Sarah with contrition in his eyes. "I should have waited until Jonathan was here to help me supervise."

Sarah didn't let him complete his apology. "Oh, Sebastian," she said, hugging him again. "Please don't apologize. This is not your fault," she added stoutly.

Martin nodded his head in agreement. "She's right, Sebastian. Relax. But I've been thinking about something since we got here anyway.

This place has been sitting empty for, what, a year or so?" he asked. Sebastian nodded. "Then, there were obviously workers here who remodeled Sarah's bedroom. I want the entire apartment swept for bugs," Martin said. "Actually, for any hidden electronic surveillance, cameras, sensors, anything. The guy could have planted something today or it may already have been here. You have someone good that can do that right away," he asked? Sebastian nodded again. "Good, get right on that and those bags." Martin gestured towards the evidence bags Will held down by his side. "I'm going over every inch of this place myself."

The two men left to do as Martin requested and he turned to Sarah. "I'd prefer it if you stayed with me, Smallest, while I check the place out. Just in case," he added but didn't say aloud that someone could still be hidden in the apartment. So, Sarah quietly accompanied him as he checked inside every possible hiding place and carefully examined every window and door again. Room by room, methodically, he searched. He looked for bugs or cameras as well, but didn't concern himself overly with that. He would leave that to the expert. Knowing Al and Sebastian, they knew someone very good at electronic surveillance. He finally finished his search, satisfied no one was hidden and no one had breached the security of any entrance to the apartment. He let Sarah sit down at her piano in her music room while he went to the security system in the small room off the butler's pantry. He wanted to go over that as well to make sure the system hadn't been compromised in any way. He would also have the expert look at it.

After Sebastian made his phone calls and gave the evidence bags to Max to deliver to someone immediately, he began dinner preparations telling Martin they would know of any fingerprint or trace evidence in a matter of a few hours; however, DNA evidence would take approximately twenty-four hours. He also said that the electronics person would be there in a couple of hours. Martin was impressed. The police couldn't move that fast. DNA sometimes took weeks or longer unless he personally harried everyone every step of the way.

Martin's cell rang. Will. He'd called earlier saying he had the name and address of the maintenance worker they suspected left his calling card for Sarah. Did Martin want Will to pay him a neighborly visit? Martin did. This time Will said without preamble, "The address was bogus. It's an empty lot."

Martin felt his scalp tighten. This was definitely connected to the attack at Paradise Cove. He knew with certainty that the guy would not be returning to work at The Dakota. Over a year on the job the manager said, over twelve months waiting to take a shot at Sarah. Someone on the beach in California, someone else here in New York. The description of this guy did not fit knife weasel. Martin's unease intensified. He no longer thought this had anything to do with Al. Somehow, he knew in his gut that what happened on the beach in California and what happened here in her bedroom was connected and that this was also connected to Danny somehow. But how? Those damn blue parrots, they nagged at the corner of his mind but he couldn't think of the significance for the life of him.

A subdued Sarah softly played her piano. Martin had never heard the music before; it was sad and melancholy. He wondered if it was something new Sarah was writing, or just something he'd never heard before.

It was a new song Sarah worked on but her thoughts were full of Martin rather than the music as she effortlessly played. He was obviously concerned about what happened here tonight, Sarah less so. She had been disgusted then embarrassed when she realized what was on her hand. Disgusted that some stranger had done that to her panties and embarrassed that Martin had to explain what it was. God, what a baby he must think I am, she thought again miserably.

Sarah wasn't that concerned, even though she glimpsed the doll they all took care to conceal from her. Men had been thinking those kinds of thoughts about her since she could remember. The fact that one had taken advantage of the opportunity of being alone in her bedroom for a few moments didn't really surprise her. Had she seen the knife in the doll she might have been more concerned.

Sarah floated in a state of near bliss the entire day. Just being with Martin, knowing he watched intently as she rehearsed with Yuri gave wings to her feet. She felt she could do anything now that Martin was back. Still, she was careful. She remembered her vow and the fact that Martin came back virtually as soon as she made it. She was intensely aware of the fact that Martin acted as though the ways they used to communicate had never happened. She reminded herself again that Martin had chosen 'normal' when it came to a woman for his wife. Therefore, she would do everything in her power to be as normal as possible. She wondered again if Martin was testing her. If so, this was a test she would pass at all costs. Sarah already spoke to Sebastian before they left for New York. She asked that Sebastian feel free to be completely honest with Martin and Will in all aspects of her life. She had none and wanted no secrets from Martin. Except one. She asked that Sebastian not tell him of her illness when she was sixteen. She explained no further and she knew he thought her romantic interest in Martin was behind the request. Since it was partially true, she let him think that.

It was interesting, she learned more about what Martin had been doing the last four years from his partner, Will, than she did from Martin. She could read Will's mind and though she hadn't been intrusive or looked for information, much of it just leaked out of him as he observed Martin with her. She knew Martin was still a loner with very few friends. She knew something terrible had happened to Will's daughter, Jace. Something that was so bad that Will's mind always shied away from the details. But what did come through was the fact that Will believed Martin had rescued both he and his daughter, that an unbreakable bond of trust existed between the two men, that Will's family invited Martin into their home and their hearts, and that Martin was now a part of this noisy, busy, loving, African American family of Will's. That his wife Tess and their three children, Jace, Theo, and Cara, all accepted Martin as one of them. She learned that Martin played a lot of Scrabble with thirteen-year old Cara, that Martin taught all of them self defense, that he taught fifteen-year old Theo boxing as well, that he ate many meals with them, usually cooking his famous chili every couple weeks or so. All that and more came through from Will, as did his fondness and admiration for his partner, his love for and pride in his family, his integrity, and his intelligence. Sarah understood how Martin became so close to this man. Martin had always, always longed to be part of a family. He tried to create his own and fate had cruelly taken them from him. This family now adopted him, and Sarah understood how happy it made him, how comfortable he was with them, by Will's perception of Martin as an integral part of his family.

The arrival of Anton interrupted her reverie. She rose to greet him as Sebastian introduced Anton and Martin. Anton was a thirty-five year old, tall, thin, black hipster with a thick Cockney accent and a large tote bag of equipment. "Sarah, me darling!" he exclaimed, dropping his bag and tilting his head and upper body in a partial bow of greeting.

"It's good to see you, Anton," Sarah said, with the same small, half bow of greeting. Turning to Martin, she said, "Anton is an old friend. He taught me everything I know about computers."

"Which is considerable, mate," Anton said to Martin. Then turning to Sarah, cocking his thumb at Martin, said, "And what about 'im lovey? 'e all right then?"

"Martin is my oldest and dearest friend. You can trust him completely," she said to Anton.

Martin's heart warmed at her words as Anton turned back to him and shook his hand enthusiastically. "Well, all right then, mate. Any friend of Sarah's and all that."

Anton went to work immediately. He started in Sarah's bedroom. Taking various pieces of equipment from his bag he began to carefully walk Sarah's bedroom, scanning for any electronic signals, monitoring his equipment carefully, adjusting and calibrating as he went. After making three complete circuits of her bedroom and carefully scanning all furniture and vents as well, he then went into Sarah's bath. After just a few moments, "Bloody Hell!" came from his lips. In the vent near the ceiling over the toilet and opposite the shower, he found a tiny wireless camera with a full view of the sink and shower beyond. It appeared the field of view did not include directly down, so it did not spy on Sarah on the toilet, just pretty much everywhere else in the bathroom.

A bolt of fury surged through Martin. Some fucker was intending to watch Sarah shower, watch her intimate moments alone. Then it hit; this didn't make sense. Why would you plant a camera then do something like that calling card in the dresser to virtually guarantee that every square inch of the entire apartment would be searched? Discovery of the camera was almost certain. The camera had to have already been there. He turned to Anton. "Can you tell how long that thing has been there?"

Anton had carefully plucked the tiny camera from the vent using forceps. He was wearing surgical gloves. He examined it closely, turning it in his gloved fingers. "Not really, mate" he said. "It's wireless, of course, and I'm betting it's motion activated. So, the battery could last quite a while if it wasn't activated too often. I'll take it apart," he said, "see if it tells me any more secrets. I'll finish sweeping first."

He continued with the most methodical and thorough search Martin had ever seen. It was three hours later and near midnight before he finally finished. He found nothing else. "Where can I go to work on this?" he asked Sebastian, holding the one tiny camera he found in Sarah's bathroom. Sebastian directed him to the office.

Martin pondered. Turning to Sebastian he asked "Who takes care of this place when no one is here? How often do they come in?"

The apartment is closed up for an extended absence," Sebastian replied. "One of Ito's sons, John, is a student here at Columbia." Ito was the master gardener at Tall Trees, the man who transformed the extensive grounds into the jewel that was the crowning glory of the estate. Sebastian did not add that Sarah paid for John's education. "He comes once a week to take care of the terrace gardens and the greenhouse. He does a cursory check of the apartment making sure everything is secure."

"Has there ever been a problem?" Martin asked.

"Never," Sebastian replied.

"And that's it?" Martin asked. "Just this John guy? Are you sure he's trustworthy? College boy, he never used the place to have a few friends over?"

Sebastian was shocked. "Never. I'm quite sure of it. Perhaps you don't completely understand," he acknowledged by the 'come on now' look on Martin's face. "Ito and his family are part of a small, trusted circle of people we allow near Sarah. Ito's wife is Soji, our chef at Tall Trees. His two sons also work for us, albeit John is now a full-time student here. His older son, Thomas, works with Ito on the estate. Berta, our housekeeper at Tall Trees, will be here in two days to work here. Berta has also worked for us for many years. These are people we trust completely. They know the rules. We do not allow strangers access to Sarah's life or home, ever. John would never bring someone into this apartment without our knowledge for any reason. Never," he repeated.

Martin nodded. He believed Sebastian. He believed they were very, very careful where Sarah was concerned. "But, you had workman here and you've had visitors here, parties when Magnus was still alive?" Sebastian nodded. "When was the last time," he asked?

"About two weeks before Magnus' death," Sebastian said. "Magnus had one of his musical evenings where he and Sarah played classical music together. There were about thirty-five guests, if I recall correctly."

"Could that thing last that long if it were filming for about two weeks, then went dormant for a year?" Martin asked Anton.

"I think so," Anton nodded. " Let me get a good look at 'er, but I think so."

"You by any chance remember who was here that night, the musical night?" Martin asked Sebastian.

"I'm quite sure I have the guest list," Sebastian replied. "It's my responsibility to keep track of such things."

Martin was impressed. He didn't really know how a household like this was run. "What else do you keep track of?" he asked, following Sebastian into the small sitting room attached to his bedroom.

Sebastian opened his laptop. "Basically, all activities of the household. All menus for dinners with guests in attendance." At Martin's look of surprise, "We wouldn't want to serve the same meal to a guest that we have served before. I also keep track of any frequent guest's preferences as to food and drink, etc. I keep track of all approved tradesmen allowed access to the apartment. You're welcome to review the household logs and schedules anytime you like."

Martin thought again of the camera and this time his anger stayed with him. He was pretty sure someone had been watching Sarah at least since they arrived and possibly for about two weeks before Magnus' death. She had left New York for California almost immediately after his death and the camera had been dormant for almost a year. If he was right about this, Martin thought, someone's been watching Sarah since we got here. The thought made him so angry he wanted to hit something. To calm down, he went out onto the terrace into the cool night air.

Sarah was quiet as she joined him, a sweater wrapped around her. After a moment she spoke. "Someone's been watching me for awhile, haven't they?" She had grasped the implication immediately, Martin realized.

"Yeah, Smallest," he replied honestly. "I doubt that camera was planted today."

She bit her bottom lip, worrying it gently between her teeth. "You don't suppose there were any cameras at Tall Trees?" she asked suddenly with a horrified look in her eyes.

The thought had occurred to him but he gathered her in his arms for a reassuring hug and said, "Don't you worry, Smallest. We'll take care of it. Anton will go there next. I doubt it seriously," he said, pulling back to look into her face, stroking her hair, "but we'll make sure, Smallest. We'll make sure."

Interesting, Martin thought as he held Sarah. She didn't ask for Al all evening nor had he appeared. He knew Sebastian called Al but it seemed Al had a full schedule that evening and trusted Sebastian to handle things. Dickhead, Martin thought.

Chapter Sixteen

Flint's anger knew no bounds. He stared at the acolyte known as Piss and realized he didn't even care to prolong the worm's life for his own satisfaction. He coolly reached over and slit the man's throat. He had a dozen acolytes by now, all with the blue parrot tattoo over their heart given when they swore their allegiance to him and accepted their new name to reflect their lowly status as compared to him, their master and lord. They agreed to serve him in any capacity he so desired in his pursuit to discover the power behind the Blue Parrot. But he realized now they were useless, worse than useless, dangerously flawed. They could not be trusted to do what was demanded of them but nothing more.

He waited, with Piss in place, for over a year for the Eastin girl to come back to New York. He placed Piss there when he had his first inkling that the flash of a female he kept seeing in relationship to the Blue Parrot was the singer, Sarah Eastin. He ordered Piss to place the camera in the girl's private bath, but was hugely frustrated when he learned nothing from watching her. His prurient interest in seeing her nude could not make up for the fact that he learned nothing, saw nothing of her connection to the Blue Parrot.

He was right, though, all along. He got a good look at her, finally, in the vision he had when he killed the old man, her guardian. He decided to have Lazlo kill the old man simply out of his frustration at not being able to see more visions of the girl, figure out the puzzle. The camera told him nothing new. But, when the plane went down and the old man died, he saw Sarah Eastin's anguish in his vision. She went to the old man, traveled to him somehow in those final moments, she'd been with him as he died. Flint had seen it all and his desire to know how she did it consumed him. She learned from the Blue Parrot, that much was obvious. He would find out everything about the Blue Parrot if he had to tear the girl apart, limb-by-limb. But first, he decided, he would let his human slave breed her. He was beginning to suspect that's what the Blue Parrot's interest in her was. Was he training her so that she could provide him with offspring? It was an interesting thought. She was certainly beautiful enough.

But for now, his decision was made. He would destroy all of his acolytes. He would keep only Lazlo, his cold, blonde, willing, slave. The remaining acolytes performed poorly and could no longer be trusted. Piss's little charade in the girl's bedroom proved that. He realized that Piss simply played out Lazlos' fantasies of fucking and then killing the Eastin bitch, and it made him intensely uncomfortable to know that the acolytes saw that deeply into not just his, but Lazlo's mind when he was controlling Laszlo.

Flint left Lazlo, departing in a flash of anger and contempt. Laszlo straightened his spine. He always felt deflated, depleted, less than himself when his master left his body. From now on, he would have to handle all of the interactions with the Eastin girl himself. It was too important. After all, he could not afford to fail his master. If he did not deliver the Blue Parrot, his own life would soon be worthless. He wondered, uncomfortably, what else the Eastin girl was capable of. Certainly her powers, even the Blue Parrot's powers, couldn't be stronger than his own master. No, he was learning from his master by leaps and bounds. No one could be more powerful. With his master's help, he would find the Blue Parrot. Then, the master would no doubt give him the Eastin girl to use as he liked. The master had no interest in such things as sex.

Chapter Seventeen

It was breakfast the morning of opening night. Alexander showed up for breakfast three mornings ago and now joined them every morning. Martin heartily wished he would go back to ignoring Sarah. At least it was only breakfast so far. They saw neither hide nor hair of the guy beyond that for which Martin was grateful. Sarah didn't seem to care. She certainly never complained at his lack of attention other than his current fixation on her weight.

When Al showed up unexpectedly three mornings ago at eight am, it surprised Sarah. She just sat down to the breakfast table when Al arrived and demanded she get on the scale and let Julie weigh her before breakfast. Now Martin himself thought Sarah's weight a bit too low, especially if she kept this pace up for another six weeks. It was just the dictatorial way that Al went about it in front of everyone at the table that pissed him off.

"I'm fine, Zander," Sarah said in a conciliatory voice. "I don't need a weigh in."

"What is your weight as of this morning?" he asked in a patient but condescending tone of voice. When she didn't reply, he said, "That's what I thought. On the scale, now please."

No one else said anything. Martin thought of speaking up but decided not to. He was trying to understand the dynamics of their relationship but so far this guy really just pissed him off. He glanced at Will. He could see that his partner, too, was surprised and displeased at how Sarah was being treated by Al. Sarah finally rose from her chair and left the room with Julie following silently behind.

"You're a real prick, Al," Martin said after Sarah and Julie left the room.

"This is none of your business, Stone," he replied. "Stay out of it. I know what's best for Sarah."

"96.3 pounds," Julie said quietly to Alexander when they came back.

134

"Damn it, Sarah!" Alexander had heat in his voice. "You know the rules. You drop to 95 and I'm pulling you! Yuri can shit little bricks for all I care! I will pull you out of that role," he threatened, pointing his finger at her.

Sarah said nothing, just sat and began eating her breakfast. Martin watched the thunderclouds build in Al's expression.

Finally she spoke. "Zander," she said, again in that conciliatory voice, "you know I always lose weight when I start a new role. It will all come together, it will all even out. Once my body gets used to the role, I'll adjust, I'll start gaining the weight back." At the look on his face she added, "I've only lost six pounds for heaven's sake."

"6.7 pounds," he replied coldly, "and you're too close to the cutoff point for my taste now. I prefer my wife not be skin and bones."

Sarah blushed but said nothing more.

Martin was amazed at this. She would never, never let him get away with talking to her like that. He was sure of it. Then he realized, he may have yelled at Sarah in anger at times, he knew he did his fair share of ordering her around when she was young; but, he had never, never been cold and cutting to her in speaking. His dislike of Al grew.

He listened as Al began to dictate instructions to Sarah and Sebastian. Sebastian was now to monitor not just what she ate, but how much and when. Her calorie intake and energy output was to be more closely monitored by Julie and Sarah was to eat what and how much she was told to eat and when.

After his tirade, it was Julie who finally spoke up. "What's gotten into you, Alexander? Why are you being…" she searched for a word and went ahead and finished with "such an ass about this"?

"Because I'm tired, Julie," he said with more composure. "I'm tired of paying people a small fortune," and he looked around the table at that, "and finding that I am still pulling her back from the edge of danger. So everyone, just do your jobs. And you," he pointed at Sarah, "you, young lady. You will obey me."

Sarah blushed deeply but finally nodded and said, "Yes, Zander." It made Martin sick. What was going on here?

This morning he watched Sarah struggle to eat the portion that was given to her for breakfast. It was the fruit and yogurt she loved, this time with walnuts added. There was also a slice of buttered toast, a glass of fresh squeezed orange juice, and a glass of organic whole milk. When Sarah was stressed, he knew her appetite was the first thing to go. He felt bad for her but knew she had to eat it all. So far, she had only managed to gain back one of the pounds she had lost. She assured him that once the ballet opened it would actually be easier on her, just the one performance a night. She would regain the weight easily. But Sebastian had told him privately the previous day, defending Alexander, that Sarah's weight could plummet dangerously low in a matter of days if not monitored carefully.

Martin had been helping Sarah as much as possible from the beginning, appreciating that the level of physical demands on her body he witnessed cried out for the individual attention a coach or personal trainer gave to any top athlete. He knew from personal experience of feeding this finicky little girl when she was young that she did much better with smaller portions of food more often. So, he tempted her with high calorie treats she loved, such as Dove Bars or Sebastian's homemade caramel nut brownies, and joined in the treat with her. He observed her diet carefully over the first few days and found it to be extremely healthful; she got enough protein from nuts, beans, and dairy. What she ate was good, he thought, but her appetite and stomach size were small so it was hard for her to consume enough volume to support this level of energy output. So high calorie, low volume treats were in order. At least she hadn't lost any more weight, even if she has only regained one pound, he thought. "Are you nervous?" Martin asked Sarah sympathetically.

"Not really," she replied. Then, with a huge smile for Martin that made Alexander clench with jealousy, she said, "I'll get more nervous as the day goes on. I get distracted, forget things. You'll see," she laughed. "I turn into a total space cadet just before curtain."

"What's going on in your mind?" asked Will intrigued.

"I guess I start living the role in my head," she said. "I get totally wrapped up in the character I'm dancing so when I step on the stage, I am her."

Sarah danced a physically difficult and emotionally demanding role. The ballet, loosely based on 'East of Eden' and the bible, had Sarah dancing Eve as she went from innocent maid to an evil woman bent only on the domination of Adam, and her eventual descent into madness.

Sarah and Yuri disagreed loudly and vigorously at times during rehearsal, Yuri not believing her aggressive enough, seductive enough, triumphant enough for his vision of Eve.

Martin watched her relationship with Yuri with interest. Sarah was not the least bit submissive with him. She gave as good as she got, slapping Yuri across the face at one point, snapping, "Touch me like that again and I will kick you in the balls." This was in response to him grabbing her in the crotch during the last lift, attempting to get a rise out of her. She whirled back on Yuri, still angry, saying, "And it's difficult to get the point across that you want with YOUR choreography in this section. You want me to be domineering but you've given me mincing little steps." Sarah stalked away.

Yuri swore softly in Russian and called a short break. He sat beside Martin while Sarah stayed on the other side of the room, doing stretches, cooling down. Yuri watched her for a moment then swore in Russian again. "I don't know why I put up with her. She is so difficult, she make me crazy. But no one else can dance like Sarah. No one else could be my 'Eve'."

Martin smiled at him. "Come on, surely Sarah's not your only great dancer. After all, she doesn't even do it full time."

"You think I don't look for another partner all this time?" Yuri asked. "I start to look for another partner from the first damn day I dance with Sarah when she is only fourteen. She is so much trouble; I do anything to find another partner. But never do I find anyone who is even close. And you're right, the ballet is not so important to her. The rest of these dancers, and me, the ballet is our life! But Sarah, it is only a diversion, a way to make music come to life with body. She can take it or leave it and mostly she leave it. She won't even dance for entire season. She give me only crumbs and still, I crawl on my belly for those crumbs. I wish to god I find somebody less difficult to dance with! She so stubborn."

"She doesn't seem like the difficult one to me," Martin said with a chuckle. "You're the temperamental one."

"Me!" Yuri exclaimed. "You think me temperamental? Just because she not scream and cry, doesn't mean she not temperamental. She is ice queen. I get blue balls just dancing with her. She never show her true passion until actually on stage. And she never let me, Yuri, touch her. I must be in character, in role always, or she not dance with me. Even when we ballroom dance at Benefactor's Ball, I must be Fred Astaire or Gene Kelly or some damn thing other than myself or she won't dance with me!"

"Well, maybe she doesn't like you, Yuri." Martin smirked. " Maybe you've hit on her one time too many. After all, your reputation is the great cocksman. Maybe she doesn't want to be another notch on your belt. Is she the only female in the company you haven't slept with?" Martin asked.

"I give up on her long time ago. I tell you, not just me but no one get close to the ice queen. That girl let no one touch her."

Sarah approached them from across the room. "I want to show you something, Yuri. Martin, will you help me?"

Martin knew what she was up to. She practiced this move at home with him several times. He rose and assumed the position she taught him, Yuri's position at this point in the ballet. She danced up to him and twirled about him, swirling her hand across his chest seductively as she twirled. Hmmmm... this was nice, Martin thought. She hadn't practiced this part with him at home. Martin thoroughly enjoyed it although he didn't even attempt any of Yuri's moves. He just stood and enjoyed Sarah's caresses. After several seductive passes, Sarah twirled away from him then ran lightly back. Martin was ready and she jumped up, his hand in front of his chest supporting her foot as she stepped up from his bent knee to his hand, then stepped up and arose on his shoulder. She stood upright, then on point, then lifted her arms above her head, extended her right leg high behind her, threw back her head, and all but crowed her triumph over this man as Martin slowly rotated, arms slightly outstretched, looking up at her in dazed wonder. A highly theatrical move but Sarah was mesmerizing and Yuri knew he had his ballet, his masterpiece.

Sarah and Yuri practiced the move over and over and Martin knew it was not particularly difficult for her although the role demanded much of her small frame. Harder still was the emotional toll the role took on Sarah as she reached somewhere inside herself to find the woman who desired nothing but vengeance and was domineering and cruel. He could tell she regretted the role already and the ballet had yet to open.

Well, tonight would be the test. Martin was no judge of such things but Sebastian, Jonathan, and certainly Yuri were, and they were all enormously excited. They expected a huge success. This was a bold move for Yuri's career. He was not only the principal male dancer, he was the creator and choreographer, setting his ballet to Vivaldi's Four Seasons; the innocent, the seductress, the domineering cruel blade of a woman, the descent into madness. It was Yuri's first totally original work and would make or break the remainder of his career. Sarah was only twenty but Yuri was thirty-five, nearing the end of his dancing career, at least at this demanding level. He needed the next phase of his career to be incredible. He wanted to leave people stunned with this performance.

* * *

They were right, Martin thought. They were all right. It was a magnificent, huge, standing ovation success. Sarah and Yuri were pelted with a mountain of flowers. The audience still thundered their approval with their hands, the ovation going on bow after bow. Martin was off to the side backstage, but he could see Sarah, quivering with exhaustion, holding herself gracefully, proud of her and Yuri's accomplishment. She glanced to the side, right at him, and smiled radiantly then turned back and accepted yet another bouquet of flowers. Martin was happy for her and so very proud. What he had witnessed tonight had been sheer perfection and he had to admit Yuri was a huge part of that equation. Damn, that guy could move; he was one hundred percent male, confident in himself, strong and assertive when he met innocence. Eve's conquest and eventual domination of this powerful male animal was what made the ballet so compelling. And the audience loved Sarah in every permutation. Even her descent into madness earned their passionate applause.

Martin felt a surge of jealousy when he recalled Sarah and Yuri's passionate seduction pas de deux. He was sure every man in the audience had the same reaction he had every time he saw it. It was completely 'G' rated as far as the body parts she touched. It was completely 'X' rated in how she touched. It always made Martin hard as a rock.

They were home by now, Sarah already showered and in her robe. Another of Sarah's idiosyncrasies, unless she had a function she had to attend immediately after the ballet, such as the Benefactor's Ball next week, Sarah preferred to just change out of her costume, remove her makeup, and go home to shower and change. She did so after classes and rehearsals as well, preferring to go home sweaty to showering in her dressing room.

Martin was still a bit surprised and Will was flabbergasted. Even on opening night, Sarah stayed for none of the festivities; the cast parties, of which Will gathered there were to be several, the champagne toasts, the general merriment. She literally left the stage, changed, removed her makeup, and left for home. The only person allowed backstage as Martin sat with her through these activities was Alexander, who congratulated her, brought her even more flowers, (ridiculous in Martin's opinion), and said he would see her again in a few days' time.

Martin was glad they just came straight home as he now had Sarah to himself. Even Sebastian and Will went to bed. Martin waited until now, until they were private and alone. He approached her, took both her hands in his and said, "You were amazing tonight, Smallest. I'm so proud of you. The whole ballet, the whole thing was great," he continued. "But you, Sarah, you were brilliant. You slay me, baby," he said, and gently stroked her cheek with two fingers.

Sarah glowed with happiness at his praise. She smiled shyly and could think of nothing to say, so she just hugged him. It felt so good to have her arms around him; it made her weak with pleasure. She released him and stepped away. Careful. Her heart was thundering in her chest. Careful, she reminded herself. Not too close.

"You never had a champagne toast." Martin indicated the chilled bottle resting in the ice bucket Sebastian left.

Sarah politely refused a glass when first home. Now she smiled at Martin, her face glowing and beautiful and unadorned, her hair wet from her shower and combed straight back. "I'll have a glass now if you'll join me," she said.

Martin answered with a smile and opened the bottle of champagne, pouring two glasses. He toasted Sarah with, "To Smallest. The best tiny dancer ever to float on air," and raised his glass.

Sarah floated on air now for sure. She twirled with pleasure, her wineglass her partner in this dance. This has been one of the best days of my life, she thought with satisfaction. Martin saw her do something difficult, demanding, and totally on her own. Just herself, Sarah, with no help from her special abilities, totally normal. Of course, she thought with a momentary flash of pain, it didn't help before. She had just come off stage after a memorable musical performance when Martin walked away before. She pushed the memory away. She didn't want to think about that now. Martin was here now, that's what mattered.

Chapter Eighteen

They saw almost nothing of Al in the past week. Everyone was busy with their routine for Sarah. Only Will had little to do. He exhausted every lead looking for the guy who had been in Sarah's bedroom but to no avail. He was right, Martin thought, the guy never came back to work and his fellow workers knew next to nothing about him. They learned nothing from the doll, readily available anywhere, or the knife, which turned out to be a cheap souvenir letter opener, also readily available. No fingerprints were found and the DNA had no match in any database. Martin's frustration and unease grew and he was glad he was there to keep a close eye on Sarah. Will had been out doing some exploring of the city, even went to a hockey game. Paul was working on some writing, something work related, and Julie worked at a nearby clinic, so everyone else was busy. Martin wasn't really busy, he supposed, but he spent every waking minute with Sarah and was enjoying it hugely.

He was glad for Will, therefore, that Tess and the kids arrived yesterday. They were all guests at the apartment at Sarah's insistence, and all would be attending the performance tonight as well as the Benefactor's Ball after. All except Cara and Theo who were deemed too young for the ball. They would be driven back by Max after the performance and delivered personally to Sebastian at home. Alexander was escorting Sarah. Tonight he intended a public announcement of their engagement. Tess would be attending with Will and Jace was excited to be going with Martin. "It's not technically a date, Jace," he explained. I'll be your escort but I'll be working. I'm sorry, but I'll be paying attention to Sarah, not you. Hope you're OK with that."

Jace was thrilled just to be attending. She was still incredulous, they all were, that she was in Sarah Eastin's home, that Martin and their Dad were on such close terms with her. Wait 'til their friends heard. They had been given strict instructions not to talk about this trip beforehand with their friends on penalty of being left behind. No one had disobeyed. Are you kidding? Miss this, the trip of a lifetime, a ride on a private jet, all the famous people they were bound to meet including Sarah Eastin herself? Not likely. They were now under strict instructions: no talking, texting, tweeting, or otherwise communicating about this visit to anyone until they were home. Then they would be allowed to tell their friends about their amazing experience, not before. They didn't really understand what the big deal was, but since both their Dad and Mom demanded it, they complied. They wanted to meet her. Sarah Eastin.

Tess and the kids were awed by the penthouse. Tess was especially taken with Sarah's master bedroom/greenhouse suite, but she was equally impressed with the suite she and Will were given, Magnus' former room. Jace and Cara were housed in the room that was first intended for Martin and Will, and Theo now bunked in with Martin.

Will was glad to see his family and happy to get out with them, show them around The Dakota and it's surrounding Upper Westside neighborhood. He also wanted a chance to talk to his wife alone. They had spoken and seen each other virtually every night via FaceTime since he left. He even gave Tess a somewhat virtual tour of the apartment but he wanted this time alone to express some of his concerns to his wife. Tess was good at listening to him; maybe she would understand this strange girl better than he did. He and Tess settled on a bench in the Strawberry Field section of Central Park. The early October weather was pleasantly crisp; a fine day for an outing in the park. He warned the kids to stay within view and let them roam and explore all the tributes to John Lennon.

"I haven't wanted to say too much on the phone in case I was overheard, but there's something very strange going on here," he said to Tess, troubled. He explained about Sarah, how solitary she was. "She has no girlfriends, Tess. None. She's somewhat friendly with her doctor, Julie, but they aren't friends like Jace has friends, like any of our kids have friends." He scratched his head in frustration.

"What are you trying to say, Will?" his wife asked him.

"I'm not sure," he said, perplexed. "Something ain't right here, Tess. This little girl here, besides me and Martin, she just has a couple of old men around her, Sebastian and Jonathan. Them and two doctors," he added. "She's supposed to be engaged but her fiancée ain't never around except to bark orders at her. They never touch, Tess," he added. "Not that

I've ever seen. But Martin and her, they have a powerful thing between them. It can be hard to be in the same room with them at times, there's so much electricity between them. Yet neither one of them will do a thing about it. It's the damnest thing," he said, shaking his head at the folly. "White folks," he summed up. "Go figure."

"Do you think he's in love with her?" Tess asked.

"Hmpph," snorted Will. "I know he is. The man can't sleep without having wet dreams and I've never seen anyone take so many cold showers."

"I didn't ask if he lusted after her," Tess said dryly to her husband. "I asked if you think he's in love with her?"

Will nodded his head yes. "See what you think this weekend," he said. "I think the reason that Martin won't touch her is because he's in love with her. He can't take his eyes off her. But he doesn't want to trifle with her. And this lifestyle, all this money, it's blown his mind. He doesn't know how to deal with it and he doesn't want to deal with it."

Tess nodded. "And the girl?" How do you think she feels about him?"

"She's even more obviously head over heels than he is. She's not as skilled at hiding it. That girl would eat him with a spoon if she could," he continued and Tess laughed. Ah, it was good to see his wife again. Will had thoroughly enjoyed their private reunion in bed last night. They had been apart over three weeks, a rare occurrence in their marriage. "Tess, I tell you, it's almost cruel what he's doing to that little girl. She's so shy and scared, she don't know which way to jump."

"But she's engaged to someone else," Tess interjected.

"I know. I tell you, that engagement is another strange thing, Tess. Alexander Gregory is pushing that for financial reasons. He wants a wedding ring on her finger by the time she turns twenty-one."

"Oh, Will, that's terrible. You don't think he loves her at all? What about her? Why would she say yes?"

"I don't know, Tess," Will said, troubled. "I don't know. I do know Al's in charge though."

He thought back to the argument about the dress the previous evening, before he left for the airport to pick up Tess and the kids. Alexander and Sarah were discussing what she would be wearing to the

Benefactor's Ball. Or rather, Alexander was telling her what she would be wearing, and she was not happy.

"Zander, it's a black and white ball. I'm not wearing a red dress. I don't want to stand out like that. It's...," she abandoned that sentence and finished with, "I don't want to stand out like that."

"I'm announcing our engagement, Sarah. I definitely want you to stand out like that," Alexander said with finality in his voice. Will could see Martin's hackles rise.

Sarah switched tactics. "Please don't make me wear red, Zander," she said quietly to him, a pleading note in her voice. "I'll wear anything you want in black or white, but don't make me wear the red."

Alexander was pleased. He got what he wanted. He had a white dress in mind for Sarah all along but it was a very daring dress. She'd said anything black or white...

Will saw the dress tonight as Sarah came out of her dressing room ready for the ball. He heard Martin's sudden intake of breath. The dress was of a lightweight, white silk, with thin shoulder straps and a softly draped low cowl neckline. Sarah had to be braless in it as the open back plunged down below her waist, the dress held on her body by only a couple of thin white silk cords across the back. The silk fabric brushed enticingly across her bare nipples. The dress was fitted at the waist and from there, down her hips, was a short cascade of shimmering crystal glass beads, gathering and causing the silk fabric below her hips to flare and flow around her like water when she twirled or moved. Perfect for dancing. Alexander had insisted her hair be up and adorned her ears with diamonds. Will didn't think she liked them but she didn't object. She also, of course, wore her engagement ring. She needed no other adornment, she looked breathtaking he had to admit.

His women were equally stunning he thought, beholding his Tess in a gorgeous black dress with copper tones in it that made her look regal, and his Jace, dressed to kill in a white, strapless, tightly fitted, beaded sheath. Will thought he and Martin looked pretty good in their tuxedos as well and was pleased as punch to be escorting his women to the ball. Even Cara and Theo had dressed in eveningwear for the ballet and Will thought his family looked pretty damn sharp.

The ballet was a huge success again that night and Tess and Jace were buoyant with pleasure. They were ardent fans of Sarah's dance but had never seen her live before. This was so much better than their wildest fantasies.

They arrived at the ball, Martin and Jace entering directly behind Alexander and Sarah, but giving them some space. Alexander put Sarah's arm through his just before they entered the room, Martin noted. There was a collective buzz of recognition as they entered. Then Yuri approached, bowed and kissed Sarah's hand, and escorted Sarah and Alexander into the ballroom personally to the applause of the room at the entrance of the two ballet stars. Yuri then bowed to Alexander and walked Sarah to the middle of the dance floor and immediately swept her into a waltz at the opening strains from the orchestra.

Wow, he didn't waste any time Martin thought, watching Yuri and Sarah dance. After the applause from their first dance alone died, the dance floor began to fill up while Yuri and Sarah danced another waltz. Martin looked around. Dinner had been served and mostly cleared away. Waiters were still removing a few plates at the farthest tables. It was obvious that the room had been awaiting the stars' arrival. Every eye in the room was on Sarah and Yuri. After a third dance, Yuri finally relinquished Sarah's hand to Alexander, who swept her into the next dance. Martin watched from the sidelines but didn't dance with Jace. He knew she was impatient to dance and he smiled at her in sympathy, but he needed to keep his eyes on Sarah.

Sarah knew Alexander intended to make his announcement soon. She felt nervous, frazzled. The stage didn't bother her but this kind of social situation, with every eye on her, was nerve wracking. She asked Alexander for a break first, a chance to go to the ladies room before his announcement. He nodded, bringing her to Martin with her request, asking him to escort her there and back. Martin nodded and Tess and Jace decided to accompany them, Will trailing along. They did not go to the closest ladies room. Will, having checked it out for her prior, sent them to a ladies room not likely to be in use. After a quick check by Will, the ladies entered while Martin and Will lounged against the wall outside, waiting. Three young women approached, expensively dressed, slightly tipsy, obviously guests at the ball. They went to enter the ladies room, looking Will and Martin over on their way, when Martin said, "Ladies, this room is in use. Would you mind finding another?"

The thin blonde with far too much makeup for Martin's taste answered, "It's for guests at the ball and we're guests at the ball," and swept by him, her girlfriends tittering behind.

Martin was irritated, but let it go. It was a public restroom.

Inside the restroom, inside one of the stalls, Sarah knew immediately it was Blaine Towers and her cronies who had entered. She could hear her voice; Blaine was being loud enough for her benefit. "Poor Alexander," Blaine said. "No wonder he's climbing the walls. That girl has ice water in her veins."

"Who are the cute guys hanging around outside?" her friend asked.

"Her new bodyguards," Blaine snickered. "I hear she pitched a fit at first."

"If she's not fucking Alexander, maybe she's fucking them," Blaine's friend offered. "That one guy is really cute, I'd do him."

Sarah came out of the stall to see Blaine Towers chopping up a mound of cocaine on a little mirror on the vanity of the bathroom. Ignoring her, Sarah went to a sink further down and washed her hands. Tess and Jace had also emerged from their stalls by now.

"Bet the black guy has a big dick," Blaine said, directly to Sarah this time, glancing at the two black women to see the effect of her words.

Sarah ignored her and went to the hand dryer. Blaine followed, carrying the mirror of cocaine. "Don't be such a prude, Sarah, have a little fun," she said, proffering a little straw to Sarah.

Sarah looked at her. "I don't believe Alexander ever introduced us," she said coolly. "That black man you were discussing is this woman's husband and her father," she said indicating Tess and Jace. At that, Sarah hit the button on the hand dryer and blew the pile of cocaine into Blaine's face. "Oh, sorry," she said politely while Jace giggled.

Blaine, furious, grabbed Sarah's arm. Tess opened the door immediately and called for Martin, who was there instantly. He grabbed Blaine's arm then tightened his grip when she didn't let go of Sarah.

"Let go now or I'll break your arm," he threatened quietly. He pulled Blaine away from Sarah. He saw the angry expression in Sarah's eyes and the cocaine in Blaine's hair, face, eyebrows, eyelashes. He smiled when he realized what must have happened. "Don't be an idiot," he said to the angry blonde dusted with cocaine. He turned his gaze to include her two friends. "I suggest you all get out of here now and don't come anywhere near Miss Eastin again. I'm a cop," he said, flashing his ID, "and I'd be more than happy to bust you. I'm guessing your Daddy wouldn't like that," he said, recognizing Blaine. The three women fled and Martin turned to Sarah. "You, OK, Smallest?" She nodded.

"What happened here?" Will asked.

"Mean girls," Jace and Tess answered in unison, laughing to ease the nervous tension.

"Bullies," Tess said. "But Sarah showed them and with class!" Tess laughed again. Sarah smiled somewhat bleakly and they left the ladies room.

Alexander swept Sarah up almost immediately for his announcement. "Ladies and gentlemen," he said to the hushed room, "I can't tell you how proud and pleased I am to say that this lovely young woman has agreed to be my wife!" He held Sarah's hand aloft exultantly then kissed it. Sarah smiled and executed a small bow towards Alexander. The crowd thundered their approval, surging forward to congratulate the couple.

Martin watched the crowd carefully, never taking his eyes off Sarah. He said quietly to Jace, when everyone's attention was elsewhere, "I want to know, word for word, exactly what went down in that bathroom, Jace."

Jace told him then said, "I'm embarrassed I didn't say anything. I guess I was too surprised. But if I see her again, I will kick her bony ass!" She was angry at how Sarah had been treated. "Who is she, Martin?" Jace asked.

"Pretty sure that was Blaine Towers, Howard Tower's daughter." Martin replied.

"Well, she's the one who's the stone, cold bitch," Jace concluded. "Sarah never said a word to her until the very end."

Alexander and Sarah came off the dance floor. Sarah asked if she could leave yet and Alexander tightened his mouth in annoyance. He motioned to the waiter to open the chilled bottle of Cristal he himself

148

brought in for Sarah, watched the man open it, then poured and handed a glass to Sarah. "Not quite yet, my dear," he said smoothly. "Relax, try to enjoy yourself. And smile, Sarah," he said, bending to speak quietly in her ear. "Everyone's watching you. You won't have to do this again after today." Then still smiling, he straightened and joined her in a glass of champagne. "Remember, I want you to meet Howard, Sarah. I want your opinion."

Sarah sighed. She was tired. The ballet was a demanding one and her feet hurt. She really didn't want more dancing and she especially didn't want to meet a stranger. A stranger who promised, from what she could tell so far, to be just as disagreeable as his daughter. But, she had promised, so she said, "Just five minutes. That's all I promised." Alexander nodded and led her off. Martin followed.

Howard Towers waited with growing impatience. People waited on him, not the other way around. But this little beauty was worth the wait, he thought, savoring the sight of Sarah from across the room. His little game neared its conclusion. Even more delightful, his daughter helped deliver the little morsel to him. Alexander Gregory was learning that if he wanted to move in social circles in New York City, he had to deal with him. He was very gracious to Alexander during their few meetings. He would be glad to make the introductions Alexander needed, he said, and had been most generous with his time and connections thus far. Finally, he made his request. He was a generous benefactor to the ballet and a big fan of Sarah's. He wanted just a few moments alone with her. Perhaps a private word at the Benefactor's Ball? Howard Towers was a multi-millionaire, real estate tycoon and used to getting what he wanted. Still, he was a little surprised at the ease with which Alexander consented.

He didn't realize Alexander was looking for a way to get Sarah alone with him for a few minutes. According to Alexander's father, Sarah was an infallible judge of character. He wasn't so sure about that but he was trying to figure Towers out. Towers wanted something from him, of that he was sure, especially since the daughter, Blaine, had come on to him so strongly. Alexander was having quite a bit of fun romping with Blaine but she was a bit too inquisitive about Sarah for his taste. It was worth a shot to see what Sarah thought of Towers. He could be a very useful connection for him in New York.

Towers waited near one of the terraces and nodded his head courteously in greeting when introduced. "I've heard so much about you, young lady. I'm looking forward to a little private chat." After a few other pleasantries, he attempted to take her hand and lead her towards the terrace. Martin made ready to follow. Sarah politely pulled her hand away and looked at Alexander with a question in her eyes.

"It's all right, Princess. Howard is a new friend. Why don't you two get to know each other for a few moments," he said, leading Martin away by the elbow. Martin resisted. "Give them some privacy," Alexander insisted, looking at Sarah.

Sarah smiled at Martin and said, "I'll just be a minute," and stepped out onto the terrace with Howard Towers.

Alexander led Martin away across the room with an admonishment, "You don't have to breathe down her neck every second. Give them five minutes before you join them." He walked off.

Sarah didn't like Towers immediately. He was arrogant, aggressive, far too forward. He led her out on the terrace then immediately tried to draw her into his arms. She stepped away saying, "It's too cold out here after all. I think I'll go back inside."

He pulled her roughly to him and tried to kiss her. She pulled away saying, "No," firmly, then stepped on his instep with the heel of her shoe and bore down when he didn't desist. That only angered him and with frightening speed and strength he backhanded her across the face, threw her back against the stone rail of the terrace, and forced his mouth over hers, his tongue down her throat.

Sarah struggled uselessly. She saw stars and her head spun from the blow to her face. Her hip was on fire where the glass beads were grinding into her, broken by the stone rail. He was just lifting her dress when Martin arrived in a fury.

Martin had been watching from across the room in mounting concern. He then saw one of Towers' bodyguards stand before the door to the terrace, effectively blocking anyone from entering at the same time he saw the other terrace entrance being covered by what could only be another one of Towers' muscle guys. His eyes locked with Will as they both realized the implications at the same time.

Martin sprang into action, running at the first guard, disabling him, and getting through the door with lightening speed while Will went for the second guard at the other door. Martin saw Sarah struggling with Towers while he held her up against the railing and attempted to lift her dress. Martin yanked the guy off Sarah and punched him hard in the face, breaking his nose. Towers slumped to the ground and Martin kicked him aside. He pulled Sarah to him as Will entered through the second entrance. Sarah was shaking, trembling from head to foot. "We have to get her out of here fast," he said to Will. "Before anyone sees fuck face here." He indicated Towers on the ground holding his bleeding face. Will nodded, pulling out his phone and dialing Max.

Martin and Will walked Sarah quickly through and out of the ballroom. Curious glances followed them but Martin kept them moving. Sarah stopped suddenly outside near the parking structure where they were to meet Max. She turned to a large stone planter and bent over and vomited. She took several deep breaths, trying to steady herself, then got violently ill again. Martin said nothing, just rubbed her back and handed her his handkerchief when she was done. He glanced down at her and exclaimed, "Oh no, Sarah! You're bleeding!" Blood was soaking through her dress on her hip. Martin realized that the creep had thrown her so hard against the stone railing, he had shattered the glass beads on her dress. They were then ground into her hip as she struggled to get away.

Sarah straightened and wiped her mouth. Max was there now and Will took a bottle of water from the car and handed it to Sarah. She rinsed her mouth and spat. She shuddered; it felt like a lizard had crawled into her mouth when Towers stuck his tongue down her throat. She tasted blood and realized it was his from when she'd bitten him and her gorge rose again. She rinsed her mouth again and again but she said nothing.

"Sarah, you need a doctor," Martin said, looking at her hip again. Now he was really pissed. He should have broken the asshole's neck, not just his nose.

"Julie can take care of it," Sarah said, shudders of revulsion still running through her. "I just want to go home." She got into the car but cried out in pain upon trying to sit.

"Here, lean on me," Martin said, pulling her to him as he got in the car. She was shivering. He removed his jacket and wrapped her in it. They rode home with Martin holding her in his arms, stroking her hair gently. Once Sarah was safely inside, Martin sent Will back with Max to get his wife and daughter.

Julie was tending to Sarah in her bedroom with Martin pacing outside in the music room when Alexander arrived. He was angry, going straight to Martin and demanding an explanation. "What the hell! You punch Howard in the face then charge out of there with Sarah in tow!"

Martin snapped. He turned on Al, ready to tear into him. "You miserable, moron," he snarled. "I ought to rip your fucking head off!"

Alexander raised his fist and suddenly found himself on his back on the floor, against the wall where Martin had thrown him. Damn, the guy was fast. He went to rise.

"Don't bother," Stone mocked him. "You're good, Al, but you're not that good." Stone pointed at him, still furious. " Don't you even want to know how she is? That's right," he sneered at the look on Al's face. "Julie's in there right now picking glass out of her ass because your friend, Howard, was such a gentleman! He attacked her!"

"There must be some misunderstanding." Alexander was taken aback.

"Your fucking friend attacked her! He tried to kiss her and when she resisted, he hit her in the face and threw her against a stone railing. That dress you have her in, Al, those beads are glass. You had her in a goddamn glass dress and you served her up to your pervert friend like some kind of fucking hors d'oeuvre!" He was snarling at Alexander in his anger.

Alexander was shocked. "Sarah's injured?" he said, rising to his feet.

Martin shook his head in disgust. "Clean yourself up before you go see her," he ordered. Al's lip was bleeding where he'd hit him. "She's actually worried about your sorry ass. You ever pull a stunt like that again, Al," Martin warned, glaring at him, "I will break every bone in your goddamn body."

Sarah looked up from where she lay, facedown on the bed. There was a towel draped over her hips. Julie looked through a large mounted magnifying glass at a section of bloody pulp on Sarah's hip. Alexander was shocked. The beads on the dress had done that much damage? He looked at Sarah's face and felt lightheaded. Her lower lip was swollen. She had undeniably been struck in the face. He sat down heavily on the bed. "Oh my god, Sarah," he said, examining her face with his eyes. "Howard Towers did this to you?"

"You wanted my opinion of your acquaintance, Zander," she said, eyes full of reproach. "He's a terrible person," and her eyes filled with tears and she looked away.

"Sarah, I'm so sorry. What happened?" Alexander asked softly.

Sarah didn't answer, Martin did. He stood in the doorway looking in at them and said to Alexander. "The guy planned this, Al. He had his men block both entrances to the terrace and he was on Sarah pretty much the instant he got her out there. Why the hell would you let him get her alone like that, Al?" Martin was still very angry. "You pulled me across the room, away from Sarah."

Alexander got up and went out into the music room, Martin following. "I had no idea the guy would be such an ass!" Alexander said, angry now as well, but Martin blazed at him.

"Why would you let anyone, anyone you don't know that well have that kind of access to Sarah! Your 'friend' sexually assaulted her and was just seconds away from rape! He had his hand up her dress when I got there! I should have broken the fucker's neck, not his nose," Martin finished furiously. He took several deep breaths to calm himself. Then he looked directly at Al and said, "Tell me why, Al? Why did you do that?"

Alexander didn't answer. He honestly didn't know what to say and was still in shock over what had happened. He'd felt there was something off about Towers, something he couldn't put his finger on. That was why he wanted Sarah to meet him. She could always read people. But he had never suspected something like this, would never have asked her to check Towers out if he'd known the man was a sexual predator.

It was Sarah who answered from the doorway, a robe wrapped tightly around her. "Alexander didn't know the man was dangerous, Martin. Neither did I or I wouldn't have gone out on the terrace with him. Alexander asked me to talk to him for a few minutes, to get a sense of the man. Magnus would sometimes ask me to do the same," she said and shrugged. "I'm good at reading people," she said with a small smile at Martin. "Alexander was considering some business arrangements with Mr. Towers and had some concerns. Well founded concerns it seems."

Martin let out a breath. He actually knew what Sarah was talking about. He also always trusted her take on people. He paced back and forth a few times in the room. God he still wanted to strangle Al. Finally he stopped and pointed at Al. "You don't interfere again with my security, my coverage of Sarah. I should have been out on that terrace with her. This should never have happened. Do I make myself clear, Al?"

Alexander nodded. He was still horrified by what happened and felt ill when he thought of Towers striking Sarah, touching her. He thought of Blaine and felt a fool; how could he have been taken in by her?

Alexander left. Sarah stood alone in the middle of her music room, her arms wrapped tightly around herself. She seemed lost and far, far away. Martin went to her and wrapped his arms around her, resting his cheek on the top of her head. "Are you all right, Smallest?" he asked softly.

"Yes," she said, but she began to tremble again.

Martin hugged her tightly to him, rubbing his hand across her back, holding her to him. "It's OK, Smallest. I've got you. I've got you," he repeated, comforting her.

Sarah had been holding tightly to her emotions all night, ever since the confrontation in the ladies room. Now her tears finally came. She clung to Martin and sobbed. He picked her up, went to the couch, and sat her on his lap. Careful of her injured hip, he cradled her in his arms, holding her while he let her cry herself out. He just held her, rocking her gently, stroking her hair.

Paul watched quietly for a few moments then took Julie's hand. "Let's retire," he said. "Martin's doing a fine job of comforting her; that's what she needs now."

When Sarah ceased weeping, she lay quietly in his lap, her head against his shoulder. "Martin," she asked softly, "what made that man think he could touch me like that?" She shivered with revulsion again, remembering Tower's mouth on hers, his tongue in her mouth. She felt her gorge rise again at the thought and fought back the urge to vomit.

154

"He's a bastard, Sarah. He knew he had no right to touch you; he also knew he was stronger than you." He hugged her to him tightly. "I'll teach you how to handle garbage like him," Martin promised, looking into her face. "You don't ever have to let a creep like that touch you."

Martin held Sarah and felt her gradually relax. She finally fell asleep in his armss and he was content to sit and hold her, watching her sleep. He thought again of Al. Every day that went by his conviction grew that Al was wrong for Sarah. Tonight was a perfect example. Martin felt Al wanted only to show Sarah off. She was upset, hurt, and scared after tonight's events and Al had left her again, left her to the hired help. Martin actively disliked the guy.

Chapter Nineteen

The routine returned to somewhat normal with Sarah dancing on stage the very day after the Benefactor's Ball. She seemed more subdued since the events of that night, even withdrawing subtly from him, and Martin's heart ached for her. He realized that he had always politely but firmly shut down any display of sexuality from her, ever since she was old enough to discover those feelings. It had been necessary when she was young, but now he realized that she no longer trusted those feelings in herself, that she was deliberately trying not to get too close to him for fear of rejection and his heart ached further for her.

He realized that she thought he was not attracted to her and was crushed by his rejection. What a colossal mistake he'd made in never discussing these things with her. She had just been so young. He had discussed sex in general with her, the birds and the bees, attraction between the sexes, but he had never discussed he and Sarah specifically. Never directly addressed her crush on him and he should have. But how could he tell a girl so young, one he loved so deeply, how twisted up and difficult he found sex. Why he so totally hid that part of his life from her, never discussed girls he'd met, girls he was seeing.

Danny had been able to be open and free with Sarah when he met Julie. Little Sarah seemed delighted by the romance, filling him in on all the details every time they'd meet. Martin hadn't been overly interested in girls yet. He was focused on getting through Officer Training, getting his goals underway. When Martin did finally discover a way to indulge his interest in women, well, it certainly wasn't something to discuss with an eight or nine year old.

Now it seemed that Sarah didn't trust her own sexuality. She was attracted to Martin, but since she thought he didn't desire her back, she'd withdrawn. Martin ached to tell her it was him not her, but could think of no possible way to begin that conversation.

They had seen little of Alexander the past week. He joined them virtually every day for a meal but left soon afterward, after assuring himself that Sarah was following her diet and doing well with her weight.

Martin had only one real conversation with him all week. When he'd heard on the news that Howard Towers was in the hospital with several broken bones after an unidentified assailant beat him, Martin approached Alexander on the terrace. "I was wondering what you were going to do about Towers," he said quietly.

"The guy has a history," Al replied, "once I knew the types of questions to ask, where to look. He's a trophy collector and he collects young girls. Most of the assaults take place in under five minutes and he roughs them up but doesn't hurt them badly. No one presses charges; no one wants the notoriety. He deserved what he got," Al said, turning away.

"No argument from me. You do it yourself or did you send someone?" he asked somewhat condescendingly.

Al turned and looked at him. "I wanted to see the look in his eye when I broke every bone in his fucking hand. He won't be touching anyone he shouldn't for awhile."

"What about the daughter?" Martin asked. Just the look on Al's face when he informed him of Sarah's encounter with Blaine told Martin that Al was sleeping with Blaine. "Damn it, Al!" He was pissed. "You let one of your little fuck buddies have a shot at Sarah! What the hell is the matter with you? What was she even doing at the ball if you were bringing Sarah?" he demanded.

"Don't worry, I took care of it," Al promised. "I don't get even with women the same way." Blaine had been surgically removed from his life. The bitch had actually gone to his apartment after her father assaulted Sarah. He'd had Max escort her out, drive her home, deliver every scrap of everything she'd left behind at his place including lingerie, music, endless bits of makeup and toiletries, and not spoken to her or returned a message since. Blaine was going to find that social acceptance worked two ways. She and her father would now be social pariahs, ignored, left off every important guest list. If either of them ever so much as entered a building again that Sarah was in, he would take harsher measures.

* * *

Today was going to be a different day. They were headed to Memphis, Tennessee, for a charity ball, attended by the First Lady. It was a benefit for abused children and Sarah would be performing a song specifically for the event. The song was her gift to the First Lady's charity. All proceeds from the song would go to the children's center. When invited, Sarah had expressed interest in attending,but it didn't seem her schedule would allow. Alexander and Jonathan had worked their magic, however, and they were flying to Memphis by their private jet this morning.

Alexander arrived at the apartment, frustrated. His efforts to find out about Martin's childhood had been largely unsuccessful. Everything he did know about the guy didn't fit with dates and times with Sarah. For instance, it appeared Stone was born in Australia. How did he end up in a missionary school in China? And how convenient that there had been a fire at that missionary, all records destroyed so no proof existed that any of them ever lived there. The information on Stone's Army career and marriage was pretty much as he'd told them. But Alexander could find virtually no information on the guy prior to his Army career. No school records, nothing. Apparently, a friend of his father had pulled some strings and got the guy into West Point. Prior to that, there was nothing on Stone except what was given as part of that application. There were no copies of transcripts from other schools. Stone was accepted on the basis of the entrance exam and personal interview. The application said Stone was seventeen, his father died when he was eight, his mother when he was thirteen. Gavin McCook, known as Doc, was listed as his guardian. McCook was a former Army surgeon, now a rancher in Montana. None of these dates and places matched up that he could see. When Sarah was three and in a missionary in rural China, Stone was thirteen and on a ranch in Montana from what he could tell. He realized there was little evidence either way. There was something he wasn't seeing here. Sarah and Martin undeniably knew each other, and well.

His and Sebastian's attempts to draw Stone out had also not been successful. At one point, when Alexander asked a question of Stone and met with silence, he'd even asked, "What's the big deal about your childhood? You and Sarah, neither one of you will discuss it. You might as well tell me," he'd said, only half joking. "I'm marrying her, I'm bound to find out sooner or later."

"I don't have to tell you shit, Al," had been Stone's terse response before walking away and adding, "As far as I'm concerned, if Sarah doesn't want to tell you about her childhood, that's her business."

Well, Alexander, thought. Time to push some different buttons.

The flight to Memphis was uneventful and Martin reflected that there were some things about Sarah's lifestyle that he did relish. The ease of getting from A to B in that jet was one. No airports, security lines, it was easy peasy. Being a virtual prisoner of her schedule and her apartment, that he was not envious of.

They arrived at the historic Peabody Hotel in downtown Memphis. The suite had already been thoroughly checked by Jonathan, and Sarah had been checked-in in advance, so they went directly to the room. Sarah had a large suite with a sitting room and grand piano and two bedrooms, one off either side of the main room. After checking the suite out again, Martin asked dryly, "Where are you staying, Al?"

"I have a nearby suite," Alexander answered stiffly.

"Fine," Martin replied, throwing his luggage in the smaller of the two bedrooms of Sarah's suite. "Will and I can bunk in there. Unless you want Sebastian to sleep there," he added politely at the look on Al's face. "In that case, I can sleep right there," and he pointed at a couch in the main room near Sarah's bedroom.

"Sarah?" Alexander inquired.

"Martin and Will are fine in that room," she confirmed. "Sebastian has a room down the hall. "I'm fine here, Zander," she said with a smile. "What time do I have to be ready?"

"Not until six. You have a few hours to relax. Enjoy yourself," he said and turned to leave.

"Can I go out?" Sarah impulsively asked. "It's a beautiful day and there's a big park right there," she said pointing out the window.

"I don't think that would be a good idea, Sarah," Alexander said distractedly, looking at his cell phone. He looked up. "This suite has been checked out, Sarah. It's safe. You have an important performance tonight. Better not risk it, best not go out," he said as he walked out still looking at his phone.

Sarah tried to hide her disappointment but Martin could tell she was as she looked out the window at the park below. But she turned and went to the piano instead and began to play. He went to her. "Sarah, I want to check out the venue for later. Will you promise to stay here with Will?" he asked. "I'll only be gone an hour or so." She nodded and continued to play.

When he returned she was still playing and Will was listening appreciatively. Martin listened as well until she finished that piece then he asked, "So, are you going to soften your approach for tonight for Al, or are you doing it your way?" This was in reference to the discussion Alexander and Sarah had in the plane on the way.

Alexander felt Sarah's song was too forceful, that along with the accompanying video, it would leave patrons not just touched, but ill. "Most people lob soft balls at these things, he'd said. "You don't want the old ladies passing out or barfing in their plates."

Sarah smiled at Martin. "I always listen to Alexander," she said then added with her impish smile, "then I do what I want. It's his problem to deal with the aftermath," she said with another grin.

Martin laughed. "Good girl. Give 'em hell."

Sarah blew the audience away with an electrifying performance that night. Her song was Benetar's hard rock anthem, 'Hell is for Children'. She screamed her chorus of 'Headed for Hell' at the audience to the flashing images of children, neglected and abused, abandoned, beaten, tortured, raped, and murdered. The images were close-ups, horrifying, heartbreaking, and they pounded the audience, assaulting them along with the beat of the music. Sarah's voice included them all, indicted them all in this hell that these children had lived. Even herself. This is society's problem she was saying by her song. We are all guilty. We all need to stop this from happening.

No applause followed her performance, only stunned silence. Then, the First Lady rose, lifted her hand and placed it on her heart and said in a clear and carrying voice, "I pledge. I pledge to do all in my power to end this kind of hell for children."

One by one, the guests rose and pledged with one voice. The donations were the highest the charity had ever received.

160

Sarah was silent on the trip back to the hotel. She knew both Paul and Alexander were dying to question her but so far they had refrained. When they were back in the suite, Paul finally congratulated Sarah on her performance then said, "Sarah, something like that, that obviously came from a deeply personal place."

She looked at Paul and decided to finally say something to him. With a smile she said, "If you're asking if my childhood was hell, it wasn't. It was magical, thanks to the two bravest boys I ever knew." She smiled at Martin then and said to the assembled room, "Good night all. I'm tired," and retired.

She didn't sleep, however. She'd been having more and more difficulty sleeping; the bad dreams were happening more and more often. She didn't want Martin to know so she spent most of the night she should have been sleeping in bed thinking about him instead. The desire to touch him almost overwhelmed her at times. She loved watching him move and took every opportunity she could to watch him work out. She knew he could tell how she felt about him but he still never acted on it. He never would she thought miserably. You're not what he wants, Sarah. She wondered what type of woman was. She had seen Martin express no interest in any woman since they had met again.

Sarah tried touching herself, touching places she wished Martin would touch. It didn't help. It didn't feel how it felt when Martin did touch her. His touch to her face on greeting was the most erotic thing he did to her and Sarah longed for that touch. It always made her want more, though, and more was not forthcoming. The ache in her womb and nipples, the wetness between her legs, these things were not relieved by her own touch and she could find no relief from her thoughts of Martin, her fantasies of seeing him naked. She guarded herself carefully when around him, not wanting to give herself away. But she knew he knew and it humiliated her. Another thing she was hopeless at understanding, what to do with these feelings when only Martin caused them in her, and he seemed to be the only male she knew who was uninterested in her. Because he really knows me she thought, miserable again.

After virtually no sleep, Sarah rose to find that Alexander had changed his plans. Since today was dark at Lincoln Center, he decided to take care of some business in Memphis and not return to New York until the next morning. "You stay here and amuse yourself, Sarah," he said, gesturing vaguely around the room.

Sarah jumped at the opportunity. "I'd like to go to Graceland, Zander. It's not far away."

She had a hopeful look on her face but Alexander said immediately, "Oh, no, I don't think so, Sarah. That's not a good idea. We haven't checked it out. You stay here," he said somewhat patronizingly. "Maybe we can check out a club on Beale Street tonight when I get back."

Sarah swallowed her disappointment and nodded. Alexander left and she went to the piano. "It's OK if you want to go to the park to run," she said politely to Martin. "I'll stay here with Will."

Martin left but got on his cell phone instead of heading out to run. He made several calls to check out details then went back up to the suite. "Still want to go to Graceland?" he asked.

"Zander said no," she shook her head.

"Sarah, you're twenty years old. You don't have to have his permission to leave your room. I know your restrictions. Max can drive us, he can do the advance check at Graceland. If it turns out we can't go in, well then we'll have had a nice drive on a beautiful day. You've been cooped up here already the better part of two days. What do you say?"

"Really!" she said, her face lighting up.

"I don't see why not. Wear something nondescript. Let's see if we can't do this without you being recognized."

"Magnus and I used to do that all the time," Sarah said smiling. "I'll be right back." She returned in plain jeans, plaid sneakers, and a plain white tee shirt. Her hair was pulled back in a ponytail. Martin gave her one of his LAPD baseball caps; and, with her sunglasses on, she was any slight girl. He gave her a thumbs' up and they headed out the door, stopping to let Sebastian know where they were going.

"Don't worry, got her backpack in tow." Will patted it.

Sebastian did not approve. "Alexander will have a fit," he warned.

"Well, Al will just have to get over it, won't he?" Martin said mildly.

"At least let me pack you a picnic lunch," Sebastian scolded. "What did you plan on eating on this excursion?"

Martin grinned at Sebastian. "I was kind of counting on you to handle that," he admitted.

Sebastian bustled about packing a small hamper which he handed to them for the car. "You had better call in regularly," he warned Sarah. "Alexander will be concerned."

* * *

A perfect day, Sarah thought. The drive to Graceland through the Tennessee countryside was beautiful and bucolic most of the way. Graceland itself, while tacky, delighted Sarah, although they spent more of their time on the grounds than in the house.

"I didn't know you were such a big fan," Martin teased Sarah.

"Elvis!" she replied shocked. "How could you not be? He was wonderful," she vowed. "I love his music."

They walked and explored, Max and Will giving them plenty of space, and Sarah finally just relaxed and gave in to the enjoyment of her day out with Martin. They were both having the time of their lives. On the way back to Memphis and the hotel, they passed a country carnival and both impulsively decided to stop. Max was nervous, but there seemed to be no agricultural contaminants, so Martin and Sarah strolled about, enjoying her anomimity and freedom.

Martin won Sarah a huge stuffed rabbit at the target-shooting booth and he laughed with delight at the expression on her face as the hawker handed over the prize. The rabbit was as tall as Sarah. She turned and presented it to the first child she saw that was big enough to accept the huge prize and Martin laughed again at her enjoyment of the moment. His heart swelled with love as he watched her cavort with the child and the enormous rabbit. She could live a lot more normal life than they're allowing her he thought with a pang. The restrictions on Sarah's life chaffed at him after only a couple of weeks. He wondered how much of it was really necessary.

They finally left the fair full of good spirits and Sarah fell asleep against his shoulder in the backseat as Will dozed in the front passenger seat while Max drove. Martin removed his jacket and covered Sarah with it as she slept; the evening had grown cool. He watched her sleep, the music from the car radio playing softly. He could watch her all night.

She'd been asleep for about an hour when she suddenly opened her eyes, awake. Martin had his face turned to her, watching her. They were very close. She moved closer and softly kissed his lips. She seemed shocked by what she had done and began to move away immediately. Martin stopped her gently then kissed her back. She responded immediately and he deepened the kiss.

Sarah was like a woman drowning. She couldn't stop; the kiss was too intoxicating. His breath was warm and he tasted wonderful, just like she'd imagined. She felt Martin pull back to look at her and heard herself whimper ever so softly, "Don't stop, please don't stop." He bent and kissed her again, gathering her to him for an embrace, and she was lost. Her heart raced as she kissed him back, her body trembled and she pushed herself against him.

Martin sensed her need. He yearned for her but realized that she, too, longed for him. His girl, he couldn't help but think of her that way, his girl was desperate for his touch. He held her and stroked her and kissed her and knew he had to help her find some release, some understanding of what her body was going through. He knew he couldn't deny her this time, she was too insecure, too frightened to take another rejection from him. He heard himself speak up to Max while he stroked and comforted Sarah. "I like that song, Max. Turn it up a bit; don't wake Will though." Max turned the music up and Martin turned to Sarah.

"Shush," he whispered softly, kissing her gently, face, lips, neck, stroking her hair, "I know what you need, baby," he said softly in her ear. "I can take care of you, Sarah." He continued to stroke and kiss her, covering her small moans of pleasure with his mouth. "Shh, baby, shhh" he murmured, continuing his caresses.

Sarah melted under his touch, squirming to get even nearer. He pulled up her tee shirt in the darkness and unsnapped her front opening bra, freeing her breasts. He looked at her to see if she really wanted him to continue, she placed his hand on her breast. He stroked her nipple gently and felt it respond immediately. He fondled her breast, covering her sounds with his mouth again. He then lowered his lips and licked and suckled her nipple. He heard her quick intake of breath, the small moan of pleasure she tried to stifle as she held on to him for dear life. He moved to her other breast, teasing the nipple of the first with his fingers as he suckled.

Sarah's hips began to move in a rhythm as old as time beside him as she pushed her mound against his leg. He knew she was unaware of what she was doing, she was all sensation at this moment. He unzipped her jeans and stroked his finger inside against her panties. He looked at her with a question in his eyes and her eyes answered him. "Lift up a bit," he whispered in her ear. She did, and he slid her jeans down under the cover of his jacket. He then slid his finger inside her panties; she was as wet as he'd known she would be. He slowly slid her panties down her thighs to her knees and whispered gently in her ear, "Open your legs a bit, baby." He kissed her face as he slowly stroked his finger around the edges of her sex, teasing her, tantalizing her.

His mouth moved from hers to her nipples and back to her lips. She was trembling with desire, with need. Martin's cock was so hard he thought it might break, but this wasn't about his need, this was about Sarah, so he ignored it. He hoped he wasn't going to come in his pants, that would be embarrassing.

He finally lightly touched her clitoris with his fingertip and she reacted as if electrified. He held her close as her body jerked, saying softly, "Shhh, baby. Let me take care of you." He softly stroked her clit, which was as hard as a little pearl by now, and slipped his finger inside her. She moaned with pleasure and pushed herself deeper onto his finger. God she was tight. He stroked his finger inside her and felt her tremble with desire, arching into him.

She was a virgin; his finger confirmed his guess. He could feel her hymen, the opening almost too narrow for his finger. He stroked slowly inside her, using his thumb now on her clitoris. She was so close to orgasm, he could feel her entire body trembling, straining toward release. "Let yourself feel it, Sarah," he whispered in her ear. "Let yourself go, baby. I'll always catch you." He dipped his head down and caught her nipple again in his mouth, this time he drew deeply on it.

Sarah's explosive orgasm consumed her, her entire body shaking and arching as she clung to him. She was dimly aware that she was supposed to be quiet as Martin held her and covered her cries with his kisses. She shuddered again as his hands, his wonderful hands, fingers, and lips, kept that amazing sensation sweeping through her body. Sarah hadn't known she could be aroused like this. She had no idea that an orgasm would be so intense, so powerful. And the connection she felt to Martin, it was divine, almost like their old bond. She collapsed into his arms, breathing heavily.

Martin held and stroked and gentled her. He could feel her heart racing, the tremors that still rocked her body. He smiled to himself and thought, *frigid, my ass.* He'd known Sarah wasn't frigid. She had far too passionate a nature. He thought of Al with another stab of dislike. Just because she doesn't like your touch, pal, doesn't make her frigid. He knew that's what Al, Paul, Yuri, most of the men in Sarah's life thought. He was glad he helped her understand that wasn't true about herself, but he was a trifle worried about what he had just done. He had no right to touch Sarah. But, Christ, it had felt good. It had felt so, so damn good.

He smiled at her reassuringly in the dimness of the backseat as he helped her get dressed again. She lay against his side in silence, his arm around her as she stroked his hand.

"Why did you do that?" she asked softly after a few moments, turning to look at him.

He looked back at her. "Because I've wanted to for a very, very long time," he answered honestly.

"Really?" she asked, sounding puzzled.

"Really," he replied. Then added softly, "Sarah, I know I have no right to you. I know there's no way I'd fit in your life." He stroked her hair softly with his hand. "But it doesn't stop how much I love you, how much I want you, have always wanted you." He stroked her hair softly. "I won't touch you again, not while you're engaged to him." He added hesitantly, "Poaching on another man's woman, that's not behavior I admire. I don't understand this thing with Al." He looked at her, his eyes troubled. "Sarah, he should be able to make you feel the way I just did. If he doesn't, you shouldn't marry him. Why do you let him order you around like he does, talk to you the way he does? I don't get it, Sarah. That's not like you."

Sarah snuggled closer. "Please, let's not talk about Alexander now," she said. "Not now."

Martin noted she hadn't been wearing her ring that day at all.

166

When they arrived back at the hotel, an enraged Alexander met them. They were later than intended, due to the stop at the fair, but Martin had called Sebastian and communicated that personally, even through he knew Max had been in communication with Sebastian all day.

Alexander was furious. She had defied him and gone out, and Stone had been the instigator. He had finally gotten some very personal information about Stone today and he figured it was about time Sarah knew about it. He pointed at Martin. "You, you're fired! I want you and your partner out of here now."

Martin didn't seem perturbed. "You can't fire me, Al." He turned to Sarah, "Do you want to fire me, us?" he amended, including Will with a nod of his head.

"Of course not," Sarah said, turning to Alexander. "Please don't over react. I'm fine. Everyone knew where I was every step of the way. Martin and Will took very good care of me," she said with a smile, attempting to placate him. It did no good.

"There's a few things you should know about your buddy there, Sarah," he said, not bothering to hide his anger, stabbing his finger at Martin. "And he's not someone I want around you any longer." He turned to Martin. "I know about the club, the private club you and your military buddies are a part of." He turned back to Sarah. "This guy is into sick shit, Sarah, S & M, things you don't want to know about."

Martin went very still, Alexander continued to rage. "He likes to hurt women, Sarah. He likes to tie them up. He likes to gang up on them."

Sarah turned away from Alexander. She had stopped listening when he said that Martin liked to hurt women. She knew that wasn't true. She stopped listening to the rest. She turned to Martin. To her horror he said quietly, "This is one time you need to listen to Al. I'm sorry, Smallest." He finally looked directly at her. "I'm every kind of fucked up there is when it comes to sex, Sarah. You need to listen to Al. I'm not for you, baby."

"I don't understand," she said. "You like to tie up the women you make love to?"

There was a long silence. "I don't make love, Sarah," he finally said, and at the look of confusion on her face added, "I don't have lovers.

I have sex partners, and I don't make love. I fuck. I fuck hard." At that he walked quietly from the room asking Will to please stay with Sarah.

Sarah was devastated. She stood there, not believing her ears. So, Martin stayed away from her because of himself? Oh god, what had that terrible woman done to him? She knew it was bad, that Martin had suffered terribly under his mother's hands, but they left. They got away when she was only three, but Martin was thirteen. There were so many things she didn't understand from those days. Her mind shied away from memories of the barn, the barn of her nightmares. Her thoughts went back to Martin. She didn't believe most of what Alexander was saying and didn't even understand some of it completely. She put her hands over her ears at 'dominant and submissive' and asked Alexander to stop. "Please stop. You've made your point," she added quietly. She asked Alexander to leave. He did, after warning her that he didn't want Martin around her any longer and asking Sebastian to make sure he stayed with Sarah.

Sarah paced. Will sat quietly. He wasn't positive about what had happened in the backseat on the way back from Graceland but he was pretty sure. When he woke from his nap and realized what was up in the back seat, he decided that feigning sleep was his best option so he hadn't moved. But he wasn't deaf either.

He, too, was surprised by Al's tirade, perhaps not as much as Sarah, but surprised. He'd known Stone for a bit over three years now and had never known him to have a woman. Women were very obviously interested in him; he was a good-looking guy. Stone did like women, Will decided a couple of years ago; he did see the guy look. He just never saw him take any action or heard him talk about women. He wondered what the widower did about sex, after all, he was a young guy. However, it was none of his business and Stone never volunteered any information about his love life.

Sarah turned suddenly to Will and Sebastian and said, "He doesn't hurt women. I don't care what Alexander said," she said, defending Martin. "I don't know about all the rest of that, but I know he doesn't hurt women." She lifted her chin defiantly.

Will was proud of her. He knew in his gut that part of it wasn't true as well. He knew firsthand of Martin's gallantry towards women; he was protective of them. He remembered the risks Martin had taken to rescue his own Jace and nodded his agreement at Sarah.

"What does it mean, Will?" she appealed to him a few minutes later. "Is he trying to tell me that's the only way he can make love? I don't understand. He was married," she added, as if that somehow made a difference.

Will shook his head. "I don't know, Sarah," he said honestly. "This is the first I'm hearing about this. Martin has never talked about women before. But I know one thing. I don't believe he likes to hurt women either. I don't believe that for a minute."

Martin returned in about an hour and Sarah felt a rush of relief. A tiny part of her thought he had left for good. He walked up to her, looked at her carefully and said quietly, "I understand if you want me to leave."

Her response was to wrap her arms around him, saying, "Nothing's changed, Martin. You're who you've always been; I'm who I've always been. And I know one thing," she pulled back to look him in the face, "you don't hurt women." She softly stroked his face. "You would never do that, I know."

He let out a huge sigh of relief; he hadn't even realized he'd been holding his breath. "Thank you for that, Smallest," he said shakily. "That means a lot to me." He smiled bleakly at her, hugged her back, then stepped away, as if his touch would contaminate her, she thought, her heart constricting for him.

Martin looked at his partner next. He didn't know where to begin.

Will started first. He was leaning against the wall with his arms crossed. "You owe us some explanations here," he said, nodding his head at Sarah. At Martin's look, he said, "If she's grown up enough for what happened in that back seat, she's grown up enough for an explanation from you. I've realized for a while now, Stone, that you also wanted me here as some sort of chaperone. OK, here I am. After what you just told us, tell me why I shouldn't tell you to get the hell out of here." He stood there looking at Martin. He was a father, had a daughter Sarah's age. He had that Dad look in his eye.

Martin ran his hands through his hair then faced Sarah. "I do tie women up, restrain them, during sex. But I'd never hurt them, not even if they wanted me to," he added, shaking his head. "I.., I just don't like to be touched." His eyes pleaded for understanding. "I just need to control the act," he said, hands through hair again. He looked directly at Sarah.

"I've never been into S & M and I left the dominant/submissive thing behind long ago. I'm pretty dominant, especially during sex," he said with a rueful half laugh at Sarah, "but the submissive thing in a woman got old fast. The club is not some nefarious den of iniquity," he continued. "Will, you're welcome to visit sometime if you like. It is a club for men who like to share their women," he said carefully, looking at Sarah.

"Why?" Sarah asked curiously.

"Various reasons," Martin said. "For me, Doc introduced me to it when I was young, about nineteen or so. I did hurt a girl, once," he said, pain in his eyes as he looked at Sarah. "I didn't mean to," he said, "but I did. We'd been seeing each other for a few months. We arranged to meet for a drink and she was talking to some guys when I got there. Just talking, but it pissed me off. I shouldn't even have approached her when I was angry. I hurt her, Sarah. Not badly, but I hurt her."

"You beat her?" Will asked.

"No," Martin replied, shaking his head. "God no. I got too rough during sex. I didn't pay attention to her; I hurt her. Not badly," he said again, "but enough that she needed medical attention. She should have busted me for assault but she didn't. She actually forgave me almost immediately." He shook his head at the memory. "After I apologized to her, I never saw her again. I couldn't look at her without guilt. I never wanted to do that to anyone again," he said to Sarah, anguish in his voice, in his eyes. "I never wanted to use someone like they didn't matter, like I'd been used," he finished quietly. "I was just so angry so much of the time." Martin paced the room, his nervous energy apparent.

"Doc took me in hand," he said. "He took me home from the hospital after making sure the girl was going to be fine. He introduced me to his new wife and the two of them took me into their bed. I became the third in their relationship, their sexual relationship," he clarified. "They taught me all about how to give pleasure to a woman. Doc told her I didn't like to be touched, so she let me tie her hands with a silk cord." He smiled at the memory. "It freed me," he said, "to know I could relax, she couldn't touch me; and, to have another person there to watch over me, make sure I didn't go too far. And it was good for her, an occasional walk on the wild side. And when she needed to stroke and caress someone, she had Doc there. It worked for us, for them," and he shrugged.

He looked at Sarah again and said neutrally, "It's what I do now for sex. My friend, Mac, and his girlfriend, Katie, I'm their third," he said. "Usually on Friday nights."

Will knew Mac was Martin's Coast Guard buddy, the one stationed in San Pedro who let Martin keep his trailer on the lot. He remembered Katie as a little round thing, cute, earth mother type. She was a masseuse, he remembered.

"Other than that, it's just me and my hand," Martin finished, looking at Sarah. "I'm sorry," he said a moment later. "I shouldn't have touched you like that earlier tonight." He looked earnestly at her. "I just didn't want you to think there was something wrong with you, baby. You're perfect," he said "Just the way you are. Perfect." His expression pleaded for understanding.

Sarah went to him. "I'm not sorry," she said sincerely. This time it was she who stroked his cheek. "I'm not sorry at all."

So, Martin was damaged goods as well, she thought. She didn't care. If he didn't want to be touched sexually, well then she would refrain. She didn't really think he would have a problem with her touch, he never had. But then she blushed as she realized she had never touched him in those places. She hadn't seen Martin naked since she was a small girl and they used to swim together in the high meadow. She felt a stab of jealousy about this Katie girl, information about her coming out of Will. She was a masseuse. Then she realized her jealousy was misplaced. Martin wasn't in love with this Katie, he was grateful that she was the other man's responsibility. She sensed he liked both of them, Mac and Katie; and, while a friend to both and an enthusiastic sex partner on occasion, was otherwise aloof from their relationship. Sarah was actually heartened; Martin was not in love with someone else. Her spirits lifted.

Will wasn't quite sure what to make of his partner's revelations. He also realized that Martin had revealed, somewhat obliquely, that he had been sexually abused as a child. It sounded to Will like he had searched for a safe, acceptable way to have sex with women and finally found an approach that worked. It did not sound good for Sarah, he reflected. It was certainly not the type of relationship she was looking for, he thought.

Sarah flatly informed Alexander that Martin and Will were staying with her. Sebastian had been in the room quietly sitting off to the side the entire length of Martin's confession to Sarah about his sex life. Sarah informed Alexander he was welcome to ask Sebastian if he had any questions, but the two men were staying. The flight back to New York was quiet and uneventful.

Chapter Twenty

Sarah and Martin became even closer than before. His honesty about his relationships, or rather lack of relationships, with women opened him up. He no longer had to hide from his partner either. It was a relief although he worried how the family man side of his partner would take the information.

When they were alone, Will said quietly, "Guess we can add sexual abuse to that def com 4 childhood."

Martin snorted and looked away but eventually nodded yes. "My mother," he finally said. He looked at the wall in their small bedroom rather than at his partner. "You know my back?" he said, referring to the heavy scarring that covered his entire back.

Will was under the impression it was something that had happened to Martin while captured by the enemy on one of his missions. Most of the guys on the squad were under that impression, although Martin never spoke of it.

"Another gift from my mother, on my thirteenth birthday," Martin said. "Generous bitch," he added bitterly.

Will was shocked. His own mother did that to him? Will didn't know what to say. He was virtually certain that type of scarring had been done by a horsewhip. The kind of whipping that killed people. Now he knew why Martin didn't talk about his childhood.

"God," Martin continued. "Danny and I always hid Sarah when the shit was coming down. She was so little. They never touched her," he added fiercely. "We made sure of that. She was only three when we got out of there. I really hoped she didn't remember any of that shit, but she hasn't forgotten anything I don't think." He looked bleakly at Will, "Damn her for fucking up Sarah's life, too," he said about his mother. "Damn her to hell."

Martin was worried about Sarah. He watched her struggle daily with the role she was dancing. She hated Eve she confided to him, hating becoming her each and every night. She was having more difficulty than ever sleeping and her weight was dropping again.

Alexander arranged another break in her schedule. Just for three days then Sarah would return for the final week of performances. But for three days he would take her to Monte Carlo. His yacht was waiting there for them. She would have a safe and comfortable place to relax in the sun for a few days. She wouldn't have to deal with a hotel. And there would be just one small party onboard, the European announcement of their engagement.

Martin rolled his eyes. This guy was too much. If the Monte Carlo break was for Sarah to relax, a party was exactly the wrong thing and Al knew it. It pissed Martin off again. What a selfish prick the guy was. Sarah acquiesced quietly as she did to most things Alexander requested.

Martin seethed quietly on the way to Monte Carlo, watching Al work his phone, play his little cat and mouse game with his eyes with the flight attendant while Sarah listened to her music, oblivious to Al. He was determined that Sarah see through this guy, call off the marriage. He could not imagine her spending the rest of her life tethered to this domineering asshole. He wanted to shove the guy's phone down his throat.

The yacht was impressive he had to admit. Sarah had been given the largest stateroom, the one Al undoubtedly used most of the time. It had a masculine, nautical flair. It was a two-room stateroom, a small sitting room led forward to a bedroom with glass all around in the bow of the ship. Martin went back to the small sitting room and dropped his bag on one of the padded window seats. It would do for a bed for him. "I'll bunk here," he said after he saw the room assigned to him down the corridor to the aft end of the ship. "Will, you can have that room to yourself. It's too far from Sarah."

Sarah did seem to relax once onboard. They were anchored far offshore. No other ships were nearby. It was private and quiet and sunny. That is, it was until the helicopters showed up, buzzing the yacht. Soon, a flotilla of small boats crowded them as well. The word seemed to be out; Sarah Eastin was onboard and the paparazzi were circling.

They all did their best to enjoy the remainder of the day despite being spied on, swimming, lazing in the sun, drinking, and eating. They watched some dolphins playing nearby and Martin and Sarah dove in to swim with them. They were both excellent swimmers, totally at home in the water. Will watched them with envy. He could swim but not like that.

Paul and Julie looked on while Alexander spent time, as usual, with his phone. Sebastian and Jonathan were onboard as well. The crew onboard would handle everything but Sarah's food; that Sebastian would take care of personally. Otherwise, he and Jonathan were free to relax and take some time off as well.

The following day was a different story. Sarah was nervous. Martin could tell she hadn't slept again. He wondered why Al couldn't just call the party off. What the hell, the guy could have a party anytime, seemed to have them all the time. Why inflict this one on Sarah? He spoke to Sebastian. Sebastian agreed that Sarah was looking a bit stressed but said this would be the last of it. After this party, Alexander would not impose any further social obligations on her. Martin shook his head in frustration and said quietly to Will, "So, why the hell does she have to do this one? What's the big deal? The whole world knows they're engaged. It's been in all the papers. Why another party? Sarah hates them. After the Benefactor's Ball, you'd think the guy would let up on her."

Will shrugged. It was strange to him as well; Monte Carlo on a yacht. Why did it feel to him that Sarah saw it as some sort of punishment, some ordeal to be endured?

Sarah made it through the party although Martin felt she was wound tighter and tighter, holding herself together with sheer will power. About sixty people came on board; many were famous faces he recognized, recording artists, models, film stars. Will was suitably awed but Martin was too busy watching Sarah to take much interest. Ah, so this is Al's world, he thought, watching him moving effortlessly through the crowd. He played the perfect host, making everyone feel at home, his charm on full display. The Benefactor's Ball had been the dance world. This was a different crowd, one where Al reigned as king.

Sarah was beautiful in a brief, bright pink sundress and matching sandals. She wore little to no makeup, just some lip-gloss and mascara. Martin thought she was stunning, even if she did look a bit tired. She smiled and played the gracious hostess to Alexander's host, but Martin noted that her hand trembled when she thought no one was looking, and he caught her looking longingly towards her bedroom more than once. When Martin judged that Sarah couldn't last much longer, Al finally called an end to the festivities by inviting all on board to a nightclub onshore. Arrangements had been made; the band was waiting. The group merrily made their way ashore in various vessels, Alexander indicating at the last minute that his bride-to-be would not be joining them. She needed her beauty sleep for the ballet soon to come.

Sarah deflated in gratitude when they all finally left. She was exhausted. It was not yet dark but she said goodnight to all. She was going to bed.

About forty-five minutes later, Martin saw Will's eyes widen. Turning to look behind himself, he saw Sarah, nude except for her panties, walking down the hallway from her stateroom. She was hugging the wall and walking very quietly, looking behind her, very much like someone hiding. She stopped and cringed. Her stare was vacant; she didn't see them, she was seeing something else.

Martin said quietly to the group, "She's sleepwalking. Let me see if I can wake her." He had been sitting talking with Will, Sebastian, Jonathan, Paul and Julie who had elected to stay on board rather than go to the nightclub. The crew had pretty much cleared away the effects of the party and the small group was just relaxing when Sarah appeared.

Sarah quickly continued down the corridor and hid herself in the aft section of the ship, trying to make herself very small as she crouched behind a chair. Martin approached her slowly and crouched down himself. "Smallest," he said quietly. "Time to wake up now. You're dreaming, Smallest," he said. "Time to wake up." He waited quietly.

Jonathan approached and reached over Martin for Sarah's arm. She reacted instantly, leaping up and running across the deck. The helicopters were back suddenly, buzzing and circling. Martin raced after her but she climbed up on the railing of the yacht and looked over her shoulder at them. The look on her face was that of terror and she leapt over the side. Martin kicked his shoes off and dove in after her instantly. He had hold of her almost immediately and could see that she was dazed, confused, still in the grip of her nightmare.

With help from above, he hauled her wet, virtually naked, and shivering back onto the ship. Goddamn those helicopters. No way one of them didn't get a shot of her going overboard. He had to get her inside.

She skittered away from them once onboard, still looking dazed. She glanced down at herself and suddenly began to scream. Her screams were bloodcurdling, terrifying. Martin could see and hear the flashbulbs popping, even over the sound of the helicopters. He grabbed hold of her but it was difficult; she was wet and struggling in the grip of her nightmare.

With Sebastian's help, he got her inside, into her stateroom. As he struggled to control Sarah, he saw Sebastian take something Julie proffered and he realized with a shock that they had a straight jacket. They were going to attempt to restrain her with it. Sebastian had a hold on Sarah as Martin pulled back to protest. Sarah's head hit the wall with a resounding 'thwack' and he winced and pulled her to him.

He grabbed the straight jacket from Sebastian and tossed it across the room. "No fucking way are you putting her in that," he said, and cradled Sarah in his arms. "Sarah," he tried to stroke her face, she was still thrashing and screaming in the grip of her nightmare. Suddenly she caught hold of Martin's hand near her face and began to suck furiously on his index finger. He let her, cradling her and rocking her in his arms while he crooned soothingly to her. She began to calm, still suckling his finger while he stroked her back and her arm and her hair with his other hand. Suddenly, she seemed to relax, all the tension left her body and she let go of Martin's finger.

Paul watched and listened carefully. They had never known how to stop these terrifying episodes, hence the straight jacket or the padded restraint bed they used at home. When Sarah began screaming in the grip of these terrifying nightmares, destruction, shattering glass, and hours of wordless screaming followed, until she finally wore herself out. Martin had stopped it in matter of a few minutes.

Sarah now lay spent in his arms. She began tracing a pattern familiar to Paul on Martin's chest and stomach with her index finger. He didn't know what the pattern was; he had just observed her do this action in thin air after these episodes. She now traced her pattern on Martin's body. Martin had removed his wet shirt, however his pants and the rest of he and Sarah were both so wet that Sebastian brought towels to them.

The hair on the back of Paul's neck rose when Sarah spoke. She spoke in the voice of a very small child. "Can we watch the stars tonight, Martin?" Her finger moved on his chest.

Paul realized she had regressed; in her dream she was that small child.

"Sure, Smallest," Martin answered soothingly. He now began to repeat constellations with her, Sarah speaking in her singsong child's voice.

Martin corrected her finger a couple of times and Paul realized that Sarah was tracing the constellations she was learning on his body. He could tell it was a familiar and comforting routine. They must have spent a lot of time doing just that under the night sky he realized.

Sarah finally dropped off to sleep in Martin's arms. "She should be OK when she wakes up," Martin said softly to Sebastian and Paul. "She'll be back to herself. She just gets caught up in the nightmare sometimes; she can't break free."

"What was that with your finger?" Paul asked. "Why did she suck on your finger?"

Martin made a wry movement with his lips before he answered, quietly, "When she was really little, we didn't have one of those baby things, pacifiers. I let her suck on my finger when she was scared," he said. "It would help keep her quiet."

"Do you know what the dreams are about?" Paul asked.

Martin held Sarah, stroking her hair softly. Finally he looked at Paul and nodded. Then he shook his head and said softly, "Don't wake her," silencing Paul temporarily, but only temporarily, Martin knew.

Shaken by Sarah's dream, his mind raced. Tonight's events disturbed him more than he cared to admit. He thought these nightmares something Sarah had outgrown. She'd had them with terrifying intensity when she was a very young child, then again after Danny had been killed. He was shocked to see that Sarah was still so deeply troubled by them. Martin finally laid the sleeping Sarah down on the bed and covered her carefully. Her hair was still wet. He picked up one of the towels and blotted her hair, soaking up some of the moisture.

"How often does this happen?" he asked Paul and Sebastian quietly in the sitting room of the stateroom a few moments later. He left the bedroom door open so he could see Sarah. Martin picked up the straight jacket still lying on the floor where he threw it. He looked at it a moment, looked at them both accusingly, then walked over to the window and flung the offending object out to sea. He watched it tumble before it hit the water, floated a few minutes, than sank. "She's not crazy," he said quietly, but with heat in his voice. "I've had nightmares like that; they're so real, you feel like you're living it again. She just has trouble breaking out of the dream sometimes. You've got no right to truss her up like that," he said, nodding his head towards the window where he threw the straight jacket.

He walked back in and looked at Sarah. When he smoothed her hair away from her face he saw that the side of her face was beginning to bruise where she had hit her head. He winced and looked back at Sebastian and Paul.

Sebastian had also been watching carefully as Martin quieted Sarah. He spoke now. "We only ever restrain her to prevent her from harming herself," he said as Martin looked at Sarah's face. "She has had these dreams since she was a child. She was much better for quite some time but the dreams began again about four years ago," he said, carefully watching Martin. "They occur with frightening regularity every couple of months or so. We have no way of stopping them. I would be most interested to learn how you managed to calm her so quickly."

Martin looked at them both silently.

It was Paul who spoke next. "My god, man," he said, anger in his voice now. "If you have any idea what these dreams are about, how to help her, you must tell us!"

Martin still said nothing. He finally looked at Paul. "She's really never told you anything about them?"

"She's never told me anything," Paul said flatly. "Not about the dreams, not about her childhood, not about you. Don't you think it's time someone ended this?" he gestured around, "this self-imposed house of pain she lives in. We all love her, care about her, and we've been helpless, helpless to do anything." He looked at Sebastian.

Sebastian looked at Martin and made a decision; he prayed it was the right one. He could see by the look on Martin's face, by his inner struggle, by how he held and cared for Sarah, that he loved her deeply still. Sebastian didn't know why Martin left Sarah four years ago. He'd heard the man's honest confession to Sarah about his sex life. He knew this man was damaged somehow, perhaps as damaged as Sarah. He could only pray that the man loved Sarah enough to try to help her now. "Sarah actually did mention you once a few years ago. You're the 'dark boy with the laughing eyes', aren't you?"

Martin didn't reply but Sebastian could see by his eyes that he struck home. "Your reluctance to speak about this," he gestured at Sarah, "your reluctance to speak of your childhood, Sarah's dreams, it's because whatever it is that happened, what's causing her nightmares, it happened to you, didn't it? You and Danny," Sebastian amended.

Martin didn't answer.

Paul burst out with, " We've had thirteen years of silence! Enough!"

Martin finally looked at Paul. "I'm not telling you a fucking thing, Paul. Not until I talk to Sarah first. You shrinks, you think you can fix anything just by talking about it. Well, you're wrong. Some things can't be fixed, Paul, they're just broken." He was angry, tired of people pushing him to reveal Sarah's secrets, his and Sarah's. "I'll talk to her when she wakes up," he continued. "I'll even encourage her to talk to you. But it's her decision," he said turning away. "Now, if you guys don't mind, I'd like to try to get some sleep too."

Alexander was back onboard early the following morning, angry. He ignored Martin and thrusting a tabloid newspaper at Sebastian, he growled, "Where is she, goddamn it."

"She's still asleep," Martin answered before Sebastian could. He glanced at the tabloid and winced. Sure enough, someone got a shot of the topless Sarah, a terrified look on her face, jumping overboard. Martin didn't even bother to read the headline. He suddenly realized that Al was pissed at Sarah and he felt his anger stir. "Where the hell were you last night, Al? I know Sebastian tried to get a hold of you. Your fiancée had a crisis here and you were nowhere to be found."

"My phone must have been turned off," Alexander said coldly.

"If you're going to turn your phone off every time you're off getting laid," Martin said angry, "you're going to be out of touch a lot."

"I'm not here to discuss what I did last night," Alexander said eying Martin with barely masked fury, "but what the hell went on here with Sarah."

Sarah walked into the room, still in her robe. "What is it, Zander, what's wrong?" she asked, looking around at the tension between the two men.

"This is not exactly the engagement announcement I had in mind, Sarah," Alexander said, throwing the tabloid in her face.

Sarah looked at the paper and went pale. She gazed in shock at Martin then back at Alexander. "I'm sorry, Zander," she said, panic in her voice.

"Don't you apologize to him, Sarah!" Martin exploded. "You think she had some kind of orgy party here last night?" he yelled at Al. "Take a look at the expression on her face in that photo, Al. She was sleepwalking, having a nightmare. My god, you're a selfish prick! Don't you give a shit about her at all?"

"Please stop it!" Sarah was near tears.

Martin backed off but still glared at Al.

Horrified, Sarah only vaguely recalled last nights' events. She'd had the dream, the terrible one, the one in the barn, the one where she was covered in Martin's blood and she was sure he was dead. But then, suddenly, she was safe with Martin again, under the night sky, looking at the stars. The stars were Martin's gift to her, she was sure of that when she was a baby. She was always safe in Martin's arms.

Alexander said, "This is none of your business, Stone. This is between Sarah and I." To Sarah he said, "How could you let yourself be caught in such a compromising position? What were you thinking?"

Martin had had enough. "One more word out of you, Al, and I swear to god I'm tossing you overboard. Get off her back, I mean it Al," he warned.

Sarah was devastated. Her plan to help Martin think she was normal, or at least could act normal, was shattered. She was grateful he helped her find her way out of the dream. That was her problem with these terrible nightmares, she would get caught, would be unable to get back to the here and now and her terror would grow. She was afraid of being trapped in the nightmare forever, reliving it over and over. That, or the one about Danny. Memories and fear of those nightmares could keep her awake literally for weeks with just short catnaps until finally her body would give in and she would have to sleep. Now Martin had seen, had seen that she still couldn't control some aspects of her mind. He had gotten a glimpse of what she was trying desperately to hide from him. Sarah was also very afraid that someone else had seen. Flint could see her when she was unprotected, caught between the world of sleep and wakefulness. She only felt his presence. That's why she called him Flint, he was hard like stone and fire sparked off him. And in the twilight world of her nightmares, he could see her. She wondered again if it was possible he brought the dreams.

Her fear grew. Martin mustn't know, mustn't find out about Flint. He had warned her years ago but she hadn't listened, at least not carefully enough. She turned to Martin. "Please let me speak to Alexander for a few moments."

Martin looked at her, anger at Alexander still in his eyes. "You have nothing to apologize for, Sarah," he stated flatly.

She nodded.

When Martin left and she was alone with Alexander, she said with true contrition in her voice, "I am sorry, Zander. You're right, I should be able to control myself better. I didn't mean to embarrass you. I understand if you need to punish me," she finished quietly.

She spoke so quietly Martin almost didn't hear her as he was baldly listening outside the door. He couldn't believe his ears. Had she just said 'punish her'? He was sure she had. He opened the door and walked back into the room. "Did my ears just deceive me," he said menacingly to Al, "or did Sarah just say that you were going to punish her?" Sarah started to speak. Martin held his hand up to her. "Stay out of this Smallest. I'm talking to Al."

Just the look of guilt that flashed across Al's face told Martin what he needed to know. Without a sound, he attacked. His arm lashed out striking hard and as Al bent over, his knee connected with Al's chin, sending him flying across the room. Martin was on him again instantly and with a roar of anger, tossed him overboard.

"Martin stop!" Sarah ran to the rail, appalled. Then she saw with relief that two crew members had already jumped overboard with a life jacket to aid Alexander. He was dazed and only semi conscious, needing help to get back onboard. Martin watched without expression. He turned to Sarah.

"Tell me now what's going on here, Sarah, or I swear to god I'll beat the crap out of him. Has he hit you? You know you can't lie to me, Sarah," he added more gently.

"You don't understand," she said.

"What's to understand, Smallest? It's a yes or no question. Has he ever hit you?"

"He's trying to help me," she answered.

"By hitting you." Martin said flatly. "Some help." Suddenly he saw the bruise on the side of her face, remembered her nightmare, and his anger melted. "Smallest, please just tell me," he begged. "Let me help, baby. Whatever it is," he went to her and stroked her face lightly in his signature touch, "let me help you with it."

She said nothing but turned away and sat down, holding herself close.

"You could talk to Paul," he said gently, sitting down opposite her. "You trust him, don't you? Why haven't you ever told him anything about the dreams? Maybe he can help you."

She just looked at him.

"Sometimes the first step is the hardest, Sarah. Just take that first step." He smiled encouragingly at her.

"Not good advice when standing on the edge of a cliff, Martin," she said sadly. "Where would I stop? Where would I draw the line?"

He looked at her quizzically.

Suddenly it poured out of her; she couldn't stop. "You think I can do this alone, that I'm strong, like you. But I'm not," she cried out, "I'm not. I'm not brave like you and Danny. You think I don't know I'm a freak, a parasite! You think I don't know I drove you away, drive everyone who gets close to me away! At least you're still alive," she said with another half sob. "Maybe you should think about leaving before you end up like Danny and Magnus," she finished, turning away again.

Martin looked at her shocked.

"Don't look at me like that," she said near tears. "You of all people know what I'm talking about." She whirled about. "You act like how we used to communicate never even happened! You think I don't know you hate what I am." She faced him with sorrow on her face. "Alexander doesn't even know about me but he's trying to help me. I know I can never treat anyone, use anyone," she corrected herself, "like I used you and Danny and Magnus," she said, more composed now. "I don't know how to do this by myself," she repeated. "I asked Alexander to punish me when I go off course."

"Like having a nightmare, Sarah?" he asked skeptically.

"Yes," she answered resolutely. " I need to learn to control my mind. You should understand that. All my life," she said more softly, "I've used you, or Danny, or Magnus as my shield, my bubble to view the world through. Like a filter or a peephole in a door, I hide behind you and just take in the images and information I get filtered through you. I have to stop, Martin. It's dangerous," she said. "I don't know why, but it is. I'm doing the best I can," she said. "Don't blame Alexander. He's doing the best he can as well."

Martin just looked at her troubled. He turned and left to go check on Al. He hoped he hadn't done any permanent damage but he still felt the guy deserved what he got, regardless of what Sarah said.

Alexander sat slumped in a chair, an icepack on his face, his elbows on his knees. Stone was unbelievably fast, he never even saw him coming. His head ached and he still coughed up water. This entire operation to uncover Sarah and Martin's secrets was going dismally. He didn't know how it could possibly be true, but he was beginning to believe that Stone was the 'dark boy'; and, in his mind, that was a very bad thing. He looked up as Stone entered the room.

Martin held his hands up in a gesture that said he would keep his hands off but said, "You want to tell me, Al, why in the world you would listen to her and actually punish her? I don't give a shit what she asked you to do." Martin sat down opposite Al and said, gesturing at Al's face, "I'm sorry about that, man, but Danny and I invested a lot of blood, sweat, and tears into making sure that no one ever hurt Sarah. I don't take kindly to anyone hitting her," he said, looking right at Al, "for any reason. You want to tell me what's going on here, Al."

184

Alexander had enough. "Do you think I fucking know what's going on here!" he exploded. "Do you think any of us know what's going on here!"

In his rage he stood and heaved the closest object, a large vase of flowers, directly into the glass back bar full of glasses and stemware. The crash of glass was so satisfying in his current state of fury that he continued to hurl things at the bottles behind the bar until he spent himself. God, he wanted his father to talk to. But, he didn't have him anymore. He would have to handle this on his own. He straightened slowly and looked at Martin who stared impassively at the damage. He was unimpressed.

"You tell me, Stone," Alexander finally said. "You're the 'dark boy with the laughing eyes', right?"

Martin did not answer for a moment. Finally he said, "So what? Sarah had lots of descriptive names for people when she was little. Your father was 'the man with the music in his fingers," Martin said impatiently. "So what?"

"So what!" Alexander turned on Martin, anger flaring through him again. "So, you're the miserable son of a bitch who likes to use young girls then abandon them!" he shouted.

Sebastian hurried into the room. "Alexander!" he said with a warning in his voice.

"What are you talking about?" Martin said, steel in his voice.

"I'm talking about a lowlife prick who uses and makes promises to a sixteen year old girl but lies to her, marries someone else the day after he promised to meet her." Alexander snarled.

"Alexander!" Sebastian interrupted again, "You gave Sarah your word!"

"I don't care," Alexander answered furiously. "This asshole needs to know what he did to her."

"You better start explaining, Al," Martin said, menace starting to creep into his voice.

"You were supposed to meet her after that concert in California, weren't you?" Al demanded.

Martin slowly nodded his head in assent.

"I knew it!" Alexander hurled another bottle at the bar in his fury. He whirled back, "You want to know what you did to her, you miserable fuck! She had a complete psychotic break! We lost her for over a year," he shouted. "I thought we lost her for good." He jabbed his finger at Martin. "And you just walked away, got fucking married to the woman you already impregnated before you even left Sarah!"

Martin looked at Sebastian in shock. "Is this true?" he asked him.

Sebastian nodded slowly. "She didn't speak for that entire time," he added. "The last thing she said before we lost her was, 'the dark boy with the laughing eyes is gone and he means to never return," Sebastian finished.

Martin said nothing, just stared at Sebastian still in shock.

"Didn't speak!" Alexander was incredulous. "She didn't so much as blink her eyes for a goddamn year! We had to feed her, bathe her, exercise her. Then, when she did finally come back to us, so did the damn nightmares, the screaming, the suicide attempts." He was suddenly very tired. He looked at Stone, shaking his head. "And you want me to tell you what's going on here. I ought to strangle you with my bare hands," he finished, sitting down exhausted.

There was silence in the room. Will had joined them at the sound of raised voices. He now stood quietly as well. Some things were beginning to make sense. His heart ached for his partner, his partner and that strange girl he was somehow attached to.

Martin was stunned by the revelation of what had happened to Sarah. He couldn't believe it. He had been proud of himself when he walked away from Sarah; positive he was doing the best thing for her. During all the pain of the last four years, he had thought only of his own struggle to stay away from her. It had been so difficult, he had almost ended his own life a few times. He was careful to never listen to her music, to change the station on the radio when he heard her voice. He had ended up cutting all music from his life; it was just too painful a reminder of her. He never looked at her image when he glimpsed videos Will's kids were watching. He only allowed himself to think of her for a few minutes upon waking each morning. That was his indulgence, wondering how her day was, what she was doing. That, and his sexual fantasies of her. When he could bear it no longer, he would close himself up in his small home and give rein to his thoughts of her.

He realized now he had deluded himself. He had bought the fairy tale Sarah fed him about how much better her MCS was, how she was no longer bothered by the nightmares. He realized now, she began telling him those things when she developed her crush on him. She wanted him to believe she was grown up, outgrowing these issues.

Martin was devastated. Oh my god, how could he have been so selfish, so blind. Never once thinking of the hell she must be going through, believing she was something and someone completely different just because he saw her on the stage that night.

Suddenly Sarah was there, in the doorway. She looked at Alexander with reproach in her eyes. "You have never done anything more despicable in your life."

"What, the truth, Sarah?" Alexander answered. "Don't you think it's about time he knew the truth?"

"You want him to believe it's his fault. That somehow Martin is responsible for what happened to me. Well, he's not," she said. "None of this is his fault. I'm sorry I didn't tell you," she said to Martin, "but when you first came back, I didn't understand why you wanted to go to New York with me, spend time with me. At first I thought it was a test, you know," she laughed nervously, "you wanted to see if I could be normal. And I wanted to be, I really did try," she said. "But then, after awhile, I thought that maybe you were here because you were angry with me." At the questioning look in his eye, she said, "You were so distant at first. But now," she said, a slight quiver in her voice, "now I think you're just here, just staying because you pity me," she said, her voice small, the hurt evident. "That's the worst of all, Martin," she said, looking at him with pain in her eyes. "I don't want your pity." She turned away. She would not cry, she would not let Martin see her cry.

Martin went to her, tried to embrace her, but she pulled away. He persisted, gathering her into his arms. "Sarah," he said, looking into her face. "I don't pity you, Smallest. I love you," he said simply. "I always have."

Sarah pulled away. "But you chose her," she said, her voice full of pain. "You barely knew her, but you chose her! You gave her your baby! You wouldn't even touch me!"

"Sarah, please," he pleaded, trying to reason with her. "You were only sixteen, hell, fifteen when I left for that last deployment. There are some lines a man just doesn't cross, Sarah," he said quietly. "Not if he wants to live with himself.

And I didn't marry Becky because I was in love with her," he continued. "You're right, I barely knew her. And Drew wasn't my baby, Sarah," he continued quietly. "I hadn't seen Becky in over a year when I married her. She looked me up when I got back. She was in a bind, the baby's father left."

He was silent a long moment. "I guess I was desperate. I couldn't think of how to live without you," he said with a strained laugh, running his hand through his hair. "It suddenly seemed like a solution. I would marry Becky, we'd raise the baby, have more babies. Guess I must have been temporarily insane."

He looked at Sarah again and said quietly. "Becky was a nice girl. I don't want you to get the wrong idea. I just didn't love her. It was a disaster from the beginning. That's why I still wear the ring, to remind myself not to do that to anyone else ever again.

I don't know if you can forgive me, Sarah," he continued quietly, "but, oh Smallest, I never wanted to hurt you. Never." He looked at her, his eyes beseeching hers for understanding, forgiveness.

Sarah was astonished. So Martin hadn't left because he was in love with Becky, it wasn't even his child. Her heart contracted as she thought of Martin's pain, his struggle during the last four years. She realized they had both caused each other pain; deep, lasting, wrenching pain. As much as she considered her mind reading to be the biggest of her curses, she wished with all her heart she could read Martin's mind. Perhaps it could have saved them both so much heartache. Sarah went to him, touching his face softly, using his signature touch for her. "I don't have to forgive you," she said. "I never blamed you."

Martin hugged her to him. His mind struggled to assimilate all that he had learned last night and this morning. But as usual, his struggle gave in to this simple pleasure, the amazing comfort of having Sarah in his arms. He would sort it out. He would figure it out. He would take care of her. His heart filled with love and he vowed he would never walk away from her again, no matter what. And he would find this blue parrot bastard. He would find him and stop him before he hurt Sarah. He made the promise to himself and to Danny.

Chapter Twenty-One

It was a subdued group on the flight back to New York. Only Paul felt upbeat, hopeful. There were serious cracks beginning to form in the shell that Sarah and Martin covered themselves with. Paul felt certain it was only a matter of time before it shattered altogether. They were on the verge of something; he could feel it.

Alexander was quiet, for once not working his phone. His mind was in turmoil. What was it that bound Sarah so tightly to this guy? So, Sarah had wanted to push their relationship further. It was Stone who had resisted, refusing to seduce a young girl. His respect for Stone grudgingly went up a notch. But why, why would the son of a bitch just walk away from Sarah after sixteen years? What really happened when he came back from that last tour in Afghanistan?

Sarah sat quietly looking out the window. A small tendril of hope was beginning to bloom in her heart and as much it thrilled her, it frightened her as well. Her thoughts went again to the backseat of the car, that ride back from Graceland. She relived that time again and again in her mind. Her body shivered and her uterus clenched even now thinking about the intense and incredible sensations Martin created in her. She glanced guiltily at Zander, hoping he hadn't noticed her squirm in her seat. She realized only after they were back at the hotel, that she hadn't touched Martin at all in that backseat. Well, she kissed him and held on to him for dear life while he made her shake and moan. But she hadn't touched, or seen, his erection and she realized, flushing deeply and wishing she were sitting next to Martin instead of Zander, she very much wanted to. She wanted to see him naked; she wanted to touch him. She wanted to feel like he made her feel again. Was it possible, even remotely possible that she and Martin could become lovers? She ached with longing just thinking about it. She would have to break off her engagement with Zander, that much was certain.

Martin, too, was in turmoil. He watched Sarah, sitting next to Alexander, and realized he couldn't bear the thought of her marrying the guy. Sarah was his. It was that simple. He didn't deserve her; he knew that. But he now knew something else; she needed him. She needed him and that made all the difference in the world. He didn't know how but they would make it work. He would make it work somehow. He would do anything for Sarah. A homicide cop marrying a superstar, it was ridiculous. He knew it but he didn't care. Sarah was his.

Martin was uncomfortable with the vast amount of wealth that surrounded Sarah. Indeed, uncomfortable with the fact that she apparently made huge amounts of money with the greatest of ease. He wished he could buy a little house somewhere, live like a normal couple, thinking of Will and Tess. But he knew that was pretty much not an option. Sarah needed the space and quiet of Tall Trees; she needed that buffer from the world. She could go for brief periods of time elsewhere, like her apartment in New York, but he could see the toll it took on her. No, it was he that would have to learn to adjust.

Martin thought of his little trailer in San Pedro. It was perfect for him, only about four hundred and fifty square feet, but on the beach. He was used to and liked compact, utilitarian living spaces. He was either at work, on the beach, or sleeping. He didn't have the time or inclination to take care of a house. Well, he thought ruefully, he certainly wouldn't have to take care of anything at Sarah's. It would be like living in a hotel, the place was so large. At least it's a five-star hotel, he thought, but the thought didn't give him pleasure. He didn't like the idea of living in the world of the rich and famous. Then it struck him and his spirits lifted immediately. Sarah didn't really live in the world of the rich and famous. That was Al's world. Sarah lived in her own little world at Tall Trees and sharing that life Martin could imagine.

When they arrived back at the apartment in New York, Sarah was still torn. She had one week left to dance. She wished she could just leave, forget the hated Eve and go home, but she couldn't do that to Yuri. She couldn't take the burnish off his beautiful triumph, for the ballet was a huge success for him. She would honor her word and dance this last week. She knew she should also wait until then to break off her engagement to Zander. After all, it was the agreed upon time frame and it was only a week. But Sarah wanted Martin now. She was consumed with thoughts of him. Watching him workout wasn't enough anymore. She wanted him and she knew he wouldn't make love to her if she was still Alexander's fiancée. Make love, she thought with a shudder of desire. Martin said he didn't make love. Well then, she thought resolutely, he can teach me how to fuck, teach me what he wants me to do to him. She would tell Alexander that the engagement was off. He could make the public announcement whenever he wanted. She wanted Martin's hands on her again.

* * *

Sarah waited in the wings for her cue. Her and Yuri's climatic pas de deux was approaching. She was uneasy, had the sense of being watched. Which was ridiculous because of course she was watched, she was on stage, being watched by many. But her unease grew. Was Flint watching as well? Is that why she felt so ill at ease, so off balance? Was he here in the audience? She pushed the thought from her mind. She had no time to think of that now.

She leapt onto the stage at her cue. She danced up to and around Yuri, teasing and caressing him. The climatic moment of conquest was approaching. Sarah was focused on her task, her dance. Suddenly, as she leapt onto Yuri's body, she felt Flint's naked eye on her. Sarah faltered; she knew she shouldn't but she risked a glance. He was glaring with hatred at her. She saw him full face for the first time. Looked back at Flint for the first time in her life. A terrible truth came to her as she stared at him in shock. Sarah fell to the stage floor as she collapsed in a faint.

Martin, watching from back stage, saw Sarah falter, then fall. He reached her almost before Yuri, who was standing beneath her when she fell. She was unresponsive. Yuri signaled and they brought the curtain down. Martin carried her backstage, Julie already on her way there from the audience. Sarah stirred even as Julie arrived and she came to with a horrid start of fright. Her frantic eyes searched until she found Martin's, then she relaxed slightly and breathed a sigh of relief. There was no question of her continuing. She was shaken to the core, still trembling, cold, clammy. "I just want to go home, Julie," she'd answered softly.

"Sarah, what is it? What happened?" Martin asked her quietly, but she just looked at him, her eyes huge and fathomless. Sarah was quiet all the way back to the apartment, watching Martin, but saying nothing. Julie and Paul accompanied them back.

Alexander was there when they arrived, waiting with Sebastian and Jonathan. Sarah turned away from the look of concern on everyone's face and headed towards her suite. Martin followed frowning, everyone else trailed behind. Sarah turned to Martin and looked at him a long moment before she said, "I'm sorry, Martin. You need to leave now."

Martin looked at her with a question in his eyes. "What?"

Sarah's eyes glittered with unshed tears but she said resolutely, "You and your friend, Will. You need to leave. You need to go back home." At Martin's shake of his head, she added, "You said you would only leave if I asked you to. Please, Martin," she said, pleading now, "I'm asking you to leave."

"What are you talking about, Sarah?" Martin said. "I'm not going anywhere, Smallest. What happened? Why are you saying this?"

"Martin, please!" Sarah said, command in her voice. "I'm sorry; I can't explain. You'll just have to trust me. You and your friend need to leave, now. As soon as possible."

Martin just stared at her. She looked back trying to look firm, in command, but her hands were shaking. She tucked them in her pockets.

Martin said, "This is about the blue parrot, isn't it Sarah? You've remembered something. You need to tell me," he commanded, taking her arm as she tried to turn away. "Damn it, Sarah, I am not leaving here," he said heatedly. "You had better tell me what's going on."

"I was wrong. I made a mistake. I should never have let you come here," she said, turning away from him. "You have to leave," she repeated. "You and Will, you both have to leave." She turned to Alexander. "Please, Alexander, tell them. Tell them they have to go."

"He doesn't tell me jack shit," Martin said, pointing at Al. "You had better start talking, Sarah," he warned. "I'm not going anywhere until you do. Is this about the blue parrot?" He left the question hanging. "I'm not going anywhere as long as you're still in danger, Sarah."

Sarah finally turned to him. "You don't understand," she said heatedly. "I'm not in danger. I never was."

It's you, it's you he's after, Martin, she thought to herself with a new stab of fear. *And I've led him straight to you.* Her heart squeezed with fear for Martin.

She adopted her haughtiest demeanor and called on her best acting skills. "I'm such an idiot," she said. "I just wanted to renew our old friendship. But you're right Martin. We live in two different worlds. I could never live in your world and you don't fit in mine," she said coolly, all the while thinking, *I never meant to put you in danger. Maybe it's not too late; maybe if you leave now it won't be too late.* She knew now that Flint was searching for the blue parrot. He was obsessed with the blue parrot and he passed his obsession along to his acolytes. But had he seen Martin yet? She didn't think so, she prayed not. She wasn't kidding; she was an idiot. She hadn't grasped the significance of the blue parrot until she saw Flint, saw his mind's obsession. She couldn't let Martin remember, it was far too dangerous.

"Now?" Martin said, incredulous. "You want to have this conversation now?"

Sarah's anxiety grew in leaps and bounds. Martin was going to be difficult about this. She should have known, since when did he ever let anything scare him off? How to get him to leave? She turned to Alexander. "Please Zander," she pleaded, "you have to make them leave."

Alexander looked at her, his concern evident on his face. "Sarah, maybe you'd better explain what's going on here. Is it true," he asked, "is this about the police case, the blue parrots?"

"No!" she cried loudly. "And I don't have to explain. Please just send them away," she begged. She went and stood before Alexander, her eyes pleading. "Please Zander, I'll do anything you ask. I'll marry you tomorrow if you like. And I will obey you," she added softly, still pleading. "Please. Just take me home," she finished, "just make them leave and take me back to Tall Trees."

Martin had heard enough. "This is total crap, Sarah. What, you're going to marry him as some sort of penance, punishment? For what, Sarah?"

Sarah turned back to Martin. "Stop! Just stop. For once, Martin, you're going to have to listen to me. I made a terrible mistake; I should never have let you come back into my life. You need to go now, it's not too late."

"Too late for what, Sarah?" Martin asked pointedly.

Sarah bit her tongue before she spoke again. She was handling this badly. "Nothing," she finally said. At the look of skepticism on his face she added, "Think of your partner, his family. You're pulling him into this as well, Martin. Please just go home, go back to your life."

"Pulling him into what, Sarah? If we're in danger, don't you think you owe it to me to tell me what that danger is?" A look of abject terror flitted across Sarah's face and Martin relented. "Sarah, don't worry," he said gently. He went to her and put his arms around her. She was trembling. He looked into her face as he said, "I'm a lot harder to kill than you might think." He knocked on his head lightly with his fist. "Very hard head. You wouldn't believe how many people have tried to kill me already," he said, his tone of voice light and joking. "I'm still here."

Martin looked deep into her eyes and he saw her fear but he also saw the determination there. She's not going to tell me, he realized. His heart began to beat faster. She was in real danger; he knew it. But she wasn't going to tell him. She wasn't going to let him help her.

She pushed away from him. "I'm sorry, Martin," she said softly. "I'm sorry for everything. I never wanted to screw up your life. I never meant to pull you into this. You've made a life for yourself," she said softly, looking at him with love and admiration. "A good life. You have important work that you love. You have a friend, a good friend," she said looking at Will. "You still have a chance," she added. "You tried to make your own family once, you can do it again," she said. "You can live that life you've always wanted, Martin, the wife, the kids running into your arms when you come home, the white picket fence... all of it, Martin. You can have all that."

She turned to Will. "He's your friend, please be a good friend to him. Don't let him come back here. Whatever you do, don't let him come back to see me."

Will said nothing; he had no idea what was going on here.

Alexander was jubilant. Sarah was finally seeing reason. He didn't really understand her reasons for defending the guy so staunchly then sending him away but he was just glad Stone was leaving. No way was he giving that prick another chance to hurt Sarah. And he would see to it that Stone paid for what he had done to her. Sarah turned to him as if she had read his mind. His neck prickled as it sometimes did when he got that uncanny feeling from Sarah, the feeling she had just seen through him.

"Send them home, Alexander. Right away. But you're to leave him alone." There was a command in her voice that he had never heard before. He looked at her and started to speak. She held her hand up and stopped him. "I mean it, Alexander. You are never to molest him, interfere in his life, his career, in any way. You will leave him completely and totally alone. Do you hear me?" she demanded.

Alexander was shocked. He had never seen Sarah like this before. Her feet were planted as she faced him. She was deadly serious. "Or what, Sarah?" he said somewhat mockingly. He didn't know what to make of this deadly serious Sarah giving him an order.

Sarah stared him directly in the eye, her expression defiant and completely serious as she said, "Or I will rip the wings off this little songbird, Alexander. I mean it. Not another note will you ever hear from me again. I will never sing or play music again, not for you, not for anyone."

Alexander looked at her in astonishment as it finally sank in. She meant it. Sarah was completely serious. He slowly nodded his understanding. His world rocked on its axis. He felt unsteady on his feet as he finally faced the truth. Not only was Stone the dark boy but Sarah was still in love with him. Enough in love to send him away from whatever danger she was in. Enough in love to threaten giving up music forever and mean it.

Martin felt panic begin to rise. "Don't do this, Sarah," he said quietly, a pleading note entering his voice for the first time. "Please Sarah, don't send me away." He reached into the small watch pocket of his jeans. He always wore Levi 501 jeans because they had that little watch pocket. He pulled out a small glass heart, about 3 inches in size. It was translucent red with the two halves of the heart clearly delineated. "See, Sarah," he said desperately. "I still have it." He held the heart out nestled in the palm of his hand so she could see it. "I carry it everywhere I go. I've never been without it since the day you gave it to me. Do you remember what you said? When you gave this to me you said we were two halves of the same heart. That's still true, Sarah. You're half of my heart." Martin was unaware of any of the rest of the people in the room. He only had eyes for Sarah. "You have to tell me about the blue parrot, Sarah. You have to let me help you, baby. Please, Sarah."

There was anguish in Martin's eyes, in his voice, and Sarah almost relented. She had never in her life defied Martin, tried to shut him out. But then she remembered what happened to Danny, to Magnus, and she knew she had to be strong. She closed Martin's hand around the heart held in the palm of his hand. "Keep it, Martin," she said softly. "It will always be true. You are half of my heart. I couldn't bear it if something happened to you."

"Sarah," Martin said desperately, "I knew there was something about the blue parrots from the beginning. I know it's important. You have to tell me!" He was almost shouting.

"You already know," she said softly. "You know everything there is to know about me," she continued. "But it's time to lay that burden down, Martin. I'm grown up now. You aren't responsible for me anymore. You've suffered enough because of me. I know what the Army did to you just before you got out, and that was mostly my fault too. I caused this; I have to fix it." She turned away, went into her bedroom, and closed the door.

Martin stared at the heart in his hand in shock. She was dismissing him, sending him away. His mind recoiled. I know about the blue parrot, he thought? How? He'd been thinking a lot about those damn parrots. They disturbed him, disturbed him deeply. Why? He didn't know. He just knew it was somehow connected to Danny. He realized that Al was saying something. He turned to him.

"Well, that was pretty definitive," Al said. "Sarah has asked that you leave. I'll have Jonathan get you on a flight out right away."

"You can't be serious!" Martin retorted. "She's in trouble, Al, bad trouble and you know it! You can't possibly think you're going to let her handle this on her own."

Alexander shook his head, clearly troubled. "I don't know what's going on with her, Stone. I never have. But she's asked you to leave and

I'm going to honor that. We'll keep a close eye on her," he added, meaning Sebastian and Jonathan, Julie and Paul.

Martin was incredulous. "You're going to let her get away with this?!"

"With what?" Alexander answered. "Firing her bodyguards? Yes, I'm going to let her get away with that. You two are out of here, now." He turned to Jonathan and Sebastian. "Call and make the flight arrangements," he said to Jonathan. "Get their things packed," to Sebastian.

Martin turned in a controlled fury. He stuck the heart back into his pocket and said, "I can pack my own goddamn suitcase," and stalked out of the room.

Will entered the room as Martin was flinging clothes at his suitcase. He watched for a moment then said, "Stone, what's happening here?"

Martin stopped, looked at Will. He calmed down looking at his partner's concerned face. "I don't know. She fired us because she's scared. She thinks I'm going to die like Danny did."

They packed the rest of their belongings quietly. Martin tried to say goodbye to Sarah but she refused to see him. That hurt; that cut deep. Sitting in the back seat of the car being driven by Max to the airport, Martin pulled the heart out of his pocket and looked at it again. His head ached. He was sick, sick at heart, nauseous, and deeply afraid for Sarah. Martin could not remember the last time he had cried; certainly it had been back in his childhood, back when he had learned just how useless tears were. Still, his throat thickened and he felt he couldn't swallow and the tears came unbidden. He looked out the window, away from Will, and let the tears fall.

Will remembered the last time he had seen that heart. He knew his partner carried it always but he hadn't known it was a gift from Sarah. Will always thought it was from Martin's wife but that showed how little he actually knew about this man he had come to love and respect.

The first time Will had seen the heart was when his partner had been shot and gravely wounded in the aftermath of the bust of the huge Columbian cartel. Will had run to his wounded partner to find him shot three times and bleeding profusely. Will tried his best to staunch the flow of blood but he only had two hands and Martin was bleeding out. He prayed. He prayed for his partner, prayed that help would arrive in time, but knew it wouldn't. Martin was only semi conscious but requested that Will pull something from his pocket. It was the glass heart and Will put it in Martin's hand. Stone clutched it and said to Will, at the obvious look of distress on his partner's face, "Don't worry, Will. I'm in the arms of the angel." Will remembered the peaceful look on Martin's face. Then Will witnessed what he privately called the miracle, though he had told no one else but Tess. He decided to tell Stone now.

"You know, Martin," he said, nodding at the heart in Martin's hand. "I never told you what happened when you got shot, when you asked me to pull that out of your pocket."

Martin looked at him bleakly. He no longer bothered to try to hide the tears on his face.

"You were bleeding out," Will continued. "I was trying to apply pressure, but there were too many wounds. I've seen a lot of gunshot victims, Martin. There was no way you were going to make it."

Martin said nothing, just looked at the heart in his hand again.

"You asked for that and I put it in your hand and you held on to it for dear life. Do you remember what you said to me?" Will asked.

Martin shook his head no.

"I remember your exact words," Will said. "You said, 'It's OK, Will, I'm in the arms of the angel'. I thought you were talking about your dead wife," Will continued. "You know, sometimes people say they see their loved ones waiting for them when they cross over. I thought for sure you were dying on me right then. But something strange happened. I never told anyone but Tess this, Stone, not even you; but, after you said that, somehow, the bleeding slowed and almost stopped. Your heart rate slowed so much that the blood stopped pumping out of you. I thought you had died for sure but you didn't. It was like that angel had her arms around you, protecting you. It was Sarah you meant, wasn't it? She was the angel."

Martin looked at the heart in his hand then looked at his partner again. "I love her, Will. I always have. God, I was such an idiot to leave her. She needs me, Will. She's in trouble and she needs me. I have to help her," he added fiercely. "I have to!"

"What are you going to do? Will asked.

"Remember. I'm going to have to remember what happened. She said I know about the blue parrot and I think she's right. It freaked me out from the beginning, I just don't know why. My memory's all fucked up, Will. They gave me a drug, Rhonopol, when they did that last debriefing when I left the Army. It fucked me up pretty bad. My memories from that point forward are fine, but the past is like swiss cheese it's so full of holes. I'm going to have to fill in those holes." He rubbed his eyes, resolution taking the place of sorrow. Goddamn it; his girl was in trouble and he had to find a way to help her. "This is somehow tied to Danny's death. I just know it," he finished.

Max pulled up in front of the airport and Martin and Will got out. Martin spoke to Max brusquely, "Thanks. I'll be seeing you." He then looked into the older man's eyes, deep concern in his own. "You take care of her, Max. Don't let anything happen to her. You have my cell; call me anytime. She's not telling us something, Max. She's in trouble, I know it. Keep your eyes open. Please," he finished quietly.

Max nodded somberly at him. He was beginning to like this cop of Sarah's.

Once in the airport, Martin and Will went to the first class lounge to await their flight back to LA. "First class," Will chuckled, pleased and surprised. "Not as fine as the private jet but a definite touch of class."

"Yeah," Martin snorted. "They fire our ass then send us home first class." He just shook his head; rich people, go figure. Martin sat and requested a drink from the attendant, "A shot of Bushmills, neat, and a glass of water." He drank the shot down, then leaned his head back and stared at the ceiling in deep contemplation.

Will ordered his own drink then called home to let Tess know the news. Will didn't like how things had ended with Sarah but he was glad to be going home. After the strangeness of living the high life with the reclusive Ms. Eastin, he was glad to be getting back to the normalcy of his life, his family, his kids with their feet on the couch, his wife's easy smile, sleeping next to her warm body. It was good to be going home, he thought, as he sighed and stretched out comfortably in his chair in the first class lounge. He looked around appreciatively as he chatted to Tess. At least he would enjoy another first, a first class plane ride. This was living.

200

Chapter Twenty-Two

As they settled in next to each other in the first class section of the plane, Martin in the window seat, Will on the aisle, Will finally spoke. "OK, you've been pondering long enough. We've got the next five hours and relative privacy," he glanced around. The first class section wasn't full and most passengers were already reclining with headphones on. "Let's start on the case of Danny's death. You tell me everything about it you do remember." Will got out the small notebook he used when they worked cases. Martin may have a near perfect memory but he didn't. He liked his notes. Interesting that Martin's past memories weren't intact. He sure had a steel-trap memory now.

Martin looked at him troubled. "One thing I remember differently than Sarah's circle, they think she wasn't there, didn't see what happened to Danny. I know she was there." He was silent for a moment then looked at Will with regret in his eyes. "I'm the fucking idiot that took her there. You gotta understand; I had no idea what we were walking into. It was just what we always did for each other. Whenever Danny was in trouble, I'd grab Sarah, hide her, and try to help. I knew his old man was dead, it wasn't that kind of trouble anymore, but I guess I thought it was Al. His new buddy, Al, was quite an operator and I thought maybe some loan shark goons were shaking Danny down. I knew Sarah saw them, saw which way they went, so I grabbed her and we went after Danny."

"OK, Stone. Start at the beginning. How did you know Danny was in trouble? Where were you, where were they?" Will asked.

"They were on the *Moonsong* in the marina at the University of Hong Kong. That part's easy. The hard part is where I was. I'm pretty sure I was on a ship in the North Atlantic. I was still in training; I'd been in for a little less than six months." Martin looked at Will, frustration in his eyes. "But I must have the timing off, because I definitely went to Sarah at the harbor the minute I knew Danny was in trouble." He stared into space, finally shaking his head. "What I do know is that I was happy

Danny and Sarah were living on the *Moonsong*. They'd been doing that for about six weeks by then and Sarah was doing much better. When they moved on board, I taught Sarah what to do if there was ever trouble of any kind. I taught her how to slip off the side of the boat without a sound and barely a ripple. I taught her how to swim when she was only about three and she was like a little seal in the water. I showed her how to swim underwater to the underside of a dock opposite the boat and to hide there by the piling until I came for her."

"You taught that to a seven year old?" Will queried. "Why? Was there someone after them?"

"No. Not that I know of," Martin replied. He looked at his partner with painful honesty in his eyes. "All this is just between us, right Will?" Will nodded his head in the affirmative. Martin continued, "Danny wasn't a fighter, I was. I was worried he wouldn't be able to protect her if something bad happened. I knew their old man was gone; we didn't have to worry about him coming after them. I was always the one to protect Sarah when their father would go on his rampages. Danny would hide her in our spot and I would come for her, take her deeper into the woods, make sure she was safe. Danny always went back to try to protect their Mom. It was pretty useless and he usually got the crap beat out of him. Martin was quiet for a moment, remembering. "So anyway, that's what I always did. I always had a plan for Sarah's safety."

"So, what happened? Will asked.

"Danny was up on deck, studying. Sarah was down below, getting ready for bed. She was in her pj's but hadn't gotten into bed yet. She heard the men come on board, heard them attack and subdue Danny, and she did exactly what I taught her to do. She was small; she went through the bathroom porthole over the side and swam to the underside of the dock. She saw them search the boat. She saw them pull Danny off, put him in a car. She got the license, saw the direction they went. When I got there, she was still waiting under the dock. I pulled her out of the water; she was shivering in her pj's. I dried her off and we went after Danny. Like I said, my first thought was that it was connected with Al. After all, the *Moonsong* had been his. I thought this was some kind of mistaken identity mix up maybe."

"How did Sarah contact you?" Will asked. "How did the two of you go after Danny?"

"She must have texted me," Martin said.

"Not thirteen years ago, Stone. How did the two of you keep in touch? You must have been close by if she was still under that dock waiting for you."

Martin shook his head in frustration again. "I don't remember, Will. I just remember pulling her out of the water. We must have driven to go after Danny. I can't remember that either. I do remember walking through the jungle and we finally came on this building out there, in the middle of nowhere. Then I heard Danny screaming. I turned back with Sarah and took her about three or four hundred yards away and stashed her in a hiding place under some bushes and told her not to move. I went to check it out.

It was some kind of warehouse makeshift medical clinic. They had Danny strapped down to a gurney. There were four guys with guns standing around and one blonde son-of-a-bitch with a ponytail and pale blue eyes, almost an albino. He was working Danny over." Martin grabbed Will's notepad and began to sketch. "I'll never forget that son-of-a-bitch's face," he said as he sketched a cruel face with hard planes, a high forehead, hair pulled back into a ponytail, cold eyes. "He looked like he was about early 30's maybe, about 6' in height, lean, maybe 180, 185 lbs. There were five of them and they were armed. I was unarmed and alone. I knew I had to create a diversion, get them to leave Danny if I wanted any chance of getting him out of there."

"Were they questioning him?" Will asked. "Did they say anything?"

"Yeah," Martin answered. "Something about subject L18, who was L18?"

"What does that mean?" Will asked.

Martin shook his head. "Then the blonde guy injected Danny with a hypo of something and pulled him off the gurney and to his feet. He told Danny, 'You'll tell me what I want to know. You won't be able to help yourself.' He had some kind of an Eastern European, Slavic accent."

"And then I watched Danny do it," Martin said quietly. "I tried making noise to draw them away but only two of them went. The blonde guy with the knife stayed on Danny. He questioned Danny again, this time with the blade of the knife held at Danny's gut. Danny fell forward on it then dropped to his knees. He gutted himself, Will, rather than tell that guy what he wanted to know.

I rushed the blonde guy but there were still two more armed guys in the room. I got them then I ran to Danny. I pulled him into the light but I could tell he was dying. He'd pretty much been disemboweled. Then the blonde guy was on me and we fought. He ran and like an idiot I went after him. I didn't catch him. He had a helicopter and he was gone. I went back to Danny and found Sarah holding him in her lap. She was covered in his blood and she was trying to hold him together. God," Martin covered his eyes. "I will never forgive myself for taking her there. Jesus, Will. He died in her arms." Martin looked at his partner, pain and grief on his face. "She still has nightmares about that night to this day. That's why she started screaming on the yacht. She looked down at herself and she was covered in Danny's blood again."

Will said nothing for a moment, then said, "We all have something we'd like to change in hindsight, Stone. None of us have a crystal ball to see how things are going to turn out. You did the best you could. What happened next?"

"I pulled Sarah away from Danny. She was in shock. I took her off to a nearby clearing, held her, tried to clean her up, and tried to figure out what the hell was going on." Martin was silent for a long moment, remembering. "Magnus and Alexander showed up. They found Danny. They went through the warehouse, found the guys I'd killed. After they searched the place pretty thoroughly, they burned it to the ground. Sarah and I sat and watched the fire. Then I took her to their place."

"You didn't let them know you were there, at the warehouse?" Will asked.

Martin shook his head slowly. "I still wasn't sure what happened. I watched them; they didn't seem to have any idea either about what the place was, what happened. Sarah was in shock; she needed a doctor. She needed Julie, she wanted to go to Magnus, so I took her there."

Martin was silent for a long minute. "Will, I said I didn't know what it was about, what the questioning meant, the subject L18. But I think I do. I guess I've known all along, I just didn't want to think that

Danny had done what he did, that he'd broken his promise." Martin looked at Will with pain and fear in his eyes. "Goddamn it," he swore softly. "I wanted to believe that it died with Danny, that it would be over with his death." He looked long and searchingly into his partner's eyes. "Will, you can never speak of this. Not to anyone, not even Tess. I need your word, man. Not a living soul, Will. It's important."

Will nodded. "You got it, partner. I'll take it to the grave with me if that's what you want." He had always hoped he could in some way one day repay his partner for what he had done for him. Martin had risked everything including his life and his career to help rescue Jace. They had been relative strangers then. Now, though he only knew the man for a little over three years, he trusted him completely.

Martin glanced around to assure himself that no one was paying attention to them. Then he said, "Sarah. It was Sarah they wanted. I'm pretty sure she was subject L18. Danny died rather than risk saying her name. He knew he fucked up." Martin looked at his partner again, trying to explain. "He never told me he did it but I'm almost certain he did. I should have known better." At Will's raised eyebrow, Martin broke out with, "I knew what Danny was like; he had to figure things out. I should have seen it coming. Even though I warned him over and over not to, that it wasn't safe, he figured he was smart enough to find a way to do it safely. He was just so fucking naïve," Martin finished bitterly. "He loved her, Will. I'm sure he never meant to put her in danger."

"What did he do, Stone? What are we talking about here?"

Martin looked out the window a long moment before he turned to his partner. "She's different, Will. She's not like other people." He didn't use Sarah's name. He looked around again before continuing. "Danny wanted to test her, test her abilities, the way she uses her mind. He wanted to know what she's capable of. I'm pretty sure he devised a program where he tested her against other subjects. He did a blind study and only he knew who the test subjects were. Thank God for that because the same night he was taken, his lab was destroyed. I'm betting it was pretty thoroughly searched first and only destroyed to cover the tracks of what they were looking for."

"Different how?" Will asked.

"Well, for one thing, she can read minds." He looked directly at Will when he said it and was not surprised by the skepticism he saw there. "I see your face, Will, but I'm serious. It's why she hates to be touched by most people; the information just floods her. But it all comes at her anyway." His mouth quirked in a wry smile. "She considers it more of a curse than a gift, and I guess it is in many ways. But that's why she's so good at reading people; she can literally read them. It's why Al wanted her opinion on Towers."

"If she can read minds, why in the world would she go out on that terrace with Towers?" was Will's rejoinder. "Didn't she know he would attack her?"

"That's the curse part of it, what she calls too much information. Look, Will, virtually every male she ever meets is thinking some version of a sexual fantasy about her. It's a bit off-putting and something she's used to filtering out. After all, just because someone thinks something, doesn't mean they'll act on it."

"So, she can read your mind?" Will said. "Knows every thought you're thinking?"

"Well, actually not me. I'm one of the few people she can't read." Martin stopped for a moment then corrected himself. "Actually, I'm pretty sure I'm the only one she can't read and I'm not so sure about that anymore." He shook his head ruefully. "I'm pretty sure now that she's just being polite."

Will looked at him blankly. "I got no idea what you're talking about, Stone. You're not making sense."

"Will, she was still just a baby when I figured out she could read our minds, mine and Danny's. He didn't believe it for a long time but I spent more time with her. I knew it was true. She started talking early for a baby, then even Danny had to admit it was true." Martin ran his fingers through his hair, his eyes troubled as he looked at his partner. "Look, Will. There was bad shit happening in my life. Things I didn't want her to see, to know. Try explaining privacy to a sixteen-month old baby girl who only understands that you're hurt. It was bad enough that she saw that, I didn't want her to know how or what was happening. So, I built walls in my mind, strong walls that I hid things behind. The more bad shit happened, the stronger my walls became. Pretty soon I imagined a fortress, a huge impenetrable vault that she was never allowed to look inside. The rest of my thoughts she was welcome to and we shared pretty much everything else in our lives. Keep in mind; she was only three when we all managed to get away. From that point on, I didn't have to hide anything from Sarah." He laughed softly. "It really was like we were two halves of the same person sometimes. And she was so smart. It wasn't just that she could read minds and therefore absorb a lot of information, but she had a curiosity about everything. I'd say at about thirteen and three is when I realized she was on the same IQ level as me. She's way beyond that now." He chuckled softly again, amazed and proud of his girl.

"What do you mean, she's just being polite?" Will asked.

"Well, like I said, she and I shared everything. We also shared a bond from the time she was born. I can't read her mind but I can feel her emotions, her body's aches and pains. It's like I'm inside her and she's inside me. No, that's not right," he corrected himself. "It's like we're connected by an invisible cord. No matter how far apart we are, this cord connects us. And I can flow through it into her and she can do the same. But, even when we're separate, we can feel the other. For example, I always knew if she was awake or asleep, even if I was on the other side of the world." He smiled at the look of skepticism still on his partner's face. "I guess I wouldn't believe it at first, either," he said, "but it's all true, Will." He looked at his partner and said again, quietly, "It's all true.

So, things were fine with us until we reached a certain age. Then the ten-year age difference really came into play. Danny was a little ahead of me in discovering girls. Well, I shouldn't say girls. He met Julie and that was it. He was gaga over her." Martin made a twirling motion with his hand. "Head over heels. Sa," Martin abruptly stopped himself from saying her name and looked around again uncomfortably. He had never spoken of these things before and had warned Danny over and over again not to. "She," he continued, "was fine with their relationship. As a matter of fact, she was fascinated by it. She knew how happy it made Danny. She liked Julie and knew Julie felt the same way about Danny that Danny did about her. She even caught them in the act one time and I had to explain the privacy thing to her again. But it was different when it came to me. I was eighteen, almost nineteen when I couldn't ignore my body any more and I became sexually active. I didn't want Sarah to know.

It was different for me than Danny," he added, shifting in his seat and looking away uncomfortably. "My search wasn't about love; it was about finding a way to fuck that wouldn't hurt anyone, me included. So I hid that part of myself from her and I never talked about girls. Until that incident I mentioned before. When I broke up with that girl, I was very upset, blown away by what I'd done, guilty, just sick inside. I tried to hide it from Sarah but I couldn't get it all behind that wall. So I finally told her that I had ended things with a girl that I had liked, that I had messed things up and felt badly.

That's all I told her but I sure didn't expect the reaction I got. She was pissed at me, Will." Martin shook his head and smiled at the memory. "Nine years old and she was a female in a snit. She let me know, in no uncertain terms, that I was hers and she was mine. We were two halves of the same whole. We had always said so.

Well, I thought she was adorable; she was so outraged at me. So I said something to her like, 'Smallest, that's true. You'll always be my girl. But not like a boyfriend and girlfriend. That's for grownups. I'm a man now and you're still a little girl. But you'll always be my little girl, you and I are family.' And she let me know that she did not consider me another brother, like Danny. What she felt for me was completely different. I belonged to her and I gather she thought I should just wait patiently until she grew up. I remember she promised me she would do so as quickly as possible, then we could be married."

Martin marveled at the memory of that young Sarah, so earnest as she said those words. "Will, this was about the age that she began to question what she was. She'd been out in the wider world for about two years now and she was beginning to understand that there were no other people like her. She was still feeling terrible guilt over Danny's death, no matter how much I reassured her that it wasn't her fault, that Danny had been the grownup who should have known better. She needed to know that I would never leave her, that I still loved her. I thought that's all it was, so of course I reassured her. I told her I would always love her and it's true. I always have and I always will. But I began to hide things from her again. More and more things. What my missions were about, my relationships with women, all things I thought were in my impenetrable vault. But I suspect to Sarah, it was no more than a curtain. A flimsy curtain she only refrained from looking behind because I asked her to."

Neither said anything for a few minutes. Then Will finally broke the silence. "So, thirteen years ago, Danny runs some tests or experiments in his lab at the University of Hong Kong. These tests are about Sarah's mind reading abilities. You think whoever killed Danny has finally figured out that Sarah was the test subject and is coming after her?"

Martin slowly nodded yes.

"And what does any of this have to do with blue parrots? Will asked.

Martin threw his head back in frustration. "I don't know," he admitted.

"I don't even need to ask who might be after a true mind reader, do I? Will asked grimly. "Could be any government in the world, any terrorist organization, and any other number of whack job cultists. You got any clue which of those avenues we should be going down?"

Martin shook his head. "Not really. The set up we saw outside of Hong Kong didn't look like a government lab but those were probably just the guys sent to bring the subject in. They could have been any thugs; hard to say who they were working for.

"Explain this bond you were talking about," Will requested. "I don't think I know what you mean by it."

Well, from the very beginning, I would always know what Sarah was feeling. If she was cold, or hungry, or wet, or afraid, or happy, I'd know. When she got just a bit older, I realized she knew the same about me. It's a very intimate connection," Martin said. After a moment's pause, he looked at his partner with some humor in his eyes. "She knows what a woody feels like and I know what menstrual cramps feel like." He raised his eyebrows at Will's reaction. "I told you, it's a very intimate connection."

"Everything? All the time?" Will asked incredulously.

"Well, after awhile you learn how to shield some things. For instance, if I was having sex, Sarah wouldn't know that because I would turn away, mentally, so to speak. What Sarah would know is that my heart rate was up, I was excited about something, I was happy, that sort of thing.

Had she cared to break my request for privacy, she could have, but she learned young not to do that."

"How did you teach her that?" Will asked.

"The only way I knew," Martin replied. "Refuse to do some of the things she loved if she disobeyed me on this. No swimming for a week, that kind of thing. It seemed to work and she hated for me to be angry with her. That was usually enough to keep her in line. If she knew she hurt my feelings, she almost never did it again."

"So you talk about this bond in the past tense," Will said. "What happened?"

"I broke it the day I walked away from Sarah at the concert," he said, pain evident in his voice, guilt in his eyes when he looked at Will. "I just wanted her so badly," he confessed. "I was like a drowning man and she was the life raft. She was all I could think of. I only survived that last tour of duty because of her and my fantasies of what I would finally have, Sarah in my arms. All I had to do was get out alive.

God, she was only sixteen years old, Will. She didn't need the train wreck I'd become. And what were the chances, realistically, that I'd be able to keep my hands off her this time? Nil I figured, and I hated myself for being so weak as to inflict myself on her, especially after I saw her perform at that concert. She was perfect, Will, absolutely perfect. She didn't need me, and I knew the only way I could keep away from her was just to surgically cut the bond, walk away and never look back. What a selfish prick," he said, disgusted with himself. "I never thought of the damage I was doing to Sarah, only of my own self-inflicted pain. God, I almost killed her, Will. I almost killed the one person I love more than anything else in this world."

Will said nothing for a while. "So, mind reading." Will finally mused. "I can't wrap my mind around it. Who else knows about it?"

"Julie for sure," Martin said reluctantly. "Everyone in her inner circle must guess some part of it. You can't live with Sarah and not realize she's different in some subtle way. But Julie and Danny did a brain scan on Sarah. I think that's what triggered the whole chain of events. I think Julie didn't realize it, but the medical lab was monitored and that brain scan sent a flag to someone, somewhere, who was very interested to know whose brain scan it was."

"Do you know the results of the scan?" Will asked.

"Not really," Martin replied. I know what Sarah knows but she was only seven when it happened. It took quite a while for her to even tell me about it. Poor kid, she felt so guilty because she disobeyed me. She thought it was all her fault, what happened to Danny. I'd argued with Danny," he explained. "Sarah was distraught, we'd never fought like that before. But I told Danny it was way too dangerous. I knew what our own government would do if they found someone like Sarah, not to mention some other powerful world interests, and it definitely wasn't good for Sarah. I made him promise he wouldn't test her. Then I made Sarah promise she wouldn't take any tests. Any IQ tests or brain scans or anything of that kind.

Then Danny asked her to lie to me. She didn't like it but he was her brother and she did it. When all this happened in rapid succession, she thought it was all her fault, for disobeying me, for lying. God, poor little girl, she was so distraught. She was so sick for so long, thinking she killed Danny. When she finally did tell me, she just confirmed what I'd already guessed. Julie helped Danny use the medical lab's brain scan off record. Both of them were startled enough about the results they didn't know what to do. Julie took the scans to talk to a colleague in the neuroscience department. That was in the late afternoon. That evening, Danny's lab was broken into; Danny was snatched. My understanding from Sarah is that Julie never got the chance to talk to her colleague. He wasn't in and when she went to the *Moonsong* to talk to Danny, she found them both gone, the disarray, the obvious violence. She went straight to Magnus with the brain scans and was there when I brought Sarah to them. As far as I know, Magnus kept them in a safe for a while. He did some research. Then he destroyed them."

"Why? What did he discover?"

Martin looked at his friend and knew he had to make a decision. He had to trust. He desperately needed help and he realized for the first time in his life he was ready to ask for it. He looked into Will's strong black face, sincerity written there. That and respect. This was a lot to swallow, Will's face said, but he was willing to hear his friend out, keep an open mind. Martin took a deep breath and said, "Most humans use less than twenty-five percent of their brain. Really smart ones, like Einstein, use about twenty-eight percent. Sarah's scan lit up like a Christmas tree. She uses about seventy-five percent of her brain or so, just on normal tasks. When she uses her abilities, she uses virtually one hundred percent of her brain."

"So what does that mean?" Will asked. "That she's really, really smart?"

"Yes, but it also means she has unusual mind/body connections that most people don't have. That's why she can dance the way she does. She is totally aware of every muscle, every sinew, every connection in her body and how to use it to achieve her goal. She can control and change her heart rate, her pulse.

She can do things with her mind, Will, that other people can't do. She can leave her body behind and travel just with her mind. Send her energy elsewhere and actually be there. To people where her body is, it would appear to them that she's catatonic. However, she can return at any time, it's totally under her control."

Will shook his head. "You're not making sense, Stone," he said. "How is it possible? You're talking about superpowers, comic book stuff. People can't travel with their minds."

"Sarah can." Martin said quietly.

The two had been relatively quiet the remainder of the flight. Will was torn. Stone was his friend, his trusted partner. He was not given to flights of fancy. As a matter of fact, it was Will who was the more fanciful of the two. Martin was pragmatic. But, the guy had been a train wreck when he first met him. Perhaps he wasn't as stable as Will thought. Then Will remembered his grandmother.

Will's grandmother would have said that Sarah had the shine. That meant her aura was just a bit brighter than others, that she was special in some way. Those with the shine often had the sight. Not that the seeing of things necessarily meant foretelling the future. It just meant one who saw things differently from others. And Sarah definitely did that. Will realized that he'd been thinking of his grandmother constantly since he met Sarah, viewing Sarah through the lens of his grandmother's eyes, trying to understand something about this strange girl that was eluding him. He decided he needed to give his friend the benefit of his doubt.

"OK Stone. Say all this is true. Who's after her? What do you need me to do?"

"Thanks, Will." Martin let out a sigh of relief. "I know you don't believe all this yet. But you will, my friend. You will. I think for now a heart to heart with Julie is in order. I want to talk to her as soon as we can, face-to-face. I have a feeling Sarah is on her way back to Tall Trees anyway.

Chapter Twenty-Three

Thank god Julie at least took his call but her voice was guarded. "What is it Stone? What's so urgent?"

"I need to talk to you, Julie, all of you," he said. "I think you probably have some questions for me, too."

"Why? Why should we talk to you?" Julie asked.

"Did Sarah ask you not to speak to me?"

"No," Julie admitted.

"Then why in the world wouldn't you want to help me? You love her too, Julie," he added quietly. "I know you do. Help her; she's in trouble."

"She won't see you," Julie said. "I've already talked myself blue in the face on that subject."

"I know. And thanks for the vote of confidence. But I don't need to see her now. I want to talk to all of you, the entire circle." At her silence he said, "you know who I mean. And make sure Paul is there. I may need his help."

"OK Stone. I'll make sure everyone is here. Be here within the hour."

"Thanks Julie." He ended the call and turned to Will. "It's on, Will. Jesus, I hope I know what I'm doing."

Martin and Will arrived at Tall Trees before the hour was out. Sebastian led them into the library where everyone was waiting. Martin acknowledged everyone in turn, Sebastian, Al, Jonathan, Paul, and Julie. He paced restlessly. No one said anything for a moment. Martin finally stopped his pacing. "How is she, Julie?" he asked, running his hand through his hair.

"Not good." Julie replied, rising to meet Martin. "She's not sleeping, she's not eating. She's running on pure adrenaline and will power. She's refusing to talk to anyone about it. What is going on, Martin? What's happening to her?"

Martin took a deep breath then just came flat out with it. "Thirteen years ago, you and Danny took a brain scan of Sarah. What did it show, Julie? And who else knew about it?" He waited quietly.

Paul watched as the blood drained from Julie's face and she sat down abruptly.

"Put your head down on your knees if you feel faint," Martin offered kindly to Julie.

"I'm a damn doctor," she snapped back. "I know what to do." But she did lower her spinning head for a moment. Of course, she thought. Martin would know; Sarah would have told him.

"Julie, what's going on here?" Alexander queried. Martin waited for Julie to speak. She finally did. She nodded.

"Yes, we actually took three scans," Julie said, "trying to figure it out. I knew Danny didn't want anyone to know. I actually didn't know it was Sarah he wanted to scan until we started. Anyway, since Danny didn't want any other assistance, I studied and practiced in the clinic so I'd be familiar with the scanner and could do it myself. But Sarah's results were so unusual, I didn't trust it, so we base lined the computer, reset everything, and scanned Sarah again. Same results."

"What was so unusual about it?" Paul asked.

"Almost her entire brain was lit up and engaged," she finally said quietly, looking at Paul. "Always about seventy to seventy-five percent, but fully up to ninety-eight, ninety-nine, maybe one hundred percent at times."

"That's not possible," said Paul shaking his head.

"I know," replied Julie. "That's why we tested Danny next. He tested fine, within normal parameters of what we'd expect to find. So we tested Sarah again." Martin winced when she said this. If the scanner was monitored, the red flag would certainly be up. "Sarah tested off the charts again," she said quietly. She now turned to Martin. "You think the lab was monitored?"

"It's one way they could have found out," he said neutrally. "Who did you show it to, Julie? Talk to about it?" His voice was kind, not judgmental as he asked this, but his eyes were penetrating as they awaited her answer.

Julie looked him directly in the eye as she answered. "No one that day. I went to the medical library to do some research on my own. I did not even pull out the scans to look at them again and I spoke to no one. I was waiting until office hours for my colleague but my own research was making me uneasy. Sarah's results just didn't seem possible. Then," Julie continued earnestly, "when I went to call on my friend, I found he wasn't in that day. So I only asked when he was expected back and I left. I told no one what it was about." She looked anxiously into Martin's eyes. "I was already uneasy about it. I really spoke to no one about what we had done." Martin nodded his acceptance of her word.

"I hurried back to the *Moonsong* to talk to Danny. It was already too late, he was gone, they were both gone," she amended. "The boat was a mess. It had obviously been searched. I was terrified. I knew I had the proof of what they were looking for in my purse. I somehow just knew those brain scans were behind what was happening. I didn't know what to do. So I went to the smartest man I know, my Uncle Magnus. I told him what Danny had been doing, testing Sarah. I told him about the scans, explained what I knew so far, and gave the scans to him."

"Father knew about these tests!" Alexander exclaimed. "I don't believe it! He would have told me."

Martin nodded his approval to Julie. "It was the smartest thing you could have done. Magnus would have done anything to protect her." Martin turned to Alexander. "You and I. We need a cease-fire. You don't have to like me, Al, but I know you care about Sarah. I am not going to let her face this alone. You can help or you can get out of the way." Alexander finally nodded. "Go on, Julie." Martin requested.

Julie nodded. "He put them in his safe. We both spent some time researching those results. Magnus didn't want to talk to Sarah; she was too traumatized. Finally, he decided the safest thing to do was to destroy the scans, so he did. He explained his decision to me," Julie said, "and then asked me to watch him destroy them. He threw them into the fire in front of me and we both watched them burn," Julie said. "I'm sure he never made a copy of them," she finished. "He wouldn't risk Sarah like that. I'm also sure Magnus never told anyone, including you," she turned to Paul, "about the scans. I know I've never spoken of them before now to anyone but Danny and then Magnus. I've never even spoken to Sarah about them."

Martin believed her. She had no reason to lie. "I believe you, Julie. It's just that someone has finally put it together. Someone knows who Sarah is."

"Do you mean that someone has finally recognized 'Sarah Eastin' as the little girl they were looking for on that boat all those years ago?" Julie asked.

"I don't know, Julie," Martin said, a troubled look on his face. "I think so." He turned to Paul. "Paul, Sarah said I know about the blue parrot, about what's going on here. But I can't remember." Martin picked up a sketchbook and showed them some sketches. "I remember a lot," he said. "That's the guy who killed Danny. I definitely remember his face. Have any of you ever seen this guy anywhere?"

They all looked at the sketch. Julie shivered at the look of cold cruelty on the face, but shook her head no. She hoped she would never meet the man who owned that face. She looked closer, so this was the man who killed Danny. Why? Was it really the brain scan? Would that man stop at nothing to get his hands on Sarah? Was he still searching for her after all these years?

Julie felt unbelievably tired. She was shocked that she had told Martin and the others so easily about the scans. She realized she was relieved; it was no longer her sole responsibility. She honestly didn't know what the scans meant, what Sarah was capable of, but she realized she trusted Martin to take care of Sarah. She turned to Paul who sat quietly, thinking about what they had learned.

"I'm sorry, Paul." Julie said softly. "Magnus and I agreed never to speak of it. I guess over the years, it lost its importance to me. It was so hard to believe Danny's death was caused by our taking a scan of Sarah's brain. It was easier to believe it was a random act of violence."

"Julie," Paul replied, "why did the scans frighten you so much? Why did you immediately think of them as the cause of Danny's disappearance?"

Julie was silent for a moment. All of them were waiting for her answer. "I guess because it freaked Danny out so much," she answered finally. "It was as if he realized he made a huge mistake, and if he could have turned back the clock and not taken the scans, I think he would have. I was pretty sure we had just screwed up the test somehow, that the scanner was not operating correctly – even though we tested her three times."

"How was Sarah through this?" Martin asked.

"Quiet," Julie replied. "Danny was upset about it and Sarah didn't understand why. I could tell she was afraid she'd done something wrong. Danny told her over and over never to tell anyone she'd taken the scan. She did tell you, though, didn't she?"

"Yes," Martin said, "but not for months. God, Julie, you know she blames herself. She believes Danny was killed because of her." He turned to Paul. " I know you all believe that Sarah wasn't there, didn't see what happened to Danny, but you're wrong. Danny died in her arms. Her nightmares are of that night, of being covered in Danny's blood."

"That's impossible," Alexander said. "Julie was with Sarah at the apartment in Hong Kong when Father and I went after Danny. She was there with Julie the whole time."

"How was she then?" Martin asked Julie. "What did she say to you?"

"Nothing," Julie replied. "She was very traumatized. She didn't speak at all."

"Was she catatonic?" Martin asked.

"That would be a good description," Julie replied. "She was non-responsive."

Martin said nothing, just looked more troubled and concerned than before, if possible.

"So, you believe Sarah saw her brother's death?" Paul asked.

"I know she did, Paul."

"Martin," Paul said carefully. "You do realize that what you're saying is not possible."

"Look, Paul, all of you, I know you have trouble believing this, but I know what happened. I was there too. And I don't believe that Sarah saw Danny deliberately fall on that knife, but she knows he did because I saw him do it. She'll have gotten that much from my mind, my memories." Martin looked at Julie; she was very pale. "You didn't know that, did you Julie? Danny deliberately fell on that knife rather than give up Sarah's name. The guy who was working Danny over, the guy in that sketch," he pointed at the open sketchbook, "he wanted to know who subject L18 was, who the brain scan belonged to. He'd drugged Danny by then and Danny knew he wouldn't be able to keep from speaking, so he fell on that knife."

There was shocked silence around the room.

Sarah walked into the room. She looked at Martin with reproach, then Will. "I asked you not to let him come back," she said quietly. Will just shrugged and shook his head.

"Sarah," Martin said with controlled heat in his voice, "this wasn't your fault then and isn't your fault now. You have to let us help you." He gestured around at the people in the room. "Every person in here loves you, cares about what happens to you, wants to help you. You trust them, don't you?" He looked searchingly into her eyes. "It's time to trust, Smallest."

Sarah looked at him a long moment before she turned away. She picked up the sketch of Danny's killer, looked at it a moment without expression, then tossed it in the fire.

Martin sighed with exasperation and straightened his shoulders. "It doesn't matter, Sarah. I'll just draw another," he said dryly, picking up the sketchbook. "I'm going to keep drawing and working with Paul until I remember. It would be faster if you would help, but I'll do it myself if I have to." Martin stared her down.

"You do remember, Martin," she finally said softly. "You just don't believe it. Go home. You should go home." She looked around the room. "You ask if I trust these people. The answer is yes; I love them and I trust them. And you have just put them all in jeopardy, Martin. You have to leave this alone. Please."

"You know I won't, Sarah," he said flatly. "You say we're all in jeopardy? Well then, information would be helpful. We can all defend ourselves much better if we know what we're up against. You've seen him, haven't you? The guy in the sketch, Sarah; you've seen him recently, haven't you?" The fear in Sarah's eyes caught at his heart. "You know you can't lie to me, Smallest," he said softly. "Why, Sarah? Why won't you let me help you?"

"Because this is my fault!" she cried out. "You say it isn't but it is. It's all because of me. You tried to warn me, even as a child, but I didn't listen. I went anyway. Especially after you were gone so much, when you went in the Army, I went all the time, Martin. On my own, when you told me not to." Sarah's face was filled with self-loathing. "This is all my fault. I've led him here. I have to stop this." She straightened her shoulders resolutely then turned and left the room.

Martin stared after her aghast. He looked back at the others. "She's going to face him alone. She's going to meet him on her own!" He was incredulous.

"Who? She's going to meet who?" Alexander demanded.

"The asshole that killed Danny!" Martin retorted, starting after Sarah.

Alexander put up a restraining hand. "Hold on a minute, Stone. Sebastian, Jonathan, keep an eye on her," he requested. "She's not going anywhere, Stone. You want to explain what's going on here?"

"You don't get it, Al. She doesn't have to leave here to meet him," and he pushed past Alexander towards Sarah's room. They all followed, trailing in his wake. No one knew what to say.

Chapter Twenty-Four

Sarah refused to see any of them. She locked herself in her bedroom and asked them all to leave. Martin refused. His angry voice could be heard through her bedroom door as he argued with Alexander about admittance. They were all milling about in her sitting room. She blocked them all out.

She was more resolute than ever in her decision to take care of this herself. She was telling the truth when she said it was her fault. All of her life Martin tried to warn her about the dangers of traveling to Top of the World. She had been so young when she discovered it, a baby really, which reflected her name for the place. She was childlike in her conviction that this magical place, which she had found at the top of what she knew as the world back then, was hers. It could never hurt her. After all, she could leave in the blink of an eye. But Martin knew better. He warned her that someone was watching their journey. He said that it was just a glimpse, more a feeling really; but, it was a bad feeling, an uneasy feeling he got when they traveled there. A feeling that something malevolent was watching, waiting, a predator waiting for prey.

She had the easy confidence of a naïve child, so certain she could skip away before any danger could befall her. She never realized that over the years, she revealed enough of herself that the man was able to find her here in this world. He connected the dots. The little girl he caught rare glimpses of grew up into a very recognizable face. But, it was what else she learned that night, the night that she finally looked at him when she was on the stage, that frightened her so deeply. Flint had a totally mistaken impression about her. He only wanted her to get to the one who was the blue parrot. He was obsessed with the blue parrot. He perceived the blue parrot to be powerful, to have powers beyond his comprehension. He had to be distracted from that. He thought he could get to the man who was the blue parrot through her; she had to get to him instead. She knew she had little chance of besting him; he'd already killed Danny and

Magnus. She knew he was ruthless. But he would not expect her to be willing to die to stop him and she was willing. She would not sacrifice another person she loved, not Martin. Martin had been right all along; she had just been too willful to see it.

She could feel Flint's presence nearby. She felt the internal heat she always felt when she realized Flint was aware of her. Her temperature began to climb immediately. Sarah knew she wouldn't have much time with Martin here. She would have to go with Flint quickly, before Martin had a chance to try to stop her.

Martin paced impatiently in Sarah's private sitting room. He was getting more and more pissed. No one seemed to understand that Sarah was in immediate danger except him and he couldn't explain why or how he was so certain, he just knew. Al was ready to throw him out; he had to think of something, do something before that happened.

His memories were driving him crazy; they didn't make sense. He couldn't seem to separate the intense fantasy life he and Sarah had lived as children from the reality of their lives. He knew there was something important, something crucial he was missing, something he wasn't understanding. But the harder he tried to remember, the more he saw the same frustrating image, a pile of leaves. What did it mean, this pile of leaves? He tried everything, even drew the pile of leaves over and over, but he could draw no inference from it. It just intruded on his memory again and again.

He threw the sketchbook down in frustration. His frustration grew until it threatened to overwhelm him. Martin paced then stopped and willed himself to let his anger go. Just let it go, float away. He took several deep breaths. He took several more. He stared at Sarah's door. She wasn't being willful. She was frightened but determined. She was that brave, scared little girl in the barn again. His mind quickly jumped away from that memory.

Martin looked again at the sketch of the trees, the pile of leaves that was haunting him. Like the final click of a tumbler falling into place to unlock a safe, Martin finally remembered. He looked at the little pile of leaves, realized that was where Danny first laid her as a baby, in a grove of trees, and it all came flooding back.

Sebastian picked up the sketch and looked at the image of the woods with the pile of leaves at the base of a tree that was so troubling to Martin. Martin and Paul had been discussing the sketch, trying to decipher why it was so compelling to Martin. Finally Sebastian said, "You said these woods were woods from your childhood," he gestured at the sketch. Martin nodded. "But you grew up in Australia," Sebastian said. "Queensland, correct?" Martin nodded again. "These are yew trees," Sebastian said. "They grow primarily in Great Britain. Certainly not in Australia."

Martin didn't have time to think about the implications of Sebastian's words. His scalp tingled; he felt the energy in the room change. He whirled towards Sarah's bedroom door and kicked it in in two sharp, swift kicks. A shocked Al and Will followed close behind as Martin confronted Sarah. Sarah had backed up to the wall opposite the window that overlooked the ocean. Alexander looked around; there was no one else in Sarah's room.

"Don't do it, Sarah," Martin warned, steel in his voice. "I'm serious, don't you even think of talking to him. Don't, Sarah. You don't know what you're doing."

Alexander was shocked and pissed. Stone had actually kicked down Sarah's bedroom door! The guy was too much. Who the hell did he think he was?

Sarah's heart was hammering in her chest. Her temperature was rising rapidly; she felt light headed, woozy. She looked at Martin with sorrow; she hadn't meant to drag him into this. "He'll never stop, Martin," she said. "He'll kill everyone I love if he has to, but he'll never stop until I go with him." Sarah's gaze looked beyond Martin.

"No, Sarah!" Martin started towards her.

Sarah froze in place. Suddenly a scream tore from her throat as she was flung across the room like a rag doll. She hit the corner of a dresser with her hip then fell to the floor. She tried to scramble out the way, but unseen hands grabbed her and threw her up against the wall. Her head bounced off the wall with a sickening thud and Martin roared in anger. Bedlam broke out in the room as everyone scrambled to try to help Sarah, but no one could see or touch whatever or whoever attacked her.

Shock froze Sarah's limbs, her mind. She had not anticipated this savage attack. She thought she would be taken to meet Flint. Instead, Flint's messenger had attacked without a word. Her head spun as she tried to hang on to consciousness. She realized with horror that the man was ripping her clothes off of her. She screamed and struggled as she felt him shred her panties as he ripped them off her. The savage blow broke her arm as she attempted to defend herself and the pain traveled through her body and exploded in her brain. She felt Martin, felt him push at her mind as he attempted to bond with her. She resisted. She had to lead her attacker away from Martin, but she felt her world tilt, felt darkness close in, and she felt herself falling.

Martin bellowed in frustration and fury. Adrenaline pumped through his veins; he had to bond with Sarah to help her. He was certain he could restore the bond as easily as he had broken it. The problem was, Sarah had to let him in and she was resisting him. She met with Danny's killer, had let the man's energy travel to her. He couldn't touch the guy unless he was in the same state of energy and he had to bond with Sarah for that. He screamed with rage and impotence as he watched what the guy was doing to Sarah as he broke her arm, tried to ravish her, ripped her clothes off her.

Finally, Martin felt it, his opening. Sarah was losing consciousness, and just before she fell down into the abyss, Martin caught her. He bonded with her instantly and turned, protecting the unconscious Sarah behind him as he faced her assailant. Martin could see the man clearly now. The blond motherfucker was shocked to see him; he hadn't anticipated this. Martin attacked; dealing savage blows to the head then midsection of Sarah's assailant. Ponytail was rattled; he hadn't expected to meet any resistance. He charged Martin. Martin grabbed Ponytail in a headlock, twisted and broke his neck as he lifted and bodily threw the guy through the large window onto the rocks and the ocean below.

There was shocked silence in the room. Martin moved first. It seemed to Sebastian that Martin, who had sunk to the ground in an apparent stupor, was the only person who had any understanding of what had just happened. Martin now crawled towards Sarah and cradled her in his arms. "Julie, she's hurt bad, Julie." He looked at Julie. "Her temperature. It's spiking out of control."

224

Julie came out of her shocked silence. She didn't know what had just happened, didn't understand what her eyes had just seen, or not seen. But the doctor in her kicked in and she crossed to her patient immediately.

"What the hell just happened here?" Alexander demanded loudly. He surveyed the damaged room.

Will finally crossed to the shattered window and looked out at the rocks below. "Well, I'll be goddamned, there is a body down there."

Paul crossed to the window and looked out as well. He felt faint. He was positive he had seen no one else in Sarah's room. But he had felt him. He pictured the bizarre scene he had just witnessed. Sarah seemed to see someone, someone who terrified her. Then, unseen hands attacked her, hurling her across the room. They had all grabbed at empty air, trying to protect her, but the unseen force had a devastating impact on Sarah. Paul looked at the blood spattered on the wall where Sarah's head had bounced off with that sickening thud. He recalled the sound of the bone in her arm snapping and felt even more lightheaded. He couldn't make sense of it. "Did anyone see him when he was here in the room." Paul gestured at the body on the rocks down below.

"Well, he's down there now." Will said, looking at his partner. "I'll go check it out." He headed out to the terrace asking Jonathan, "What's the quickest way down there? Got a good flashlight?"

Martin only had eyes for Sarah. "Julie, what's her temperature?" he asked anxiously.

"104 degrees and climbing," Julie said. "We need to get her cooled down fast. She'll start seizing somewhere between 105 and 106 degrees."

Sebastian ran to the tub and began running cold water. He then left to get ice. Martin carried Sarah carefully to the tub. "Julie, her arm's broken for sure. She probably has a concussion; she took a hell of a blow to her left kidney. Julie nodded. We'll do x-rays and a full body scan later. Right now, we have to get her cooled down. Julie snapped a temperature gauge on Sarah's fingertip then monitored her blood pressure and pulse as Martin carefully lowered Sarah into the tub. Sebastian arrived with ice and they added it to the tub, Martin laving the icy cold water over Sarah's chest and face and arms. She was so hot he could feel the steam coming off her. He looked anxiously at Julie. "It's not working, Julie. Her temperature's not coming down."

Sarah's eyes began to flutter behind her eyelids. Her body began to twitch. She was only semi-conscious, incoherent. "She's going to have a seizure!" Julie warned.

Martin's response was to splash into the large tub beside Sarah. The icy water took his breath away for a moment but then he ripped his tee shirt off and clasped Sarah's near naked body to his chest. Careful of her broken arm, he cradled her to his body.

"What are you doing?" Julie cried out.

Martin ignored her. He held Sarah to him and whispered softly to her, "Let me help you, baby. Feel my temperature, Sarah. Let me help you, baby." He held Sarah to him and rocked her softly in the freezing water of the bathtub. He finally looked at Julie. "I can help her, Julie. I can help her regulate her temperature, bring it down." He turned his face back to Sarah, closing his eyes, concentrating on her. Gradually, he felt her body begin to cool as his began to heat up. It was as if he transferred some of the heat out of her body to his.

Sebastian watched amazed. So, Martin knew what to do about the fevers as well as how to manage the nightmares. He continued to cover the few glass and mirror surfaces of the bathroom with large, soft towels. He wasn't risking flying broken glass, even if it did look like Martin knew how to head off the seizures.

Julie was also amazed. She helped Martin climb, shivering, out of the tub, still cradling Sarah in his arms. Martin held Sarah until her temperature reached almost normal. On impulse, Julie checked Martin's temperature. She was right; his temperature was 103.6. "How do you feel," she asked Martin dryly. "Is that how this works, you transfer the fever from her to you?"

Sarah stirred weakly, her eyes fluttering open. Martin smiled down at her then said to Julie. "I can take it. I just take the edge off. Help her get her own body to reset her temperature. The fevers usually dissipate right away for me." To Sarah he said softly, stroking her hair away from her face, "Hey baby, wake up now. You're here with me, Smallest." He watched Sarah struggle to focus, to become fully awake. She floated away again and he just held her, waiting patiently. Her face was already

226

beginning to bruise and swell where she'd been struck. He winced as he looked down at her frail body, at the damage that bastard had inflicted and was glad he'd removed that particular threat forever.

But now he knew; knew what Sarah must have realized. How could she think she could face this guy alone? He shook his head at her folly, brave but foolish, his girl. But she was not out of danger. Ponytail was definitely just a messenger boy. Flint was still after Sarah and Martin had confirmed something he had only guessed at before. Flint was responsible for Sarah's terrible fevers. When he was able to find her, to focus in on her, he sent heat, terrible heat, the only energy he seemed able to project. He craved to know and understand the power he felt around Sarah and he would never stop until he had fulfilled his terrible thirst. But the ultimate irony was Flint didn't realize Sarah was the source of the power he felt. She was a small, insignificant female to Flint. Significant only because the blue parrot was interested in her. The misogynistic bastard thought Martin had the abilities, that he was in charge. Martin chuckled sourly as he realized that gave him an edge. Not much, but an edge. That's what Sarah was trying to hide. She didn't want him to know that Flint was after him, was waging this war against Sarah to flush him out. She'd intended to confront Flint herself and catch him unawares, kill him even if she died herself in the attempt. Ice cold rage shot through Martin when he remembered Ponytail striking Sarah, ripping her clothes off. The bastard had put his hands on Sarah. Why had Flint allowed Ponytail, his human avatar, to attack Sarah?

Martin turned to Julie. "Julie, you need to take care of Sarah, but I don't want her going to a hospital, not now. Not unless we absolutely have to. She's not out of danger. Flint deliberately had her attacked. It may have been to flush her out of here, get her to go to a hospital."

"You don't think that guy was working alone?" Alexander asked.

Martin shook his head no. "He was just the messenger boy. Flint wanted him to hurt her."

"Who the hell is this Flint?" Alexander was almost shouting in his anger and frustration. He had that surreal feeling again, that what was happening around Sarah was happening in a dream. He looked at Sarah, looked at the destruction in the room again and said, "We can get portable x-ray equipment here and pretty much anything else you need right now Julie."

Julie was examining Sarah's head injury. "That should be OK unless she doesn't come to soon or I determine she has a serious head injury. Right now, her pupils are responding, so she should be OK. Sarah?" Julie began to massage Sarah's hands, her face.

"The fevers aren't over either, Julie. That bastard uses them to weaken her. Keep a temperature monitor on her. I want to know if her temperature changes by even a half a degree." Julie nodded again.

Martin turned to Alexander. He needed to take control of this situation fast. "Al, we're going to need to move that body. I don't want him associated with Sarah in any way."

Alexander breathed a sigh of relief. He'd been wondering how in the world to broach just that subject with the two cops. Will came back into the room. "It's the guy from your sketch, for sure." He showed Martin, then the rest of them the photo he'd taken of Ponytail with his cell phone.

"He dead for sure?" Martin asked.

"Completely and totally dead." Will answered dryly. "No ID on him." Then Will showed them another photo. Ponytail had a tattoo of a blue parrot over his heart, virtually identical to the one George Fulton had only larger. "We any closer, Stone, to figuring out what the fuck is going on here?"

Martin looked at everyone's questioning face and slowly nodded yes. "But not now," he said. "First things first. Sarah's hurt and I'm not leaving her for a second. Not until I get a chance to talk to her and that's going to be a while. Will, can you and Al handle moving the body?" Will started to objec, then just looked around the room and nodded yes. "Take it south of here at least a mile or two and dump him on rocks just like the ones here. Go over the body with a fine-tooth comb first. Find out anything about him there is to find out." Will nodded and he and Alexander left the room.

Martin could feel Sarah beginning to gain consciousness; he felt her as she slowly rose to the surface of a murky pond. She finally broke the surface and opened her eyes. He smiled reassuringly at her. "Hello Smallest." He felt her relief at seeing his face, felt her brief spurt of

228

happiness before panic seized her. "It's OK, baby," he said trying to gentle her. "Don't move, Sarah. You're hurt, baby. You're hurt pretty bad. Julie's going to take care of you." He stroked her hair gently. "Don't worry, Smallest. We'll take care of you." Sarah struggled to move then cried out in pain. "Don't move, baby," Martin instructed, stroking her face gently. "Your arm's broken. Stay still, Smallest, stay still."

"Oh Martin, you don't understand," Sarah cried out.

"Shush, baby. I do understand, Sarah. I understand everything now. I remembered." He gently stroked her hand as he held it. He kissed her hand and stroked it on his face. "We'll face him together, Sarah. You're not in this alone. You and me, Sarah." He stopped her protests with a shake of his head. "Hush, rest now." He looked deep into her eyes. "I won't let him have you, Sarah. I'll never let him take you. You're mine," he said simply. "I'll die before I let him touch you again," he vowed. He kissed her tears away and held her while Julie examined her.

"Sarah, baby, you're exhausted. You need to sleep. Julie's going to give you something to help you sleep. Don't worry," he gently shushed her protests. "You'll be safe, Smallest. You can sleep. I'm bonded with you now, I'll watch over you. I'll shield you from him, Sarah. If I have the slightest hint he's found you, I'll wake you, baby. It's OK, Smallest," he repeated soothingly. "You need to sleep. I'll stay with you until you wake," he promised. "I'll be right here the whole time."

He held her until he felt her body finally give in to her exhaustion and the effects of the drug and she fell asleep in his arms. Martin arranged Sarah carefully on the bed so as not to aggravate any of her injuries and lay down next to her. They had moved Sarah's bed into her sitting room and he could hear Jonathan and Sebastian in the bedroom, cleaning up broken glass and hammering to secure the broken window. "I need to sleep too, Julie," he said, his own exhaustion suddenly overwhelming him, "just for two hours. I just need a couple hours sleep. Wake me in two hours or if Sarah's temperature changes at all." Martin dropped instantly off to sleep.

Julie stared at him in amazement. After all that had just happened, Stone just went to sleep like flipping off a switch.

Chapter Twenty-Five

Martin woke in exactly two hours, refreshed, his decision made. He told Sarah earlier that it was time to trust; he was going to take his own advice. He knew she loved and trusted these people. He would do the same. He needed help; he didn't think he could do this on his own. He knew Sarah was far too frightened to agree to talk to her family, her loved ones. After what had happened to Danny and Magnus, she wouldn't risk it. He was going to take that decision out of her hands. She might be angry with him but it would be done.

Will and Alexander returned. Everyone looked at him expectantly. Paul finally spoke first. "Sebastian, how about you and I make some coffee for everyone? I have a feeling this is going to take a while."

Martin paced, running his fingers through his hair. "I did remember finally," he said. "It was the pile of leaves. It finally clicked into place and when it did, it was like one of those trick pictures that suddenly reveal themselves clearly." He stopped and looked at them all. "Before I go on, I need your word, each of you. I need your oath that nothing will go beyond these walls; that you'll never tell anyone else what I'm about to tell you. I'm dead serious. Consider this a blood oath." He looked earnestly at all of them. "I need your help but I won't ask you for it until you've heard me out. Then you need to decide. But whatever you decide, I need your word now that you won't ever talk about this. That you'll keep Sarah's secret." Martin looked at them each in turn. They all gave their word.

Martin resumed his pacing, running his fingers through his hair again. He stopped by Sarah's bedside and gently felt her forehead again. He took a deep breath and hoped she would forgive him for what he was about to do. He turned back to Sarah's circle. "Everything Sarah and I told you about how long we've known each other, how I helped raise her as a baby, all of that is true." Martin paused before he continued. "What you don't know is that the first time Sarah and I actually met, in the flesh so to speak, was when I walked into Tall Trees the day after she was attacked in Paradise Cove."

There was confused silence in the room. Paul said gently, "You're not making sense, Martin."

"I know," Martin said, a nervous laugh escaping. "And I don't really know how to explain this. It's all so unbelievable that I didn't believe it myself. I've spent years thinking I was crazy but I'm not. I just couldn't separate reality from fantasy with Sarah; but, now I know, it was all real."

"What the hell are you talking about, Stone?" Alexander said impatiently. "You better start explaining what happened here tonight."

"Precisely how did you arrange this little charade we saw here tonight? Jonathan broke in, staring at Martin with a coldly contemptuous look.

"You think I engineered what happened here tonight?" Martin asked incredulously. "You think I had anything to do with Sarah getting hurt!" He glared at Jonathan in anger.

"Calm down, everyone," Paul said, gesturing for Jonathan to sit down. "We've asked Martin for an explanation. Let him give it. You can't believe he hurt her," Paul said to Jonathan. "I don't know what I saw tonight, but it wasn't Martin attacking Sarah."

"No," Sebastian said slowly. He'd seen flashes, glimpses of the man with the ponytail, like looking at a film that was so faded the image was almost gone. Then, when Martin appeared to go limp, Sebastian got flashes of him, attacking the man with the ponytail. "Let Martin speak," he said. "I'm most interested to hear what he has to say." Sebastian poured coffee and sat and waited, an expectant look on his face.

Martin looked at them all again. "My Dad used to say, 'it's best to begin at the beginning.' I can't think of how to tell you this without telling you my story." His voice shook, he cleared his throat. "I've never done that before." He glanced at Paul. "I know this is going to sound unbelievable, but please hear me out. I'll be able to explain what happened tonight. I'll prove what I'm telling you is true. But, this is going to take a while." Martin looked at them.

Paul nodded. "Let's get started then. Begin at the beginning." He gave Martin a small smile of encouragement.

Martin took a deep breath then began like he was reading from a case file. "I was born in Queensland, Australia. My father's name was John, he was American; mother's name, Constance, she was the Aussie. We lived on a large cattle station in a very remote part of Queensland. Part of our land touched on the ocean; the main house and ranch operations were located there. Most of the station went inland, for miles of open rangeland. I was an only kid; there were no other kids for miles and miles. White kids, that is." He looked at his partner, Will. "There were plenty of aborigine kids but I wasn't allowed to associate with them by decree of my mother. I was home schooled by radio." Martin paused, took another deep breath. "My dad was in the military, he was gone a lot. My mother ran the cattle station, was in charge of the ranch hands, the whole operation really. It had always been in her family.

I don't remember much of my real early childhood," he said, looking at Paul, "but I know my mother was never really in the picture. I had an aborigine wet nurse, Maria, who I adored. I remember my Dad a bit from those first couple of years, but it was mostly Maria and her husband, Joseph, I remember. There were about four or five white ranch hands, aborigines did the rest of the work. They had their own little village on the station, inland from the house by about a mile or so. I loved it there. Spent a lot of time there with Maria and Joseph, playing with the other kids until my mother put a stop to it when I was about four.

I don't really remember much about my mother's reasons; I just remember all the yelling and arguing and my father finally giving in. My mother said I was far too old for a wet nurse. It disgusted her that aborigine mothers sometimes put a child as old as three or four on the breast. She didn't want any of the aborigines in the house anymore; she didn't want me playing with their children. My dad was home during this time, so I didn't care that much at first. He was teaching me to swim and was spending a lot of time with me, so I was in heaven. I did sneak away a few times and met up with David, my best buddy at the time. He was one of Maria and Joseph's sons and was about the same age as me. We were milk brothers, the aborigine term for two babies nursing at the same time. Every time I'd get caught with David, my mother would go off the deep end, but my Dad would stick up for me. So, I knew there was this kind of war going on between the two of them about me, but I didn't pay it much mind. I just learned to be sneakier when meeting up with any of my aborigine friends.

Then, right around the time I turned five, my dad left for another tour of duty. My mother told me she was tired of me disobeying her. My dad wasn't there to interfere any longer; she was setting the rules.

I knew my mother didn't like me. I had no idea why but it was just one of those things I knew. I just didn't know yet that she hated me." Martin felt the terrible memories pulling on him, like old, wet, heavy clothes, weighing him down. His hands were getting clammy; he wiped them on his pants. "I did pretty good for the first week or so. Then she caught me swimming with David. Rather, one of her ranch hand spies turned me in.

She beat the holy crap out of me," he said quietly. "She used her fists, then a cane. She beat me so badly, I literally crapped myself, then passed out. She threw water on me and when I came to, she beat me some more. I thought she was going to kill me." He paused, sat down and looked at the floor. Then he resolutely continued. "She threw me in my room with just a pitcher of water to drink and locked me in. I couldn't even crawl for the first day. On the third day, I crawled out the window. I hadn't eaten; I was lightheaded and stank to high heaven. I was still in the clothes I'd crapped myself in. I got on my bike and made a beeline for Maria.

It was like heaven." Martin smiled at the memory. "She took me in her lap and cried. She cleaned me up, fed me, fussed over me. This caused a huge stir in the village. There is virtually no child abuse in the aborigine community. They treasure their children; indulge them. They never, never hit them. There was a meeting and they decided that Joseph, as the head of the village, would go and tell my mother that it would be better if I just lived with them until my father came back." Martin said nothing for a long moment.

"What happened next?" Paul asked gently.

"Instead, my mother and two of the ranch hands came back practically dragging Joseph. I was still in Maria's lap." Martin's voice thickened with emotion as he recalled the events of that terrible day.

"David was standing next to us. My mother pointed at him, asked Joseph if this was his son. When he nodded yes, my mother grabbed David and cut his throat. Just like that. Right in front of his parents." There was shocked silence in the room. Martin looked at his partner, Will. "Five years old," he said. "And his crime was to go swimming with me."

"Jesus," Will said. "Didn't someone do anything to stop her?"

Martin shook his head. "As far as I know, nothing's ever happened to her for what she did. But that was it; her war against me was on. I learned that she would stop at nothing and I knew that I was alone. So, you get the picture of the next five years of my life."

"Did you ever see Maria or Joseph again?" asked Paul.

Martin nodded. "Believe it or not, they didn't abandon me. The relationship just went way underground. The aborigines became my network of spies; I always knew where she was, what kind of mood the bitch was in. I doubt I would have survived without Joseph's help, that and my cave. Joseph helped me find and camouflage my cave, my hide away. It's where I went to hide from her, where I went to recover, to lick my wounds." Martin cast a nervous glance around the room. He couldn't believe he was speaking of those days. He had never done so, not to anyone.

He took another deep breath. "Cut to my tenth birthday. I was in my cave, even more upset than usual. I hadn't seen or heard from my dad at all since just before my eighth birthday. Somehow, I was always sure I would hear from him on my birthday." He shot Paul an embarrassed look, then continued. "But instead, my mother beat the shit out of me again, then informed me that I wouldn't be hearing from my dad. He'd been dead for almost two years and she'd never told me. She saved that little tidbit of information for my birthday." Martin shook his head at the memory. "I had just about cried myself out. I was pissed at myself; I knew tears were useless, but I couldn't seem to help it. I was just lying there, looking out of the cave. I had that floating feeling you sometimes get after strong emotions leave you wrung out. What do you call that, Paul? Disassociation?"

Paul nodded.

"I was doing that a lot by then. Suddenly, it was weird, but I noticed the view outside the cave had completely changed. My cave looks

234

out over the ocean, but suddenly I'm looking out at a forest, a wooded area. I had never seen trees like that before, yew trees." Martin looked at Sebastian. "Well, this finally gets my attention. Am I dreaming? I sit up and my ass still hurts like hell and my nose is bleeding, so I'm not dreaming.

Then I hear someone coming. I see this boy clutching this bundle. He's got a big dog with him, one of those big sheepdogs. He kneels down and rakes a small pile of leaves together with his hands, puts the bundle in it, tells the dog to stay, and the boy turns and runs away."

"I felt the baby, Will." Martin looked earnestly at his partner. " I didn't just hear her cries; I knew she was hungry and alone and afraid. She was just lying there in a pile of leaves with this knitted blanket around her. So I didn't even think about it. I just got up and went to her, picked her up. She hadn't even been cleaned up. Her cord was cut, but not tied off. I used a piece of yarn from the blanket to tie her cord off then used my tee shirt and water from my canteen to clean her up as best I could. I was pissed. Who leaves a tiny baby like that out in the woods? And she was hungry. I had nothing to feed her so I let her suck water from my canteen off my finger.

When the boy finally came back for her, I could see he was in bad shape. Looked like his arm was broken from the way he was holding it. I was holding the baby when he came back. The kid looked like he saw a ghost or something then he passed out. But he had brought a backpack of supplies for the baby, including a bottle, so I fed her, got her cleaned up proper, changed. By then I'd realized something very strange was going on. Who was this kid with the baby? He looked like he was about my age. I'd never seen or heard of him before. I would know anyone who lived near our station. It was the woods that really got to me, fascinated me as well. We didn't have forests and woods like that in Queensland. I knew something bizarre was happening.

The boy, of course, was Danny and when he finally woke up, I was rocking Sarah to sleep. He was acting very strangely still. It was like he couldn't see me. The baby knew I was there; she reacted to me like any baby. Hell, even the dog knew I was there. But the kid couldn't see or hear me and it was freaking him out. He kept looking around wildly, insisting that I put the baby down, and I realized he was afraid for her. So,

I wrapped her in the blanket, put her back down into the pile of leaves, and handed the bottle to him. He passed out again. This time when he came to, I just waited. He checked Sarah over from head to toe. Discovered that I'd cleaned her up, taken care of her, and he calmed down a bit. This time when he asked who was there, I picked up a stick and wrote in the dirt, 'A friend'. Man, you could have knocked him over with a feather he was so surprised.

We didn't really need much in the way of explanations; just two kids getting the snot beat out of them on a regular basis. I don't know why but we became friends instantly. Maybe because I had this connection to the baby from the beginning and because I admired Danny for what he'd done. He got the baby out of the line of fire, so to speak. I gather his old man on a rampage was not something you wanted to see. It cost him a broken arm, nose, and a couple of ribs, but he kept the baby safe. So anyway," Martin continued ruefully, "Danny and I became blood brothers on my tenth birthday. We swore an oath to take care of her, to help each other. He told me her name was Sarah and he left her with me for three days that first time, until his father left the house. Good thing that bastard was gone most of the time. It was pretty horrific when he was home."

It was Sebastian who broke the silence this time. "Are you saying that you were in Queensland, Australia, and Danny and Sarah were in England when you first met?"

Martin slowly nodded his head. He looked at Paul. "What would you say to a patient who told you this story?" he asked.

Paul slowly shook his head in the negative. "It's not possible, Martin. I would work with that patient to try to show him the basis of his fantasy. Sometimes we can believe something so strongly that it seems true in the face of all evidence to the contrary."

Martin chuckled grimly. "I thought that's what you'd say. I guess I did believe I was crazy, but that wasn't until years later, when I got out of the Army. I never questioned my relationship with Sarah when we were young. She was just a part of me. I was bonded with her in some way. I could feel her, sense her all the time. I could go to her and she could come to me anytime." He ran his fingers through his hair in frustration at the looks of disbelief on everyone's face. He wasn't explaining this well.

236

"Look, if Sarah had a nightmare or got scared, I'd suddenly find her in bed with me, back in my room in Australia. She was a real as you are standing there. I'd see her, feel her. Her head would make a dent in the pillow. She'd hold on to me, tell me the bad man was chasing her and I'd comfort her. It took me a while to realize that when Sarah came to me, no one could see her but me. She was invisible to everyone else. When I came to her, she could see me but I was invisible to anyone else. I realized that it was as if our energy was traveling but our actual bodies stayed behind."

He struggled to find the words to explain. "I realized that all the time I spent with Sarah, in the woods, in England, my body was still behind in my cave. I would have appeared catatonic to anyone who found me there. I learned that I had to go back to my body on a regular basis. I couldn't eat with Sarah; I had to feed my physical body back in Australia. If I stayed away too long, I'd come back to find I'd pissed myself. I learned that I could maintain a connection to my body, be aware of it on some level so I could take care of myself.

I didn't like Sarah to come to me in Australia. I didn't think it was safe. I didn't want her anywhere near my mother, near the house or the barn. But she would come to me in my cave. She also always knew when I was hurt or scared or angry." He was silent for a long moment. "I can see that you all think I'm off my rocker." He smiled. "Can't say I blame you. I can prove it."

Alexander sat quietly, assessing Martin. This was the most preposterous thing he'd ever heard. He was waiting for the follow through. Martin was setting some kind of hook with this crazy story, to what purpose Alexander couldn't imagine. "This I've got to see," he said, looking Martin directly in the eye.

"I'm bonded with her again," Martin said. "It's how I fought off Ponytail. You all saw the damage he did in there," he gestured towards Sarah's bedroom. "You saw what he did to Sarah. Did any of you see him? Did you try to stop him, grab empty air?"

Sebastian nodded slowly. "I didn't see him but I caught a flash of something. I felt a presence."

Alexander was annoyed at Sebastian for playing into the guy's hands. "This is bullshit. What are you trying to sell here, Stone?"

Martin looked at Al for a long minute. Then he sat in a chair. "This is what I mean, Al." Suddenly Martin seemed to go limp, he slumped back in the chair. His eyes were vacant then they closed. Sebastian's hair stood on end; his entire scalp tingled as he watched. He did not see but rather felt Martin get up and cross the room. Martin's body did not move in the chair; but, unseen hands smoothed Sarah's hair back from her face, straightened the blanket around her. Then, a vase of flowers got up from the table, floated across the room, and was dumped in Alexander's lap. Alexander jumped up cursing, staring incredulously at the vase, still floating upended near him. The vase floated back to the table.

A pad of paper and a pen moved, the pen writing of its own volition. The pad of paper floated in front of Will's face. Will's face was priceless to see. This is kinda fun, Martin thought, with the same sense of glee he experienced as a kid when he discovered these amazing things. The words appeared on the paper, written by an unseen hand wielding the pen. 'You recognize my handwriting, Will. Is this it?' the words said. Will's hands began shaking. He reached out but could feel nothing. The pad of paper floated in front of his face. He grabbed the pad; Martin let him take it. Martin went back into his body. He opened his eyes and sat up. "Sorry about that, Al," he said dryly, looking at Al's wet trousers. "Couldn't resist."

Sebastian sat stock still, his heart hammering. So this was really it, they were about to learn about Sarah.

He turned to find Paul's confused face, looking at Martin, then Sarah. Paul's mouth was dry, his mind a blank. What had he just seen?

Alexander was furious. He didn't know yet what scam Stone was up to, but if he thought he was going to pull one off on the master of the long con, he was wrong. Alexander bit his tongue, waited, and watched.

Julie felt like she had finally realized something she had known on some level all along. She thought back to those terrible days right after Danny had been murdered. She remembered Sarah's small body, so full of pain and sorrow, racked by terrifying fevers they couldn't control. She remembered how she'd several times had the fancy, when she was sitting up late and exhausted with the sick child, that someone had just cradled Sarah, had just held her and comforted her. Sarah had always been better for a while after those episodes. In her own grief and loss over Danny, she had fancied that somehow it was the spirit of Danny, still taking care of his little sister even after death. Julie had especially felt this because the child had turned to this unseen presence for comfort, had nestled into to it and finally relaxed her little body and slept, a healing and restful sleep. Julie realized with a shock of recognition that what she had actually witnessed was Martin comforting Sarah, not Danny's spirit.

Jonathan sputtered in self-righteous outrage, "This is the most preposterous thing I've ever heard of. You can't possibly expect us to"

Julie held up her hand to cut him off and said, "Wait, Jonathan. I want to hear this." Sebastian smiled encouragingly at her. Julie looked at Martin and slowly said, "I've seen something like this before. You helped take care of Sarah after Danny died, didn't you? You helped with the fevers."

Martin nodded.

No one said anything for a moment. Finally Paul spoke, "Go on, Martin. Pick up where you left off, please."

Martin nodded again but Alexander broke in with, "Just to be clear, you're saying you're in Australia and Danny and Sarah are in England, but you and Sarah can communicate and go back and forth whenever you want." The sarcastic edge to his voice was unmistakable but Martin ignored that and simply nodded yes again.

Everyone looked at Martin expectantly. Martin looked at Will for support. His partner was looking steadily at him, his face betraying nothing. He was wearing his 'take in information, try not to judge it yet' face. The face he wore when they were working a case and got some surprising information, some facts that didn't yet fit.

Martin was heartened and continued. "Well, that's kind of what the first three years of Sarah's life were like. Her mother was very sick; I don't know if she even realized Sarah had been born. There was this woman, Peg, who took care of their Mom and was some kind of housekeeper. Their father was hardly ever there. It was mostly me that took care of Sarah from the beginning, Danny and me. But Danny always had his nose in a book, so it was really me that took care of Sarah. After all, I was bonded with her in that strange way. I took her everywhere with me as I explored their place. We spent most of our time in the woods. And, that's where I always took her to hide when her father was there."

"Is that where the star gazing ritual started?" Paul asked.

Martin nodded. "I'd give her my finger to suck when she was scared. I needed to keep her quiet even though we were a ways from the house. I couldn't take the chance that a baby's cry might be heard on the wind. By the time she was just a year or so, she knew these times we hid out meant that bad things were happening to Danny. So, to distract her, I taught her the constellations. I had a kind of perch up in a tree with a nice opening in the canopy above us where we could see the sky. Sometimes I would sing to her, real soft. When she was about two, I wrote a song about her. She loved that song." He smiled at the memory. "I would sing that over and over to her."

"Tell me more about her parents," Paul asked.

Martin shrugged. "I don't know much more. Her mother's name was Laura. I don't know her father's name or what their last name was. You must remember, I couldn't really communicate very well with Danny. I mean, we could write messages, but mostly we communicated through Sarah. And Sarah was still just a baby. Plus, I didn't spend much time in that house with them at all. Peg was pretty spooked by any suggestion of me; she didn't even really like to be around Sarah."

"What do you mean," Paul asked.

Martin tried to remember and explain as clearly as possible. "I didn't like Sarah to spend a lot of time around Peg, either," he said. "She seemed to think that Sarah was cursed or jinxed or something. I didn't like Peg because of that. It was something to do with the circumstances of Sarah's birth. I gather that Sarah was born prematurely because their father beat their mother. Their mother never recovered from that beating. She was in a wheelchair and just sat and stared out at the sea. She didn't seem to be aware of Sarah's existence. None of this was Sarah's fault, so I didn't understand the attitude and it pissed me off. But I gathered, as time went on, that Peg was afraid. Believe it or not," Martin ran his fingers through his hair with a snort and a chuckle, "I'm pretty sure their father didn't know that Sarah was alive. Peg and Danny let him believe that she died that night. After all, he tried to kill the baby when she was born. They just let him think he was successful.

I think Peg was terrified that he would discover the truth and kill them all. I don't know. I'm not really sure what Peg was so scared of, what was really going on in that house. I do know that everything that Sarah owned, everything that related to a baby in any way, was kept in one small backpack that Danny could grab, along with Sarah, and hide until their father left again. After a few slip ups in the beginning, I was careful never to let Peg sense me, see me touch Sarah. I could tell it freaked her out and that she thought that somehow the baby was strange." Martin stopped for a long moment, staring at the floor. Finally he looked up, looked at all of them in turn. "From the first moment I became aware of Sarah, I never thought of her as strange or odd in any way that was negative. To me she was miraculous, incredible, magical, wonderful, and she was mine. It was as if she'd shown up on my birthday as some kind of answer to a prayer and I was one hundred percent convinced she was my responsibility. I was fiercely protective of her, still am," he said.

"Sarah was only a few months old when I began to realize she could read my mind. She was also pretty good already at letting me know what she was thinking, what she wanted. Danny didn't believe me at first. Actually, he didn't believe until Sarah started talking, which she did at a little over a year old. I didn't realize she could read more than just mine and Danny's mind, until I realized that she knew what Peg thought about her. Danny swears Peg never actually said this in front of Sarah, but she thought that a baby that was conceived in a violent rape, beaten, then thrust into the world too early, these children,"

"are cursed and can bring only pain and suffering." Alexander had cut Martin off and finished the statement for him, his voice raw with emotion, a look of pain and horror on his face. Martin stared at Al in surprise. Alexander sat down heavily. He suddenly didn't know what to think. His mind recoiled from the image of where he had last seen those words.

Paul, Julie, they all looked at Martin and he realized that they were familiar with the statement. All except Will who was puzzled at the sudden change in demeanor in the skeptics in the room. He had counted Alexander, Jonathan and Paul as skeptics, Julie and Sebastian as more open minded, more accepting of what they'd heard so far. But suddenly the skeptics were shaken.

Will looked at Paul but it was Alexander who spoke, his voice heavy, thick with emotion. "Sarah wrote those words on the wall in her own blood when she tried to kill herself." He could still see the terrible words, dripping down the wall; Sarah's look of despair as she turned the deadly shard of broken glass into a dagger and used it on herself. Alexander felt fear squeeze his heart as he looked at Stone. Good god, was it possible that any of this was true?

Martin looked at Al and saw that his resolve was beginning to crack. He also saw that the guy was truly torn up over what had happened to Sarah and his animosity towards him softened just a bit. "What happened?" he asked quietly.

Before Al could answer, Paul interrupted with "I think we should stay on track. Take all of this in order as it happened. Martin, let's go back to your assertion that Sarah can read minds."

"She can," he said bluntly. "Most of you here know it on some level. Even you, Will," he said, "and you've only been around her a few weeks. It's why she doesn't like to be touched. Then she gets flooded with information from the other person. But, this input, this avalanche of noise and information, it's coming at her all the time anyway. That's why she prefers to stay somewhere isolated, quiet, with only a few people close by that she knows and trusts. It's exhausting for her otherwise."

Sebastian sat up straighter. He knew instinctively and immediately that this was true about Sarah. He'd had the uncanny realization that Sarah knew his thoughts too many times in his dealings with her. She had always professed ignorance when he delicately approached the subject a few times and he had never pushed her on it. Now he looked directly at Martin and asked, "How does it work? How does she do it? What can she read?"

"So," Martin said dryly, "at least one person believes me." He looked at Sebastian when he answered. "I really don't know how it works, she just can hear your thoughts, what's going on inside your head. There's more," he said quietly to Sebastian. "She's a telepath as well. If she knows you, she can communicate with you no matter where you are. It's how we communicated every day with no one else ever being aware of it. No matter where I was in the world, I at least said good morning to Sarah, then said goodnight every night."

"So, you're a telepath too?" Will asked, still with a healthy dose of skepticism. "Don't tell me you're a mind reader too."

"No," Martin shook his head. "It's all Sarah. I sure as hell can't read minds and I'm not a telepath. It's just that when connected to Sarah, I can contact her as easily as she can me."

"So, that makes you a telepath in my book." Will said.

Martin tugged his hair in frustration, trying to think of a way to explain. "Sarah can talk telepathically to anyone she wants. I can only speak to Sarah and then only when we are bonded. Look, we're getting off track here again."

Paul nodded in agreement. "Let's get back to how you discovered these things about Sarah. How old was she?"

"She was still a baby when I started learning about how different she is. Look," Martin cleared his throat nervously. "I knew she knew when I was hurt, she just didn't know why, what was happening. I hid that from her. But she knew I was angry, too, full of rage at times. So angry, that sometimes I felt like I wanted to lash out at something, anything. But then I'd remember her, see her, and that rage would all dissipate because I knew I had to take care of her, and that if I let the rage out, it would destroy everything. So, even as young as two, she showed me a way to get away, to escape with her. Go on adventures. Leave my body and my shitty life behind and go amazing places with Sarah, like under the sea in the body of an octopus, or take to the skies in the body of an eagle. We did it every chance we got, hours and hours and days and days on end." Martin shook his head, amazement on his face at the memories of those days. "That's pretty much what our life was like, the first three years of Sarah's life. Hiding from her father, my mother. Me and Danny usually in some stage of broken and injured or recovering. Danny buried in his studies, me and Sarah roaming the natural world like two feral children."

Martin stopped and drank some of his coffee. "I know one thing," he continued. "If I could have left my body behind, there in Australia, and stayed with Sarah permanently, I would have. But I realized I needed my body, needed it to stay alive. My energy was tied to my body. I realized that we had to find a way to get away, all of us, them from England and me from Australia. We had to find a way to be together in the same place." Martin shook his head ruefully. "I was beginning to understand that either Danny or I wasn't going to make it one of these times, they were going to kill us. The abuse level had increased dramatically with my mother. When I hit puberty, she really stepped up her game. Either Danny or I was going to buy the farm one of these times, and that would mean a death sentence for Sarah as well. I didn't think we could take care of her and keep her safe with just one of us. It was tough enough with the two of us. Then, the shit hit the fan." Martin stopped at the memory, ran his shaking hand through his hair. This was so much harder than he'd anticipated. He would do anything for Sarah, though, so he took several deep breaths to calm himself.

"You said 'the shit hit the fan," Paul prodded gently. "What happened?"

"It all came down at once, almost. At their place and mine. It started the day before our birthday, my 13th and her 3rd. Her father showed up and it was bad. Real bad. He surprised them and Danny almost didn't get Sarah out in time. Her backpack was still in the house. It was a plain, navy blue, school looking pack, but Danny was terrified his old man would look inside it. See baby stuff. Plus, she kinda needed that pack. Everything she'd need for a couple of days in the woods with me would be in there. But I took her away anyway, up into the woods to our safe spot.

She was very upset, very agitated. She knew what was happening to Danny back at the house with the bad man. I could usually distract her with music or the stars but she was having none of it. She wanted to help Danny and to tell the truth, so did I. So we went back and I stashed her in hiding outside near the perimeter of the property and I went in to check things out. I was still learning about how far away from Sarah I could get when traveling." He looked apologetically at Paul, then Sebastian. "You understand; this was difficult. I had to stay aware of Sarah as it was really through our bond that I was there at all. But I also needed to see what I could do to help Danny. I had to look, but I didn't want Sarah to see. I thought I could handle it, you know, sort of mentally cover her eyes, tell her to not look; but, I know she saw a lot, either as it was happening or later in my memories. It took me years to learn how to effectively block her seeing my thoughts.

Anyway, I went in and saw that Danny was out cold. Their mother was dead. Their father had finally beaten her to death. I heard

Peg; she was locked in a closet and banging to get out. Their father was pouring and drinking a brandy. I didn't really know what to do, so I decided to let Peg out of the closet. She went straight to their mother and saw she was gone and started wailing. I was checking Danny over again, making sure he wasn't dead. I heard their father startle, drop his glass. Sarah had heard Peg wailing and started for the house and her father had seen her! I was with Sarah in a flash, grabbed her and ran with her, but he started out of the house. He'd seen her. Danny had finally come to. He saw his father start out the door after Sarah. He picked up the hunting rifle and blew him away."

"Danny shot and killed his father?" Paul asked.

Martin nodded. "I took Sarah with me and went for help to the monks. Unbeknownst to their father, Danny had been taking some martial arts classes from two Shaolin monks that showed up in their village. They seemed to be the only adults who realized something was amiss at Danny's and might be willing to help. Peg also stepped up. She made sure Danny and Sarah were long gone with the monks then she took responsibility for what happened at the house. Said she had killed their father in self-defense after he had beaten his wife to death in a drunken rage. Said the boy had taken off weeks ago, she didn't know where. Sarah was never mentioned to the authorities. The monks took Danny and Sarah to China, then to their monastery in Tibet, Sun Tao."

"Is that what Sarah's nightmares are about?" Paul asked. "Are the events of that day haunting her?"

"Not really," Martin replied. "She does sometime dream of a nameless dread, a need to hide. But that's not the bad nightmare. That's what came next," Martin said quietly. "I was supposed to join them, a monk was to have come to escort me. But Danny's father had changed the plan; they had to leave much earlier. I wanted to get away right away, but my mother had other plans for me on my thirteenth birthday." Martin looked miserably at the floor, then at Paul. "I've never told what happened that day in the barn to anyone, but it's what Sarah's other nightmare is about."

He took a ragged breath, then another, steeling himself. "When I hit puberty, about twelve or so, I was stronger, I started fighting back. So, she enlisted her ranch foreman to subdue me. Tie me down. Then, she'd beat me and he'd fuck me." Martin continued to look at the floor, expressionless.

"They moved the games to the barn; she had manacles hanging from the rafters. On our birthday, I was supposed to meet Sarah in my cave. But I didn't show because I was hanging in the barn. My mother had flayed every bit of skin off my back with a horsewhip. The foreman had finished fucking me with his dick and had moved on to using handles of farm tools. I was barely conscious. I knew I was going to die, hanging there in the barn." Martin's voice was bitter, the memories acid on his tongue.

"Suddenly, I knew Sarah was there. I was terrified she was coming in the barn. She knew she wasn't allowed, she must never come near there, but when I didn't meet her, she got scared and came looking for me. I tried to warn her off; I yelled at her to go back to Danny but she didn't. She came in the barn and freaked out when she saw what they were doing to me.

Like I said, I was barely conscious, so I don't have a clear memory of what happened, but she later told me she threw the foreman across the barn with her mind. Just flung him away from me. He landed across the barn on a pitchfork, dead. She grabbed the whip from my mother and lashed her across the face with it, then tossed them both aside.

Then she just turned into a scared little girl. She ran to me, clinging to my thigh while I hung here and bled all over her. I guess I passed out for a while. When I came to, she was crying and had wet herself. She thought I was dead. I kept telling her she had to leave, to go back to Danny, but she wouldn't. She said Danny wasn't here, he couldn't help me. She had to find someone to help me. When she said she would go for Joseph, I agreed immediately. I just wanted her out of there. I didn't understand what had happened, how she stopped the attack. I was terrified that my mother would turn that whip on her.

So little three-year old Sarah went for Joseph and brought him and Doc back. They were the ones who found me hanging there. Doc saved my life. He was an Army buddy of my dad's. Turns out he'd been trying to get custody of me after my dad died. My dad had confided in him his fears about my mother, and when my dad was killed before he could get me away from her, Doc tried. He'd never even gotten as far as seeing me

246

yet, but it wasn't for a lack of trying. Anyway, as soon as I could be moved, he had me airlifted to Montana, then to his ranch, and that's where I lived for the next four years."

"But Sarah was in Tibet." Will interrupted.

Martin nodded. "She was actually still just on her way to Tibet, but Danny carried her unresponsive body most of the way because she was with me in the hospital in Australia, then Montana, almost continually. She was terrified to leave me, she was very afraid I was going to die. And it took me a while to realize it, but she was very, very frightened by what she had done in the barn. It was weeks before I was well enough for us to talk about what happened. I didn't really want to talk about it but I realized Sarah thought she had been bad. That I was angry with her as well as, well; angry at the world. I reassured her that I wasn't mad at her, asked her to tell me everything that happened when she went into the barn. She was full of remorse because she had just thrown the bad man, hadn't even thought about it, just threw him and it killed him. And even though she knew he was a very bad man, she was sure she was a bad girl for killing him instead of just stopping him."

"God, Paul. I didn't know what to do, what to say. I was just thirteen; she was just a baby. I just held her, told her I loved her. That she was the bravest little girl who ever lived. That she did the best she could and that she saved me, saved my life, and I would do the same thing for her.

So, that's her nightmare, Paul. The inside of that barn."

Paul was silent as were the others. No wonder the bond between them was so strong, Paul thought. They were survivors.

"So, the next four years in our life had a pattern," Martin continued. I was in Montana. I talked to my guardian, Doc, about going to Tibet, but I obviously couldn't explain about Sarah so he wasn't buying it. It wasn't too bad, though. I had a good solution. I virtually lived in the high meadow, supposedly watching a flock of sheep, lots and lots of time on my own when I was actually at Sun Tao with Sarah.

Doc let me get away with staying up there in the mountains, alone, since he really didn't know what else to do with me. I was one pissed off kid. A disaster at school; got into fights if anyone even looked cross-eyed at me. But, even though Doc didn't know it, I was actually attending classes at Sun Tao with Sarah and Danny, and taking martial arts classes there, from Master Po. So, I was learning. Doc finally said he didn't know what it was going to take for me to heal from what had happened; he was going to trust me and let me guide the process myself. As long as I passed quarterly tests for school and came down to the ranch to have a civilized meal once a month, then I could stay in the high meadow and educate myself.

So, Sarah and I were both in relative safety and could spend as much time as we wanted with each other in either place. But, actually, it was around this time that she introduced me to another place. A place she called Top of the World. It's like another dimension or an alternate universe. It was a place we could live out intricate fantasies, other lives.

Sarah knew I was angry, angry at everything and everyone but her. She somehow knew, even at her young age, that I needed to get those feelings out, needed to act on them, but in a positive way. She took me to a world where I could be a hero, fight the bad guys and win. Protect the weak and innocent. Direct the rage where it needed to go, to the villains and monsters. We spent an enormous amount of time there as different people. It was there, in Top of the World and with Master Po in Sun Tao, that I learned to fight.

I knew even then that Top of the World was a real place with real consequences. Dead there is dead here. It's not a virtual world but a real one somewhere else. I was always in charge when we went even though I couldn't have gone without Sarah. But she was still so young, that even though she usually chose a character close to my age, usually another boy, I would be the one to decide where we would go once there, how long we would stay, plot our general course. That's where the Smallest nickname really came into play. I was worried that it was too much danger for her and so I wanted to call the shots.

Also, I sensed from the beginning that someone was watching Sarah, watching for glimpses of her as we traveled to and from Top of the World. Something predatory, like a leopard hidden in the grass. It gave me the creeps, but not enough to stop going. It was too addictive, this world Sarah took me to. I learned I could hide her; shield her from those prying eyes when we went back and forth. And when the man Sarah began to call Flint directed his wrath, his fire at Sarah, I could shield her from his heat. He couldn't find her, couldn't direct his fury at her. He couldn't seem to see or sense me.

I warned her not to go there alone; it was too dangerous. For a long time, when she was small, I think she obeyed me, only went with me. But now, I think that's why she feels so guilty. She's been going on her own and he's finally found her. I know she feels that Danny and Magnus died because of her.

This was before Danny died, though, and these were mostly great years. We spent virtually all our time together. Thanks to Sarah, I began to heal. I realized I had developed a distrust, almost a hatred of women because of my mother. But I loved Sarah and she was a girl. She opened my eyes, showed me what honor and valor meant. And, she trusted me and loved me unconditionally. It made all the difference in the world." Martin laughed a hollow, mirthless chuckle. "God knows what I would have become without Sarah."

"I never really told her what my mother and her foreman had been doing to me, she was too young understand any more than they were hurting me. Sarah's afraid of herself because of what she did in that barn." He looked earnestly at all of them in turn. "You have to understand something about Sarah. She's all about love. She reveres it, looks and watches for it in all its forms. She admires love and kindness all the more because she sees, hears, and feels all the other negative emotions that come with any group of people. She's bombarded and battered by them, so she seeks love and kindness and uses it like a balm to help her survive all the rest of the shit the world seems to dish out.

Do you have any idea what it's like for Sarah?" he asked quietly. "It's a nightmare to know and be aware of every terrible thing that's happening right now, out there," he gestured loosely towards LA in general. "Every person that's getting beaten, raped, robbed, abused, taunted, humiliated, right now, this very moment. Those are strong emotions; they call out louder than anything else. And what are you supposed to do with that? Especially as a young child, but even as an adult, what the hell are you supposed to do with that? It's not like you can save all of them. So what is the point of having all the worst of humanity thrown in your face all the time? That's why she chooses to only surround herself with people who mostly personify those emotions of love, kindness, and calm.

The thing I don't understand, Paul," and here Martin looked searchingly at Paul, "is why she can accept that other people that she loves and cares for, people like all of you, and me, have faults, we're not perfect. We sometimes have uncharitable thoughts, do questionable things, but she forgives that in us. In me especially," again Martin chuckled, but there was an edge of anxiety in his voice. "So why, Paul, can't she accept herself? Why does she have this expectation of perfection for herself that no one could live up to?"

Paul looked back at Martin with compassion. "You've told me some startling things tonight," he said. "Things that will take time to digest, to understand. But I do know Sarah very well, her character, her deep sense of justice, her intelligence. My thought is that she understands and accepts that all people are flawed, have a side to themselves that they must overcome, a better nature that needs to be nurtured, for lack of a better term. You've admitted you had, and still have to a degree, some anger issues from your childhood and Sarah helped you to resolve them. My thoughts are that Sarah, too, has some anger issues she has yet to resolve and I think she is deeply afraid of what she might do, what she is capable of doing, should that side of her nature get the upper hand. I'm beginning to understand her desire for punishment." Paul looked reflectively at Martin then said, "I can't imagine what it must feel like to know that you can kill with a flick of your mind. No wonder she wanted someone else to be in charge for awhile."

Paul looked at Alexander and was filled with compassion for him. This was difficult for all of them to understand and accept, but Alexander was still more focused on the closeness of the relationship, the love that was evident between Sarah and Martin. He was beginning to realize that his dream of marrying Sarah was just that, a dream. He looked like a man who'd just been hit by a truck, a truck named Martin Stone. Paul hoped his friend would survive the collision but knew he would never be the same.

"So, you're saying this Flint character caught on to you two from going to Top of the World," Will clarified. "This guy is from another dimension, another world?" Will looked skeptical.

Martin nodded his head yes but added a quizzical twist of his eyebrows. "I know it sounds crazy," he said. "I did think I was crazy for a few years there. When I got out of the Army, after the debriefing I went through, when I began to try to look closely at my memories of Sarah, I got caught up in that. Trying to figure out what was real and what wasn't. Fucked my head up pretty thoroughly because for the first time I didn't believe Top of the World was real. Then I started believing that maybe all of it was a fantasy. Listen, we're going to have to wait until Sarah wakes up and is ready to talk to learn more detail about Top of the World. All I can tell you is that when we go there, we physically leave; our bodies disappear with us. We then inhabit the body of the person whose life we choose to share for that particular adventure, with their permission. Rather like we politely ask an eagle to share his flight for awhile."

"And these people in this other world, they freely let you into their minds, their thoughts?" Sebastian was fascinated and mystified. "Why would they do that?"

Martin shrugged slightly. "Some don't. But most seem to welcome us, kind of like they prayed for strength and courage for whatever ordeal it is they're facing, and we're the answer to that prayer. I'm not trying to say they think we're gods or angels or anything like that," he hastened to add. "Just, it's rather like you welcome thoughts of your father, or someone you admire when you're facing something tough. Helps strengthen your backbone if you feel you're not alone. Helping those people in Top of the World fight the good fight, protect their families, their villages, I guess that's why I became a cop. It's the same compulsion, helping protect the weak and innocent from the bad guys. Pretty simple stuff."

"So, you're saying you and Sarah lived in this manner for the next four years?" Paul had become the unofficial moderator of the discussion. "What was Sarah's life like at Sun Tao?"

Martin nodded. "She was by far the youngest one at Sun Tao, most boys were at least eight when accepted into the monastery. She was also the only female. There were about forty monks, five masters and about one hundred and fifty boys from ages eight to eighteen. Not only were there no women at all living there, women also didn't come to Sun

Tao, it was rather cloistered. So, while she liked it there and she liked Master Po and most of the monks, she was definitely an outsider.

It was weird, I guess, but because Master Po was blind, he was the only one who seemed to see me. His other senses were heightened so he could feel and hear me move. He couldn't hear me speak and he couldn't smell me, but he always knew when I was with Sarah. Also, it wasn't a problem for him to train me, he didn't use his eyes, he used his other senses.

I continued to be the primary caregiver for Sarah as soon as I was well enough. I mean, she was only three when they first arrived. They didn't really know what to do with such a small girl child and their focus was really on Danny. He was a genius and they were determined to give him a decent education and access to as much learning as he wanted.

Sarah was sick and terrified by what had happened in the barn. She'd started wetting the bed and that humiliated her. She was just so much better with me there to put her to bed at night, make sure she didn't drink too much water before bedtime, tuck her in, chase the nightmares away. And I loved doing it," Martin continued quietly, glancing at them almost in embarrassment at confessing his softer side. "Since my Dad left, I'd never had anyone to love or love me back. No one but Sarah, this brave, scared little girl. I loved telling her stories, teaching her things, singing to her. We had total freedom at Sun Tao or in my meadow to explore and we roamed everywhere together. I taught her how to swim in the pond in the high meadow. But mostly, when I wasn't either training with Master Po or in lessons with Sarah, we were in Top of the World. This went on until Danny and I turned seventeen and Sarah was seven."

Martin got up and poured another cup of coffee before continuing. "I was worried about the plan from the beginning. I wanted to go into the Army. I had earned my first dragon," he gestured slightly at the mark on his arm, "but I wasn't interested in earning my second dragon, becoming a Shaolin. They taught me all about fighting, discipline, hand-to-hand combat, and I'm glad that it was the Shaolin who got a hold of me. Their entire martial art form is based on purely defensive moves. The only offensive moves are those to protect a weaker victim. It's never about instigating violence of any kind, it's about protecting yourself and those too weak or young or small to defend themselves. But they had taught me all they could and now I wanted to learn about weapons, modern warfare. I wanted to fight the good fight on a global level." He laughed deprecatingly at himself, shaking his head at the memory. "Seventeen and I'm going to save the world. What an ass. Anyway," he continued ruefully, "Danny got that scholarship and there was no question that he was going to take it. Sarah definitely couldn't go with me but I was worried about her going to Hong Kong with Danny from the beginning. She was used to me taking care of her and Danny could be very absentminded. Also, no one but me seemed to understand what going to a big city like Hong Kong with millions of people would be like for Sarah. She had always lived a very isolated existence, even at Sun Tao. But it was there I realized that she was better at handling all the thoughts and emotions swirling around, all the testosterone of one-hundred and fifty boys," he added with a wry quirk of his mouth, "with me there to sort of buffer things for her. No one really took my objections seriously, even Sarah had no idea what it would mean to live in a city; she'd never been to one. And there weren't a lot of solutions; she couldn't stay at Sun Tao."

"But, it turned out I was right, Hong Kong was terrible for Sarah at first. She couldn't handle it; she was terrified most of the time. When I was with her, I could understand why, see what she was feeling, going through. It was like being caught up in a giant kaleidoscope that has her helplessly tumbling every which way with images and sensations bombarding her from every direction. Every one of her senses was on overload. I could help calm her when I was with her. She could sleep and I realized I was sort of shielding her, like I shielded her from Flint when we went to Top of the World. Problem was, to do that kind of shielding, I have to concentrate on her and I couldn't do that 24/7; basic training is pretty intense.

We practiced with her trying to use Danny as a shield; but, like I said, you have to pay attention to, be aware of the person you're shielding, and Danny was usually somewhere else in his mind, concentrating on the mysteries of the universe," Martin said with a fond smile at the memory of Danny's look of surprise when Martin or Sarah would finally get his attention. "Sarah didn't feel it was right to intrude on Danny's thoughts or into his mind since the connection with him was not as natural as it was with me, and it was definitely one-way. Danny couldn't bond with Sarah like I did. Still, it was better than nothing and then Danny got the *Moonsong* and living there was much better than the dorm housing Danny had at first.

And Sarah told me all about Magnus, 'the man with the music in his fingers'. Sarah had still never seen or heard a piano, so she didn't know what to make of the instrument she saw in the dreams, but she told me all about the man she said she saw making the music. She, too, saw him in dreams for weeks before she met him." Martin looked directly at Sebastian and Paul. "It's the only reason I trusted you guys at all," he said. "But she was young still and I was just beginning to learn to trust her assessment of people. Anyway, she told me for weeks that 'the man with the music in his fingers' was coming to take care of her. She was very confident about this, told me not to worry. She knew I had even considered deserting from the Army in order to take care of her."

"Well, she was right. Magnus did show up and they connected almost immediately. It wasn't a bond like she and I have," he said, addressing his remark to Al. "As far as I know, I'm the only person who has that two-way bond with Sarah. But, Magnus was very interested in and receptive to Sarah. She was able to use him as a pretty effective shield from that moment forward. That's another thing she feels guilty about," Martin added. "She loved him but she never confided how he helped her. God, she seems to think she's some kind of parasite, can only live off of some poor unwitting host. And that's my fault, Paul," he added miserably. "I was so worried about Sarah's abilities being discovered before she was old enough to take care of herself, I urged secrecy all the time. I guess that was just part of my nature by then, but I was also under no illusions of how bad the consequences for Sarah would be if it became known how different she was. Danny was burning with curiosity to figure out Sarah and now he had a university and a medical lab at his disposal. We had our first real arguments ever and I made him promise not to test her in any way. Made her promise not to take any tests, not to let anyone do medical tests on her brain, no IQ tests, nothing. God, poor little girl, she was already far smarter than I was and she was only seven, but she was probably younger than that emotionally, she had been so sheltered. So, you know what happened. Danny couldn't resist and he tested her anyway and he got her to lie to me about it."

"You said she saw Danny die, but she was with me at the apartment in Hong Kong." Julie said.

Martin shook his head. "Remember you said she seemed catatonic, non-responsive most of the time. That's because she wasn't there, Julie." Martin replied. "Her body may have been there, but she was with me trying to rescue Danny."

There was a long silence. Finally Paul spoke. "What are you saying, Stone?"

"I told you, Sarah can travel out of her body," Martin replied. "All those times you thought she was catatonic, she was just someplace else. I took her with me when I went after Danny. I didn't know about the tests you and Danny had been giving Sarah. I didn't know about the brain scan. Danny had promised me he would never do that. I warned him over and over how dangerous it could be for Sarah, but I guess he never really believed me, not until he saw the scan anyway. Then I guess it hit him that I was right; there are people who would do anything to get their hands on someone like Sarah. But when I took Sarah with me to go after Danny, I knew none of this. I thought it was some gambling buddies of yours, Al, and they made a mistake grabbing Danny. I would never have taken Sarah if I'd any idea of what was going on.

Paul, that's her other recurring nightmare. I can still see her, little Sarah, her hair in pigtails, still wearing her pajamas, sitting on the ground, covered in Danny's blood this time, trying to hold him together." He turned to Alexander. " You saw Danny's body. You know what happened to him. What you don't know is that Danny died in her arms."

Alexander looked at Stone in shock. Sarah had seen that? He couldn't believe it and said so. "I saw neither one of you, it's not possible you were there," he said flatly looking at Stone, trying to grasp what he was saying. It was just too preposterous.

"Alexander," Martin said carefully, using his full name for the first time, "I suppose it was only natural that you and I would be antagonists at first. After all, we both love the same girl." He looked frankly at Al. "But here's the thing; I think you do love her. I think you love her enough that you need to open your mind and listen because this is the crux of the problem, this is what all of this has been about from the beginning." Martin gestured at the damaged bedroom, then threw his arms out to encompass it all. "Alexander," he said softly, "we need to be on the same side."

Alexander attempted to stare Martin down but the guy just looked back at him, sincerity and patience written on his face. Either he was telling the truth or he was the best actor Alexander had ever met. Well, Stone was telling the truth about one thing. He did love Sarah and he also believed that Stone truly loved her. Didn't mean the guy wasn't crazy but he would at least listen. Actually, he was beginning to admire Martin's brass balls. Evidently Stone was a guy who enjoyed high stakes games as much as he did. Alexander broke the tension in the room with a small chuckle. "Go ahead and call me Al, Stone. Coming from you, anything else would feel un natural. So, tell us, what is the crux of the problem?"

Martin looked at them all. "Sarah was right. I did know all along. I was the blue parrot."

Chapter Twenty-Six

Martin looked at the shocked faces around the room and understood their difficulty. He had grappled with the mystery of his relationship with Sarah for years and had finally concluded he was temporarily insane. It would take time for them to grasp the truth.

"I was on board the U.S.S. Bainbridge in the North Atlantic in the middle of a dangerous maneuver, but I went to Sarah immediately when I got off the firing range. She was still under the dock in her pj's, waiting for me like I'd taught her. When she told me what happened, I knew I needed to go after Danny right away. That meant I needed privacy and some time alone aboard ship. So, I did the only thing I could think of in a pinch. I wrote that note and took Sarah to your place in Hong Kong. After you guys opened the door and I knew she was safe, I went back to my ship and I walked up to this guy in the mess hall. The guy was a dick and I always just avoided him before, but that day I just walked up to him and without a word punched him in the face in front of plenty of witnesses. The fight didn't last long. No one was really hurt but dickhead; I did break his nose. But, I got what I needed. I was thrown in the brig for twenty-four hours of solitary. I just laid down on the cot and left, went straight to Sarah."

"She was with you, Julie, at the apartment. Everyone else left, acting on my note which was heartening, but I still wasn't sure where you stood in all this, Al." He looked apologetically at Al. "I knew Sarah and I had the best chance of finding Danny quickly. After all, Sarah could leave her body safe at the apartment with Julie and take both of us to wherever Danny was immediately. I just had to figure out how to keep her out of the way once we got there but get in to see what was happening to Danny on my own. I solved that by stashing Sarah in the jungle and 'borrowing' a blue parrot's body so I could fly in and see what was what.

And what I saw horrified me; they were torturing Danny. I had to stop what ponytail guy was doing to Danny immediately, but how? I flew in the window straight at the guy's face and went for his eyes. There was a moment when our eyes connected that he realized that there was a different intelligence inside the parrot. That the parrot was acting on orders from someone else. I don't know, it was just a flash," Martin ran his fingers through his hair in his habitual nervous gesture, "but I think that's when Flint became obsessed with blue parrots. He wants to find out who it was and he's finally figured out that Sarah knows."

"I thought you said Flint was from another world?" Will interjected.

"He is," Martin said. "I'm not being very clear here; sorry about that. Flint is from Top of the World, or at least I'm pretty sure he is. He can definitely see into that world and the nether land that's the entrance to it," Martin clarified. "Ponytail is the guy who kidnapped and tortured Danny and he's the one who attacked Sarah and was killed tonight. But he's just Flint's messenger boy. I think Flint uses him here on good old earth much like we used the people we met in Top of the World. He's definitely on the other side though; Ponytail definitely embraced evil. So, Flint was there inside Ponytail, saw the blue parrot. Flint is Ponytail's master and my guess is Ponytail recruited the other guys to help him implement Flint's original plan, which was to find out whose brain scan that was.

But after that confrontation with the parrot in the jungle, and when I abandoned the parrot and came back to try to rescue Danny and those guys I killed couldn't see their attacker, well Flint became obsessed with trying to figure out the mystery of that blue parrot and the energy that attacked them. Here's the ironic part. The misogynistic SOB has been looking for and spying on Sarah for years and has never once considered that it's her, that she's the one with the abilities. Sarah's right, the asshole is looking for me. He thinks I'm the one with the power." Martin shook his head at the blind stupidity of the man but was grateful for the edge it gave them.

No one said anything for a moment then Paul said, "It makes sense. You said Sarah was a very small child when you first started going to Top of the World. You were the one setting the rules; she obeyed you without question. You shielded her; he couldn't see you. All those things would lead someone who only got glimpses of Sarah to believe that someone else, someone more powerful was in charge."

No one spoke for a few moments; everyone was trying to absorb the incredible story they'd been told. It was Alexander who broke the silence. "Why did you leave her Stone? Why did you walk away, marry someone you admit you barely knew? Why did you hurt her like that? Why did she say that what happened to you in your final debriefing was her fault? Why is it classified information?"

Martin shook his head. "Slow down, Al. That's a lot of questions." He took his time formulating his answer. There was no reason any longer not to be totally honest, at least about his own motives. "You know I was Special Forces. A killing machine for the US government." He closed his eyes and shook his head at the painful memories. "What a dewy eyed, naïve recruit I was. Just like most of us who sign up for god and country. Well, guys like me, we're not supposed to question things. That's one thing Uncle Sam doesn't like in his expensive, highly trained, extremely effective killing machines.

I'd had enough. I made my decision that this tour would be my last. I wasn't going to reup when my ten years were over. When I met Sarah in Hawaii for that leave before my last deployment, I told her I was getting out of the Army. I hadn't seen her in awhile, although like I said before, we communicated, touched bases so to speak, virtually every day. I had been wounded and was recovering at the hospital in Hawaii, so I had some time on my hands. I hadn't actually seen her in about ten months, almost a year. She was fifteen at the time.

I met her on the beach in Hawaii at your place, Jonathan. We sat and talked for hours. It was wonderful to see her again. She was so happy I was leaving the Army. She understood why I joined and she was supportive of the things I felt I needed to learn, things the Army could teach me. But she hated the violence, the necessity of it, the institutionalization of it. And on some level she was still afraid for me all the time, just like when we were kids. So, she was delighted with my decision.

After we talked for hours, we decided to go for a swim, always one of our favorite things to do. Sarah was wearing this little terry robe thing, and when she took it off, holy shit! I nearly swallowed my tongue.

She was wearing this little red bikini, and, wow!" Martin's throat was dry just at the memory and he swallowed now remembering exactly how he felt when he saw Sarah that day. He shook his head guiltily. "There was no way to hide my reaction from Sarah. She knew she scored a hit and she was pleased as punch with herself." He smiled at the memory. " I knew she knew it, but I still didn't want her to see I had wood, so I dove in. We swam awhile while I tried to recover my equilibrium. It seems my little girl had grown up while I wasn't looking and she was fucking hot. As soon as we got out of the water, I hustled her back into her robe and I never met her on the beach again for the remaining two months of leave."

Martin looked at all of them with a plea for understanding in his eyes. "For Christ's sake, she was only fifteen; I was twenty-five. I told you, our bond is very intimate. She was delighted she finally had me notice her as a woman, but she was still very innocent. She just wanted to flirt with me, try out her feminine charms.

I still met her everyday, but at that park in Kapiolani Beach. In public, but no one else knew we were meeting there. I was learning Kurdish and Sarah was great with languages, so I had her help me. We spent a lot of afternoons sitting in a big banyan tree, both of us on different limbs, while I practiced. To anyone watching, it just looked like what it was, a guy practicing a foreign language out loud on his own. Sitting removed from everyone else so as not to disturb or intrude on them with his recitations. And that's what it was, except I was practicing with Sarah and she was usually flirting pretty outrageously with me. I didn't really mind. We kept our distance and I stopped hugging her when we met. That's when I started just touching her cheek. I knew how much my touch resonated within her. Knew I probably shouldn't even do that much, but I couldn't not touch her at all." He shook his head.

"This was the first time our bond was actually kind of painful for me. I was terrified of showing Sarah too much, revealing my brand of sexuality to her, scaring her. I was careful to keep her at arms length except for that caress on her face as greeting when we met."

"Man," Martin chuckled. "I still think of Kurdish as a pretty sexy language from those afternoons of watching and practicing with Sarah." Martin smiled at the memory. How engaging and beautiful the young Sarah had been as she tried her wiles on him, confident she could trust him to let her spread her wings and try to fly close to the sun without getting scorched.

"What I did," Martin continued, "in retrospect wasn't so smart, but it's how I coped at the time. I spent the entire afternoon with Sarah, every afternoon in the park. Then I'd go back to the base, to the nurses' quarters, find the first one who was willing and available, and fuck her brains out. That's how I met Becky. She was one of the nurses. After the first few days, I kinda stuck with screwing Becky when I got back from the park. Her schedule made her available, she was willing, didn't expect me to talk much or romance her and it was easier than trying to negotiate with someone new every time. It also seemed to cut back on the jealousy, gossip, and petty stuff since those women all knew each other, compared notes, etc. What can I say," Martin shrugged. "It was a pretty fucked up thing to do, but Becky was a grown up and she didn't seem to mind being my fuck buddy. It gave me some breathing room with Sarah or I think I would have been chewing my way through that tree we were sitting in."

"I did kiss Sarah, just once, before I left for Afghanistan. Just a kiss but a real kiss. Almost blew the top of my head off, her too. I shouldn't have done it; I know that now. But it was amazing, that kiss. Like nothing I'd ever experienced before. I could feel it from Sarah's perspective and she from mine." He remembered how desire flared up between them like nothing he'd ever felt for a woman before or since. It was like something elemental, as basic as breathing or his heartbeat; it felt like a necessity. And from Sarah he had felt a much more grown up desire that time. He pulled himself back to his narrative.

"But she was also scared for me. She didn't know what my mission was; just knew it was dangerous. They all were. She was terrified she would never see me again; that somehow I would die and she would never have been kissed, been made love to. Not quite sixteen and she was afraid she would die an old maid." He chuckled ruefully. "So I did kiss her, that one time. And I held her and comforted her. I promised her that I wouldn't die. I did that before every deployment from the very beginning, but this time I also promised that I would come back to her, for her. The two of us would finally be together in the same place, at the same time. In real life time as Sarah used to call it when she was small. I did promise her that," Martin said, despising himself for breaking that promise.

"That last deployment, it was a tough one. A real tough one," Martin said quietly. "I don't know how I survived it and I realized that I wasn't really supposed to. It was turning into what could only be a suicide mission. Sarah and I had virtually no opportunity to communicate at all. I think I was only able to talk to her about three or four times over the course of a few months, then only for a few minutes." He leaned forward, his elbows on his knees, gazing at the floor without seeing, his mind completely engaged in another place and time.

"I don't know, I never meant to go down that road, but I couldn't help it. I thought about her day and night. Fantasized about her constantly. Played that kiss over and over again in my mind. I was gone, way gone on a girl way too young for me. I knew I couldn't act on it, even if by some miracle I made it out of Afghanistan alive and got to see her again. But I couldn't help it. I couldn't stop thinking about her. It was like fantasizing about Sarah in my arms, making love to her, was my reward for getting killed. Pretty fucked up, I know." Martin looked at them, sympathizing with their feelings. "I didn't say I was thinking too clearly at the time.

Then I was wounded, shot. I was alone in a cave up in the hills and surrounded by the Taliban. The wound got infected; I was feverish, delirious. Sarah knew I was in trouble, badly hurt. She could feel it through our bond, so she broke her word to me. She was never to come to me when I was on a deployment. Never, for any reason. I made her swear to that every time before I left. But she did. She came to me in that cave and she took care of me, nursed me, fed me, saved my life again. She also became my invisible eyes. While I was insensible inside the cave, she monitored the enemy, memorized their routine, completely got the lay of the land for me."

"When I was well enough that she knew I would live, but still too weak to get up, to get back to duty, she took me to the Top of the World again. I could leave my tired, sick body behind for a while and experience the exhilaration of Top of the World. This time, she was a beautiful woman, tall, with long dark hair, my age. No more boys close to me in age so we could be buddies on an adventure together. She was a beautiful, alluring woman named Ariel and I was a ranger, a loner named Hartshorn, traveling through on a mission to rescue the prince. We became lovers. I knew on some level that it was Sarah, fifteen-year-old Sarah I was playing this charade with, not Ariel, but I didn't care. I was in heaven and she was too. I don't have any excuses. I knew it wasn't Sarah's body I was fucking but it was her. She was feeling and experiencing all the sensations of that body she was inhabiting and she could feel me as well. We couldn't get enough of each other. It's the only time in my life I've ever made love to a woman. I didn't hold her down or try to restrain her. I made love to her and she to me and it was glorious." Martin was silent a long moment. He met their gaze directly, looked them all in the eye, his expression a bit defiant and defensive at the same time.

"Thanks to Sarah's help back in that cave in Afghanistan, I not only accomplished my mission, but I survived it. The Army wanted to know how; they wanted details. I was still in pretty bad shape, pretty fucked up mentally and physically. The debriefing they put me through, well it almost finished me off. They used drugs and sensory deprivation. I spent six weeks in a straight jacket in a padded cell, drooling all over myself and feeling like I was going to shit my brains out right through my ears, terrified I would tell them about Sarah. They used Rhonopol on me. It was the same drug that Ponytail used on Danny but I didn't have the option of suicide. I was strapped down pretty securely. I didn't know what to do. I was out of my mind, desperate that I would be the one to reveal Sarah, put her in danger, in harm's way. It felt like I was standing on the edge of a cliff, my toes hanging over, balancing ever so precariously so as not to fall.

I did the only thing I could think of. The only way I could devise to keep her safe. I knew I would tell them about her. The compulsion to talk was already strong in me. So, I stepped off the edge of that cliff into freefall. I decided to tell them everything, every detail about Sarah, our visits to The Top of the World, spending time under the ocean as an octopus. Everything. The more fantastical the detail, the more I wanted to impart that information. I told them everything about Sarah except for one thing. One small word I kept in my impregnable vault. One word I never revealed. Her name. I never said her name. I said her name was unpronounceable so I just called her Smallest.

It worked. They knew the drug forced me to tell the truth, tell them what I believed happened. I got a psych discharge. They decided I was just crazy.

They finally cut me loose and I went straight to California, straight to Sarah. I got the shock of my life. I knew she made those two movies, although I didn't know she won another Oscar. I knew she had a couple of hit records, was dancing in a ballet company, but I had no idea she'd become this incredible superstar back home. I felt so stupid. I'd been so busy fighting, trying to stay alive, that I'd lost touch with what was happening back in the States. And Sarah never talked about that stuff when we were together. I mean, she talked about her music, the things she loved. But she never said, 'the song is #1' or 'I won an Oscar', nothing like that. I realize now it's because the money and fame are pretty meaningless to Sarah, that's why she never mentioned it. So that's the first time I realized there was this huge frenzy around the 'superstar, Sarah Eastin'. I went to that Jam concert, there were thirty thousand people going absolutely nuts for her.

I'd never seen her on the stage before and she was incandescent. She lit up the universe. She blew my mind. And I realized I had no right to interfere in her life. She was only sixteen years old and she had it all. She didn't need me. I had to finally admit that Magnus and you had done that for her, Al. Not me." Here Martin stopped abruptly. He knew it was important to tell the truth, the whole truth. He just didn't want to do it.

He looks miserable again, Paul thought with compassion. He admired Martin for finally daring to talk about this.

"What I just said is all true," he admitted quietly. "But the real reason I didn't meet Sarah after that concert was I didn't have the guts. I was too afraid to face her. I'd been thinking a lot about what I'd gone through in that debriefing and I decided that the Top of the World memories couldn't be true. It wasn't possible. That was just a short step that led to me questioning all my memories about Sarah. I questioned my sanity. After all, I was the kid who was raped and beaten by his mother. I spent most of my time alone. Which scenario was more likely to be true? As a lonely kid I made up a little girl to take care of and love and over the years, she somehow morphed and merged into memories and fantasies of the superstar 'Sarah Eastin'? Or that I actually knew a superstar, just didn't know that one little fact about her?

I was terrified. I couldn't face her. I knew that if I got backstage to see her and she looked at me with no recognition, no idea of who I was, I wouldn't be able to take it. I needed her to be my Sarah. I desperately needed her to be my Sarah and I couldn't face testing it. I knew I would blow my brains out if she didn't know me, if my entire life was a fantasy, if I really was crazy. So, like a coward, I walked away. I've faced enemies with ten times the numbers or strength I had and not been so mortally afraid before." He bit his lip. The memory of that day was still brutally painful.

Suddenly Martin was bone tired again. He felt like he'd been talking for hours. He looked frankly at all of them and told the truth again. "I need to sleep," he apologized. "I've been operating on little or no sleep for days. I should wait for Sarah to wake anyway before saying more. She deserves to hear the rest of this." He went to Sarah, asleep on the bed, and stretched out next to her. At the look on Al's face he said, "I'm not leaving her. Not for an instant. I want to be here when she wakes up. You're welcome to stay as well," he said, stretching out to get comfortable.

Alexander was annoyed, yet again, at how presumptuous Stone was. To just crawl on the bed and lie down next to her like that? Sure, he was fully clothed and on top of the blanket, but still. Then Sarah stirred slightly in her sleep and turned towards Martin. He reached for her immediately and she nestled into his warmth, still deeply asleep. Alexander was shocked by the intimacy of the small moment. This was not a Sarah that he had ever seen, not with anyone. He saw Stone's eyes watching him steadily as he cradled Sarah in his arms. Alexander flushed and turned away, granting them some privacy.

Chapter Twenty-Seven

Sarah stirred slightly and Martin woke instantly. Julie smiled at him from her seat beside the bed. "Don't worry, she's doing fine. Her temperature is normal. I think she's beginning to wake up."

Martin propped himself up on one elbow and rubbed his face awake. "How long have I been asleep?"

"A little over nine hours," Julie said. At the look on his face, she added, "You obviously needed it. We all did. Everyone has managed to get some much needed sleep."

"Except you," Martin said. "Thanks for watching over her."

"You're welcome," Julie said, "and I did get some sleep. Paul spelled me for a while."

Martin looked at Sarah again, assessing her injuries in the cold light of day. He winced when he saw her shiner. The fracture in her arm was clean; it should heal well. The injury that concerned him the most was the severe blow to her left kidney. When tossed across the room by that bastard, her kidney had connected hard with the corner of the dresser before she bounced off and was thrown against the wall. He'd taken bad blows to the kidney before and knew that if her kidney wasn't ruptured, it was severely injured. That was going to hurt like hell, especially the first time she has to pee, he thought.

He could feel her struggle to wake though she didn't move as yet. She felt as if she were swimming slowly through murky water. He lightly stroked her face with his finger. "Wake up Smallest. Time to wake up." His voice was gentle.

Sarah finally broke through the surface and opened her eyes. She saw Martin smiling down at her. Happiness began to spread a slow warmth throughout her body. Martin was stretched out on the bed next to her. He was fine; he was unhurt. He had saved her from Flint, from herself. She turned to him and gasped as she felt every part of her body cry out in pain.

"Don't try to move much, Sarah," Martin warned, still stroking her face gently. "You're hurt, Smallest. Take it nice and slow." He smiled reassuringly at her.

She smiled brilliantly at him, even though her face hurt. She reached for him with her left arm. He took her hand. "Is everyone OK?" she asked him.

He nodded his head. "Everyone but you. If you ever do anything that bone headed again," he stopped at the look of contrition on her face, in her eyes.

"Oh Martin, what have I done! How can you ever forgive me?"

He saw in her eyes that frightened little girl again and he gathered her into his arms. "Shush, Sarah. You've done nothing wrong, baby. Nothing anyone in your shoes wouldn't have done." He looked her in the eyes when he said, "No more hiding, Sarah. At least not from the people you love and trust. I told them, all of them," at that he inclined his head towards the other side of the sitting room where Sarah's circle was gathered, "about us. I told them everything, Sarah."

Her eyes widened in alarm. "You told them about me?" she asked.

He nodded yes.

"Oh Martin," she protested, her eyes filling with regret, with censure. "You shouldn't have." She closed her eyes momentarily and took deep breaths to steady herself. "He's never going to stop. I've put everyone in danger. I have to put an end to this." She closed her eyes again. She couldn't bear to see the look she knew must be in Martin's eyes, the look she had dreaded all of her life, the look that would condemn her for her weakness, her selfishness, the look that would confirm why he had turned away from her.

Martin turned her face to him. "Look at me, Sarah." He stroked her face gently again with his fingertips. "Please, Sarah," he asked softly. But she couldn't. She kept her eyes closed and willed herself to disappear, to hide again as she had as a child. But she had never hidden from Martin. Never, and she couldn't now. She was ashamed of her weakness and turned away from him on the bed.

Martin felt his heart ache anew for her as he watched her struggle. How could he have left her so unprotected, so vulnerable? Had he really been so sure she was a figment of his imagination, so concerned about his own survival, he had spared no thought for hers? She had been the only thing that mattered to him throughout his entire childhood, and he had abandoned her. Cut her off cruelly, walked away into another woman's arms. He would spend the rest of his life making that up to her, making sure she never felt alone or abandoned again.

"Sarah, I was afraid you'd be angry with me at first. I don't blame you." He spoke softly and refrained from touching her, just continued to lie beside her propped up on one elbow, watching her carefully. "You don't trust me anymore, and after what I did to you, I can't say I blame you for that either. I have some explaining to do, Sarah. But baby, I told them because I just couldn't risk you or them anymore. No matter what you decide about me, Sarah, I can't leave you alone to face Flint."

She slowly opened her eyes and looked into his. Her heart began to beat faster. She reached out in wonderment and touched his face. His eyes were warm; his smile was gentle. The judgment she feared was nowhere to be seen in his expression.

"I love you, Smallest." He lightly kissed her lips, her bruised face. "We're in this together, baby. You and me, we belong together. I should never have left you, Sarah." He cradled her to him, burying his face in her hair, breathing deeply of her scent. "Oh baby," he said softly, " I've been through some rough times in my life, but nothing was as hard as the last four years, trying to live without you. I can't do it, Sarah. I've tried and I've tried, but I can't do it. I need you too, Sarah. You need me and, baby, I definitely need you." He held her and rocked her gently stroking her hair. "I'm so tired, Sarah, so fucking tired of trying to figure out how to live without you. I need music back in my life, Sarah. I need you.

I made some mistakes, some bad mistakes. I urged secrecy for so long, I didn't realize that I was leaving you so alone, so isolated. I think a part of you thought there was something shameful about you, something that needed to be hidden. It's not true, Sarah. You're amazing, a miracle. I just was so worried about protecting you until you were grown up enough to not have someone take advantage of you.

You're grown up now, Sarah. We should have started this a long time ago but we can start now. No more hiding. Let me help you figure out who you are, what you are. It's time to understand as much as we can about what you're capable of. Maybe it's finally time to understand the past too, Sarah. I think we need to know more about your parents. Who they were."

Sarah stared at Martin in amazement. He wasn't angry with her; he wasn't even disappointed in her. He said he loved her. The words filled her with joy. She didn't know how she could feel so happy. She was in pain and the worst had happened. She had exposed everyone she loved to the danger that was Flint. Still, her heart leapt with happiness and she could feel it shivering throughout her body.

She could feel Martin; she was bonded with him again. She could feel his happiness, his utter joy at having her in his arms. She felt whole again. His body was so strong, so warm. She fit perfectly in his arms. Even as the thought crossed her mind that she hadn't washed her face or brushed her teeth in she didn't remember how long, a strong wave of lust swept through her. She shivered and blushed to the roots of her hair. She knew Martin had felt her reaction and she was embarrassed. She had just been attacked by a madman, assaulted and beaten. But when Martin held her, all she could think of were his hands on her.

He chuckled softly and looked into her eyes again. "There'll be time for that soon," he promised softly. "I want you to be well before I make love to you. I've waited for you for a long time, Smallest. I can wait until you're ready." He was silent a moment, looking into her face, her eyes. "We'll learn how to make love together, Sarah. I don't ever want to treat you like I did those other women. Maybe that's why I had so much trouble being touched by them. I only wanted your touch, Sarah." He kissed her cheek, nuzzled her neck. Shivers of pleasure danced up and down her spine.

She reached for him, held him in her one good arm. Sarah was happier than she could remember being in so very, very long. But anxiety soon intruded. Martin told them about me. She thought of Alexander and her resolve faltered. Would he hate her now? Oh god, he knew about Magnus. Of course he would hate her now. How could he ever forgive her?

Martin felt her happiness change to anxiety. He looked closely at her, *"What is it baby, what's wrong?"* He tested out his telepathic communication with her for the first time since they remet. Sarah was surprised but her delight in Martin finally communicating with her as only they could was overshadowed by her thoughts of Magnus, then Danny. Martin felt it, the huge weight that was crushing Sarah, squeezing down on her chest, making it difficult for her to breathe. *"Sarah, talk to me. What's happening?"* He held her carefully, sat up and pulled her closer to him. "Julie," he said. "She's having trouble breathing."

"It's my fault," she said into Martin's mind. *"First Danny, then Magnus. It's my fault!"* she repeated fiercely to Martin. *"Zander will hate me now that he knows. He'll hate me."*

"Like you hate yourself," Martin finished for her. He pulled her close, trying not to aggravate any of her injuries. He just held her and rocked her gently for a few moments, letting her feel his love for her. Letting it calm her.

Alexander, Paul, and Sebastian entered the room on hearing that Sarah was awake. Jonathan followed shortly. Sarah buried her face in Martin's shoulder, unable to face them.

"Sarah, do you remember Master Po?" Martin spoke softly but aloud so that all could hear.

"Yes." His stern but kind face flashed into Sarah's memory, his sightless eyes that could see more than most men with keen eyesight.

"Remember how he described life as a gigantic tapestry. One so large we can't hope to see the entire pattern with our limited vision. That in the warp and weave of this tapestry, every stitch has it's place and is important to the strength of the entire tapestry." Sarah nodded and Martin continued, "He said that some very few people were different, special. Now, these special people are all different in different ways, some good, some bad. Just like all the rest of us, they have to choose their path. But, what these few special people all have in common, they all change the pattern of the tapestry. Their karma, or whatever you want to call it, is so strong, it changes the weave of the tapestry; a new pattern emerges."

Sarah nodded again, speaking softly, "Master Po was talking about Danny when he told us that story. He said that's why the two monks came to our village, they were drawn to Danny."

Martin stroked Sarah's hair gently for a moment before answering. "I know that's what he said, Sarah, but I find it interesting the monks only showed up after you were born. Danny'd already been going through hell there for ten years." He smiled ruefully. "The monks have their own form of blindness, Sarah. They weren't looking for a little girl and they were blinded by Danny's intelligence. But you're as smart as he was and you're the unique one, Smallest. Danny wasn't able to use his mind in any of the ways you can. No, baby. I think Master Po was talking about you, even if he didn't know it."

Martin looked steadily at her. "Sarah, I bear a large part of the blame that no one has tried to help you understand yourself, train yourself. When you were small, we concentrated all our time on me it seems. We only explored your talents in so far as they brought us to Top of the World where I could play my hero games." He shook his head in dismay. "I should have helped you more, Smallest. I'm sorry."

"You did help me, Martin. You're the only one who did. But I learned young, being sheltered by you, that I could use you to help me cope. I tried to be more self sufficient, tried to use some of the coping tricks you taught me, like concentrating on one thing, blocking everything else out, but it was so hard. So, I took the easy way out. I used other people like I used you. I hid behind Danny." Sarah stopped and laughed bitterly. "It was more like I hid inside him. Just looked at the world from the safety of my little pouch, hidden inside Danny like some burrowing baby kangaroo. Then, after he died, I used Magnus that way." She finally looked at Alexander. "You don't know how right you were when you called Magnus my 'shield' against the world. Over the years Flint finally got a good look, not only at me, but also at Magnus.

I didn't listen to you, Martin." Here Sarah began to rock in distress. "I went to Top of the World, not a lot, but I went. I actually think he can see me anytime I travel now, even here. I should have stopped." Her voice faltered. "I know I should have stopped traveling but I didn't. He knew how important Magnus was to me. He saw over the years." There was anguish in Sarah's eyes, face, as she looked at Alexander. "I should have told him, I should have warned him."

"You knew, Sarah? You knew this Flint character was going after Father?" Alexander asked, concern and disbelief on his face.

"No" she said. "I didn't connect Flint with what happened to Danny yet. I didn't know he would hurt Magnus. But I should have told Magnus what I was doing. I knew Flint was watching for me, that he was dangerous. That what I was doing was dangerous, wrong. I just couldn't resist going, doing some of the things that we used to do together, Martin. I should have trusted Magnus, told him what I was doing. I wouldn't have been so lonely and he would have been more aware, alert. Perhaps he wouldn't have trusted that pilot, that plane so easily."

"What happened, Sarah? How do you know this Flint was responsible for Father's death?"

"I'm sorry, Zander," Sarah said softly. "I didn't know how to tell you without telling you about myself, without putting all of you in danger. You've never really wanted to acknowledge any of these things about me. You would become very angry with Magnus when he would go down that avenue."

Sarah, silent for a moment, finally said. "I only knew about it as it started happening. I could feel Magnus' sudden spurt of terror and I went to him immediately. The plane was going down; the pilot frantically working the controls, but it was crashing. I was horrified but Magnus was calm. He knew I was there. He said goodbye and that he loved me. He told me to tell you how much he loved you, was proud of you and he told me to let you take care of me."

A tear slipped down Sarah's cheek. "I only knew it was Flint after the plane crashed and I knew Magnus was dead. I was devastated. Then I felt him, heard him." Sarah shivered with revulsion. "Flint was jubilant. He killed Magnus just to prove to me that he could get to me." Sarah closed her eyes and looked away from Alexander. She couldn't bear to see the judgment she knew must be there. "That's why I decided to stay at Tall Trees, Zander. I didn't want to ever use anyone again like I had used Magnus. I was afraid that Flint would see, would strike again." Sarah was rocking and holding herself in her distress. Pain flared through her from her injured hip and kidney. She wanted to curl into a ball and hide.

Martin pulled her gently into his arms, kissing her hair, stroking her, gentling her. He looked at Alexander, wondering how he was taking the news of his father's death. Al had said nothing yet. It wasn't up to him to absolve Sarah; she needed to hear it from Al. His heart ached for her as he felt her fear, her guilt, her longing to see Magnus again. She loved Magnus with all her heart and she had not been honest or forthcoming with Magnus because of him. Martin realized the magnitude

272

of his mistake. But he had never really understood when he was younger the depth of her feeling for Magnus, Alexander, Sebastian, all of them. After he lost his father, he never allowed himself to love anyone, have feelings for anyone but Sarah. At least, he never allowed himself to admit those feelings. It was only after he tore himself away from Sarah, ripped the only love he allowed himself from his life, that he realized he had no one. No one else.

Then, by some miracle, he had been partnered with Will and fate and circumstances had combined to forge a friendship. Being admitted into Will's life and family had transformed Martin and he had slowly let a few other friends become trusted, true friends; his Coast Guard buddy, Mac and Mac's girlfriend Katie, and his closest friend from his Army days, Randy, and his wife Alexa. The last was still a surprise to Martin. Alexa had been Becky's friend. He was surprised she held no animosity towards him. He certainly blamed himself for Becky's death.

It was interesting, letting go of his one love had opened him up to the realization that there were all different kinds and levels of love. Watching Will and Tess with their children, the obvious love and respect on both sides, had also been transformational for Martin. It was mesmerizing for him to watch this happy family, even through their squabbles. He couldn't get enough.

He now understood how important Al's opinion of her was to Sarah. He hoped Al was the man his father had been. Al had to know he lost her to Martin. If he still thought that engagement of theirs' was on, he was more delusional than Martin thought. Still, Al was part of Sarah's family and he knew she was afraid she had lost him. Martin looked frankly at Al, waiting for his answer.

Alexander finally sat down. He looked sadly at Sarah. "Oh, Sarah. Why? Why didn't you tell me?" He leaned over, elbows on knees, hands clasped before him. Before he could speak, Sarah shook her head.

"It's worse than you know," Sarah said miserably. "I've done a terrible thing, Alexander. Terrible." Sarah rocked in her distress and finally looked directly at Alexander. "He asked me to trust you. Before he died, Magnus asked me to trust you, to tell you everything. He asked me to be honest with you, to let you help me, and I gave him my word that I would. But I couldn't, Zander, I couldn't. I'm a coward." Sarah looked at Alexander and said softly, "I thought you would blame me; you'd hate me." She winced and looked away. "I was too afraid of being all alone. I didn't keep my word to Magnus."

Alexander looked at her again, pain and betrayal in his eyes. "I would have trusted you enough to tell you anything," he said, his voice raw with emotion. "He was my Father, Sarah! How could you keep such a secret from me?" He rose and turned from her, fighting the urge to run from the room, the house, the unreality of the last few hours. At the sound of Sarah's distress, he turned back. His anger melted immediately. Sarah turned away from them all, was trying to separate herself from Martin, who held her firmly, still being careful of her injuries.

Alexander went to her but Sarah flinched away from his touch. "I understand, at least I'm trying to." He looked at her with compassion. "Sarah, I know how much father loved you. You were the daughter he never had. And I know you loved him. There is no question in my mind on this. If you can read my mind, then you know it."

Sarah did not answer, just withdrew deeper into herself.

"It's OK, Smallest, you don't have to talk now if you don't want to." Martin soothed her gently. He looked at Alexander, the others. "She's not ready yet. Give her time." He held her gently, pulling the blanket closer around her. "She'll talk when she's ready." He looked compassionately at Al. "She'll come around. You're the one person she's afraid to face right now. She knows how much you loved your father. How close the two of you were. Give her a little time, Al," he asked. Alexander nodded and walked away.

Martin lay next to Sarah and held her gently. "Why don't you go back to sleep for awhile, Sarah. You're so tired, baby. You need more sleep. I'll be right here. I won't leave you, not for an instant." He held her and felt her inner struggle against the weariness that was wearing her down. "You don't have to be afraid to sleep anymore. I won't let anything happen to you, Sarah. I promise." He felt her finally give in to the security of his arms, felt her falling back into welcome sleep and he held her until he felt she was deeply, peacefully, sleeping, her body already beginning to rejuvenate and heal.

Martin then rose and went to join the others in the sitting room, keeping the bedroom door open and Sarah in full view. He ran his hands distractedly through his hair then turned to Paul. "I don't know what to do, Paul. She's so scared, I don't want to push her." He looked at Paul, then Will with painful honesty in his eyes. "She's convinced I did the wrong thing in telling all of you. She seems to think this is something, some challenge she has to meet on her own. She's trying to shut me out."

"Perhaps she is right," Jonathan said. "None of us know what Sarah is, who she is, what she's capable of. Perhaps this is best left to her discretion."

"No way," Martin was shaking his head decisively. "I don't care what the rest of you do, but no way is Sarah facing Flint on her own. That is not happening." He glared at Jonathan. "Sarah is no kind of fighter, no warrior. She may have powers that even she doesn't understand, but she'll be a lamb led to the slaughter if Flint gets a hold of her now. Sarah's so innocent; she doesn't even understand what that kind of evil is. There is no fucking way I'm letting her face him!"

Martin turned away in a fury but realized his anger was misspent. He turned back to Jonathan and the rest of them, an apology in his eyes. "I'm sorry. I can't expect you to understand what's at stake here when I'm just starting to understand. And I've known Sarah all her life!" he added with bitter irony in his voice.

"Look, I don't want to face Flint either. Not yet. Not without a lot more information. Not before Sarah is a lot stronger. But one thing I do know, no matter what happens, she has me. I will take him down." Martin looked directly at all of them. He was not boasting; he was delivering a solemn vow. "I will never let him have her. I'm asking for your help now, all of you. If we help her, if we support her, we can keep her safe and we can figure out Flint's game and stop him."

Martin looked at each of them in turn and when they nodded, he nodded his head in assent. It was done. A fellowship was formed.

"We need more information." Martin said. He looked at Al. "I think you and Will should go to Sun Tao, find Master Po if he's still alive, and bring him here. I think you should go as quickly as possible." Alexander nodded. Will did not look surprised. He knew how his partner's mind worked.

"Jonathan, I want you to go to England. I want you to find Peg, their old housekeeper. See if she's still alive. See if you can unearth the story of Sarah's parents." Martin looked coolly at Jonathan, then turned his glance away and looked back with more warmth. "You'll be good at disarming the gentry. If anyone can charm the secrets out of that set, it's you, Jonathan. Your help would be appreciated."

Martin waited and Jonathan accepted graciously. "Of course," he bowed his head in assent. Martin realized he was being too hasty in judging Jonathan harshly. Sarah loved and trusted Jonathan, which would have to be enough for him for now. So far, he saw Jonathan only as an old British foreign office type. A real stickler for the rules; a fussbudget.

He turned to the one man, besides Will, he knew in his bones he could trust. "Sebastian, I'd like you to stay here with Paul and Julie. I'm worried about her. She's about at the end of her rope."

Chapter Twenty-Eight

When Sarah awoke, Martin was stretched out next to her. He woke almost immediately and turned to her with a smile. She smiled back tentatively; she couldn't resist the gentle humor in his eyes. The dark boy with the laughing eyes she had called him. And, in spite of the horror of his childhood, that's how she remembered her time with him; laughter and love, acceptance and protection, loyalty and bravery. He reached out to her now and stroked a curl out of her face.

"Hello. Welcome back," he said softly. "Feeling any better?"

She tentatively nodded her head. She didn't seem to hurt quite as much as before. She struggled to sit up and Martin assisted her. Her bladder was screaming for release and her hip throbbed dully, but the pain was bearable.

Martin winced sympathetically and said just to Sarah, *"The first time you pee, that injured kidney is going to hurt like hell. I've taken a lot of blows to the kidney, so I know you're best off to just let go, let 'er rip. I'll hold on to you, baby."*

He picked Sarah up carefully and headed towards the bathroom. He set her carefully on the toilet then helped her with her panties. *"Julie's got a catch basin in there,"* he let her know at the inquisitive look on her face at the strange contraption below her. *"She needs to measure the blood in your urine, see how bad you're hurt."*

Sarah released her bladder and the pain shot through her with a fury, taking her breath away and dimming her vision.

Martin held her tightly then lifted and carried her back to the bed. *"It'll be better soon, baby. The worst is over now."* He held her until her trembling stopped.

Sarah lay quietly for a few moments, enjoying the feel of Martin's arms around her even through the pain of her injuries. *"What now?"* she asked Martin. *"Where do we go from here?"*

"Easy," he answered, looking at her with affection and humor. *"We get you well again. Strong. Then we'll figure it out together, Sarah. Whatever it takes, that's what we'll do. But, we'll do it together, baby. And the people we love, they'll help us, Sarah. That's the way it's supposed to be. That's why we'll win, Sarah. That's how we'll beat Flint, because we'll stand or fall together. It's like one of the games in Top of the World. We choose the side of right; we choose to stand up to evil. Only this game is being played out here, on Earth."*

"But these are people I love that could die," Sarah said sadly, softly.

"The people in Top of the World risked their lives as well, Sarah," Martin rejoined softly. *"We could escape in a flash, will ourselves home, but they couldn't. Those battles were just as real to them as this is to us."*

Sarah nodded, acknowledging the truth of Martin's words. *"Why, Martin? Why is this happening? Why am I like this?"*

"I don't know, baby. I don't know. But I'm willing to help you find out. Tell you what," he said, settling her comfortably in his arms. *"I want to know everything about the last four years. Everything about the time we were apart. I don't want any secrets between us, Sarah."* At her silence, he said, *"OK, I'll start if you won't."*

He cleared his throat even though he wasn't speaking aloud. *"When I saw you at that concert, I was so proud of you. You blew my mind, Sarah. You were fantastic."* He kissed the side of her neck, caressed her shoulder. *"I can still see you, up on that stage. I was amazed. Amazed and terrified. I suddenly lost faith, Sarah. I didn't believe. I mean, guys like me, we don't get girls like you, Sarah."*

Sarah looked at him in wonderment.

"Oh, baby, I didn't have the balls to come and see you. I suddenly felt sure you couldn't be real, not for me, and I couldn't take it. I was afraid you wouldn't know me, would look at me like just some guy, another fan, and I would lose it. I would lose it all; my whole life would be wiped away as a lie.

And even if you did know me, I reasoned at the time, what good could I possibly be to you? You didn't need me. I was terrified that I needed you so much I would just overwhelm you with my problems, that I

278

would do something irredeemably wrong, end up hurting you." Martin was silent for a long moment.

"But mostly I was too scared, Sarah. Too scared that I would find out you weren't real. I left the concert and went straight to see Becky. Randy and Alexa told me she was in town and that she was having a tough time; she was pregnant and the guy abandoned her. We talked for a few hours and I guess, in my desperation, it seemed like a solution. I asked Becky to marry me and she said yes. We went straight to a justice of the peace.

It was a disaster from the beginning," he continued ruefully. *"You're not the only one who's made mistakes, hurt people, Sarah. I've done my fair share. Becky thought her hero had rescued her. She remembered me from Hawaii as this red-hot lover and she was determined to be a good wife. But, turns out, I couldn't get it up for her at all,"* Martin admitted quietly. *"All I could think of was you."* He stopped in embarrassment then continued. *"I never did consummate that marriage. Becky let it go at first. She thought it was because she was pregnant, but her pregnant body didn't bother me; I liked it. She looked happy, peaceful most of the time.*

I just, well, I just didn't want her. And I didn't want to talk about it either. I didn't leave her many options. After she had the baby, she was more insistent; she wanted a husband in her bed. I actually got her off a few times, just with my hands and mouth, just to get her off my back, but I couldn't, you know." He stopped again.

Sarah could feel his embarrassment and she really didn't understand it. There were a great many people she couldn't get aroused by. She wondered why a man would be embarrassed by it; were all women supposed to be arousing?

"Sarah, I was pretty insensitive to her. I wouldn't be a husband to her and I wouldn't talk about it or go to therapy. She thought it was Post Traumatic Stress from battle and I let her think that. I got a job as a cop and figured I was working full time, bringing home my paycheck, taking care of her and the baby, and she should just let it go. I even told her if she wanted to find someone to fuck, fine, just don't shove it in my face.

The baby was a few months old by now. We were fighting all the time and I was tired of it. That evening she got on me again and I'd just had it. *So when she said she was leaving, taking the baby and leaving, I said fine. Go. I was tired of it all.*

I knew how upset she was; she was crying pretty hysterically. I never should have let her leave. I should have been the one to go. But I didn't. I sat there ignoring her and she ran out with the baby. Wrapped her car around a pole on Highland Boulevard. Killed them both instantly." Martin was silent remembering.

Sarah turned in his arms to face him. She stroked his face gently as he looked into her eyes.

"*She didn't deserve that, Sarah. Becky didn't deserve what I did to her. You feel guilt because you never told Magnus about yourself. I understand*," he said, his guilt over Becky and her son filling Sarah's senses, "*I feel it too, Sarah. I never told Becky anything about myself, what I was going through. She was in the dark from beginning to end. She was a nice girl,*" he repeated, "*even if I wasn't in love with her.*"

Martin and Sarah held each other in silence. Finally Sarah said softly into Martin's mind, "*I was with the whales. That's where I went after you first left. I saw you leave the concert, go to her. I thought it was your baby she was carrying. I saw you choose her and I couldn't stand it.*" Sarah's face burned at the memory and Martin held her close to comfort her. "*You broke the bond, Martin. You broke our bond.*" Her heart trembled at the memory and he realized what a shock it must have been to her system. "*I knew then that you meant to never come back. I didn't know what to do. I didn't think I could live with people by myself; it was too hard. So I ran away with the whales. I didn't stay connected to my body; I just left it. I didn't want to ever come back.*"

Sarah was silent for a moment, remembering the sad peacefulness of her time of mourning, her time spent with a pod of nine whales led by Eartha. "*Time passes very differently with the whales. A year passed in no time at all and Eartha was insisting I go back. They had given me succor and sanctuary as long as they could. I was being sent home. I didn't know what to do. I couldn't live as a whale anymore than I could live as a human.*"

Martin felt the contentment in her body at her memory of her time with the whales. He felt the deep peace and floating sensation of the sea and her connection to it. He also felt her sense of loss and displacement at being forced out of that watery home, back to where she felt just as alien, perhaps more so, for being so alike and yet so utterly different from other humans.

"Magnus, Julie, Sebastian, Paul, they all tried to help me. They all did the best they could but I didn't know how to be alone. I didn't understand, I still don't understand why I'm the way I am. Why is Flint drawn to me, why does he see me? Peg was right about me."

"Stop it! Stop it now!" Martin commanded out loud, turning her face to him. "Peg was full of shit, a superstitious old woman. Of one thing I'm perfectly certain, Sarah." He looked searchingly into her eyes. "It's that you're good. You're a good person; you inspire it in others. Look at me; I'm a perfect example. If it weren't for you, I'm sure I'd be in jail instead of a cop. You're not perfect, none of us are. But you try, you try your best all the time to be the best person you can. That's all any of us can do." He gathered her back into his arms and held her close. His girl needed a lot of reassurance just now.

As the day slipped away, Martin stayed with Sarah. He left her to her deep thoughts, her contemplations. He didn't try to intrude. He simply stayed with her, waited for her, took tender care of her, and waited some more. At times he was rewarded with a small smile; mostly Sarah was silent and distant. She finally dropped into a troubled sleep and Martin sat silent watch over her.

He stayed with her for the next three days. Helped her take her first hesitant steps in the garden then walked with her as she regained her strength. Martin coaxed her to eat while he took obvious enjoyment in the food Sebastian prepared for them. Martin waited patiently, seemingly sure of the fact that Sarah would return to him when she was ready.

The morning of the fourth day, after Julie's examination and Sarah's protestations that she felt better, Martin realized it was true. He knew her body was feeling better, healing quickly. He'd taken a lot of beatings in his life and he was surprised at how quickly Sarah's body was recovering. He could feel her injuries and thought Sarah was healing in less than half the time it would have taken him. But now he realized she was feeling better emotionally as well. He grinned at her as she requested a bath from Julie. *"Want some help washing your hair?"* he asked wickedly so only Sarah could hear.

Sarah blushed deeply but she nodded yes. Suddenly she was shy, she didn't want Martin to see her bruised and battered body.

Martin seemed to understand. He filled the bath for her then helped her step in with her robe bound tightly around her. He then politely turned his head to give her privacy and held his hand out to take the robe from her as she held on to him and lowered herself into the water.

Once she was ensconced in the bubbles, Martin turned back to her. *"Lean forward,"* he suggested, *"I'll wash your back."* He rubbed soap into the soft cloth then softly washed and massaged her back. He could feel her relax into his touch and his heart was lightened. He washed the rest of her body thoroughly, never probing into private places. He let her relax into the water, into his touch. He leaned her back gently, took the shower wand and washed her hair, shampooing suds through her thick curls and rinsing carefully so as not to get soap in her eyes.

Sarah fell under a kind of spell under his ministrations. She felt relaxed and safe; and, slowly, without being aware of it, she became aroused. It felt so good to have Martin near, touching her. She shivered at his touch on her back and the shiver went all the way through her, making her womb clench with desire, her breath catch in her throat.

Martin looked at her, his eyes liquid with his desire. His gaze never left hers as he picked her up and wrapped a thick, warm towel around her. He carried her to the bedroom and set her on the bed. He politely turned his gaze as he handed her a clean camisole and panties but turned back with a smile when he felt her struggle. He helped her pull the camisole over her head and pulled it down on her body. *"I was hoping to go the other way with these,"* he teased, as he helped her pull her panties up and smiled at her blushing face.

Sarah pulled the blankets around herself protectively, but she turned to look at Martin almost immediately with a question in her eyes.

"What is it? You can ask me anything, Sarah."

"Can I see you?" she asked shyly. *"See where you were shot?"*

Martin pulled his tee shirt off without a word and sat on the edge of the bed near Sarah. She reached over and softly traced the entrance scars on his shoulder and chest of the three gunshot wounds he'd received just over two years ago. *"It was you, wasn't it?"* he asked softly. *"My angel."*

282

"I couldn't let you die." She said as softly and she motioned for him to turn. She lightly traced the larger exit wounds in his back and shoulder. *"Why did you get shot?"* she asked quietly, still softly stroking his back, his shoulder.

"Columbians." He shrugged. *"Sore losers. You saved my life yet again, Smallest."*

"Yet, you seem determined to throw yourself in the way of danger," Sarah said with a small smile.

Martin smiled a slow, lazy smile at her and her heart did a flip-flop.

He was thoroughly enjoying her touch on his skin, his chest, his back. This was such an unusual sensation, but a welcome one. He knew she could feel his heart racing when he looked at her. He smiled at her reassuringly. He would let her set the pace.

"Can I see all of you?" Sarah asked, amazed at her audacity. It was as if she was thinking it, so she just spoke the thought into his mind. Her face flamed as she looked at him.

Martin looked at her for just a moment, a small smile playing across his lips. Then he stood and in two smooth motions, unbuttoned, then pulled off his jeans and underwear and stood before her. The beauty of his body took Sarah's breath away. His thighs were so strong, his chest and arms lean but muscled. His erection throbbed and Sarah gaped at the size and hardness of his penis. She hadn't expected that and paled when she considered it. He smiled reassuringly at her again. She reached out to touch him.

He gasped slightly with pleasure at her touch as she lightly stroked his hard length. *"You're welcome to explore."* Even his telepathic voice was thick with desire in Sarah's mind. *"Don't worry,"* he said at her tentative grasp, *"You won't hurt it, baby."* He felt her grip him more firmly and he shuddered with desire. He kept still, letting her explore, watching her face.

Sarah brimmed with curiosity and desire. She slowly stroked his erection and reveled in the alive feeling of Martin in her hand. He loved the way her hand felt on him; she could feel his desire mounting, his need. It fed her own need and she moved closer to him. She saw a bead of moisture on the tip of his cock. On an impulse, she swiped it with her finger and tasted it. Martin smiled at her as she said aloud, puzzled, "I thought it would have a taste."

"That's not semen, Sarah," he explained gently. "That's precum, kind of like a natural lubricant."

"Oh," she replied, embarrassed. "I shouldn't have done that, I guess."

"You can do whatever you like," he whispered back, nuzzling her face, her neck. "Can I see you now?" he asked, pulling back to look in her face. She nodded yes, ducking her head shyly when thinking of her bruises. But Martin just stroked her face gently, kissing her bruises before pulling her camisole over her head. He swallowed deeply, looking at her with reverence before asking softly, "All of you? Can I see all of you, Sarah?"

She nodded yes and he slowly slid her panties down then tossed them aside. He looked down at her, his eyes shining with need, dark with desire, but he held himself back. He swallowed deeply again, looking at her. "Oh god, Sarah," he groaned. "You are so beautiful, baby."

He lightly stroked her nipple and it responded immediately, hardening to a little bud beneath his fingertips. "Will you open your legs for me, Sarah?" he asked hoarsely. "Let me see you, baby. Let me see all of you." His heart nearly stopped as he looked at Sarah, saw the trust in her eyes as she parted her legs to show him her sex. "Oh baby," he crooned with desire, covering her with his body. "I've been dying to taste you, dying to smell you," he said as he buried his nose in her hair and clasped her to him.

He covered her with kisses until she swooned with pleasure and tried to climb on his body. "Slow down, baby. Take a deep breath," he commanded as he laid her on her back and slowly spread her legs. He lowered his head between her legs and slowly licked the edges of her sex, teasing her with his tongue, lapping at her juices.

Sarah writhed helplessly in equal measures of pleasure and impatience; her body already demanding release. She cried out, gasping with surprise and pleasurable shock as his mouth sought her swollen clitoris and suckled it gently.

He slowly teased her with his tongue while he slid his finger inside her and stroked gently. *"Oh baby,"* he breathed reverently. *"You taste like a ripe peach on a summer day."*

Martin continued stroking and licking and delicately suckling Sarah until he felt her orgasm overtake her. She convulsed and shuddered under his hands and tongue and he brought her to orgasm again and yet again until he felt she could take no more. He then raised his head and gathered the limp and trembling Sarah in his arms.

"Will you trust me, Sarah?" he kissed her neck, gently nipped at her nipple with his teeth. *"Trust me to take care of you, baby?"*

She pressed herself into his arms; it felt so good to feel his bare skin against her body, her nipples.

They kissed deeply and Martin felt Sarah's desire rising again to match his own. He wanted to take her now, while she was still shuddering from her orgasm, while the wonderful sensations were still in her body. He knew her first time would cause her some pain and he wanted to get that over with as quickly as possible.

He reached for a condom and began to unroll it over his erection.

"What are you doing?" she asked him, then *"no, please no,"* when she realized what it was. "I want to feel you, Martin, inside me," she whispered, "not some piece of latex."

"Baby, I made sure I'm clean; but, Sarah honey, you can get pregnant even on your first time," Martin said gently, looking into her eyes.

"I won't, Martin," she said softly into his mind. *"I'm not ovulating now, I won't get pregnant. Please. I want to feel you inside me."*

He understood her unspoken plea. She wanted the one thing she had never had from him. She wanted to feel him spill his seed inside her, the final proof that he wanted her. Without another word, he tossed the condom aside. If he got her pregnant, they would deal with it. He wanted what she wanted. He wanted desperately to lose himself inside Sarah, fill her with himself.

He held her close while they kissed, the kiss deepening and spinning his senses. Her breasts burned against his chest and he caught her aching nipples in his mouth, both of them straining, their heart's hammering in their chests.

Martin could not remember ever being this hard; his dick throbbed with an intensity and urgency he'd never felt before. Sarah pressed her hands around his shaft, feeling the hardness and the extent of his desire for her. Martin groaned and thought he would go mad if he couldn't bury himself in her soon.

He rubbed the engorged head of his cock against her sex, teasing her clit, then pressed slightly at the opening to her vagina, letting Sarah get used to the feel of him. He could feel her heart beating wildly in her chest. He felt her fear but he also felt her desire.

He was torn. He wanted her so badly his legs were shaking; he couldn't have stood if his life depended on it. But he didn't want to hurt her, wondered wildly for a moment what type of god designed a universe where women experience pain before pleasure when it came to sex.

He pressed his entrance further, stopping again when he met the resistance of her hymen. It was Sarah who took measures in her own hands, holding herself tightly to him and impaling herself on his cock with a single thrust.

He felt the pain knife through her and he held himself still. *"Oh baby."* He held her still as well. *"Try to relax, Sarah."* He stroked her hair gently. *"We can stop if you want, baby. I don't want to hurt you, Sarah."*

She was so exquisitely tight and he was so excruciatingly hard he had to grit his teeth, but he just held her until he no longer felt pain from her.

Her eyes were pleading for him to continue. He moved slowly inside her, easing himself inside her until he felt her respond to him. Slowly he pulled his length almost out, then eased himself back in, deeper and deeper.

This time, Sarah cried out in pleasure; her body suffused with joy to have him finally, deep inside her, where she craved his touch. She arched her back to meet him, calling his name helplessly.

He plunged back inside her, the feel of the walls of her sex surrounding him, gripping him, driving all other thought out of his mind; just the mindless pleasure of this incredible feeling as he thrust himself over and over inside her. This need he felt coursing through his entire body. He felt it in Sarah's body as well, this desire for completion, this need for him to erupt inside her, to meld with her, to become one with her.

With a hoarse cry, Martin exploded inside Sarah. He held her to him and buried himself inside her, pumping his life force into her with deep, quick jabs of his hips.

He felt her orgasm slam into him just seconds behind his own, felt her womb and vagina clutching at him, milking every last drop of semen from his trembling body.

Sarah clung to him like a drowning woman and he held her, gasping for breath himself. He held her and stroked her while saying, "I love you, Sarah. I love you, baby." He couldn't stop saying it; it felt so good to finally say the words. To be buried deep inside her and whisper in her ear the words he'd longed to say so many times. "I love you, Smallest."

She smiled up at him, her face radiant, her eyes full of wonder. "You love me, Martin. I love you and you love me." She laughed aloud at the sheer magical wonderfulness of it all. She felt him; he was still deep inside her body. He was bonded with her in every way now. She felt how happy his body was to respond to hers, how filled with awe he was at what they had just done. She was content to just lie in his arms. Everything was different now; Martin wanted her.

After a few moments, she smiled again, "I thought you said you didn't make love. I'm no expert, but that was more than just fucking."

Martin stroked her face gently as he looked deep into her eyes. "That was definitely making love, Sarah." He shook his head amazed. "It's never happened to me before, but my whole body craves your touch. I'm inside you and I don't want to leave," he whispered.

Sarah held him tightly. "I've dreamed about this so many times, Martin, but this is so, so much better than my dreams, even better than Ariel and Hartshorn." Sarah shivered appreciatively. " You were making love to me, to Sarah. You wanted me." Her eyes were filled with equal measures of happiness and confusion.

He stroked her face gently with his fingertips, propped up on his elbows, trying to keep his weight off her. He finally gently pulled himself free of her body and rolled over, pulling her to him. *"I've wanted you since that first moment on the beach. You know the time I'm talking about."*

Sarah felt a sense of loss as his penis left her body, but she smiled at him. *"The red bikini?"*

He nodded. *"You don't play fair, Sarah. That bikini was hitting below the belt, so to speak."* He smiled down at her, happiness and satiation in all his features. He had never been so happy; he wondered if he was dreaming. Then he saw the blood on Sarah's thighs and came to with a jolt. "I did hurt you," he said, concern marking his face.

"Not very much," Sarah laughed softly, dismissing the pain, "and you certainly made up for it." She stretched luxuriously, at least as much as possible with the cast on her arm.

Martin got up and walked into the bathroom.

Sarah watched him appreciatively from behind as he walked. The muscles in his buttocks clenched as he walked; there was a graceful power in all his movements. His penis now swung freely down in front of him, no longer erect but still impressive to her.

He returned with a warm, wet, soft cloth and cleaned Sarah between her legs carefully. He was grateful to see there was very little blood, just a smear or two really. Sarah was not experiencing any pain now; indeed, she was enjoying his attentions to her pussy very much. He smiled at her. His penis stirred and Sarah stared with fascination at it. "You're not ready for round two yet, young lady. You're going to be sore for a day or two, Sarah."

Sarah pulled herself into his lap and sat facing him. She wrapped her good arm around his neck, cradling her broken arm between them. "But I want to taste you," she said so softly he wasn't sure he heard her. "You tasted me, I want to know what you taste like."

Martin smiled at her. "There's plenty of time for that, baby. No need to do that now."

"But I want to," Sarah said, looking at him from under her lashes. She was embarrassed at her lack of knowledge, but she pushed on, "Don't you like it, that I mean, oral sex," she finally amended.

Martin smiled at her, but he wasn't laughing at her. He looked her in the face and said, "Sure, I like oral sex just fine, Sarah." He lightly kissed the tip of her nose. "How are you going to give me a blow job, baby, when you have trouble saying 'blow job'," he teased. "You don't have to do everything in a day, Sarah." He pushed the errant curls out of her face and kissed her again.

He realized as he held her that she was disappointed. He looked her in the face. "You really want to do this?" he asked curiously.

She nodded yes. "I want to know what you taste like," she said looking at him, her violet eyes dark, her desire showing. "I want to make you come," she said quietly, reaching down to stroke him.

"You already did, spectacularly," Martin said, desire lancing through him again at Sarah's touch.

"But I want to make you come in my mouth," she said softly, looking into his eyes. Martin was instantly hard in her hand and she marveled at that, looking at him with a question in her eyes.

"Yeah, you pretty much do that to me instantly," he said, with a quick intake of breath. "Especially with statements like that," he continued softly. "Are you sure you feel well enough to try something like that, Sarah?"

She answered by kissing him and sliding down his body. She stopped when she was eye level with his naval. She stared at his huge erection with rapt fascination then looked up at him.

"You'll have to tell me what to do," she said softly, stroking his penis gently with her good hand.

He smiled at her. "I've never actually given anyone a blow job, Sarah."

She slapped him lightly on the chest. "You know what I mean. Tell me what you like." She asked shyly, "What should I do?"

"Well," Martin said, smiling at her. "Why don't the two of you just get acquainted first. Do whatever you like, Sarah." He stuffed a pillow behind him and leaned back against the headboard, settling in, helping her cradle her injured arm.

She looked uncertainly at him, then back at his penis. She stroked it slowly but firmly from the base to the tip and he arched his back in pleasure at her touch. Sarah leaned down and kissed him. The feel of her lips on his cock was heavenly. She then rubbed him lightly on her face, luxuriating in the feel of his masculine hardness against her cheeks, her lips, her forehead.

He watched her, amazed. She loved the feel of him, was worshipping his cock. It swelled even larger, if that was possible, and he felt he would probably burst before she even took him in her mouth. He was trembling and on the verge of coming already.

Sarah began to kiss his dick, kiss and lick. He groaned in sweet agony. She tentatively sucked on the head and at his helpless cry of pleasure, sucked harder.

Martin breathed deeply and tried to gain control of himself. He tried to move as little as possible. Sarah was still injured and he didn't want her to hurt herself pleasuring him. But holy Christmas, how he wanted to just grab her head and fuck those sweet lips of hers.

She began to lick him, long slow licks from the base of his stalk to the tip. The feeling was so sublime that Martin's heart skipped a beat. She continued and he had to close his eyes but opened them almost immediately. He couldn't take his eyes off her, the sight of her lips on his dick was better than any fantasy he'd ever had.

She smiled wickedly at him from beneath her lashes and bent to his erect staff again. Sarah took as much of him in her mouth as she could and suckled him, harder and harder.

Martin groaned in desperation; he thought he might pass out from the pleasure her lips brought him. He guided her hand to his dick under her mouth and showed her how to use it to lengthen the stroke of her mouth.

She stroked him firmly and sucked as her hand and lips went up and down on his rock hard cock. She could feel what he liked, what he yearned for, the touch that sent his senses flying, and she gave it to him freely.

Martin erupted into her mouth, clutching the sheets in his desperation not to grab her head, shouting her name at his release, rolling and bucking his hips helplessly as Sarah continued to suck him.

Sarah felt his orgasm claim his entire body. She felt and tasted the spurt of hot, thick liquid as it jetted against the back of her throat and she felt an answering surge of wetness between her own legs. She felt the deep shudder that went through Martin's entire body as she sucked him again and yet again and was rewarded with a second spurt of semen and Martin's helpless groan of agonizing pleasure.

He finally lay spent, Sarah's head on his thigh. "Sweet, sweet Sarah," he said, when he trusted his voice to speak again. "If that's you learning to give a blow job, I don't know if I'll survive it when you get it figured out." He laughed softly and pulled her to him, kissing her, tasting himself on her lips. "So what did you think?" he asked softly. "What did I taste like?"

"Umm," she snuggled into him. "You tasted wonderful," and she shivered appreciatively, sharing her emotion with him. She tried to describe it for him. "You were savory, a bit tart. It tasted very masculine," she said, kissing his chest.

Martin laughed. "Masculine, huh. Glad you like it." He smiled at her deep blush. "Oh my darling girl. You and I are going to have so much fun playing." He held her and stroked her, gently nuzzling her nipple and Sarah's body quivered in response.

Sarah was so relaxed she was drifting off to sleep in Martin's arms when she felt the change in him, felt him searching for a way to tell her something. "What is it?" she said, suddenly awake. "Tell me, Martin."

"There's something I should explain, Sarah. Something I did before I sent Al and Will to Tibet."

"You sent them after Master Po," Sarah said. She looked strangely at Martin. "You don't even know if he's still alive."

"No," Martin replied. "But you do, don't you?"

"Yes," she finally admitted to him. "They're on their way here now. Why do you want to bring him here? What do you think he can tell us that he didn't when we were at Sun Tao?"

"I don't know, Sarah. That's why I asked him to come. It's time for him to explain, tell us what he knows. But that's not what I wanted to talk about. He held her to him, kissed her face, looked in her eyes. "I love you, Sarah. I mean that, baby. I always have and I always will. And I'll be here for you every minute of every day. I'll never leave you again."

"What is this leading to, Martin?" Sarah was afraid; there was a 'but' coming, she knew it.

"Sarah, don't worry, it's fine." He could feel her anxiety spiking. "Baby, I love you and I want to marry you. I want to marry you but I promised Al and Sebastian I wouldn't for a year. I wanted you to know right away what we talked about."

Sarah stared at him stunned. "Why in the world would you make a promise like that?"

"Because it was the right thing to do. I told them," he said, stroking her gently, "you're mine and I'm yours and I won't leave you again. But," he added at the look in her eyes, "they have the right to be worried about you. They don't know me. And you, Sarah, you have the right to get to know me better. Get to know the side of me you don't know before you commit to something as legal as marriage. I told Al I would sign any kind of pre nup he wanted." He shook his head at her protests. "I want to sign one, Sarah. This isn't about your money. I'm coming into this with nothing. If you ever want me to leave, I'll leave with what I came with.

Sarah, I adore you and want you to be mine forever. I didn't promise not to ask you, I just promised not to marry for a year. If you still want me then, I'd like to marry you on this day, a year from now."

He looked deeply into her eyes. They were both still naked, spent from their lovemaking, connected to each other in some inexplicable way that Martin couldn't bear to lose. He knew she felt the same. "But I pledge myself to you now, Sarah. Now and forever," he finished softly.

"I'll marry you whenever you like, Martin Stone," she replied, putting her arms around his neck, kissing him lightly. "I don't care what you do or don't sign. And I'll be a good wife, you'll see." She kissed him deeply. She loved the feeling of his mouth on hers, the strength of his body pushing on hers. *"I'll be a very good wife,"* she promised softly.

Martin took her face in his hands and laughed at her seriousness. "How could you be anything other than a perfect wife to me," he teased. "I already think you're perfect."

He rose from the bed and went and got something from his pants pocket. He came back to Sarah. "I know you don't like diamonds, but I wanted to get you a ring. I wanted something that said you're mine," he said simply. "I thought you would like this."

He held a small golden ring out to her and she held out her hand. Martin slipped the ring on her finger; it fit perfectly. She looked at it in wonder. It was a small gold band with tiny leaves etched around it and in the center, a tiny grotto of ferns. It was a reminder of where Martin had first found Sarah as a baby and she fell in love with the delicate ring immediately.

"It's beautiful, Martin," she said, tears in her eyes. "I never want to wear another." She kissed the ring then kissed Martin.

Their kiss deepened and Martin felt the passion in Sarah, rising up to meet his. But he also felt her weariness. His girl was tired; she'd been through a lot. He pulled back, kissed her lightly on the neck, her breasts. "I think I want to sleep now, my girl in my arms." He pulled her to him and covered them both with the blanket. Sarah drifted off to sleep in his arms almost immediately and he smiled with quiet satisfaction that she was able to do so. He watched her steady breathing, waited until he was sure she was deeply asleep before he rose and went to find Sebastian.

Sebastian, Julie and Paul waited for him in Sarah's garden. He breathed in the scents appreciatively. He realized with a small jolt that he and Sarah had been closeted in her bedroom all day and evening. He was a bit chagrined but met their looks without embarrassment. They all knew it inevitable that he and Sarah would become lovers.

"She's sleeping now. She's feeling much better," he said without irony. "I think she'll be ready to talk to all of you soon. Have you heard from Will and Al?" he asked Sebastian.

Sebastian nodded. "They have located Master Po and are on their way back here with him. They will arrive late tomorrow morning."

Martin nodded his understanding. "How about Jonathan?" he asked quietly. "Is he making any headway?"

Sebastian shook his head. "So far, no," he acknowledged. He's been crawling all over Cornwall looking for the estate you described." Sebastian looked steadily at him. "He'll find it," he assured Martin. "If it's there to be found, he'll find it."

Martin nodded and turned to go back to Sarah.

"Did you ask her?" Sebastian asked.

Martin stopped and turned back. He looked at Sebastian quietly then said, "Yes, I asked her. She said yes." He smiled deeply. "I'll honor my promise, we won't be married for a year, but she's engaged to me. She said yes. She liked the ring," he added happily.

Sebastian smiled his approval.   Julie offered him her congratulations. Paul said nothing at first, merely looked grave. Finally he smiled at Martin.

"I do offer you my congratulations. It's obvious that you are both deeply in love. It's wise that you've decided to wait. You and Sarah still have much to learn about each other. I see you have started down that path already. Tread carefully, Martin. This is all very new to her." But Paul smiled at him encouragingly.

Martin knew he would take Sarah to his heart and to his bed no matter what these people thought, but it was reassuring to know they were accepting of him. As long as Sarah loved him and wanted him, they would accept him in her life. He gladdened him to know that, although he still couldn't quite imagine the life he and Sarah would live, she would still have her family, her circle of confidents around her.

The morning finally arrived, Martin still keeping a silent vigil over the peacefully sleeping Sarah. Sarah was now his and she trusted him completely. He resolved to never let her down again.

Finally he heard sounds that indicated the travelers had returned. Sebastian hastened to let them in. Martin quietly woke Sarah, told her Alexander had returned. She rose immediately and donned a robe. Her hair still sleep tousled, she held Martin's hand as he led her from the bedroom into the sitting room where the others were waiting.

Alexander noticed the slender gold ring on her finger immediately but said nothing. He knew right away that things had changed between Stone and Sarah. They were lovers now; it was obvious.   His heart clenched with pain but his face betrayed nothing.

Alexander thought back over the events of the last few days. It seems his life had changed irredeemably due to Sarah once again. Part of him hadn't believed there was a Sun Tao, a Master Po, to be found. But they had located the monastery easily enough following Stone's directions. Stone had been right, the locals hadn't offered much information about Sun Tao. It was not a place that people talked about, visited. It was spoken of, by the few who admitted of its existence, with reverence. It had not been easy to get to; it was one hell of a climb.

Master Po had been waiting for them, expecting them impatiently. Alexander had no idea how the man knew they were coming but he knew.

He was a man of somewhat indeterminate age; seventies would be his guess. His head was clean-shaven. His eyes were blind, white with cataracts, but his merry expression said he was glad to see them. He carried a staff and thumped it appreciatively to welcome them. "Welcome, welcome tardy friends," he admonished them. "I have been waiting for you for some time now. Please, rest; refresh yourselves. We cannot tarry long. We must get back to her. She is in need of my help."

Alexander was surprised. "You know who we are? Why we've come?"

"Of course," the monk replied smiling. "You are the third part of the prophecy," he said to Alexander as he bowed in greeting. "I have been most anxious to meet you for some time now." To Will he said, "You are our brother's true friend. You are always welcome here at Sun Tao." He bowed in greeting to Will.

Will was surprised. This place was like a painting in a dream, he thought. Perhaps it was because they were so high and the oxygen was so thin; Will thought that accounted for the feeling of unreality he got in looking about the monastery.

"If you know why we've come, then you know we're looking for answers." Alexander said.

"Of course, of course," Master Po said impatiently. "All in good time. But the child has been kept in the dark long enough. It is time for her to hear. This is for her ears."

"What prophecy? Alexander said stubbornly. "You spoke of a prophecy."

Master Po assessed him with his blind eyes for a long moment. Rather, he seemed to analyze the air around Alexander with his nose, his ears, his skin. Finally he said, "Ah yes, I should tell you that much. Come. Sit." He motioned for another monk to bring them some tea and settled himself comfortably on a cushion, indicating that Alexander and Will should also sit. When the monk brought their tea, Alexander realized with a slight shock that it was the same tea Sarah drank incessantly at home. He recognized the aroma immediately.

Master Po regarded the air near them as if he could feel them since he couldn't see them and then began. "I was aware of the child's birth from the beginning, yet I could not be sure it was she, the child from the

295

prophecy. My vision is not always so clear. But the prophecy is clear. A secret child, a girl child, will grow to be a young woman. In one hand she carries a shield, in the other a harp. Her shield is a mighty warrior. She will have great need of him. The harp is her voice. The third person in the prophecy carries her voice to the world. Her message is one of hope and love and tolerance. It is important for she has learned the mystery of how to speak to the secret heart of men and women. How to touch their true selves, their better selves."

Will had been astonished. This monk spoke of these things as if they were the most natural things in the world. "Do you mean Sarah is some kind of legend, some kind of…" he searched for a word, but words failed him.

"That, I do not know," Master Po said, laughing merrily. "I only know that she is the young woman from the prophecy and it is time, past time, that she learn something of who she is. She has need of my council as does our brother, Martin. We should go to them as quickly as we may."

And so they had, retracing their steps, traveling back to the jet and flying back to California in record time.

Sarah now looked anxiously at Alexander, then at Master Po. She bowed to Master Po, acknowledging him respectfully as she had at Sun Tao. Martin also bowed deeply, acknowledging the Master.

Master Po's face lit up with a joyous smile at Sarah and Martin's entrance. "Let the journey begin!" he proclaimed and flung his arms out wide as if to embrace them all.

Made in the USA
Charleston, SC
13 January 2014